RISKY BUSINESS

SAVANNA ROSE

Copyright © 2025 by Savanna Rose

All rights reserved.

No part of this book may be reproduced or transmitted in any form or by any means, electronic or mechanical, including photocopying, or by any information storage and retrieval system without the author's written permission, except for the use of brief quotations in a book review.

This book is a work of fiction. All characters and places in this book are fictitious. Any resemblance to actual persons, living or dead, events, or locales is entirely coincidental.

Cover design by Sam Palencia

Editing by Katie Ducharme

This book is intended for an 18+ audience.

This book is written in British English.

To all my people pleasers

It's time to start focusing on yourself because your happiness matters.

TRIGGER AND CONTENT WARNINGS

- parent with illness
- alcoholism (side character)
- toxic past relationship
- explanation of traumatic event
- panic attacks and anxiety

CHAPTER 1
IVY THOMPSON

"So, when I lived in Australia for three years, everyone warned me about the spiders and how big they'd be. But then I found this massive huntsman in the bathroom, it didn't affect me at all."

I stare back at my date, Adam, as I sip on my cocktail, wishing time would pass a lot quicker than it currently is.

"Wow," I say with fake enthusiasm. "Sounds fun."

"Oh, and the crocodiles. Don't get me started on the crocodiles. They're so much smaller than people say they are," he says as he leans back in his chair. "People think Australia is this terrifying place with dangerous animals, but you cannot fear the animals. They should fear us. They—"

"Have you been anywhere else apart from Australia?"

Adam pins me with a stare as his mouth presses into a thin line. "Why are you talking over me?"

My eye twitches at his hypocritical statement. "Sorry," I say sharply.

When I take another sip of my drink, instead of tasting a mouthful of my strawberry daiquiri, I'm slurping from an empty glass. Great. No more alcohol to help me through this nightmare.

"Don't tell me you've never been to Australia before?"

I shake my head. "But I've been to—"

"Oh my god," he cuts me off. "Australia is the best place on Earth."

My back presses into my chair as I sigh silently.

If only he'd let me finish one sentence.

"I can't believe you haven't been," he carries on. "You haven't lived."

My eyes almost roll into the back of my head when he moves on to how savage the excursions were. I might have been interested if he asked me something personal and didn't make everything about himself.

"I'm going to go to the bathroom," I speak over him—otherwise I'll be here until tomorrow morning.

I drag my chair out from underneath me, and Adam blinks, bewildered. "But I'm not done talking?"

"My bladder can't wait for you. Sorry."

When he scoffs, I ignore him. Reaching for my bag, I head straight for the bathroom, needing a minute to take a breather. I rummage for my phone to call my friend so she can shove some sense into me.

"Ivy?" Erin's voice echoes into my ear.

"Hi," I murmur before pressing my thumb to the speaker and sliding it onto the counter.

"What's happened? Is he a serial killer?"

A laugh slips past my lips. "Not sure how I'd be talking to you if he was a serial killer."

She tuts. "Well, something must be wrong because you wouldn't be calling me halfway through. What's going on?"

"It's not going to work out. I know I shouldn't have done this," I groan.

"Ivy, this is your first date in over three years. I'm not surprised you're feeling a little anxious."

I shake my head furiously. "No, this has nothing to do

with my nerves, and everything to do with the fact my date is so far up his own ass that he has shit stains on his face."

"What… really?"

My head falls into my hands. "No, Erin. He's barely let me finish a single sentence all night. All he's been talking about is his time in Australia, and it's killing me. I can't do this."

"Do you need me to come and shout some sense into him?"

"No," I say as I stare at myself in the reflection and flatten my champagne-blonde hair. "He's just incredibly obnoxious and I already know he's not the one."

"Then leave. Screw that guy."

"I'm done with dating apps forever."

"You've only been on there for a week."

"Yeah." I laugh to myself. "And I think that's enough for eternity. I knew I shouldn't have done this. I'm not ready. I think I'm born to be single."

Erin sighs. "You're giving up so easily."

"Yeah, I am." I sigh morbidly.

"Go and tell that *boy* you're leaving. Don't waste your time on someone who doesn't even want any of yours."

She's right. She's always right.

"Thanks, Erin."

"Text me when you're leaving."

"I will. Love you."

"Love you, too."

I touch the screen to end the call. My eyes flick up and I inhale a deep breath, smoothing down the fabric of my dress before I leave the bathroom and head back to our table.

Adam spots me from across the room, his curly blonde hair bouncing around his head. He flashes me a funny look and suddenly I'm paranoid I have toilet roll stuck to my shoe.

"What took you so long?"

My jaw clenches. Yeah, Erin was right. Screw this guy.

"There was a queue," I lie.

I don't bother sitting back down.

"Sorry to cut this short, but I need to go. Thanks for the drink."

Except, I'm not sorry. Not one bit.

He recoils like I've slapped him. "Wait… you're just leaving?"

"Yeah." I force a sympathetic smile. "I have to go."

Adam scoffs loudly and stands from his chair, the legs scraping against the floor. "You're doing me a favour anyway. Worst fucking date ever."

"Yeah, that makes two of us," I mumble under my breath.

His eyes blaze. "No guy is going to settle for someone as boring and rude as you."

I swallow the lump in my throat as he storms out of the bar. My chest heaves, realising there are multiple sets of eyes on me. Brilliant.

I knew I should have stayed at home.

When I know he's long gone, I make my escape.

My head dips, and I walk through the bar, wishing the ground would open up and consume me. As I approach the exit, my heel grazes the floor at the same time I hear a crack. Then I'm stumbling forward.

I reach out for the main set of doors to stabilise myself before I fall.

"Shit," I hiss.

My head tilts, and I raise my foot. The heel of my cutest stilettos has snapped clean off. I slump forward, pushing past the doors so I can rest against the street wall. A scream is brewing in my throat, but I keep myself together—at least until I get home.

I bury my head into my hands, listening as people stroll past, laughing and chatting with their friends. They're ready to start their Friday night in style, and I'm ready to hide under a rock for the foreseeable.

"Are you okay?"

I don't even bother to look up. My gaze remains on the pavement.

"Yes, I'm absolutely fantastic. Thanks for asking."

Poison feels like it's been injected into my veins. Right now, I have one emotion bubbling through me. *Wrath*. Fuck this night, fuck these shoes, fuck Adam, fuck dating apps. Fuck everything.

"You sure? I think your shoe is broken."

I snap my attention to the owner of the deep voice. He's staring back at me with dark blue eyes, a brunette buzz cut, and a silver nose ring.

"Thank you for pointing out the obvious." I narrow my eyes at him.

I'm trying my hardest not to be intimidated by this guy's good looks while he experiences my misfortune. This is the icing on top of the cake.

There are two guys behind him, one is smoking a cigarette and laughing at something the other guy said. I'm guessing they're his friends, and I'm grateful they're not in on this conversation to humiliate me further.

"Bad night?"

I scoff. "Bad night? That's an understatement."

The guy tilts his head and shoves his hands into the pockets of his cargo pants. "Join the club."

I narrow my eyes at him and his friends, who are messing around behind him. "Looks like you guys are having a blast."

He glances over his shoulder and shrugs. "They just got us kicked out of the bar for being too drunk."

"Oh, how I wish I was being kicked out of a bar for being too drunk."

"Go on then." His lips twitch into a smirk. "Tell me how bad your night has been."

I push up from the wall and remind myself not to put any pressure on my heel, or I'll go flying. "Well, let me see…" I trail off. "Firstly, I matched with some asshole who only wanted to speak about himself, talk over me, proceeded to tell the entire bar that no guy is going to want me. Oh, and then I broke my heel, and next, it'll probably be my ankle."

He chews on his lip as I catch my breath, realising I'm offloading to a complete stranger. I close my eyes and release a staggered exhale. What am I doing?

"And on that count," I say before reaching down to take off my heels. "I'm going home."

"Wait, wait." He reaches out to grab my arm gently. "You can't walk home barefoot. It's Friday night, and the pavement is going to be littered with glass."

I raise my brow at him, then I look down at his grip, and he quickly lets go of me. "Well, I can't walk home with a broken heel. I'll definitely end up in A&E then."

"And what if you cut your feet?"

I fold my arms across my chest, the straps of my heels hitting my shoulders. "Are you a doctor or something?"

"No, but I know when someone is being stupid."

A bitter laugh barks from my chest. "Stupid? Oh god. This night keeps getting better and better."

He curses. "I mean, you could get hurt."

"It's fine." I hold up my hand and take one step back, my bare foot pressing into the pavement. "Tonight can't get any worse than it already is."

I turn to walk down the street, being careful of any glass bottles and who knows what else. Footsteps echo behind me, but I don't look back.

"My night is bad because I came out for a drink to distract myself from stuff I've got going on at home, but my friends decided to get us kicked out, and quite frankly, they're pissing me off."

My teeth sink into my bottom lip as I slowly come to a stop. I tilt my head over my shoulder, my blonde hair swishing. "So what are you going to do about it?"

"Ditch them," he says instantly. "And ask if you want to go for a drink with me instead, because I think you might need it as much as I do."

My mouth opens, and I shut it immediately in shock.

"You want to go for a drink with me?"

"Yeah." He nods. "I could do with six shots of tequila, and I bet you could, too."

"I don't like tequila."

He narrows his eyes but smiles anyway, a cheeky yet playful glimmer reflecting in his irises. "Fine, sambuca then."

My heartbeat pounds in my throat as I stare at this abnormally handsome man—something I *really* didn't want to acknowledge again.

"My shoe is broken," I say, raising the heels in my hand.

"I'll hold you up."

For a moment, I look at him. "What's your name?"

"JJ."

I tilt my head at his Godlike confidence.

It's practically oozing out of him. I want nothing more than to peel my eyes away, but I can't remove myself from his undeniable energy.

"And yours?"

I lick my bottom lip. "Ivy."

"Well, Ivy. Would you like to go to the next bar so we can banish this shit day with a sambuca shot?"

I shove down the pounding thoughts that are telling me to go home. He's right, we could attempt to make this night better if I fall into nicer company. Otherwise, I'll be wallowing in self-pity the second I get home and striking myself out for future dates.

Not that this is a date, by any means.

JJ stands there waiting patiently for an answer.

I roll back my shoulders and shake out my stiff spine. I can't remember the last time I've done anything this spontaneous, not since the accident. I've been living in bubble wrap for far too long, and tonight might be the night to surprise myself.

"Alright, fine," I say softly. "But I'm only going for the sambuca."

CHAPTER 2
IVY THOMPSON

We walk down to the next bar. *Scratch that.* I hobble down to the next bar with assistance from JJ. The second we enter the vibrant space, I'm gasping for another drink.

As we make it to a vacant table, I perch on the edge of the chair as JJ reluctantly releases my arm. My lips twitch, offering him a tight smile as I kick off my shoes beneath the table and take a seat.

"I didn't think the bouncer was going to let me in," I admit, brushing my fingers through the ends of my hair.

JJ's brows furrow with suspicion as he leans on his elbows. "Why? Wait… god. Please don't tell me you're still in school or something."

I tilt my head and push down my laugh. "No, because I look like an extra from *The Walking Dead* with this broken heel."

"So… you're out of school?"

"I left sixth form three years ago."

JJ sinks back into his chair with relief. "Not going to lie, I don't think he was looking at your wobbly foot."

My eyes narrow on his, but he's beaming back at me. Even

though they're blue like the ocean, they should look soft and inviting, but all I can see is a mischievous glint behind them.

"I don't know if that was an insult or a compliment," I say cautiously.

JJ rests his forearms on the table. My gaze floats down to a couple of silver rings on his long fingers. The cuff of his jacket rides up his wrist, flashing a splash of ink I didn't notice before.

When I meet his gaze again, he's grinning at me playfully. "It's a compliment, Ivy."

"Unnecessary, but thanks." I blink away my blush.

"What do you want to drink?"

"I'll get my own drink."

"Why?"

"Because this is not a date."

JJ chews on the inside of his lip and has the audacity to smirk at me.

"Is it not?" he drawls.

I lean back in my chair and comfortably fold my arms across my chest. "No. It is simply two people having a drink together. Both of our nights have ended tragically, and they need fixing with some alcohol and adequate company."

His brows shoot towards his hairline. "Adequate company?"

"Yours, not mine. Obviously."

JJ releases a soft chuckle, and I wish he didn't because the sound is far too alluring for my liking.

"So it's a date if I buy you a drink?"

"Even if you buy me a drink," I clarify. "But you should know I am more than capable of buying my own drinks."

He shrugs simply. "I wasn't expecting you to pay for them when I asked you to join me."

Suddenly, I'm heating up, like I'm under a spotlight and he can see every inch of me. A thought rushes through my mind—this is so unlike me. I've never been the kind of person who can confidently talk to boys; I've always cowered away in fear of not being good enough.

But maybe I've officially crossed into *I don't give a fuck anymore* territory.

What else do I have to lose?

I shake off this warmth and remind myself we'll go our separate ways tonight, and I'll never have to see him again.

He's a metaphorical shoulder to cry on.

Tomorrow I'll be back to the Ivy I know. *It's okay to change the rulebook every now and then.*

Erin certainly would approve of me being more spontaneous. She'd probably go into cardiac arrest knowing what I'm doing right now.

The waitress makes her way over to our table. I order another strawberry daiquiri, and when JJ orders, he asks for two sambuca shots along with an espresso martini. I don't complain. I could do with a good whiplash.

"So, this guy you went on a date with." He clears his throat, and I internally grimace at the memory. "You're not giving him a second chance, are you?"

I gawk at him as he swipes his thumb across his bottom lip. "Did you completely ignore the part where he told the entire bar I was boring and no one would ever want me?"

"Mm." His eye twitches. "He's an asshole."

"Glad we're on the same page," I murmur as the waitress drops our drinks off. Two cocktails. Two sambuca shots. Just on time. "Let's not talk about my disaster of a night. What's going on with you?"

He glances down at the table, pushing the sambuca shot over to me. I sip on my cocktail, waiting for a response, but maybe he's in the same boat as me and wants to ignore the situation entirely.

"You don't have—"

"My mum is sick," he says as he crosses his arms. My brows furrow as I watch him, but he doesn't look me directly in the eye, and suddenly I feel disgustingly guilty. "She's with my dad in Germany trialling this new treatment they can't get in this country."

I press my lips together as tightly as possible, ignoring the ball in my throat.

"They left yesterday, and I couldn't deal with everything going on right now. It's too much. My dad is losing his shit. I needed a night out to distract myself from everything, but my friends decided to make it about them instead." He sighs, and my heart softens a little.

I lick my bottom lip. "I'm sorry you've been going through that."

Slowly, he drags his eyes back to mine. Those blue eyes that were once full of mischief are now filled with fear, and I wish I never pushed him to speak. I take my sambuca shot between my fingers and raise it between us.

His brows furrow as I clear my throat. "To your mother," I say as he eventually picks up his own and clinks it against mine. "May the treatment work and bless your family."

JJ flicks his eyes between mine for a moment, as if my toast was completely unexpected. "Thank you," he says gratefully.

Then we both throw back the tangy liquid. At first, it stings my throat. I can't remember the last time I had a shot. JJ's expression twists to pure disgust as he shudders and drinks down half of his cocktail after.

I laugh softly. "I thought you liked shots?"

"Not sambuca," he grimaces.

I tilt my head. "What?" I blink. "Then why did you get it?"

"Because you wanted it."

I narrow my eyes into slits. "You didn't have to get it because I wanted it."

My fingers wrap around the paper straw in my daiquiri as I take a sip. JJ's eyes watch my mouth carefully.

"No..." he trails off. "But I promised you sambuca and I wouldn't be a team player if I backed out after all of this."

The corner of my mouth twitches but I push away the intrusive smile. "Well, aren't you a gentleman," I tease.

He scoffs. "Not perfect, but I try."

I quirk a brow at him. "You don't think what you did for me earlier was gentlemanly?"

He raises one shoulder. "I can definitely do better."

When he locks his eyes on mine, there is a sparkle that makes my stomach flip.

I swallow around my clammy mouth. "Like what?"

"Dunno." He grins wildly. "I guess we'll see how this date goes."

My eyes roll. "We said it's not a date."

"Are you always this argumentative?"

My teeth clamp down on my bottom lip as heat begins to catch the back of my neck and spread across my chest at an alarming rate. "Sometimes."

"I like a challenge," he says with a subtle wink before downing the last drops of his drink. "As much as I like your honesty, princess."

My eyes narrow at him.

"You pick up a lot of girls with that nickname?"

"No, but is it working?"

I release a long sigh and shake my head. "It's a cute attempt at being charming."

"I'm flattered you think I'm charming."

"Yeah, well... it's not working."

JJ leans in again, a little too close this time. The playfulness in his expression bleeds into the wildfire in his eyes, and suddenly I realise I might be partaking in flirting. Even though I have no clue what I'm doing.

"Isn't it?"

"No."

"Well, I beg to differ because your heart is pounding like an alarm."

I jerk backwards from his close proximity. My cheeks begin to heat, despite trying to tell my body not to embarrass me now, and prove him completely right.

He laughs again and drags one of his hands over the back of his buzz cut.

"No, it's not," I respond lamely.

"Just stating facts."

I almost cut a hole in my cheek from the pressure of my teeth. My eyes narrow, and suddenly I'm desperate for another sambuca. The waitress walks by, and I call her over, ordering for myself.

"Maybe now I understand why your friends got drunk." I flash him a sarcastic smile. "Putting up with your company is way worse when you're sober."

JJ's neck extends backwards, and he exhales a long, loud laugh that has people glancing over to our table. I stare back at him blankly as he recovers and wipes at the fake tears on his cheeks.

He beams. "That was unexpected."

"Just stating facts," I shoot back.

We stare at each other for a hot minute, neither of us uttering a word. His lips twitch like he wants to continue winding me up, but he doesn't. Probably because I look like I'm seconds from having a mental breakdown.

JJ's mouth opens, and I brace myself. "Tell me what you do," he says casually.

"What?"

"What do you do?"

"You're asking me what I do?"

"Yes." He flicks his eyes from left to right. "That's how conversations tend to go. I ask a question and you answer, and maybe if you're really nice, you might ask me a question too. Were you dropped as a child?"

"Now you're pushing it." I narrow my gaze at him.

"Then tell me," he says, sounding genuinely interested.

My arms lay flat on the edge of the table as I adjust in my seat. "Well, I just finished my second year of university."

"What do you study?"

"Biomedical science."

JJ blinks once and then twice. "Shit." He sighs. "You must be super smart."

I bite down on my straw. "When I want to be. What do you do?"

"Just finished my third year in engineering." He nods. "Still got another year to go, unfortunately."

I hum with approval. "And you think I'm super smart."

He shrugs it off. "You can attempt to wing some stuff, that's for sure. Other parts you have to get your head down, but what degree isn't going to be hard?"

"True." I sip my drink. "So, is that what you want to be… an engineer?"

"No." He barks out an unexpected laugh. "Absolutely not."

I tilt my head in confusion. "Then why are you studying it if you don't want to do it?"

"It's a long story." He waves a hand.

"I wanna know," I say, shuffling forward.

JJ eyes me hesitantly for a moment before grazing a hand over his jaw. "My dad said I had to go to university. I didn't want to, but he said that's how people get jobs. He helped me pick what to study."

My face scrunches up at the thought. I couldn't imagine my dad trying to tell me what to do, he's always said I should follow my dreams and no one else's.

"What is it that you want to do?"

"Video production," he says before beckoning over the waitress to order another drink, and one for me, too. "It's always been my first love. I remember getting my first camera when I was ten, I took it everywhere with me."

"But couldn't you have done that at university?" I frown.

JJ snorts quietly. "Yeah, but it wasn't in my dad's brochure for degrees, unfortunately."

"That's shit," I state. "He shouldn't rule your life."

"You're right." He sighs. "But he can be very persuasive, and I don't want to let him down."

Something tells me that might be one of his biggest fears.

"So are you still doing video production?"

He nods eagerly. "Yeah, when I have the time. University takes up a lot of it, and everything with my mum. My dad would have a heart attack if he saw that I'm not doing well in my course."

"Are you?" I ask curiously.

"Yes." He winks. "Top of my class."

I shake my head. "Of course you are."

"Let's stop talking about me," he dismisses himself. "I wanna talk about you."

"What do you want to know?" I laugh hesitantly.

"Everything." JJ's eyes glitter at me. "I wanna know everything you're willing to share."

Well, this has definitely taken a turn from my tragic date earlier.

I suck in a breath and stare across the table at him and his boyish grin.

"Uh, when I was fifteen, I won a surfing competition," I blurt out of nowhere.

JJ's eyes widen as he leans forward. "Are you serious?"

I chuckle quietly. "Yeah, that's all I did with my brother when we grew up."

"You do not strike me as the type to surf."

My mouth falls open. "Why not?"

"I've seen your balance. Are you sure you didn't bribe the judges?"

I lean over the table to gently push his shoulder. "Are you going to let that go?"

"Never." He grins, eyes glistening. "Tell me more. I wanna know more."

"About surfing?"

"About anything. What colour was your board? I bet it was blue."

"Wrong." I smile smugly. "It was pink."

JJ taps his fist on the table. "Damn it, I was going to say that next."

When he watches me with his pretty eyes, my cheeks begin to heat.

What the hell is going on, and why am I enjoying this more than I should be?

CHAPTER 3
IVY THOMPSON

I hate to admit that I can't remember the last time I laughed this much.

The hyena type of laughing.

With my non-date.

JJ is charming, and he knows it. But not in an arrogant way, in a charismatic way. He's asking me questions, automatically raising him in my good books, which is absolutely pathetic because if this is my bare minimum, I need to get a grip.

Somehow, it's gone from being a horrific night to one I wouldn't look back on as a total disaster.

We ordered more cocktails and a pitcher of water. My mind is swaying a little, but I know I'm still in control. What I didn't expect was for the security guards to tell us the bar was closing up for the night.

Had we really spent all night talking?

JJ sneakily pays for the bill when I'm gathering my stuff, and I scowl at him across the table. All he does is smile back in response with a wink. Instead of fighting him, I thank him, and we make our way outside.

We stand on the edge of the curb, and I cling onto JJ's arm

to balance myself. I'll be throwing away these stupid heels the second I get home. I stare up into his blue eyes and feel my heart stupidly quiver—I'm blaming the alcohol.

I have no idea how this man—who is totally out of my league—spent the night with me in a bar. But I choose to ignore that thought. I had a good night—better than good. I shouldn't complain.

My ankle twists suddenly, and I'm falling back on my broken heel. A yelp escapes my throat, but before I tumble to the ground, JJ wraps an arm around my waist and hoists me into his warm, hard chest.

A flush of heat coats my cheeks as his body hunches over mine. He doesn't release me, he remains close. Our faces are merely inches apart. His eyes flick between mine, then down to my parted lips that are still trying to inhale oxygen.

There goes my heart again. *Thump. Thump. Thump.*

JJ leans closer, the tip of his nose grazing mine. I draw in a sudden breath, my entire body bursting into flames at the gentle action. Goddamn those sambuca shots because I can't take my eyes off him.

My head is telling me to go home, to call a cab, to end this night now. But I can't. Something is stopping me from moving. Instead, I lick my lips and tremble in his hold as he spreads his fingers wide against my back.

I almost lose myself to the sensation.

JJ inhales, his eyes slightly hooded. "Come home with me," he rasps. "Let me show you how much of a gentleman I can be."

My eyes flutter shut for a brief second, and I step into his hold, his warmth surrounding me like a soft hug.

I am well and truly screwed.

When I open my eyes, he's staring down at me with an unexpected tenderness. Oh god. That handsome face.

"If by gentleman you mean you'll make me a good cup of

tea to cure this hangover for tomorrow," I say with a stroke of confidence. "Then I'm all for it."

A playful smirk flashes across his lips. "I make a fucking great cup of tea."

For a moment, I expect him to drop my waist, but he doesn't. He draws me in impossibly closer until I'm throbbing all over.

"Do you have oat milk?"

"No," he admits with a small chuckle. "But there is a twenty-four-hour shop beside my apartment. I can grab you some on the way."

I slowly remove myself from his grip, but his fingers remain resting against my hip to stabilise me on my heel. "Fine," I say as I fold my arms over my chest. "You've sold me."

JJ fishes his phone out of his pocket and orders a cab to his apartment, which is on the other side of town. When it arrives, he guides me over to it before helping me into the car.

I'm trying my damn hardest to keep my breathing quiet because I am being anything but cool right now, and I don't need JJ to see how badly this situation is affecting me.

We arrive at JJ's apartment, and he guides me up to the second floor before I slip off my shoes and carry them the rest of the way. I don't bother asking who he lives with, I doubt he'd be bringing me back to his parents' house after what he told me tonight.

He shows me inside. It's clean and simple and smells like fresh laundry and thick aftershave, but mixed together, it's not too prominent.

The door shuts behind me with a soft click, and I turn to him with wide eyes. "We forgot the oat milk," I blurt.

JJ's delicious mouth twists into another soft smirk. "What a shame," he murmurs before sliding his hand across my cheek delicately. He takes a step towards me, and I flutter my lashes up at him. "But I don't really think you came for the tea."

His voice is soft like silk and seductive like sin; it makes me want to close my eyes and submit. He's right, of course I didn't come for the tea.

It's been a while. I deserve pleasure as much as the next person. And from someone devastatingly handsome? Yes, please.

"Did you, *Ivy*?"

My mouth opens, but nothing comes out. His eyes have me stuck in a trance, and his lips curl like he knows exactly what I'm thinking.

His lips drop to the other side of my jaw, brushing my skin softly. "Tell me or I won't touch you any more than this."

I tilt my head, looking up at his tall stature as he straightens his spine for a brief second. Only now without my heels do I notice how damn tall he is, and it's doing absolutely nothing for my pounding core.

"No," I whisper. "I didn't come for the tea."

JJ smirks against my jaw, and I despise how wobbly my voice came out. He's got me wrapped around his finger, and I don't even think I hate it, he can have me.

All of me.

For tonight, anyway.

"That's what I thought," he grumbles deeply.

For a moment, he pulls back, and both of our eyes are thick with desire. We know what's about to go down, and suddenly my knees are shaking at the thought. It might have been a while, but I'm willing to let myself go.

JJ takes my cheek with his other hand and presses his lips to mine. At first, the kiss is soft, delicate. It takes me a moment to feel the shape of his gorgeous mouth. His fingers slide into the back of my hair, tilting my head to the perfect angle so he can deepen the kiss.

I release a slow exhale as his tongue slips across my

bottom lip. I'm gasping when he brushes it against my own. My head twists and he steps forward, guiding me further into his apartment.

After a few seconds, his hands drop from my face, and he glides them over my shoulders and down my back until he reaches my ass and parts my thighs. My legs wrap around his waist with ease as he draws me into his arms as if I weigh nothing.

My fingers graze his buzzed hair, and I kiss him deeper, holding my arms tightly around his neck as he continues to walk. He kicks the door open, and then shut once we're inside.

JJ drops me to the bed but slides across me, our lips barely parting for a second. His fingers bunch at my sides, but he doesn't race to take off my dress, which is weirdly a relief. He's taking his time, and I couldn't be more grateful.

Instead, we explore each other through our kisses, the feel of our bodies with our clothes on. I understand that one-night stands are one-night stands for a reason, but it's nice to feel wanted and not used.

JJ parts from my lips and kisses over my jaw, down my neck, and over my collarbone. I stare up at his ceiling, trying to keep my breathing under control. He can probably hear a hurricane going off inside my chest, but his lips feel so damn divine, I don't care.

He raises up and looks down at me with dilated eyes and swollen lips. His heated gaze trails my face as he blows out a low breath.

JJ slowly flicks his fingers inside the straps of my dress. "Can I take this off?"

My breathing hitches, and the intensity of our gazes feels like a nuclear explosion. The thought of him seeing me naked is incredibly unnerving.

For a moment, I pause.

I've had a difficult relationship with my body for the past

few years, ever since the accident. This body hasn't felt like mine, regardless of the scars—physical and invisible.

My therapist tried so hard to get me to understand my thoughts, but I guess it's been psychologically imprinted into me. A mental block. *The fear of being vulnerable for someone else to see all my cracks and flaws.*

"We don't have to," JJ says, sensing my hesitation.

But his words slash into me.

I thought I'd be running at the idea of a one-night stand, but I don't want to. I want to stay. I want to push away these insecurities that have been crowding my mind for years. I want to be the woman I've always wanted to be. *Brave.*

A wave of confidence steams through me, I don't overthink it—I take it.

It's the first time I've felt empowered and comfortable in years.

"Take it off," I say boldly.

"You sure?" he asks, searching my eyes.

I nod adamantly. "Yes. Take it off."

He lowers to kiss the corner of my mouth gently. Then he flicks the straps off my dress and pulls it down my chest and legs until I am in nothing but my underwear. Suddenly, the cool air has me feeling more than exposed. I didn't wear a bra tonight because it didn't go with my dress.

But JJ's eyes soften as he looks down at my naked body. He takes his sweet time to analyse every inch of me. His gaze gravitates to the centre of my chest, right where my healed scar is. Beside my heart.

He blinks once, and then twice, but his expression doesn't give anything away.

Once upon a time, it was ugly and prominent, but now it's mostly red and flat.

His eyes dart to mine, and I bite down on my bottom lip with apprehension.

I try not to overthink. Not now.

He doesn't react with a look of disgust or shock, instead he lowers his head and kisses along the mark gently—like I'm made of glass.

Featherlight kisses.

As if he's trying not to hurt me, even though it's already healed.

"You are gorgeous, Ivy," he says before returning to my neck.

His words feel like they're being etched into my skin with his talented lips and perfectly placed hands.

I close my eyes and relax into his bed, taking a moment for myself before looking at him again. He kneels again and undoes his shirt, button by button. A sliver of flesh catches my attention before he shoves the material over his broad shoulders.

Tattoos litter his arms. Patchwork. Pretty. *Unbelievably attractive.*

But the sight of his toned stomach, beautiful smooth skin, and muscles over muscles takes my breath away.

Everything inside me tightens.

JJ takes my hand and places it against his rock-hard stomach. I tremble at the heat beneath my palm. "Oh, god," I rasp.

He tilts his head and lowers down, caging me between his two large biceps. "Oh, god… what?" His breath tickles the shell of my ear.

I swallow down my pride. "I haven't done this in a while," I admit.

JJ's head twists and catches my eye. "Do you want to stop? It's okay if you want to stop."

"No." I let out a strangled cry of desperation. That's the *last* thing I want. "I just wanted you to know."

He hums softly and presses a caress of a kiss to my pulse, and then my lips, leaving me breathless. "You are in control," he whispers against me. "We stop when you want to stop. But if you want to carry on, I want to make you feel good, Ivy. So please let me."

I raise my chest into his, grazing my nipples against his hardened torso. He claims my mouth once more, this time hungrier. He covers my body as I sink further into his mattress, into literal heaven.

My hand wraps around the back of his head, holding him to my lips as I kiss him deeper. "Please, make me feel good."

CHAPTER 4
IVY THOMPSON

A small huff of pain escapes my lips when I shift beneath the soft sheets. My head pounds at the same time I try to dampen my mouth, but it's drier than the desert.

Water. I need water before I burst into dust from the lack of moisture inside my body.

My eyes crack open as my cheek nuzzles further into the pillow. For a moment, everything is blurry, but when I blink myself into reality, I realise this isn't my apartment.

I push myself back into the headboard and rub my eyes furiously for better vision, then I glance down at the bare-chested male beside me.

Last night. My date. My shoe. Sambuca shots. JJ. Unexpected orgasms.

I almost choke when I remember everything that happened. Oh fuck. I'm in his bed naked. Double fuck.

JJ is still sound asleep despite having moved around like an earthquake. I grab my phone from the bedside table and tap the screen to discover it's barely nine in the morning. I run a hand down my face and lean out of the bed to grab my clothes as quietly as possible.

When the floorboards creak, I whip my head over my

shoulder to look at JJ. His eyes are firmly shut, and he's breathing evenly. I take another step forward and slip on my dress quickly, my bottom lip between my teeth.

I grab my bag and shoes and walk towards his bedroom door. I pause for a moment and look back, hesitating if I should say goodbye. But what's the point?

It was a one-night stand.

We both ended up here for one thing. Sex is natural.

There would be no point hanging around, waiting for him to wake up so he can make me breakfast and swoon over how amazing last night was—that's if he didn't want to chuck me out after seeing me in his bed. I'd rather throw up all of yesterday's alcohol instead.

It won't work. I'm moving home. We both go to university.

A night of fun doesn't need to end with the swapping of phone numbers or awkward goodbyes.

We both had a shit start to the night, it ended with a fantastic bang. *Literally.* There isn't much more to the story, and honestly, I hate to admit it. JJ is far out of my league. Anyone with a pair of eyes can see.

With one firm nod to myself, I twist open his bedroom door and creep outside as I order an Uber on my phone. A vibration lets me know that my driver is two minutes away, and I almost sag in relief.

When I finally make it downstairs and onto the street, the driver pulls up to the curb and looks down at my bare feet, then at the shoes in my hand.

Ah, the trusty walk of shame.

As soon as I get home, thirty minutes later, I run upstairs to my flat and jump straight in the shower, followed by downing a litre of water and placing two crumpets in the toaster.

My body stiffens as I rethink what I've just done. I left without saying a word.

I slump against the counter and bury my head in my hands, my wet hair tickling my cheeks. My phone vibrates in my pocket, and I glance at the screen. Multiple messages from Erin. Oh god. She's probably worried sick.

Without hesitation, I click on the call button and hold the phone to my ear.

It takes two rings until she answers.

"Oh, Ivy," she shouts through the receiver, and I wince. "You didn't answer my texts. I was freaking out. What happened?"

I watch my crumpets pop up in the toaster and pluck them out, pressing my phone to my shoulder and holding it with my ear. I spread a little too much butter over them as I say, "Sorry, I'm so sorry." I exhale and grab my plate before heading to the living room. "Things were a little hectic last night."

Erin is silent for a long moment. "Don't tell me something happened with your asshole date because I will—"

"No," I cut over her. "Nothing happened with him. But it did with someone else."

"What?!"

I pull the phone back and put it on loudspeaker. "It's too early for all the shouting, Erin. Please turn it down a notch. My head is aching."

"You need to spill it all. *Now.*"

So I do. I tell her everything. Every last detail.

"Holy shit, Ivy. I'm—" She pauses. "I'm in shock."

I throw my head back against the sofa. "It's so unlike me, isn't it? I've never had a one-night stand in my life."

"But it was good?"

"Yeah," I rasp. "It was almost too good."

"Did he make you come?"

"A few times. I didn't know I could do it after drinking," I admit. "But he made me feel comfortable and safe, and nothing was rushed. It was far different from what I expected a one-night stand to be."

Erin hums with glee. "So, a gentleman then?"

"Yeah." I smile softly. "I guess so."

"Do you think you'll see each other again?"

I snort and lick the crumbs from my fingers. Those crumpets didn't even touch the sides, I need at least three packs of them to fill me up. "We won't be seeing each other again."

"Why?"

"Because I snuck out of his apartment this morning without saying anything. We didn't swap numbers. It's better this way."

Erin is so quiet, I think the line has gone dead. "You didn't get his number?"

"No. I didn't."

"Why on earth wouldn't you get his number?"

I close my eyes. "It's not going to work, Erin. You know I'm going home for the summer, and I'm not sure if I'm coming back."

It's taken me almost two and a half years to pluck up the courage to visit home. Especially after what happened.

Erin groans. "Don't remind me," she whimpers. "What am I going to do without you?"

"You'll do just fine," I reassure her. "You have art school coming up, and you'd barely have time for me anyway."

"Oh, shut up," she huffs. "How are you feeling about going back home?"

I open my mouth to speak, only to shut it again because I've been deflecting the answer for weeks. I want to be confident in my feelings, but I don't know what it's going to be like after these last few years.

"Not sure," I admit. "Hopefully it can just be a clean slate and a fresh start. Push out all the bad memories. It's my hometown, I grew up there. It holds such a special place in my heart, and I don't want to resent it."

"You're strong, Ivy."

I wish I thought the same.

"Do you think you'll see Ben?"

For a moment, I hesitate at the mention of his name. I wish I could say that I'm numb to it, but I'm not. The memory of him lingers no matter how many therapy sessions I've gone to.

I clear my throat. "He's still meant to be in prison."

I haven't heard anything about his release, but he doesn't deserve to get out for the rest of his life. We all know what the justice system is like. You can commit a heinous crime and still get out for good behaviour. It churns my stomach.

"Well, let's hope he's rotting away in a jail cell and doesn't plan on getting out soon. He doesn't get to have this hold over you anymore."

My eyes shut tightly. "I know he doesn't."

"You deserve happiness."

I'd like to think so, too.

And as much as the thought of going home scares me, I'm trying to be optimistic. I haven't seen my brother, my friends, or even that beautiful sandy beach in what feels like forever. I've missed everything more than I realise.

"Thanks, Erin."

"Don't forget about me, whatever you do."

I release a slow chuckle. I could never forget Erin, even if I wanted to. If only she hadn't thrown her drink over some guy who was being a little too friendly to me at the bar we met at two years ago. A friendship was born out of instant loyalty.

"Well, come see me before you leave, yeah?"

I hum and sit up, leaning over the coffee table to look down at my phone. "Of course. I'm going on Tuesday. I still have some things to take care of at the flat and with my landlord."

"Okay, swing by tomorrow?"

"Definitely. See you then."

"Love you."

"Love you."

Erin disconnects the call before I do. I slump back against the sofa. I should get packing, but I could also do with twelve hours' sleep. I ponder for a few moments before leaping towards my bedroom for a well-needed nap.

Except, I have to force myself to think of anything other than JJ and the way I smelt of him this morning.

CHAPTER 5
IVY THOMPSON

The drive home wasn't nearly as bad as I thought it would be. I left at a good time with minimal traffic, and the sun beamed the entire way.

This is it.

This is the fresh start I need in Willows Bay.

A lot of people hate the beach because sand gets absolutely everywhere, but I chose to embrace it from a young age. Even when you find grains of sand in your shoes for days. But that's the beauty of the beach, it follows you everywhere.

And for a summer of hopeful fun, I will take it any day.

I can't believe I haven't been back in over two years.

This time will be different, I'm sure of it.

As I pull up outside my parents' house—and my childhood home—I sit in my car for a few moments and stare. Nothing has changed, it's the exact same house I remember.

The arches are still painted white, and the house is still the most perfect shade of sky blue with my favourite wooden bench on the porch.

My heart softens as I take it all in. I could never forget what my first home looked like, but today feels like I'm seeing it again for the first time. It is, and will always be, the most beautiful house I've ever laid eyes on.

I suck in a breath and pop open the car door. Once my feet touch the ground, I smile. All my memories with my parents come flooding back, even my brother—despite how much we'd argue as kids.

My hands pat my pockets as I dig out my keys. Once I press it into the lock and step inside the house with a thumping heart, a waft of linen washing and fresh plants instantly makes me feel at home.

"Ivy?"

My brother's voice booms through the house at the same time footsteps run across the landing upstairs. Then he's directly in front of me as he rushes down the stairs.

He doesn't look different, but he looks grown. Now with stubble growing out across his jaw and his blond hair wet and dripping across his forehead.

"Hey, Finn," I grin back at him.

He takes me in and then moves across the kitchen like a flash of lightning. His arms wrap around my body as he draws me into the world's biggest hug. I chuckle into his chest as he pulls me off the floor.

"God," he mumbles and squeezes me tighter. "It's so good to see you."

"You too. I missed you."

Finn pulls back slowly and analyses me. "Missed you more. How have you been?"

I nod and brush back my hair with my fingers. "Yeah, good. Really good. What about you?"

"Happy it's summer. University is a bummer," he comments. "But we don't have to talk about that. I'm just pleased you're finally here."

"Pleased to be home," I confess.

Finn tilts his head and grips my shoulder. "You sure?"

Concern is slashed across his face.

"Yeah." I flash him a smile, even though I'm not one hundred percent sure myself. I've been here five minutes. Things might be different tomorrow.

"Okay." He takes a step back. "You know Mum and Dad are away, right?"

"Yeah, Mum told me last week."

Finn hums. "Got plans for today?"

"Probably unpack and go and surprise Daisy. She doesn't know I'm home; I've been texting her all morning," I say as I shove my keys into my pocket.

"Sounds fun, sis." He ruffles my hair, and I bat his hand away. "Glad to have you back for the summer."

"Maybe forever," I blurt.

Finn's eyes widen. "Forever?"

"Well, not forever. But I mean, I probably won't go back to Chesterville, I'll probably find somewhere closer to university because the commute was a little too long. I'm not sure of everything yet."

His smile softens. "Good for you, Iv."

I hike my thumb over my shoulder. "I'm gonna grab my stuff from my car."

"I'll help," he says as he follows me out and carries my stuff upstairs. "Jesus, how much stuff do you own?"

I chuckle to myself as we enter my old bedroom to find it exactly the way I left it. "A lot, apparently."

"Girls are far too much," he mutters under his breath.

"That's probably why you don't have a girlfriend."

Finn's eyes waver for a moment before he clears his throat and recovers. He flashes me a quick smile that seems forced. "Whatever," he grumbles. "I'm too busy for a girlfriend. It would never work."

After unpacking most of my belongings, I head straight to Daisy's house.

Daisy has been my best friend since the first year of secondary school. We were paired up in music class for a project to create a Christmas song—it's safe to say neither of us has any musical talent.

Ever since then, we've been inseparable. Other friends have filtered in and out of my life, but Daisy stuck. We've been friends for almost ten years, that's something.

She came to visit me a couple of times over the past few years because I refused to come home, but she never complained. I think she was pleased to get out of this small town and experience a busy city.

As I approach her door, I quickly knock and stand back on the porch. It takes a few moments before I hear the door unlock. My best friend's eyes fall on mine, and she screams.

"What the hell?"

Before I get the chance to open my mouth to say hello, she's already pounced on me with both her arms and a leg. We almost topple backwards, but I grip onto the pillar of her house and laugh. I wrap my arms around her to hug her back.

"Oh my god, oh my god," she repeats. "I can't believe you're here. Why are you here?"

My lips curve as she squeezes me to death, then eventually she pulls back to study my face with a watchful eye. "Here for the summer, possibly longer."

Daisy's face melts to a look of awe. Her long, thick brown hair flows over her shoulders, naturally curling at the ends, with the brightest blue eyes I've ever seen.

She can catch anyone's attention instantly because she's half Spanish, and her skin turns the most beautiful bronze shade in the summer.

"I can't believe you didn't tell me," she huffs with a grin. "You're so sneaky."

I laugh. "Surprise?"

"Come in." She waves her hand into the house. "My parents are at work."

When I step inside, a very fluffy, very cute golden retriever bounds towards me. My heart bursts in my chest as he nuzzles his face against my legs. "Rufus," I beam as I drop to my knees, and he flops onto his back for belly rubs. "Oh, I missed you. Yes I have."

Daisy stands beside me with a hand on her hip. "It's been a while since he's seen you."

"Too long," I comment. "God. He's so cute."

"The cutest." She laughs softly. "And here all summer."

Rufus stands back on his feet and barks at something in the garden before racing off.

"Let's go upstairs," she says, and I follow her to her bedroom.

The second I step into her room, I'm floored with memories. Thick nostalgia rushes through my veins. We've had lots of fun in this house, getting ready for parties, sneaking her parents' alcohol from the cupboard, crying in her bathroom over stupid arguments, and endless sleepovers.

This place tells a tale.

"Come sit." She pats her bed. "You need to tell me everything because I can't believe you're here."

I shrug and perch beside her. "Not much to tell. I thought it's time to come back."

"You haven't been here since…"

"Yeah." I clear my throat. "Since what happened. But it's done; I need to move on and prove to myself that I can."

"Of course," she agrees before slinging an arm over my shoulder. "It's so good to have you back. We're going to have the best summer ever. Without a doubt. Okay?"

I smile and settle into her arms as I latch onto her wrist. "Yeah. Of course we are."

And for once, I kind of believe it.

When I get home later that evening, Finn is sitting at the kitchen island with his phone in hand. "Hey," I call out.

"Hey, did you see Daisy?"

"Sure did." I shove my hands into my hoodie pocket as he taps away at his phone screen. "You good?"

He hums. "Yeah, my best friend from uni is almost here."

"Oh, come to visit?"

"For the summer, yeah." He hops off the stool and walks to the front door.

My brows dip quickly. "Oh. You didn't tell me anyone was staying?"

"It was kind of a last-minute thing," he shrugs and latches onto the door handle. "But he's here now."

I step back and watch as he walks onto the porch and throws his hand in the air. "Hey man," he yells, and I dip between the space to see who he's waving at.

My gaze snags on a black Polo, and I see movement of arms and legs, but no face. I follow Finn onto the porch as a guy walks towards the house, head slightly down to watch the pavement.

His head tilts upwards beneath his hood, and all the air in my lungs evaporates. I think I might be choking—no, scratch that, I think I might be having a stroke.

My knees buckle, and I'm seconds from hitting the deck.

Panic crawls through my sternum, but I tell myself to keep it together because my brother cannot see my reaction. He can't see me freaking out because the guy coming to stay with us for the summer is my brother's best friend—the guy I had a one-night stand with five fucking days ago.

He flashes a devastating smile at my brother and then turns his attention to me.

Our eyes collide, and this is when I realise it might be the end of the world. No exaggeration.

His smile falters when he recognises me, but he instantly covers it.

"Did Mum and Dad say they were fine with this?" I mutter under my breath as I tell myself not to go into cardiac arrest.

Finn nods with a chilled expression. "Yeah, they're totally fine with it."

"Oh… great," I say through a wobbly smile.

When in fact this isn't great. It's far from great.

It's a disaster.

CHAPTER 6
JJ WOODFORD

I'm not exactly sure what's going on right now.

All I know is I've turned up at my best friend's house for the summer, to find the girl who left my apartment a few days ago after a mind-blowing night.

No goodbye. No number exchange. Absolutely nothing.

Alarm bells start ringing inside my head as Ivy lingers in the doorway to Finn's house. What on earth is going on here?

Fuck. Don't say she's his new girlfriend or something, because this is the sort of shit that would happen to me.

I suck down a troubling breath as I step close to Finn. We parted ways only a few weeks ago after our third year of university together, but we still hug like we haven't seen each other in years.

"How are you, man?" Finn slaps my back.

I force a smile as my gaze falls on Ivy, who is staring back at me in utter confusion. "Yeah, good. Journey could have been worse."

Finn pulls away and smiles, then beckons me into the house as Ivy steps away. Her eyes roam over my body quickly and then glance at the wall. Her teeth sink into her bottom lip, and then she fiddles with a piece of string falling from her cardigan.

She's nervous, that's obvious. I guess I'm about to find out why.

Finn turns towards me as we step inside their coastal house. The air smells like lingering sea salt, especially when I stepped out of the car. A scent I'm definitely not used to living in a built-up city filled with CO_2 emissions and rotting garbage.

"JJ," Finn starts. "This is my sister, Ivy. Ivy, this is JJ."

Okay, maybe this is worse. They're related.

I stare back into Ivy's bottle-green eyes. The same eyes that almost had me hypnotised when we first met. I remember the way they flared at me when I teased her at the bar, and boy, I wanted her so bad. Only to be left in my bed alone the next day.

Dare I say she looks even more beautiful than the night I met her.

I don't know how, but she does. And it's killing me.

These are not the thoughts I should be having now that I know the facts.

"Nice to meet you," she blurts out.

I tilt my head slowly, but Finn doesn't clock anything. My arm extends, and she glances down at it hesitantly for a moment. "You, too."

She reluctantly shakes my hand for a second before dropping it like my touch has burned through her skin. She steps away and lowers her gaze as Finn presses a hand to my shoulder.

"Let's go grab your stuff and I can show you around."

"Alright," I agree as Finn steps out of the house towards my car.

I take one quick glance at Ivy again, but now she's turned away and walking through the house, her head low.

Once we bring my belongings inside, I take a moment to

admire the decor throughout the house. There are pictures of seashells organised in a picture frame, along with oil paintings of the sea and cute ornaments of beach huts.

"You worship the sea here, huh?" I laugh.

Finn exhales a long breath, then smiles. "Yeah, our parents live, die, breathe this sort of lifestyle."

As we walk through the house, the stairs are located at the back. My eyes snag on the open-plan kitchen as we walk by. Ivy is standing at the island with a glass of water and is staring blankly at the transparent liquid.

"You need to tell me about the last two weeks back home, man," Finn says as he directs us towards the stairs.

"Uh." I glance over my shoulder as we walk up the stairs, but Ivy has her back to me. "Yeah, sure."

It's been a while since I've clicked with someone the way I clicked with Ivy. Probably because I had no expectations of that night before I met her. I haven't had real fun like that in a while.

"This will be you," Finn says as he shoves open one of the doors with his foot.

We step inside the plain but homely room. Soft duck egg blue bed sheets against a white framed bed, a simple dresser, and even more pictures of the beach cover the walls.

Finn dumps my bag down on the bed, and I follow his lead, taking in the room again.

"Will this be alright?"

I hum. "Thanks, man. And thank your parents again. I know this all came up at the last minute."

"I know you've got family shit going on and I don't want you to be alone. This place might seem boring and quiet, but it's definitely fun in the summer." He shrugs.

"I didn't think it would be boring," I admit. "Something different, but sometimes change is good."

Finn flashes me a smile and heads towards my door slowly. "Precisely."

"Hey." I catch his attention before he leaves.

When he turns back to me, I focus on his green eyes. The resemblance between him and Ivy is almost obvious now. Rich blonde hair, the same eyes. They don't necessarily look the same, but they have similar features.

I clear my throat. "I didn't know you had a sister. You never mentioned her."

"Twin," he clarifies, and I tense.

Somehow, that makes this a thousand times worse. They shared a womb.

"And besides, you never asked." He folds his arms across his chest, but something else flashes in his eyes that catches me off guard.

We've definitely spoken about family before, and something tells me Finn didn't mention Ivy for a reason. A reason I can't seem to understand. Three years I've known the guy, and I didn't know he was a twin? That screams suspicious to me.

But I drop it for the sake of our current situation.

Then he stalks forward a few steps, and I know exactly what's coming. I gulp silently but try to remain calm and collected.

"Stay away from my sister, okay? She really doesn't need any more drama."

Any more?

I'm expecting some kind of deathly glare from Finn, but instead, he looks concerned more than anything. Of course he doesn't want me anywhere near his sister. I don't think any guys want their friends to go after their relatives.

"Okay," I rasp. "You got it."

"My parents should be home in a few weeks." Finn leans back against the wall and crosses one foot over the other. "But you can have access to whatever you need. You've got a bathroom just next door, and you can use the kitchen whenever you want."

"Alright, thanks."

"I'll let you unpack your stuff. When you're done, I can show you around Willows Bay. Sound good?"

I hum and begin to unzip one of my bags. "Yeah, sure."

"Sweet."

When I'm left alone, I unpack my clothes into the wardrobe and drawers until my bags are empty, and the room feels a little more full than it did before.

I head downstairs when I'm done, expecting to find Finn, but he's nowhere to be seen. Instead, I spot Ivy leaning against the counter in the kitchen, her phone between her hands. I pause by the last step and turn my attention upstairs, hearing music blasting from one of the rooms.

Ivy doesn't notice me until I'm off the last step and walking towards her. Soon, those green eyes find mine, and she sucks in a breath. For a long moment, we have a silent standoff, and I can't tear my eyes away.

"What the hell are you doing here?" she eventually hisses under her breath.

I quirk a brow. "What am I… what are you doing here?"

Ivy's jaw crunches. "I live here."

"I see that," I state.

Her chest heaves as she begins to pace.

"Should we talk about what happened?"

"No." She whips her head to me. "Absolutely not. Finn is literally upstairs."

I lean back slightly and fold my arms across my chest. "So, are we going to pretend what happened never happened?"

"Yes," she sighs. "Of course we are."

I flick my gaze between hers. She stares right back with a hardened expression.

I'd like to know why I woke up in an empty bed, but I guess I'm not going to find out with the way she's looking at me.

"Alright, fine," I murmur under my breath. "If that's how you want to play it."

Ivy doesn't reply, and I huff out a silent sigh.

The upstairs floorboards creak, and I brace myself for Finn's entrance. I walk towards one of the cupboards and search for a glass to pretend to fill.

"You all done?" Finn's voice echoes from behind me.

I twist to find him shoving his phone into his pocket. "Yeah."

"Let's head out," he says, grabbing his keys from the counter. "I'll show you around town."

CHAPTER 7
IVY THOMPSON

The next morning, I'm up bright and early. As soon as the sunlight started to seep through my blinds, there was no chance I could lie in. I've spent all night tossing and turning.

After getting showered and dressed, I head downstairs to grab some breakfast, praying I don't bump into JJ or Finn.

Finding out that JJ will be staying for the summer is bad as it is, but knowing I could see him almost every day? I need to get out of the house as much as possible.

When my toast pops up, I slip my phone from my pocket and call Daisy.

"Ugh, Ivy," she grunts into the phone. "It's so bloody early."

"I'm sorry, but I really need to get out of the house."

Daisy exhales a breath. "Okay. Meet me at the beach huts in twenty."

I nod and butter my toast before taking it on the go. "Please bring Rufus. I need the extra love."

Her soft laugh echoes in my ears. "Okay. I'll bring him. Let me get ready, and I'll see you soon."

"Thank you," I say before taking a bite of my breakfast and heading out the door.

The sun has just risen over the horizon, projecting the most beautiful shades of orange and pink across a cloudless sky. Sunrise is my favourite. Everyone cries over sunsets, but never when the sun rises; it's severely underrated.

In those few moments, it feels like time stands still and we're given a new chance at yesterday.

As soon as I reach the beach front, I suck in a large breath of air and smile. The waves gently crash into the shore. My eyes close for a second. Peace. So much peace. It warms my heart, and I didn't realise how cold it was before now.

I'll *always* be a seaside girl.

My shoes touch the grainy sand. It's a lot lighter than I remember, but still stunning. Every inch of this beach is shining in its own glory.

I snap my head to the sound of a barking dog. Rufus bounds towards me along the beach huts. I grin and lower to the ground as he rushes into my arms, knocking me backwards. A laugh bursts out of me, and I give him a big hug as he attempts to lick my face.

"Stop it," I chuckle. "I won't taste good, Rufus."

He licks my hand, and as I gently push him away, he pants with his large tongue extended. My heart melts. Such a big softy. I wrap my arms around him and give him another hug.

Soon, Daisy catches up to us and I stand from the ground, dusting off the sand from my ass. "He's very excited to be out today." She flashes me a smile as she holds out an arm and brings me into a gentle embrace. "What's going on? Because getting up at this time should be illegal."

"What should be illegal about this?" I say, gesturing to the rising sun and orange-painted sky.

Daisy glances and places a hand on her hip. "True. It's been a while since I've gotten up for the sunrise."

My lips twist into a frown. "Why?"

"It was always our thing, and it didn't feel right doing it without you. You're the only person who could drag me out of bed at 5am to see a sunrise."

I beam at her. "But worth it, right?"

Daisy nods and looks back to the sky. "Right."

We walk down to the beachfront and sit by the dry sand, watching the water come and go in gorgeous, quiet waves.

"What's been going on?" she asks, patting the spot next to her for Rufus to sit, but he darts into the sea and splashes around in the shallow water.

A smile creeps up onto my face as I watch him. Oh, to be a dog and have absolutely no care in the world. At least I wouldn't be in the predicament I'm in right now.

My face drops within a second. "Well…" I clear my throat and focus on the sunrise. "One of Finn's friends from university is staying with us for the summer."

"Right," she says as I pause.

"And he—" I cut myself off and turn to her. "I kind of met him last week without knowing who he was, and we went on this *non-date* date."

Daisy's green eyes widen in shock. "Oh my god, what?"

"I know." I cover my face with my hands.

She tugs on my wrist and forces me to look at her as she blinks. "You need to tell me everything."

I choke down a breath, but I can't find it in myself to tell her that I slept with him. Not because I'm ashamed, but because I can't wrap my head around the idea myself. It's unlike me, and as much as she's my best friend, I don't have the courage to disclose it to her yet.

"He's staying at your house?"

"Yes."

"Are you going to tell Finn?" she asks.

"Absolutely not. It'll make the situation worse. With everything that happened with Ben—" I close my eyes and catch my breath. "I can't. Finn will freak out, and I want to have a good summer."

Daisy chews on her lip. "But what if he finds out?"

"He's not going to find out." I shake my head with confidence. *Because he can't.*

Finn is protective. He always has been. But since my accident, I saw the way he deteriorated. He blames himself, but it's not his fault.

"What's he like then?"

"Please, let's not go there." I wince.

She groans loudly. "Come on. I need the details. You've been away for years, and I want the goss. And quite honestly, Ivy, you going on a date seems pretty serious to me."

I study my best friend and her curious eyes. "First, I was on a date with someone else, and it was definitely the worst date of my life. Anyway, later on when I was leaving, my heel snapped, and JJ was standing there helping me. He offered to take me out to try and make my night better. At first I was sceptical, because I just wanted to go home. But then we went to a bar and got cocktails and shots. It surprised me how much fun we had."

"Holy shit." Daisy claps a hand over her mouth. "I can't believe this."

"Trust me. I feel the same."

"Was he nice at least?"

I nod. "He was charming, funny, and easy to be around. Stupidly good-looking. Like way, way out of my league. I'm still baffled by it, and I'm convinced it was some kind of fever dream."

"I don't even know what he looks like, but you are not out of anyone's league, Ivy. You are beautiful," she says as her brows press together.

The corners of my lips curve at her words, yet I don't always believe them. "Thanks, Dais."

"Did you want to see him again?"

"We had fun, but I left it at that."

"So, is that a no?"

"I'm not sure if I can be in a relationship right now."

"What happened when you left?"

"Nothing." I sigh. "I didn't give him my number. I knew I was moving home, and he told me he goes to university." I grip onto the sand to release it moments later.

Daisy frowns but doesn't say anything.

"Then I got home, and Finn said his friend was coming to stay. And there he was, getting out of his car."

She stares back at me with shock. "Oh my, this is like an episode of *Geordie Shore.*"

I roll my eyes at her dramatics. "Nothing is going to happen. It's not going to work, so there's no point going there."

Daisy calls Rufus back to us, shaking off his wet fur. "Well, that's a shame. Shall we go for a walk? We'll lose Rufus to the ocean if we keep taking our eyes off him."

"Sure."

As we walk down the beach, Rufus runs circles around us. Daisy fills me in about what she's been up to with university. She's yet to find a boyfriend, and I know how picky she is. They'll have to be perfect in every sense.

Two people in the distance begin to walk towards us with a small brown terrier. Rufus barks and Daisy sighs, calling out for him as he moves closer but doesn't reach the other dog.

"Honestly," she mutters. "He's made friends with the whole town."

I chuckle quietly. "Wouldn't expect anything less from him."

We walk towards the two people who have stopped so Rufus can gently greet their dog. Daisy grips my wrist. "Oh my god, do you know who that is?"

"No." I squint. "Who is it?"

"Isaac and Harriet," she murmurs under her breath. "From school. I haven't seen them in ages."

We inch closer until Isaac's eyes find mine. He does a double-take. I'm pretty sure he thinks he's seeing a ghost; except I didn't die, and everyone in this town knows that I survived and moved away without a second thought.

"Ivy?" Isaac calls out. "Oh my, how long has it been?"

"A while."

Isaac was one of my first friends at school. We had some classes together, including biology where we both thrived. But when I left, we didn't stay in contact. That's my fault, I wanted to leave everything in this town behind.

"How are you?" I ask.

I focus on his face, curly black hair, and glowing brown skin. He looks so grown up now, even with the evidence of stubble on his cheeks and jaw. Throughout school, we were mostly the same height, but he's rocketed since. At least eight inches taller than me.

"Good." He doesn't take his eyes off me. "I'm good. You back for the summer? I had no idea you were home."

I clear my throat. "Yeah, just visiting for now."

"Fair enough." He flashes me a handsome smile. "Well, hopefully I might get to see you a bit more this summer."

"For sure."

"There's a party tomorrow." Harriet catches my attention. We weren't as close as I was with Isaac, but I remember her being a nice girl. "On the beach. You guys should come. There will be a bunch of people from school coming, and it might be nice to have a little reunion."

Daisy hums. "Sounds like fun to me. Ivy?"

Isaac's gaze lingers on me carefully, and I nod. "Yeah, of course. We're there."

"Great." Harriet grins. "We'll probably start just before sunset. Bring drinks."

"Of course," Daisy says as Harriet calls for her dog to move away from Rufus. "See you then."

Isaac and Harriet begin to walk until Isaac stops and locks eyes with me, offering me a gentle smile. "It'll be really great to see you there, Ivy," he says genuinely.

"You, too," I agree.

When they're gone, we head towards the road. "That guy has had a crush on you since year seven. I swear."

I shake my head, dismissing her words.

"He asked me to the school disco in year eight, but we went as friends. That's all we were throughout high school."

Daisy tuts. "Trust me. I can tell. He's chuffed you're home. And his glow up has done him wonders."

She's not wrong. He looks great, I almost didn't recognise him at first.

"Hey," Daisy says as she dips her hand into her pocket to take out her vibrating phone. "Sorry, I need to dash off. I promised my mum I'd help her with my grandma this morning."

"It's okay. Thanks for meeting me. I needed to get this off my chest."

She cups my arm and pulls me into a hug. "You've got this. Summer is going to be good. Focus on yourself."

"Of course."

"See you tomorrow for the party?"

"Most definitely." I lean down to scratch Rufus' damp ears. "See you later."

I wave and prepare myself to head home.

CHAPTER 8
JJ WOODFORD

"What do you say…" Finn swats me in the chest as I chug down a glass of milk. "Party, tonight?"

"Sure," I nod. "People you know from school?"

He shrugs. "Pretty much. Will be nice to see old friends. I can introduce you; it will be good for you to know a few familiar faces."

"Right," I say as I place down the empty glass. "Where is it?"

"On the beach." He gestures in the direction of the sea. "Bring your own beers. Why have house parties when you have an endless beachfront?"

I can't say I've ever been to a party on the beach, considering I'm a city boy, but I guess there is a first for everything.

"What time are we heading out?"

"Around eight," he says as he grabs his phone and punches out a text. "You wanna go into town beforehand? I can show you all the decent pubs with good beer gardens."

"Sounds good to me."

When we get home a few hours later, Finn orders that we start to get ready, and he takes longer than any girl I've ever met, so I start thirty minutes after him.

Once I'm ready and dressed in an oversized hoodie and shorts, I adjust my nose ring and brush a hand over my buzzed hair.

Music blasts from Finn's room as I step out into the hall. The door to the bathroom between my room and Finn's opens. My eyes latch onto Ivy as she strolls out wearing nothing more than an olive-green towel that showcases her pale skin. Her champagne-blonde hair brushes the edges of her shoulders, droplets rolling down her arms.

She hasn't seen me yet; her eyes are glued to her phone between her hands.

"Are you going to the party tonight?"

Ivy's body jolts, and her phone almost slips from her hand—worse—her towel almost slips from her body. She clutches her arms to her chest in an iron grip that makes her knuckles turn white.

"Jesus—" she hisses, staring up at me through damp lashes. Her nose wrinkles, with the freckles over her fair skin on full display. "You scared me half to death."

My lip twitches into a smirk as I fold my arms over my chest. "I see that."

She scowls at me, and it's infuriating that she looks pretty doing it. I've never really been into the mean-pretty thing because some girls are actually spiteful, but this is different.

"Why does it matter if I'm going to the party?" she asks with a tight expression.

"Because I'm wondering if I'm going to see you there."

She stares at me for a long beat, straightening her spine. "Maybe."

When she moves to walk around me, I don't say anything else. I stare ahead at the wall and smile to myself.

Okay, we really are pretending we don't know each other.

Finn has introduced me to far too many people. I don't struggle with remembering their faces, it's remembering their names. Especially when alcohol is involved. But I made an effort to remember his closest friends, Joel and Callan.

They've been friends since year seven, and even though Finn left school five years ago, they're thick as thieves.

Now the sun has gone down, we're perched around a bonfire on blankets, others on broken pieces of log. There is a speaker near the drinks table, someone even brought a keg, which I thought I'd only see in American movies.

Willows Bay is a pretty little town, it's definitely different from city life.

It's calmer and quieter, and everything I needed to clear my mind.

As I sit between Finn and Joel, both of them try to tell the same story from when they were kids. I laugh along with them until I spot familiar blonde hair as it flaps gently in the wind.

"I'm gonna go grab another beer," I mutter as I watch her approach the drinks table.

Neither of them turns to me with suspicion. Finn tilts his head back and cackles at something Joel said, almost falling off the log. I know he loves to drink, I've seen it at university, but he's definitely starting to peak too early.

As I approach the drinks table, Ivy stands with her back to me. She's wearing a pair of boyfriend shorts and a black crop top. I pause by her as I reach for a new beer.

"I can't believe you live here," I admit as I inhale the salty air.

The beach has never really appealed to me until now. Sand is rather inconvenient, but listening to the waves is therapeutic when I'm used to car horns and midnight trouble.

Ivy turns her head towards me, and I notice she's covered those freckles with make-up and made her lashes longer and darker. I inhale again because suddenly it's hard to breathe—even being outside.

When her eyes land on mine, she flicks her head over her shoulder, glancing around at anyone who could be watching us. I furrow my brows. Does this interaction really bother her this much?

I shove my hands into my pockets. "Am I not allowed to talk to you now?"

Ivy grabs her freshly made drink and draws her arms to her chest. "I don't want anyone getting the wrong idea," she mumbles, moving her eyes away from me.

"Look," I huff. "We're going to be living together for a few months."

"Months?"

My brows raise. "That a problem?"

She recovers her expression and clears her throat, brushing a strand of hair behind her ear. "I thought it would be a couple weeks, not months."

"I realise this makes you uncomfortable," I address.

Ivy scoffs. "Of course it does." She folds her arms over her chest. That's the last thing I want her to feel around me. "You're Finn's best friend."

"You're drawing more attention to us by resisting so much." I roll my tongue over my lip. "I'm just trying to talk to you. There is no crime in that."

"I'm not drawing more attention to us."

"You are." I exhale a sharp laugh. "God, so argumentative. You weren't lying."

Those green eyes narrow at me. Oh, I probably hit a nerve bringing up our date.

"I'm sure we can get through this summer without having to bump into each other or talk to each other. You'll be off with Finn, and I'll be doing my own thing," she states simply.

I can't stop the smile that meets my face. Her eyes dart

towards the action, and she flicks them back to mine with a scowl.

"What?"

"I'm wondering if there was a reason why you left my apartment without saying anything."

Ivy's eyes flash for a brief moment. She stands there and says nothing until she takes a step back and glances down at the sand beneath her feet. "Enjoy the party, JJ," she murmurs as she walks past me.

I turn to her. "You're not even going to answer the question?"

"There's no point dwelling on the past. Is there?"

When I don't say anything in response, she heads back to her friends. I raise my fresh beer bottle to my lips, taking a well-needed swig.

I breathe sharply through my nose before heading back towards Finn. A hand touches my shoulder, and I find Callan grinning back at me.

"Ready for some beer pong, JJ?"

"Ready as I'll ever be."

CHAPTER 9
IVY THOMPSON

No one needs to tell me that my face is the colour of salami. I'm grateful the sun has set, and nothing but the fire can illuminate my complexion. My lips latch onto the edge of my drink, and I take a sip—I shouldn't even call it a sip when half my drink is gone.

I perch on one of the logs beside Daisy, who is looking in the direction of the drinks table. I clear my throat and pretend that everything is fine after my conversation with JJ, but Daisy sees *all*.

After a long moment, she tosses her hair over her shoulder, brown curls whipping me in the face. "Who's that?"

My throat closes up. "That is Finn's friend from university."

"Oh my god, that's JJ?"

Here we go.

I suck in a breath and act unbothered. "Yeah," I say, finding the colour of my drink severely fascinating.

Inside, I'm deflating because this is the last situation I want to be in.

Daisy wraps her hand around my arm in a death grip. I

wince at the pressure. "Oh my fucking god. He's unbelievable. A nose ring and a buzz cut? Holy hell."

She's not wrong. He's in a league of his own.

When her eyes find mine, they're filled with excitement. I cringe internally. Without showing my true thoughts, I simply shrug and take another sip of my cup. "He's alright, I guess."

"You guess?" Her glossy red lips fall open. "What did he say to you?"

I brush a few strands of hair from my eyes and focus on the roaring fire in front of us. "Just being friendly," I admit.

Daisy slides her lips together and hums. They're so pouty and flirtatious that she can simply look in the direction of a man, and they're on their knees for her. She's built like a Spanish goddess, and I'm your average pale blondie.

Her eyes burn into mine. "Do you think you'll go back there with him again—"

I wave a hand in her face. "No, Daisy. He and Finn are best friends. *Best friends.* That line I cannot cross. Not again. You of all people should know that."

She hums in my direction and twists to look over at JJ, who is chilling with my brother and his friends. His mouth is stretched into a wide grin, and he tilts his head back and laughs before raising his beer bottle to his lips.

Unfortunately, he manages to flash the rings he has on his fingers, and I know Daisy is probably having a seizure over there.

"He's beautiful," she huffs.

I hum.

"Were there feelings there?"

My brows press together, and I shake my head. "No. How could I have feelings for him when I literally knew him for about four hours?"

She pants like a cat in heat. "Would it be weird if I spoke to him?"

I blink once in surprise and pause for a moment. She

finally turns to me with wild eyes, and I know she's a little buzzed right now because I doubt she would have asked if she was sober.

"I don't mean to like get with him," she clarifies. "Just to get to know him."

"No." I swallow quickly. "Not at all."

Daisy dips her head to read my expression. "If it's weird, you can tell me, Ivy. I totally get it."

Maybe this is what I need, for them to get together so that if Finn ever finds out, shit might not be as bad as it could be.

Daisy watches me for a long moment.

"Honestly," I exhale, blinking back the tightness in my chest. "It's fine. He's Finn's friend. So go ahead. Knock yourself out."

She breathes in so deeply, I think she's about to take off. "Boy, I want to get to know him."

I grind my teeth into my jaw when she takes another look. A wave of unexpected jealousy hits me right in the sternum, invading my body without permission.

It wouldn't have worked out anyway, so why am I grieving something that was never there?

I knew him for one night, and even though we had fun, I was the one who left without saying anything. I have no right to feel this alien emotion. It's pathetic if anything, and I try my hardest to brush it away.

For a split second, I imagine Daisy and JJ together. They'd make a good couple.

"He's all yours, Dais." I dig my fingernails into the bark of the log.

She lets out a squeal, a sound I didn't know she could make. Her arm wraps around me, and she tugs me into a side hug. "Thanks, Iv. You're the best. Nothing will happen. Doubt he'll even fancy me. But worth a shot, right?"

"Sure." I force a smile and hug her back.

Doubt he'll fancy her? There is absolutely no chance he

won't take one look at her and ask how many children she wants to have.

She has that effect on guys, and I shamefully have been envious of how easily they will fall at her feet. Being her friend throughout high school came with amazing benefits, but a shit tonne of insecurity.

Once she pulls her arms away from me, she stands, straightens herself out, and slides her glossy lips against one another again.

Without another word, she's walking in the direction of JJ.

I have no idea where she gets her confidence, but sometimes I wish I had it.

She's charismatic and bubbly without even trying.

I need as much liquid courage as possible to even think about doing what she's doing.

Before she reaches him, I glance away, downing the last few drops in my cup before forcing myself to stare at the fire. This is far more interesting than having my heart rate increase by watching them.

"Fancy seeing you here." I jump at the voice and glance up to find Isaac hovering next to the log.

My lips stretch into a smile. "Isaac. Hi."

"Hi." He laughs hesitantly. "Mind if I sit?"

"No." I shake my head and budge up, even though the log is empty. "Not at all."

Isaac sits down beside me, holding a can of cider. "How have you been?"

I swallow the lump lingering in my throat. "Yeah, good. How have you been?"

He rests his forearms on his knees and turns to look at me. The gleam from the fire highlights his face and showcases the curve of his jaw. "Yeah, I've been okay. Same old, same old."

"Did you go to university?"

Isaac smiles. "Still there, studying biochemistry."

"Wow." I widen my eyes. Then I nudge his side playfully. "Always knew you were super smart."

He laughs awkwardly. "What about you and university?"

"Biomedical science," I say.

"Being partners in biology helped us, then?"

I smile. "Yeah. it did. But now I've got into it, I'm enjoying it a lot more than at school."

Isaac hums with approval. "Nice. I'm pleased for you, Ivy. I really am."

"You, too," I say sincerely.

"You're back for the summer?"

"Maybe for good," I confess. "Still have another year of university, but I think I'll move back home eventually."

Isaac raises his can and clinks it against mine. "Good for you. I've missed seeing you around."

My heart clenches in the softest of ways. "You have?"

"Course." He bows his head. "We were friends for years, and then I never saw you again. That kinda hurt."

I frown. I didn't keep in contact with anyone when I left, only Daisy. But that's how I wanted to move on, by ignoring this town and everyone in it until I found the courage to come back.

"Sorry." I flash him an awkward smile. "I wasn't really thinking when everything happened, and I knew I needed to leave—"

His hand cups my knee to silence me. "I know. I get it. You don't have to explain yourself to me. That was an idiotic thing to say. I'm just glad to know you're doing okay."

I stare down at his hand against my leg, then up to his soft and honest eyes. "It was an idiotic thing for me to not talk to you," I admit. "But this summer I'm sure we'll be seeing a lot of each other."

Isaac beams at me. "Most definitely." He pulls his hand away. "It'll be good to catch up and reminisce on old times."

"Agreed. Let's vow to have a good summer of friendships."

I don't miss the way his throat bobs when I finish my sentence, but he recovers quickly. "Yeah." He leans over to peer at my drink. "You wanna grab another?"

When I glance over my shoulder, JJ and Daisy are nowhere to be seen. I freeze for a moment before turning back to Isaac. "Sure," I say, standing from the log.

He holds his hand out in front of me. "Lead the way."

CHAPTER 10
JJ WOODFORD

The first rule of going to a party where you only know one person is to never get too drunk. I passed successfully and woke up this morning feeling fairly decent. Finn on the other hand texted me from his room saying he feels like dog shit.

I don't really remember seeing him in a bad state last night, but that's because most of my night was occupied by the girl with tan skin and brunette hair. Danielle, was it? *No.* Daisy, like the cow. I remember almost saying that to her last night—good thing I didn't.

I knock on Finn's door, and when he groans in response, I let myself in. "Rise and shine," I say before ripping open his blinds to let in the sun.

He covers his face with a pillow. "You asshole."

"Come on, the beer can't have got you in this much of a state."

"I need coffee and a large breakfast from the café," he mumbles into his pillow pathetically.

I roll my eyes. "Since when have you been this dramatic?"

"I don't know," he grunts, and after a few moments, he

pushes himself up from the bed, rests his back against the headboard, and rubs his eyes viciously. "Oh god. I feel sick."

A stifled laugh escapes me as I cross my arms and lean on his dresser. "Still moping?"

He flips me off and manages to stand. "Fine. I'll go get breakfast."

"You will?" My brows rise in shock.

Finn nods and stabilises himself against the wall. "Let me find my car keys and I'll go."

"I'll come with you."

He waves a hand at me—signalling *no.* "I need the space. I need time not to be judged. Are you okay with that?"

"Fine," I chuckle. "Go and bring me back a bacon sandwich with coffee and no sugar. Thanks."

Finn doesn't bother to shower before he pulls on his clothes and searches for his keys. Five minutes later, he leaves, slamming the door on the way out. I head downstairs and grab myself a glass of orange juice.

I stare down at my phone and my recent texts with my dad. My mother's treatment has started, and the doctors will know soon if it's working. I've been praying with everything I have that she pulls through, and this is a miracle for her, for all of us.

A family without my mum isn't a family. It's a gigantic blackhole.

Loud music begins to blare from upstairs, and it startles me. Then I remember—Ivy is probably home. I sip on my orange juice and try to ignore the sound as I read over my father's last message, but become increasingly distracted when I hear an awful singing voice.

The sound of a door opens, and suddenly I hear footsteps coming down the stairs. She's still singing, but almost at a whisper as if she'd used up all her energy.

Ivy's foot touches the landing, and she glances up, her entire body tensing as she sees me. "What the hell are you doing here?" she demands, slightly out of breath. "I thought you left."

"Finn went out to grab breakfast." I laugh as I fold my arms over my chest. "Said I wasn't allowed to go with him because I'd be a distraction."

She snorts. "Probably because he's throwing up down the side of the door."

The corners of my lips tilt upwards. "Nice singing by the way," I say without hiding my amusement. "Those high notes were Grammy worthy."

Ivy's eyes burn before they narrow at me. She turns and heads back upstairs, but not before I hear her mutter, "Asshole," under her breath and I chuckle.

I make my way to the living room just in time for Finn to walk through the front door. He looks worse than when he left, his skin almost grey and his eyes dark and heavy.

"You good?" I quirk a brow.

"No," he declares. "Some lady tried cutting me off at a junction and then ended up my ass the whole journey back. Almost crashed."

I exhale a breath through my nose. "Typical. Did you get the goods?"

Finn holds up a coffee and a takeaway bag. "I drank mine on the way back. It was either that or vomit everywhere."

I shake my head at his dramatics as he passes me my coffee and then throws me the bag with my sandwich inside.

"What are we gonna do today?"

"Lay as low as possible," he groans before catapulting himself onto the sofa. "But if you want to do something, feel free. I've got a date with this lovely cushion and the football."

My brows hit my hairline. "Really?"

"I have games to catch up on."

"Funny, I thought you were over football after you ditched the team last term."

Finn narrows his eyes at me. "I had to. I was falling behind in class."

"Oh…" I trail off. "Not because of Maya—"

"Do not bring up her name," Finn warns me. "I beg."

I raise my hands in defence. "If only you'd talk to me about what happened."

If there's one thing I know about Finn, he keeps his cards close to his chest.

He practically fell in love with Maya the moment he laid eyes on her in second year, and now? I have no idea what happened between them because he won't open up to me.

I'd never push him, but it frustrates me to see him suffer.

"Nothing happened," he grumbles before reaching for the TV remote. "Now shut up and watch the game."

"Fine," I huff. "Whatever."

We get through twenty minutes of the first game when I hear footsteps echo down the stairs. I twist my head to see Ivy strolling past. She doesn't glance my way as she reaches the front door.

"Bye," she says quietly.

"Bye," Finn groans into his pillow like a sloth.

My phone vibrates beside me and I glance at it.

> UNKNOWN NUMBER:
>
> Hey, it's Daisy. It was so cool to meet you last night. I was wondering if you'd want to meet up another time, alone. Just us two. It would be nice to get to know each other.

I clear my throat and glance at Finn. "You know much about Daisy? She was at the party last night."

"You mean that smoking hot brunette, Victoria's Secret model lookalike?" He manages to pick his head up from the pillow an inch to look at me.

"Uh, yeah. I guess that's her." I give him a bemused look.

Thinking back to last night, there was a lot going on and

new people to meet. From what I can remember, she was pretty with the dark, alluring, mysterious vibe going on that most guys would find sexy.

Finn snorts to himself and turns back to the screen. "She's Ivy's best friend. Total man-eater."

Ivy's best friend.

Well shit. I wasn't expecting that. Does she know we hooked up?

"Why?" Finn mutters.

"She just texted me asking to hang out."

His mouth hangs open now, and I have his attention. Then by some miracle, he pushes himself up from the sofa. "She texted you?"

I nod once.

"Fuck, you have to text her back. She is hot."

"Sounds like you might have something for her," I state suspiciously.

Finn scoffs. "She's Ivy's best friend, man. That would be fucking weird."

Right. Of course. Just like how Ivy and I would probably be weird, but the damage has already been done.

He settles back into the sofa. "You should text her back."

My eyes are glued to my phone, gazing over the words again. I mean, yeah, she's cute, but something inside me isn't pushing to reply.

Any guy would jump at the chance of going out with her given her confidence, but I'm not interested. I only gave her my number because I didn't want to seem rude. She's a nice girl, but I like a little more chase.

I lock my phone without replying and focus on the football instead.

CHAPTER 11
IVY THOMPSON

"Come on, Daisy," I huff as I chuck a pillow at her across the living room. "These job applications aren't going to write themselves."

She rolls her eyes, long lashes fluttering against her cheek. She glances away from her phone and exhales a low grunt. I mean, I don't want to be helping her with her gap year job applications either, but I'm being a good friend because I know she won't do them herself.

"Iv," she grumbles with a frown. "Why hasn't JJ messaged me back?"

Now she has my attention.

I open my mouth, and it turns bone dry. "You texted him?"

Daisy nods and shuffles closer to me on the sofa. "Yeah, after the party. He gave me his number and I dropped him a text the day after, but he still hasn't replied. It's been days, Iv. *Days.*"

My heart pangs for her because I know she struggles to take rejection, mainly because she's rarely rejected, and when it happens, it hurts her a thousand times harder.

I have no right to dictate who she can speak to. I know I

can't be with JJ, so I can't gatekeep him. For all I know, they might work out and end up happily ever after, married with two kids in their semi-detached house in the city.

God. What am I even thinking?

"Maybe he's busy, or he hasn't been on his phone," I say with as much optimism as I can give. "I don't know."

"It's been four days. Ugh." She stares down at her phone screen and blows out a morbid sigh. "Where is he today? Is he in?"

I shake my head. "Went out with Finn earlier."

"Do you think he doesn't like me?"

"Dais, I have no idea. You met him once. Maybe he's trying to settle first. Let's focus on these job applications. I said I'd help you. Not gossip."

She narrows her eyes at me, and I look back to the laptop, praying she hasn't seen through my sudden defensiveness. But when she moves to sit next to me, I release a silent sigh of relief.

"Fine," she grumbles. "But only because I really need a job so I can save up and go travelling after university."

"Exactly." I point at her. "So put your phone away."

For thirty minutes, we scroll through potential jobs and highlight pages for her to come back to when she's ready to apply.

The front door opens, and I already know who it is without looking, but Daisy glances over my shoulder, her eyes lighting up like fireworks.

Finn and JJ are talking amongst themselves.

"Hey." Daisy grins widely, fluttering her eyelashes.

"Hey," Finn responds.

My eyes are glued to the screen as I act interested in these job adverts that are starting to all blur into one.

"What are you guys up to?" she asks.

"There is a storm coming, and we're gonna go to the beach and try out the waves. I'm gonna teach JJ how to surf,"

Finn explains, and I suck in a breath, finally turning towards them.

"A storm?"

"Well, not yet. It's brewing, which makes great baby waves for this one." Finn swats JJ on the shoulder.

I stupidly watch the action, then drag my eyes up his broad chest before resting on his dark blue eyes. I shudder at the intensity behind his stare. Yeah, it should be illegal for anyone to look that damn good.

"Can we come?" Daisy sits up on her knees.

Finn glances between JJ and Daisy and flashes a devilish grin at the three of us. "Sure. The more the merrier, right?"

JJ doesn't show any reaction as he turns to my brother. I glance at Daisy and shake my head with wide eyes. "We've got applications to do, remember?"

She waves me off and drops her eye into a subtle wink. "Those can wait, can't they?"

They sure can't.

I don't want to be stuck between my best friend, my brother and the guy I've been trying not to think about for the past two weeks. The last thing I need is to witness Daisy getting it on with JJ. I need to keep my distance for my own sanity.

"Oh come on, Ivy." Daisy grips my hand in a pleading gesture. "Just for a little while. It'll be fun. Right?"

Her gaze lands on JJ, and I flick my eyes to him. "Yeah, definitely."

"Great," Finn says loudly. "We're just gonna get changed and then head to collect our boards from the beach huts."

When they disappear upstairs, Daisy turns to me with a quiet squeal. "I might actually get to talk to him today," she whispers. "Maybe I got the wrong number, and that's why he didn't reply."

"Maybe," I murmur under my breath.

After getting changed and heading out, we walk to the beach front, which takes no less than a minute.

Finn walks towards our sunshine-yellow painted beach hut. "You having a go, sis?"

I blow out a breath. "Not a chance."

He turns to me and frowns. "Why not?"

My shoulders raise and drop heavily. "It's been a long time. I've probably lost my spark. I bet you'll be great, though. You've always been good at surfing."

He flashes me a cocky wink as he sorts through the beach hut and calls to JJ to come take one of the boards. I wrap my arms over my chest as he walks into the little hut, and JJ's tall stature looms over me as he stands in the doorway.

I freeze as I stare up at him.

Never in my life have I thought a man could pull off a buzz cut, until I met JJ.

When JJ takes the board, he glances down at me, and his brows furrow when he notices me staring. I clear my throat and avert my gaze.

"Need help with anything else?" I ask to act busy.

"Nope, I'm all good."

I back out of the hut before we begin to overcrowd it, just in time for Daisy to flash her flirtatious eyes at JJ.

We walk towards the seafront, listening to the waves crash against the shore. I close my eyes for a brief second and enjoy the sound. I've missed the calmness of the beach.

I glance down the coastline, there are plenty of other people who have the same idea. Brewing storms give the best waves and perfect weather to practice.

As we reach the ocean, they drop their boards, and I glance at JJ as he takes his T-shirt from the back of his neck and pulls it from his torso. I try not to let my eyeballs fall straight out of my skull at the sight of his rippling abs. I've seen them before, but I was slightly intoxicated then. Right now, it's like I'm experiencing it for the first time.

Daisy is practically drooling at the sight of him.

I don't blame her.

Finn slaps JJ's shoulder, and they take their boards and head towards the sea. I perch on the buttery sand, and Daisy exhales a sound somewhere between a sigh and a moan.

I draw my legs up to my chest and watch as Finn attempts to show JJ how to surf. The sun gleams down on us, and the water reflects off the light as it glitters across the waves. It's truly breathtaking. Something I'll never get bored of admiring.

They both laugh as they fall from their boards, then try again immediately.

It warms my heart to see my brother like this. We've adored the beach since we were kids; it's technically part of our souls.

It is us. It's our home.

Daisy begins to take off her sundress, revealing her ruby red bikini underneath. I take one glance at her tan and toned body, and that reminds me, I won't be taking my clothes off today—especially since my best friend is an absolute bombshell.

The boys' laughter echoes over the breaking waves. Daisy steps closer. "Can I have a go?"

JJ nods. "Sure, take my board. Finn can show you. I need a second out."

Daisy's expression falls flat at his words. She flicks her dark hair over her shoulder and walks towards my brother with the board anyway.

I tried to convince her every summer when we were growing up to let me teach her how to surf, but she said it was never for her.

JJ grunts as he lands on the sand beside me, water droplets falling over his sculpted biceps. I glance away, pretending that I didn't spend three seconds eye-fucking his strong tattooed arms.

Instead, I focus on Finn as he tries to keep Daisy up on the board; she screams when she falls in.

"I think having balance is the key," JJ hums.

The corner of my lip twitches. "Not so easy, is it?"

He turns to me with a small smile. "Who got into surfing first, you or Finn?"

"Finn convinced me when we were kids," I shrug before dropping my legs to stretch in front of me. "He was a great teacher, and we'd do it every weekend we could."

"Why aren't you out there showing Daisy how it's done? You won a competition, Ivy."

I chew on the inside of my lip as I push my blonde hair behind my ear, startled by the fact he remembers my silly competition. "I haven't done it in a while," I admit. "Been away from home for too long."

Because something is holding me back.

For a split second, I stupidly glance back at JJ when he remains silent. He frowns at me, and I take in his handsome features before fixating on his silver nose ring.

"How come?"

I tear my eyes away.

His question runs around my head for a few moments, and I subconsciously pull up the material of my top. It's already covering my chest, but I do it anyway. I might have taken my clothes off around JJ, but that was the liquid courage talking.

The scar beneath begins to burn for no reason. I know he's already seen it, but I don't like having my clothes off for other people to stare.

Most people in this town know what happened a few years ago, and I can't handle the unapologetic attention. It makes my skin crawl and my anxiety spike, it's better to keep covered up to save the questions.

It's not hard to Google this town along with my name.

I come up, the first result.

"I bet you're great at it," JJ offers when I don't respond.

He leans forward and wraps his arms over his legs, muscles flexing with the movement. *Damn him.* My heart flutters and I clench my fists, allowing my nails to dig into my palms.

"Great? I was fantastic," I deflect.

JJ grins at me, and I internally fumble.

"Yeah, I could tell by the balance of your feet when your heel broke."

My eyes narrow at his playful tone. "Oh my god. Let it go. That was completely different," I shoot back. "How was I meant to balance with only one heel?"

JJ laughs, and it sends an earthquake of a shiver down my spine. The sound makes me feel like I don't know myself at all.

"It was a good night," he comments.

My throat tenses, and I suddenly find the sand rather interesting.

"I haven't had fun like that in a while," he adds.

The back of my neck begins to heat. *Me neither,* I want to say, but I keep it to myself. It's not worth the pain in the future.

Daisy screams from the sea, and we turn to see her standing up on the board, grinning from ear to ear. I cheer her on from afar before she catapults herself into the water.

After a few moments, they come out of the sea, soaked from head to toe.

"Did you see?" Daisy asks JJ with excitement behind her eyes.

He nods with encouragement. "Yeah, you did better than me."

"Doubt it." She pushes away her dripping hair that cascades down her toned back. "You were great."

Finn glances between them and smirks to himself. "Should we get beers?"

"Absolutely." Daisy claps her hands together.

JJ stands up from the sand, and I follow his lead. "Sounds good to me."

"Actually…" I trail off quietly. "I might head home."

Finn whips his head to me, brows pinching. "What? You've got nothing better to do."

I scowl at him. "I might, thank you very much."

"Come on." JJ's voice catches me by surprise. "One beer."

When he stares at me, I don't miss the way his eyes sparkle. They're pleading with me to come with them. I want to be strong enough to decline and tell them again that I'm busy. But we all know that's a lie.

"One beer." Finn folds his arms over his chest.

"Fine." I roll my eyes. "*One* beer."

Daisy wraps her arm over my shoulder, soaking the side of my T-shirt, but I don't push her away. "There's my girl."

CHAPTER 12
JJ WOODFORD

After getting dressed in dry clothes, Finn takes us to *The Pearl and Oyster Bar* along the seafront. Ivy and Daisy are trailing behind us, speaking in hushed tones. I've resisted the urge to glance over my shoulder a thousand times.

Finn steps closer to me and places an arm over my shoulder. "Don't worry, bud," he says lightly. "I've got you and Daisy."

Then he drops his eye into a wink. A sleazy one at that.

"What do you mean?"

He scoffs. "What do you mean, 'what do you mean?' I've seen the way she looks at you, man. She wants you badly. So I'm going to do my hardest to wingman the hell out of you."

"I barely know the girl," I mumble under my breath.

Finn shrugs. "Don't need to know someone to get laid."

My organs churn a little uncomfortably, and I plummet into flashbacks of that night with his sister. We sat down for hours, getting to know one another, sharing parts of our lives, teasing one another.

I might not have *known her* known her, but I felt like I did. And the thought of sleeping with someone before trying to know them at least a tiny bit leaves a sour taste in my mouth.

Our night together was fun because of the time we spent endlessly talking. It built the tension, it made me feel like I had known her for years. It was easy to laugh and fall into conversation with her.

And this thing with Daisy feels different. *Wrong different.*

We stop outside the bar and grab a table. The weather is blistering today, but with the gentle breeze in the air from the nearby storm, it's about to cool down significantly.

I slide into one of the seats first, Daisy diving over to sit beside me. Finn taps Ivy and pulls her away, dipping his head towards her ear so he can whisper something.

Then he clears his throat. "We'll go grab the drinks," he says as Ivy nods, glancing away. "What do you want?"

"I'll have a Stella, please," I pipe up.

Daisy's eyes flash my way. "Me too."

"Alright." Finn claps his hands together.

I stare at the back of their heads as they walk into the building. Ivy has barely looked at me today, and it's driving me insane.

"So." Daisy clamps a hand on my arm. I blink at the action, focusing on her dark red nails. "I've been wondering why you haven't texted me back since the party?"

My mouth falls open a little as Daisy flutters her long lashes and waits for me to respond. "Sorry," I exhale after a few moments. "I've barely been on my phone since I've been here. Just settling in with Finn. I didn't mean to ignore you."

Her shoulders relax a couple of inches, and I despise myself for lying, but I don't want to upset her.

"Oh." She swipes her long brunette hair over her shoulder. "That's okay. I was just wondering if you wanted to meet up sometime. Have dinner or something. Nothing too crazy, would be nice to get to know you a little better."

Heat spikes my neck, and I blame the beaming sun. I stare back into her hopeful eyes, and I take a slow breath. "Yeah," I rasp awkwardly.

Daisy's face explodes with happiness.

"Okay, so I was thinking we could go to this really nice restaurant not too far from here," she begins. "If you like fish, they have—"

As she rambles on, I glance past her head. My eyes settle on Finn and Ivy at the bar. Our drinks are being made and placed onto the counter. Ivy shoves her hand into the back pocket of her denim shorts and turns to face our table.

For a moment, our eyes meet, and she blinks before looking away quickly. Daisy presses a hand to my forearm and shakes me.

"JJ?" She frowns, and I pull back, averting my attention. "Were you listening?"

"Yes, sorry. The restaurant with fish."

"Yeah." She grins. "Do you like fish?"

"Some," I admit.

Finn and Ivy return with our drinks. Ivy is now facing Daisy as she sips on her cider silently.

"So." Daisy leans on her elbows. "You need to teach me more about surfing."

I study Finn as he raises an eyebrow. "I can't believe you've never learnt how to surf. You've been here every summer when we've done it."

She shrugs. "Guess I wasn't interested in it then. Ivy, why didn't you do it today?"

"Hmm?" Ivy glances up at the sound of her name. "Not really feeling it. Maybe later in the summer."

I already know she's lying.

It's much deeper than not feeling it. I saw it in her eyes.

Those eyes that were wild and awake the night I met her, now they're reserved and hesitant.

The shape of her scar is imprinted into my mind, and I desperately want to know what happened to her, but Finn hasn't told me anything, so I won't probe.

"You know, one time," Finn says loudly, clapping a hand

onto Ivy's shoulder. "We decided to go surfing when we really shouldn't have. Coast guard said it was too dangerous, but we knew it would be worth it."

"We almost drowned," she deadpans.

He holds up a finger at her. "See keyword, *almost*. Anyway, we were surfing together, and this massive wave crashed over both of us. We lost our boards and resurfaced, but Ivy was covered head to toe in seaweed. I've never heard someone scream so loud."

Ivy scowls at him, but the corners of her lips lift. "It was terrifying." She shakes her head. "Not as bad as you completely losing your shorts to the sea. I still remember how those old ladies almost had heart attacks as you walked by."

Finn tips his head back and laughs, and Ivy soon follows after him. If I could see my eyes right now, I'm sure that they've dilated at the sound. It's smooth and gentle. Seeing her smile makes me smile, even if it's a little detached.

"No, that's not the worst bit," Finn recalls. "I left my fucking housekeys in my pocket and Ivy didn't have one with her. We didn't own wetsuits at the time. Big mistake."

Daisy's expression widens. "Why didn't I hear about this?"

"Because I told Ivy that if she told anyone, I'd make her life hell. It was fucking torture. We had to wait for our parents to get home, and fuck, if I had a pound for every time someone stopped to point, I'd be bloody rich."

Ivy is still grinning at her brother, and I can't take my eyes off her. Not for a single second.

"We tried to get him into my shorts and T-shirt," Ivy says as she sips her drink again. "But those arms and legs were going nowhere in my clothes."

Finn wipes his eyes as he leans back, continuing to chuckle. "Ah man. Those were the days."

"I would have killed to see that," I add, and Finn shakes his head.

"No, you wouldn't have. It was traumatic for everyone involved."

My eyes gravitate back to Ivy, there is still evidence of a smile on her lips. I find myself studying her, every little curve and those tiny little freckles on her nose that have somehow become darker since earlier.

"So, JJ." Daisy changes the subject, and I wish she didn't. I want to know more about them, about their summers together. "What brings you to this little coastal town?"

I clear my throat and turn to her. "Just a change of scenery. It's boring where I live."

"Well, are you enjoying it?"

"So far, so good."

Finn elbows me from across the table. "It's only begun, brother. It's going to be the best summer ever."

"We should totally plan something fun." Daisy sits up on the bench and glances around at all of us. "Right, Iv? Now that you're home and we've got the summer to ourselves. We should do something."

I find myself staring again, and Ivy knows it, but she avoids my gaze anyway. "Uh, yeah, sure."

"There's another party next Friday," Finn says.

"We're there." Daisy grins across the table at him. She then turns to Ivy. "Why are you so quiet today?"

Ivy's green eyes snap to her, and her forehead wrinkles. "No reason."

Daisy frowns and pulls back. "You sure?"

Pink tones invade her cheeks, and I don't want to stare to increase her embarrassment, but none of us looks away.

"Just adjusting to being home." She shrugs simply.

"Oh." She leans forward to grab her hand. "You have all of us. Being home doesn't have to be scary."

Scary? I quirk an eyebrow in confusion.

Why would being home be scary?

"Let's change the subject," Finn declares loudly, and Ivy

glances towards him gratefully. "Mum and Dad said that they're going to stay out in Vietnam for a little longer. That means we should have a barbecue around ours?"

Ivy nods in agreement. "I like the sound of that."

We finish our drinks over the next fifteen minutes, then Finn goes to the toilet, and Daisy's phone begins to ring. I don't get to see who it is before she stands from the table and walks towards the beachfront for some privacy.

Then I'm looking at Ivy again, and she pushes her empty glass further on the table. She catches me red handed and tilts her head, eyes narrowing into slits. "Why do you keep staring at me?"

"Didn't realise staring was illegal," I say with a playful tone.

Ivy wraps her arms around herself, but she can't be cold. "You just stare very intensely. You're making me think there's something wrong with my face."

"There is absolutely nothing wrong with your face, Ivy," I state sincerely.

Not a single thing.

I want to know what the hell makes her feel so insecure, when the reason I'm looking at her is because I can't stop myself. It's a natural pull.

She inhales deeply and shakes her head, a hand running through the ends of her hair. "It's just, when people stare at me, I…" She pauses, and I bite my lip to stop myself from cutting in, but she doesn't finish her sentence anyway.

"You what?"

Ivy glances up at me, eyes softening when she notices that I'm not trying to be intrusive. "I guess it makes me feel a little self-conscious."

That's the last thing I want her to feel. Not because she has something in her teeth or has an awkward laugh, but because when I look at her, I want to see that carefree side of her to come out like it did the night we met.

She lit up the entire room, not just with her beauty, but her aura.

And I know something is suffocating that light inside of her because when she smiles, it doesn't quite reach her eyes. It's as if she's trying to look happy, putting on a front and failing miserably.

And that doesn't sit well with me. At all.

"Ivy, I'm not looking at you because—"

"Where's Daisy?"

I glance up at Finn as he approaches our table. Ivy leans back and points to where she's on the phone.

"I'm gonna head back." Ivy excuses herself from the table.

Finn's expression warps suddenly. "Now? Why?"

"I've got some reading to do before the summer is over, and I'm tired." She shrugs simply. "I'll see you guys at home."

As she walks away, she waves at Daisy to say goodbye.

An unsettling feeling flutters in my stomach as I watch her.

I suck in a slow breath as Finn claps a hand on my shoulder.

"Another beer?" he asks.

"Sure."

CHAPTER 13
IVY THOMPSON

The next morning, I wake up to texts from Erin asking how being at home is. I smile at her caring nature and quickly give her the low down that JJ is staying with us for the summer.

A flood of texts comes in straight after, and I groan into my pillow.

IVY:
> I promise to call you later, okay? I'll explain everything then

ERIN:
> You better. I want to hear EVERYTHING.

My lips continue to curl at her message, despite the fact my stomach churns at the thought of addressing it again.

As I glance around my childhood bedroom, a wave of nostalgia hits me in the chest. Even though I've changed it a thousand times over, I still remember the pink painted walls when I was seven, and the boy band posters when I was thirteen.

I definitely have a box of school memorabilia somewhere.

School wasn't necessarily the best time of my life, but there were moments that made me happy. I mostly kept my head down and did my work with no questions asked. I wasn't necessarily popular, but because Daisy was my best friend, that meant I was invited to parties with her.

After peeling myself from my bed, I rummage in my old cupboard to find it used as storage for my father's pickleball hobby. I'm not surprised to see that he swapped out my stuff into the loft to make his stuff more accessible.

I step into the hall and stare up at the rectangular outline on the ceiling. I gently pull down the string and let the ladder fall into place beside me. My fingers latch onto the metal and give it a good shake—I've never trusted ladders.

My foot slides onto the metal ledge, and I move one step at a time. I peek my head into the loft, but everything is pitch black. I grip onto the ladder and press my hand to the landing to push myself up so I can stand.

But as I reach forward to grab the handle inside, my sock slips, and suddenly I'm falling. A scream echoes from my lips at how fast everything happens. My life literally flashes before my eyes.

My heart pounds inside my chest as I fly through the air, trying my hardest to grab onto something or tangle my legs onto the ladder. But it's too late.

Seconds before I hit the ground, my arm scrapes down the jagged side of the ladder, piercing my skin. My back cracks beneath me, causing the floorboards to creak.

I groan and close my eyes at the influx of pain. My spine feels like it's been snapped in two, as for my arm, I take a quick glance at it and study the crimson droplets falling towards my elbow.

My stomach literally flips. No. No. No. No.

The door down the hall bursts open, and I hear footsteps darting towards me. "Oh shit," JJ curses as I tremble. "Ivy."

He drops to his knees beside me, and I make the mistake

of turning to look at him because, for whatever reason, he's shirtless. I squeeze my eyes shut and take in a large gulp of air, giving myself a second to recover.

"Are you okay?"

"No," I murmur.

I might as well have fallen fifty feet from the roof; this feels no different.

JJ places a hand on my shoulder. "Here. Sit up."

I attempt to nod as he slides his hand under my back and pushes me into a sitting position. My head spins aggressively, and a wave of nausea hits me. He positions his knee behind me so I can rest my shattered back against it. His other hand is now gently rubbing my shoulders.

Am I dreaming? This must be a dream of torment.

"What were you doing?"

I huff out a breath. "I have a memory box somewhere," I grunt. "I think my dad put it in the loft. I underestimated the reach for the light switch. Socks were a stupid idea."

JJ sighs harshly. "Maybe write a note to yourself that you shouldn't go up there alone. Someone is meant to hold the ladder."

My eyes snap open to meet his dark blues. "Right," I croak.

He drops his gaze and looks down at my bloody arm, and when he winces at the sight, I know it isn't good. "We need to clean this up," he says, inspecting the wound. "You've cut yourself open, Ivy."

"I don't know if I can stand," I admit. "Not right now."

"It's okay." JJ shuffles impossibly closer to me. This time, I rest all of my weight on his knee. "Give yourself a minute."

I inhale deeply and close my eyes, trying my hardest not to throw up everywhere. Holy hell, I am so stupid. Why did I think I could do it by myself?

A few minutes tick by, enough to get my thoughts in gear and to stabilise my mind. "Okay. I'm ready."

"Alright," he says and helps me up off the floor. I stumble into the side of his body, my head hitting his hard shoulder. "Don't fall on me again, otherwise you're really making a habit of it."

I whimper at his words. "Please, no jokes. It's the last thing I need."

JJ stifles a soft laugh. "Sorry. Just trying to lighten the mood."

"We have a first aid kit downstairs," I say as he wraps an arm around my lower waist.

He practically carries me downstairs with one arm as I almost fall limp in his grip.

When we make it to the kitchen, JJ takes my waist in his hands and hoists me up onto the counter with ease. *Far too much ease.* I don't miss the way his fingers linger for a few more seconds than necessary. But his warmth gives me an unexpected comfort.

"Where is it?"

"Cupboard." I attempt to point with my good arm.

He's gone in a flash and comes back with the kit. I look down for a brief second and study the dried blood that has clung to my thigh and the droplets that rest on the white counter. I suck in a breath and squeeze my eyes shut.

"JJ—" I moan as he rummages through the kit.

My stomach acid crashes into my sternum, making the nausea rise in my throat.

Oh god. Blood. Blood. Even more blood. The coppery smell. It's invading my nose.

"JJ," I whimper again.

I'm moments away from falling off this counter with my spinning head.

"Give me a second, princess. I'm right here."

I grip onto the counter, but right now I don't have a second because I find my mind growing darker and darker, my vision almost fading into nothing. A presence approaches me, a large hand at the back of my neck, delicate fingers brushing my skin.

"Ivy," JJ says as he places something cold against my lips. "Take a sip of this. It'll help with your sugar levels. Don't faint on me."

I lean forward a fraction and allow him to pour the liquid into my mouth. *Coke.* I slurp it down, enjoying the sensation of the fizzy sugar.

"That's it." His fingers continue to caress my neck. "Good girl."

He pulls back the can slowly, and I open my eyes.

"Okay." He takes my arm again, and I resist the urge to look down at his rippling, tattooed biceps. He hasn't put a shirt on, and now that might be the reason why I faint. "Let me clean this up, then I can bandage it."

"Does it need stitches?" I ask as my stomach rolls.

"I don't think so," he says.

I lick my lips and press my head back into the cupboard door. "You know first aid?"

He glances up at me with a cheeky grin, blue eyes gleaming. "Sure do." He takes a damp washcloth and removes the blood from my open wound. I look away and grip his arm with my fingers.

"How?" I ask desperately. "Talk to me, please, because I need a distraction."

"Okay, but you can't laugh."

His fingers gently stroke my arm in soothing motions. I don't dare look back at the damage. "I won't."

"My mum used to take me ice skating when I was younger," he starts, and I focus on his soft hands as he takes his time. He definitely knows what he's doing. "And for ages, she wanted me to be a professional skater, but I was too much of a liability. I was like a kid on crack, the coaches didn't know what to do with me."

I bite down on my lip as he begins to put something on

my arm, drying the skin. "I would fall over all the time because I just wanted to mess around. My mum made sure I knew basic first aid in case I hurt myself or anyone else. Especially with those blades, they can do some real damage."

My mouth twitches into a frown. "Why would I laugh at that?"

"I guess no one really knows I ever did it, or suspects as much."

"Were you good?"

"No." JJ laughs gently, and it makes me smile, warmth and calmness washing over me. "Not at all. I felt bad because my mum really wanted me to try it, but it just wasn't for me. I got into other things as I got older and into other sports, but video production has always been my passion."

I finally pluck up the courage to look at my arm, a bandage now in place and not a drop of blood in sight. My lungs constrict, and I watch his gaze as he inspects his handiwork.

"I remember you telling me about it," I whisper.

JJ glances up, and it makes me realise just how close we are to each other. Practically sharing the same breath.

"What do you make your videos on?"

"Anything that inspires me, really." He shrugs. "Nature. People. Kind of like realism, I guess."

"That's cool."

"There," he says before placing my arm back into my lap. "Leave the bandage on for a few days, and then take it off to see how it's healing. Might need to replace the gauze if it's still a little gooey."

I nod once, heat rippling down my spine. "Thank you."

When JJ doesn't move away instantly, I look down at his nose ring and my heart thumps. Why are nose rings stupidly attractive on the right man?

"I didn't realise you were squeamish around blood."

My throat goes dry at his words. "I never used to be, but sometimes the smell and the thought set me off."

"Did something happen?"

I run my tongue over my bottom lip and dart my gaze to the window. "A while ago, yeah."

JJ shifts from one foot to the other. "Has this got something to do with the scar on your chest?"

His eyes meet mine, and for a few moments, I say nothing.

"Yeah," I say eventually.

When his expression warps into something I can't read, I resist the urge to run. He presses a hand to the counter beside my leg and studies me carefully. "What happened?"

"It's from an accident a few years ago. Don't worry, I didn't have open heart surgery or anything."

I try to keep my tone as neutral as possible, but there is a slight tremor to my voice. It's been a while since I've spoken about it to someone new, not in the last few years anyway.

"Accident?" he repeats as his brows crease. "What kind of accident?"

The air inside my lungs becomes non-existent, and the look in his eye has suddenly turned intense. A demand to know, and it makes butterflies of dread erupt inside my stomach.

"It doesn't matter, JJ." I brush it off.

"Does being squeamish affect your studies?" he asks after a few moments.

"What?"

"You said you study biomedical science. That's like medicine and doctor stuff, right?"

My mouth parts at the fact he remembers. "Oh." I blink. "Yeah. I'm not really squeamish when it comes to other people. It's weird, some kind of mental block I have when it comes to myself."

"Because of the accident?"

"Yeah."

The kitchen turns silent, and I wish he had never brought it up in the first place because it makes me feel seen, and I'm used to hiding in the shadows.

It's the reason why I hate him staring at me so much, because I fear he'll be able to draw all my insecurities to the surface and analyse every inch of me.

It wouldn't be hard, I doubt I'm very subtle.

I wish I was more like Daisy. I wish I was more like anyone… but me.

JJ's mouth opens, but I get there first. "So, you and Daisy, huh?"

I scold myself for blurting the first thing I could think of when it's the last thing I want to talk about with him. He blinks at my direct question and clears his throat, pushing himself up from the counter, putting distance between us.

"Uh." He folds his arms over his bare chest, and I use every bit of strength inside me not to look. "Yeah… she's a nice girl."

My mouth stretches into a forced smile.

"Yeah, she is."

"So, the loft." JJ brushes his hand over his buzzed hair. "You want me to grab whatever you need?"

"Yes," I exhale quickly. "Please. It's in a green box with gold lining. It looks like a Christmas box, but it's not."

He hikes his thumb over his shoulder. "I'll go grab it."

"Thank you," I say as he walks away.

The front door opens moments later, and I turn to find my brother strolling into the house. I frown at his presence because it's early in the morning.

"Where have you been?" I raise a questioning brow.

"Nowhere."

I narrow my eyes at him and his scruffy attire.

"Suspicious."

Finn walks towards me, and he's immediately drawn to my arm. "What happened?"

"I fell from the loft. But I'm okay. Luckily, JJ was here."

He tuts. "Be careful, man. Dad always told us how slippy the ladder is."

"I know, I know," I mutter under my breath.

"Are you okay?"

"Yeah, I'm okay."

JJ emerges from the stairs a few moments later, now in a black T-shirt. "It's on your bed, Ivy."

I press my lips into a thin line. "Thanks."

"Hey." Finn swats JJ's chest. "Joel and Cal are heading out across town, there is this new park they've just built. We're gonna chill and play football. You down?"

"I'm there."

Finn makes his way upstairs, and JJ loiters for a second or two. He catches my gaze and flashes a soft smile that does something to my soul.

"You good?" he asks.

I press my lips together and breathe out through my nose. "Good as new. Thanks."

When he leaves, I slump against the counter and press a hand to my face.

Yeah, this is going to be harder than I thought.

CHAPTER 14
JJ WOODFORD

"So we've got sixteen burgers, fourteen sausages, chicken skewers, cheese, buns, onions, gherkins, coleslaw, potato salad," Finn lists off as he points to everything on the kitchen island. "Do you reckon that's enough?"

I turn my head to him. "To feed a football team? Yeah."

"It's better to have more than to scrounge for the scraps."

"True." I nod in agreement. "When's everyone getting here?"

He snorts. "Define everyone."

"Joel, Callan. Anyone else you invited."

He shrugs and walks towards me, wrapping an arm around my shoulders. "Joel and Callan are on their way. But do you know who is coming? Your girlfriend."

I shove him off. "She's not my girlfriend."

And I *don't* want Daisy to be my girlfriend.

There is nothing there.

No spark.

No chemistry.

It's bland and I can't force it.

"Why so uptight, man? Honestly, that girl has it bad for you."

I ignore him as he walks towards the barbecue in the garden to turn on the gas canister and get the food cooking.

The storm that's been brewing is predicted for tonight, so we decided to do something for lunch. The next few days are likely to be written off due to the bad weather.

When I hear a knock at the door, I push myself up from the counter and open it.

Daisy stands there with two handfuls of alcohol. I flash her a forced smile.

"Hey, you." She grins, stepping forward and planting a kiss on my cheek. The stickiness of her gloss makes my skin itch, and when she's out of my view, I raise my hand to wipe it off.

"Hey," I say, closing the door behind her.

She whirls on the spot, holding the bags with drinks above her head. "I brought the goods."

"Hey, Daisy," Finn shouts from outside.

"Who's ready for a drink then?" she declares.

Finn nods as he heats up the barbeque, prepping the tongs and plates on the side. "Hell yeah, I'm down."

I watch Daisy as she unpacks beers, ciders, and bottles of wine.

"What do you want?" she calls out to him.

"A beer."

She throws him a beer without barely looking.

"JJ?"

"Yeah, sure. Thanks."

Daisy takes two out of the cardboard holder and twists off the caps. She hands me one and then clinks the glass against mine, bright blue eyes glittering at me. "Cheers," she says before latching her lips onto the bottle and taking a long sip without breaking eye contact.

"Where's Ivy?" Finn asks as he steps back into the kitchen. "I told her we'll be starting soon."

She reaches into her pocket and taps the screen. "She bumped into Isaac earlier, so they'll probably be here soon."

My eyebrow twitches without permission. "Good for her." Finn heads back outside.

"Who's Isaac?" I ask Daisy.

"Oh." She presses a hand to the counter before perching on a stool. "He's this guy from school who has always fancied Ivy, but never said anything to her. But now she's back and he's had this incredible glow up, I really hope it works out for them."

I clear my throat and take a sip of my beer. "Right."

"So, JJ." Daisy flicks her dark hair over her narrow shoulder. "How have you been? I haven't seen you in a few days."

I flash her a small smile. "Yeah, good. Just been spending time with Finn and his mates."

"Yeah, of course. You probably want to make the most of the summer."

"Yeah."

"So, what are your parents doing right now?"

The mention of my parents makes my stomach turn to cement. I study Daisy as she props her chin on her fist and flutters those long lashes at me. I could tell her about my mother, but I don't want to. It doesn't feel right.

My mouth opens to spurt out some sugar-coated lie, but a knock at the door saves me. I step back from the counter like it's lava and yell, "I'll get it."

I press down on the handle and open the door to find Joel and Callan with even more beer in hand. I greet and welcome them inside, and as I move to close the door, I spot familiar blonde hair whipping in the distance.

Beside her is a tall guy with dark hair that looks freshly cut, and a beaming grin. I don't recognise him, but I do notice the way Ivy laughs brightly beside him at something he said.

They make their way to the house and Ivy glances up,

sobering her expression when she realises I'm watching them. "Hi." She forces a smile at me.

"Hi." I nod.

The guy I'm presuming is Isaac steps closer and holds out a hand. "Hey man, I'm Isaac."

I glance down at his hand for a second before taking it. "JJ."

After gathering inside, I help Finn plate everything up on the kitchen island. Daisy is latched to my hip, explaining what jobs she applied for this week. If I'm being brutally honest, I'd rather watch paint dry than listen to her talk right now. I feel like an asshole, but I can't help it if I'm not interested. And it's hard to even pay attention when I can see Ivy and Isaac talking across the kitchen.

I have to give it to him, he's a good-looking guy, and the way Ivy looks up at him? Yeah, I might have the green-eyed monster festering inside me right now.

My fingers clench around the base of my beer bottle when Daisy places a hand on my arm. "Are you zoning out again?"

I turn back toward her to find her pouting at me; those glossy lips are so shiny I can almost see my reflection in them. "Sorry, what were you saying?"

"I can't believe they rejected my application," she murmurs. "I had a telephone interview, and they said I talk too much. Can you believe it?"

My eyebrows raise subtly. *I sure can.*

"Guys," Finn calls, his words slurring slightly. "Come get some food."

Ivy walks past her brother and smiles. "Thanks for this, Finn."

He leans down to kiss the top of her head, a slight wobble in his step. "I told you this would be the best summer ever, and I will make sure it is. Even if the food is a little burnt."

She chuckles quietly. "Still, thank you."'

We all grab platefuls of food, and my stomach growls at

the mouthwatering smell of it wafting into the summer air. I don't waste any time, I dig in until my plate is clean.

Finn attempts to pile up the empty plates once we've finished eating but ends up dropping them in the sink. Isaac rushes to his side to help. I have no idea how Finn gets himself into this state so easily.

I've seen how he can drink himself to oblivion at university, and I'm starting to wonder if it's becoming an issue.

"So," he slurs to Isaac. "What are your intentions with my sister?"

"Oh my god," Ivy groans. "Don't do this, Finn."

Finn ignores her and attempts to roll his fluttering eyes. "I presume you like my sister."

I glance at Isaac, who seems a little taken aback. "Yeah, Ivy's great," he responds.

He steps closer to the poor lad, almost squaring up to him. I know how protective he is of Ivy, but I underestimated him when he's this drunk.

"You hurt her." He points a finger at him. "And I'll dig your grave for you."

I flinch a little at the harshness of his tone. Ivy storms over to Finn and grabs his arm, he sways at the motion. "That's enough. You need to go to bed. You're drunk and being annoying, and trust me, it's not cute."

"Whatever," he grumbles. "I'm barely drank—drunks. I'm barely even drunk."

Ivy breathes out a heavy sigh through her nose. "Leave Isaac alone. I don't want your overprotective shit right now, especially when you can barely stand up. You wouldn't even win against a plastic bag right now, let alone Isaac. So stop it."

I glance at Joel and Cal and they nod, stepping towards Ivy so they can take Finn into their arms. They carry him through the house and upstairs—needed for when the storm hits and he decides to go and do something stupid.

Daisy stands up to help clean away the food. Ivy and Isaac

whisper beneath their breaths by the sink, but I can't hear what they're saying. I frown at her trembling tone.

A loud gust of wind rockets through the back door and Daisy walks towards it, poking her head out at the dark sky. "Yikes," she mutters. "I think the storm is starting early."

"You better get back," Ivy says and then glances at Isaac, "you too."

"Yeah, I probably should." He grimaces at the sky.

I say goodbye to Daisy, and Isaac gives me a smile. "Good to meet you."

"You too." I return the gesture, even if it's a struggle.

Isaac offers Daisy a ride, and she happily takes it. Joel and Cal come downstairs to say Finn is safely in bed and they're heading home before they're stuck in the storm.

Ivy turns back to the kitchen once everyone is gone and starts to tidy up, uneaten food in the fridge and buns in the bread bin. I stand beside her and help wash up all the plates and utensils.

"Does Finn always get drunk like that?" Ivy asks.

I stall for a moment and look down at her. "Uh, yeah. I guess."

"He's a mess," she tuts. "I swear he had like three beers."

"Three beers? Na, more like nine. He downs that shit like it's an Olympic sport and discards the bottles so you'll never know."

Ivy closes her eyes and shakes her head. "He's such a liability."

"Tell me about it," I say as I glance down at the bandage on her arm. "How's it healing up?"

"Yeah, it's fine. Thanks again."

My heart thumps as she grazes her fingers over the bandage before looking up at me with darkened lashes that make her green eyes brighter. *So beautiful*. It hurts to look at her and her freckled nose and arched cupid's bow.

"It's the least I could do after finding you on the floor," I say with a soft smile. "You scared me. For someone as small as you, there was a lot of blood."

Finn might have told me to stay away, but that doesn't mean I have to listen.

How can I stay away when being around her makes me lose my breath?

We might have only known each other for one night, but there was so much more to it. It felt so much more than one night. The devastation I felt after I woke up alone was surprising. Normally I wouldn't care, but with Ivy? I cared too much.

I desperately wanted to know why she didn't stay. Then the endless thoughts started pouring in. *Did I do something wrong?*

I'd like to think she would have told me by now if I had.

Ivy's cheeks turn to a pretty shade of pink, and she nods, busying herself with tidying up again. Soon the kitchen is spotless, and the weather has taken a turn for the worse. Never in my life have I heard it rain so aggressively.

I walk towards the open door and glance up at the dark clouds. It might as well be midnight sky.

To my surprise, Ivy stands beside me, leaning on the opposite door. "I love it when it rains here," she says so quietly, I'm not even sure she wanted me to hear. "It's refreshing."

"I've never seen it like this before."

Her eyes glisten as she turns to me. "It's relaxing. I love the sunshine, but this is a close second."

I keep my eyes focused on her as she speaks, and she catches me staring—again. A strike of lightning flashes through the sky, and her lips part slowly as she wraps her cardigan around her body.

Then she sits down on the floor by the back door and stares up at the clouds. I perch beside her, drawing my legs into my chest. She doesn't tell me to leave, probably because she's not looking at me. She's fascinated by the storm, and I can see the calmness reflecting in her eyes.

The clouds are lit up by strikes of silver lines over and over until the thunder erupts, and I'm sure the floor vibrates. It sounds like something from an apocalypse movie.

Ivy twists towards me after we sit in silence for a few minutes, she copies my actions and hugs her knees into her chest. "How is your mum?" she asks with such delicacy that it sparks something inside my heart.

I open my mouth and lick my bottom lip. "Okay." I lower my gaze to my knees. "She started her treatment, and she's in good hands with my dad. That's why I'm here, because I couldn't sit at home by myself all summer waiting for an update. So far she's reacting to it, but it hasn't been long enough to know if it'll help her in the long run."

"Well, I hope the treatment works," she says softly. "I'm glad she's able to receive this kind of treatment. And like you said, she's in good hands."

My teeth clamp down on the inside of my cheek. "I'm a little surprised you remembered."

"Why?"

"Well, we were a little intoxicated." I shrug. "And I've started to realise that people don't like talking about sick people."

Ivy's brows pull down into a tight frown. "Really?"

"Yeah." I exhale a long breath. "A mention of illness, treatment, possible death. People don't want to know. So I appreciate you asking about her, it honestly means a lot."

She stares back at me, the whites of her eyes glistening as she listens. I'm not sure what flashes past her face, but it looks like empathy or consolation. It practically sets my heart on fire from the way she looks at me, not with pity or sorrow, but genuine understanding of how I must feel.

"Well, if you want someone to talk to. I'm here."

"Thank you," I whisper.

"How are you feeling?"

I shrug. "Okay, I guess. I'm just glad I have company."

"I'm sorry for what I said at the party." She chews on her lip.

My brows furrow. "Sorry for what?"

"I probably didn't sound very welcoming." Her eyes fall an inch. "But you are welcome here. I don't want you to be alone at a time like this, I was just… startled by your arrival."

My lips curl to the side. "Well, the feeling is mutual. I panicked and thought maybe you and Finn were together or something when I saw you."

Ivy pulls a face. "Ew. So gross."

"Yeah," I chuckle.

She stares back at me with big green eyes, and I glance down at her lips that have been torturing me for weeks. I'd be a fool if I said I didn't want to kiss the shit out of her again. Until neither of us can breathe, and she's panting into my mouth for more.

A gust of wind sends the rain splattering into the kitchen, droplets coating Ivy. She yelps at the coldness, and before I know what I'm doing, I lean over to grab her waist and tug her along the kitchen tiles where it's dry.

The warmth of her leg spreads into mine as I position her beside me. It stretches across my skin with comfort and calmness. She glances up at me, and I tilt my head down at the same time.

She swallows, eyes becoming wider, then dilating as she takes me in.

My gaze floats back down to her mouth, and her cheeks tint even darker. I lean closer, just an inch, until I can feel her breath on my lips.

A line of lightning zaps through the sky at the same time a roar of thunder claps in the air.

We jolt apart, and Ivy turns away, hiding her heated face behind her blonde hair.

I bite my bottom lip. My heartbeat rattles in my ears, blood soaring through my body with adrenaline.

I know I should stay away, but I don't think I'm strong enough to.

For a while, we sit side by side in silence and enjoy the storm.

CHAPTER 15
IVY THOMPSON

The storm flew by our town faster than expected, which is a miracle, so we're hoping there will be minimal damage. As I approach the kitchen, I glance outside to find my brother standing in the beams of sunlight, not a single cloud in the sky.

Finn has his phone to his ear, a face full of concentration. I decide not to disturb him and turn back to the kitchen to make eggs on toast for breakfast.

When the patio door slides open, I glance over my shoulder as Finn stares down at his screen. "Morning," I call out to him. "Who was that?"

"Hey." He taps away at his phone before giving me his full attention. "That was Wendy down at the seafood restaurant at the marina. I got a job there for the summer."

My brows hit my hairline. "Salty Sea?"

"Yeah."

I stir my eggs around the pan to make them scramble. "I didn't know you were looking for a job," I admit. "But congrats. Proud of you."

He flashes me a grin and rests his elbows on the counter.

"Yeah, I didn't want to get a job, but I need one if I want to fund this summer."

"What about your student loan?"

His green eyes flick to mine and he tilts his head. "I spent a lot of it last term, and I desperately need to make the money back."

"A lot?" I quirk a brow.

He grimaces at my question. "I'm in my overdraft."

"Oh god." I turn off the stove. "What were you even spending your money on?"

I watch his shoulders rise and drop dramatically as if the answer is obvious. "Going out, takeaways, you know… the standard student stuff."

For a moment, I pause as I plate up my breakfast and turn to face him. "Has this got something to do with your excessive drinking?"

"What are you talking about?"

"The fact that you like to drink to the point you almost blackout. You were drunk and you threatened Isaac with digging his grave for him."

Finn's eyes widen, and relax the next second. "I was only joking."

"No, you were about to kill him," I state.

He waves me off. "So? I had one too many beers. I wasn't going to hurt the kid. I was just being protective. You know me."

I snort at his choice of words. "Yeah, you're right, I do know you, and your drinking habits don't seem healthy, Finn. If you've lost all your money from going out, then that explains how much you must be drinking. And if it's not alcohol, then it's drugs, and I pray it's not the latter."

"Ivy." He runs a hand down his face. "You're reading too much into this. Did you not go out and splash a bit of money on alcohol and have a good night out? The last term is always a little chaotic, celebrating exams and papers. It was harmless. I promise."

I keep my eyes trained on him for a long moment. "Alright," I exhale in defeat. "But it's your last year coming up. You need to focus on getting the grades you've always wanted; going out isn't going to help with that."

"No." He winks. "But it will give me lots of fun memories."

"Yeah, if you can even remember them when you're paralytic."

Finn shoots me down with daggers. "I got a job, alright? No need to go all Mum and Dad on me."

My eyes roll. "I'm not going all Mum and Dad on you, Finn. I'm your sister and I'm worried about you."

"And I'm trying to make it right." He holds up his arms in defence.

"Alright," I say, trying my hardest to give him the benefit of the doubt. "Congrats. I'm pleased you're taking the reins on this one."

He draws back and shares a small smile with me. "Thanks, I appreciate it."

I dig into my breakfast as Finn looks at his phone.

"There's another party on Friday."

My eyes narrow into slits. He can't be serious. "You just got a job, Finn."

"And they're changing the rota every week," he huffs. "I'm not working this Friday. I need something to live for. You coming?"

I hum suspiciously. "Maybe. Not sure what I'm doing yet."

"Alright. I'm gonna go take a shower," he says before turning to the stairs.

When I'm done with my breakfast, I clean everything away and slump on the sofa to find my phone vibrating. Isaac's name flashes across the screen and I beam. His messages always make my day a little better—I have to admit.

> ISAAC:
>
> Hey, how are you?
>
> I was wondering if you wanted to go and grab some ice cream or something tomorrow and take a walk down the beach?

My heart warms at his message.

> IVY:
>
> Hey! I'm good.
>
> Yeah, I'd love to. What time?

> ISAAC:
>
> What about 2 at the beachfront, near that fancy ice cream shop?

> IVY:
>
> You mean the one that charges a fiver for one scoop

> ISAAC:
>
> Yeah, but I'm paying, so you don't have to worry about that

My face stretches into a wide smile. His messages don't necessarily give me butterflies, but they make me feel something. I chew on my lip at the waves that wash through me.

"What's got you so smiley?"

I jump at the sound of JJ's voice as he enters the kitchen. I tear my eyes from my phone and quickly lock the screen.

"Oh, umm," I mumble as JJ quirks a brow with clear interest. I need to ignore how unbelievably good-looking he is because I need to focus on Isaac—*I must focus on Isaac*. "Nothing. Just made plans for tomorrow."

JJ's eyes glitter against the kitchen lights. "What plans?"

"With Isaac," I admit.

The creases on his forehead push together quickly as he studies me. "Oh, that's—" He pauses. "That's nice. He seems like a good guy."

"He is." I nod. "How are you and Daisy?"

The words feel bitter on my tongue. We both need to pretend that night we had together never happened, for the sake of my brother and everything that went down all those years ago.

"Okay, I guess." He shrugs and brushes a hand over his head. "She wants to go out, but—"

"You should," I blurt. "Go out with her. I know she really wants to get to know you."

JJ blinks at me in surprise. His mouth parts, but before he says anything, he stops himself. "Uh, maybe."

"If you do, I'm sure you'll have fun," I say quietly.

"Mm."

Our eyes remain locked on one another's for a moment too long.

My heart pounds against my ribcage, the back of my neck beginning to heat.

I can't find it in me to take a small breath, not when his eyes latch onto mine like he's trying to unravel my brain and find out how I'm really feeling.

My phone buzzes in my hand, and it drags me away from this silent conversation. Saved. Literally *saved.*

I give my attention to the next message Isaac just sent me, but I physically can't read the words. Not when the tension between me and JJ is suffocating me to death.

Goddamn this. I should have just chosen my vibrator that night instead.

CHAPTER 16
JJ WOODFORD

Daisy's hand creeps along the open café table as we sit outside on the beachfront, her fingernails gingerly brush mine. They're painted a rich Barbie pink and are pointy at the ends.

"I'm so happy you agreed to come out with me." She props her chin onto a fist and flutters those dark eyelashes at me. "I was starting to get worried."

I flash her a smile. Why did I listen to what Ivy said? *Oh, probably because she's going out with Isaac, and you decided to be bitter about it.*

"I didn't hear from you yesterday." I clear my throat. "I thought you might have changed your mind."

Daisy's lips stretch into a wide grin. "Did I not make it clear enough how much I wanted to go out with you?"

"Yeah." *Maybe a little too much.*

"So." She grips my fingers with those claws and draws my attention back to her. "I heard back from a job that I applied for."

"Yeah?"

Daisy nods, dark curls slipping past her narrow shoulders. "Said that my interview was good and they want me to come in to do a group interview, see how well I mix with other people."

"Congrats. Which one was this for?"

"It's for a marketing company that works with specialised sports."

My eyebrows raise. "That's cool."

Her eyes glimmer in my direction as she roams them across my face and exhales a long sigh.

I shift in my seat. "So, tell me about your university degree," I say, because I need her to talk about something before she brings those googly eyes back.

"Well…" She trails off, and I prepare to listen.

A gust of wind ripples through the air as I glance along the beachfront where people are strolling with fluorescent beach towels over their shoulders, and sunburnt noses. Daisy is still talking, and I'm picking up on every other word as best as I can.

My eyes wander from person to person until they fall on a familiar face.

Isaac.

My gaze shoots to the person next to him, blonde hair half tied up in a messy bun. She's wearing the cutest ribbed dress with short sleeves and socks and trainers.

Isaac says something that has Ivy cackling, and both of them have ice cream cups in their hands. I study Isaac's gaze as it's locked on Ivy. He's not just looking at her, he's beaming.

And I can read that look from a million miles away. *Because he likes her.*

Ivy's lips move, and Isaac grins. A part of me wishes I could be a fly on the wall in their conversation, but I'm too far away to hear anything. I don't even realise that my fist has clenched on the table until Daisy clears her throat.

"Everything okay?" she asks hesitantly.

I drag my eyes back to her and relax my hand. "Yeah," I rasp. "All good."

Daisy hums. "So yeah, that's where I'm up to with my degree."

And I have no recollection of our one-sided conversation. "Sounds good." I force another smile. "Things are looking good for you."

"Hopefully." She sinks her teeth into her lip.

"What's going on between Ivy and that Isaac guy?"

She blinks at my question and pulls back.

I clear my throat and rest my elbows on the table. "Because of what Finn said at the barbecue. He wouldn't have reacted like that if it wasn't serious, right?"

Her hand brushes those long locks across her back again. "I mean, they've been close since school. They lost touch when Ivy left for a few years, but I know how bad Isaac had it for her. He never really told her or anything, but now I guess he's got that confidence he didn't have before. But who knows what might happen."

"Didn't Ivy like him in school?"

Daisy shrugs. "Ivy was quite… shy at school. She was reserved, and I don't think she felt like she was good enough. Which I don't understand because to me, she's beautiful. But everyone has their own flaws and insecurities."

She's not the only one who thinks she's beautiful.

I glance back over at where Isaac and Ivy were standing, but they're nowhere to be seen. My eyes fixate on Daisy's again, but this time she's studying me.

"Look, JJ," she starts, "I know you and Ivy met before she came home."

My eyes blink quicker than the speed of light. She told her about us? And she was still happy for her best friend to try her luck with me? My head *aches*.

"I'd never tell Finn or anything, don't worry." Her hand

comes back to caress my wrist. "I guess you guys knew that nothing would come of it. Ivy made that very clear to me."

I hate that my heart twitches at her words, bruising my ego because I thought what we shared was somewhat special, even if it only lasted one night.

Maybe I am delusional.

"Yeah, I suppose," I mutter.

"So, what's your usual type?"

"I don't really have a type," I lie.

"Not even Ivy?"

I shrug. "No."

I don't even know why I said it because she is. She doesn't need to tick boxes next to certain traits and features, I just know she's my type because of how I felt when I was with her. Before I brought her back to my apartment, we were in the bar talking for hours on end, like time didn't exist.

"Oh." Daisy's cheeks darken. "Would you say I'm more your type?"

My teeth graze my bottom lip as I study her carefully. She's pretty, don't get me wrong, but she doesn't make my stomach flip like someone else does.

"Sure," I say through a forced smile, even though the word burns my tongue.

I don't want to upset the girl, but I have no idea what else to say.

I sit here for another hour or so, listening to Daisy and her endless rambling, but I tell myself to listen when my brain wants to ponder.

Soon after we say our goodbyes, I head home alone. When I reach the house, I find Finn adjusting his shirt in the mirror, slowly remembering that he got a job at a local restaurant.

He looks at me out of the corner of his eye as I shut the door behind me. "Hey," he calls out and tucks in his shirt to his black lined trousers. "How was your date?"

"Fine," I mumble and walk straight towards the kitchen.

I latch onto the fridge door and haul it open, searching for something sweet to drink. "Just fine?" Finn's voice sounds deflated as I grab a can of Diet Coke and crack the lid.

I slump my back against the counter as I meet his eyes. "Yeah. Fine."

"Hmm." He narrows his eyes. "What happened?"

"Not much."

Finn's eyes hold my stare before he backs away and holds his hands up in defence. "Alright, whatever. I've got to go to work. I'll be back sometime tonight."

"Bye," I say as I watch him leave.

The front door opens a few moments later and Ivy emerges in that little green dress that clings to her hips. I can't even look as she strolls in because it grates on me knowing that Isaac got to enjoy her today—her company, her face, her laughter.

She's smiling as she walks in, even when she locks eyes with me.

"Hey," she says cheerily before dumping her bag onto the sofa.

"Hi," I say.

"You okay?"

I hum. "Yeah, you?"

Ivy sinks her teeth into her bottom lip. "Yeah, I'm great."

I watch as she walks away, heading upstairs with a spring in her step, wishing I had been on that date with her instead.

CHAPTER 17
IVY THOMPSON

When I wake up the next morning, I take a quick shower and slide on my underwear. I catch a glimpse of myself in the mirror, and for once, I can't drag my eyes away. The redness of my scar is darker than usual from the temperature of the shower, and I find myself sinking into my heels.

It's not just one scar, but multiple across my body that are less noticeable. My lips slant to the side as I analyse my body, grazing my fingers across my skin.

Sighing heavily, my eyes droop at the sight. I haven't felt myself in a long time, no matter how hard I try to mask it. Smiling through it is the only option I have left.

It reminds me of the pain and the fear I endured when I woke up in the hospital, when my body changed forever. When all I want to do is look at my body and not despise what I see.

As I throw on some clothes and head downstairs to grab some breakfast, I find JJ in the kitchen. He hasn't noticed me yet, but he's sitting on one of the stools. His hands are together in front of him, and he's looking directly at the countertop.

I walk to the fridge, my senses immediately heightened as I feel his eyes on the back of my head.

"Morning," he calls out a little gruffly, as if he woke up not too long ago.

My head whips over my shoulder, and I smile softly. "Hey."

JJ is devastating in the mornings. He's devastating all the time, but today he looks particularly good with a white T-shirt clinging to his chest and carving his biceps like marble.

"Ivy," he strains. "Can we talk about what happened the night we met?"

I blink in surprise, my throat tensing. "Why?"

There is no need to bring it up. What's done is done. We can't change it.

"Because I want to know why you left. Did I do something wrong?"

My brows furrow. "No. You did nothing wrong."

Everything he did was right. So fucking right.

JJ takes a breath of relief. "Then why did you leave without saying anything?"

"Because it was just easier." I sink my teeth into my bottom lip.

"Easier?"

"Yes."

"How?"

My hands throw up in defeat. "Because there was no point in hanging around when we both go to university. We both wanted a distraction, and we got it."

JJ's brows raise. "Oh, I was just a distraction?"

"I didn't mean it like that." I shake my head. "I just didn't want you to wake up, see me and realise you made a big mista—"

The stairs creak loudly, and I shut my lips when I hear Finn say, "Morning, fuckers."

Oh, the irony in that statement.

"Morning," I call out to Finn and glance back to the fridge.

Finn steps to my side as I pull out the tub of butter, and I turn back to the counter to find JJ's eyes already on mine like magnets. They're practically pleading—*pleading* that this conversation isn't over, and I hate what it does to my stomach.

I take a breath because looking at him makes me question my entire existence.

JJ has been going out with Daisy. He took her on a date. You don't take someone on a date that you're not even remotely interested in, and I get it, Daisy is the most beautiful girl I've ever met.

Finn starts telling JJ about their plans for the day, and I drown them out by cooking breakfast. I can't bring myself to meet his eyes again, so I keep them low, even though I can feel his gaze burn into the side of my head like a pair of lasers.

When they leave, Daisy texts to ask if I want to go for a walk around town and stop off for a glass of wine. I've got nothing better to do, so I get ready and meet her at the beachfront. She wraps her arms around me in a tight hug, and I return the gesture. It feels like it's been a while since it's been just us two.

We've both been busy.

"How are you?" she asks as we walk past the parade of bars and restaurants.

I wrap my arms over my chest. "Good. I've been good. What about you?"

Daisy turns to me with a wide grin. "I went on a date yesterday with JJ."

My eyes flick to the lapping waves against the shore. "Oh yeah?" I say as cheerily as possible, despite the hollowness in my chest. "How was it?"

"I don't know." She shrugs slowly, her grin slipping

slightly. "He's cute and everything, but he doesn't seem entirely that interested. Which I don't get, because why would he agree to meeting up with me? Maybe he's just super laid back."

My brows begin to furrow at her words. JJ might have been having a bad day yesterday. He seemed agitated when I got home.

"Are you going to see him again?"

"I don't know." She sighs. "We didn't mention it or anything, but I'll probably see him at the party on the weekend."

"Oh, yeah."

"What did you do yesterday?"

I drop my arms to my sides. "I met up with Isaac, we got some ice cream and caught up with each other. It was nice."

Daisy's expression explodes. "I can't believe you didn't tell me! Do you like him?"

"Yeah." I nod slowly. "I like him."

Her head slumps, and her eyelids hang low. "You know what I'm trying to ask."

I suck in a breath as the wind whips past us. "He's nice, but I don't know if I like him like that. I enjoy his company, and being with him feels easy."

Daisy wraps an arm around my shoulders and tugs me towards her. "I'm so proud of how well you've been doing. I know it's probably still hard for you, but you're amazing, Ivy."

My lips curve into a smile. "Thanks, Dais."

We walk for a little further until we settle at a wine bar and buy a bottle of white between us. We don't talk about JJ or Isaac anymore, which I'm beyond grateful for. We discuss Daisy's plans for getting a job, what I might do after the summer is over, and some ridiculous stories whilst we've been away at university.

Our laughter fills the bar, and it brings me so much joy.

As much as I've loved making new friends, Daisy has been my longest friend, and being with her feels like family.

I finish my glass of wine when Daisy looks out at the path between the seafront and the line of restaurants. "Oh shit," she says under a hushed breath.

"What?"

"Julian and Tom and all those idiotic boys from school are coming in."

My stomach lurches at her words. *Julian and Tom.* They're two of Ben's closest friends.

Shit. I curse to myself in my mind and glance down. "It's fine." Daisy cups my hand. "Doubt they'll come over. I haven't seen them in years."

"Yeah," I murmur.

She continues to talk when I feel a presence near us, but I don't dare look up. "Daisy Garcia," a voice shouts across the bar, and I want the floor to swallow me whole. "Holy shit. I haven't seen you in forever. Still hot as ever."

I hear Daisy suck in a breath and place her elbows on the table, turning her head to the perpetrator. "Julian, it's been a while."

"Are you back for the summer?" Julian decides to lean on our table and I hate his cocky arrogance.

"Yep," Daisy speaks bluntly. "I am. That's why I'm here."

Three of them are now standing around our table. Julian laughs loudly, and I cringe at the sound. "Ah, Daisy. Always playing hard to get."

My eyebrows scrunch together at his words. Still an asshole, I see.

"Nope, not really," Daisy says with a dismissive tone. "Just trying to enjoy some quality time with my best friend."

They all turn to look at me, and Julian's eyes widen, like I wasn't even sitting here in the first place. "Oh shit." Julian grins at me like a Cheshire cat. "Ivy, you're back. Didn't even notice you."

I keep quiet because I have nothing to say to these assholes.

"Did you hear Ben should be getting out of prison soon?" Tom steps forward, crossing his arms over his chest. He's staring me directly in the eye, and I want to shrink to the size of a pea.

I knew it was soon, but I didn't know how soon.

Daisy's gaze narrows on him, she's ready to pounce and claw his eyes out for even bringing him up. We all know they were friends, but what he did to me is a thousand times worse than Tom hating me for having a friend of his put behind bars.

"Oh, fuck off, Tom." Daisy snaps.

"What?" Tom exhales as if he doesn't care that it'll upset me. "She might not have known, and it's probably a good idea for her to have a heads up. I mean, no one heard from you for years after, everyone thought you topped yourself or something."

My nostrils flare. I don't want to bite, but I can't stop myself. "Leave us alone, Tom."

"Agreed," Daisy grumbles. "Leave before I put my fist down your throat."

Julian blinks at Daisy's loud voice, but then he grins back at her. "It's cute when you get all feisty."

Daisy's expression turns to stone, she's about to explode, but I don't want to cause a scene.

"I always wondered how you managed to bag someone like Ben," Tom says in a tone that tells me he's trying to be as malicious as possible. "He might have been a bit crazy, but that chap was one good-looking motherfucker. He didn't deserve to go to prison. All because you had to go and cheat on him, didn't you?"

"I didn't cheat on him." I clench my fists. "It was a shitty rumour. I'd never cheat on anyone."

Julian chuckles and folds his arms over his chest and takes a glance at Tom. "Oh, please, we have our sources."

My eye twitches at his words because whoever these 'sources' are, they're bullshit. I never cheated on Ben, and whoever made it up ruined my life.

"We know it's true, Ivy. Why are you trying to deny it?" Tom scowls deeply at me. "It's disgusting."

Bile rises in my throat at the memories. I stand from the table, no longer able to sit around and listen to this shit. I stare Tom directly in the eye and tell myself to calm my breathing as I say, "Go fuck yourself. All of you."

I push past the three of them, ignoring their petty laughter. Daisy soon follows, and I wrap my arms over my chest, wishing I could instantly be home in my bed.

"Hey." Daisy runs after me and grabs my arm. "Are you okay?"

No. I want to scream. I'm about to have a fucking breakdown because no one will let me forget.

"I'm fine." I steady my voice.

"Ivy." She squeezes my arm gently. "Ignore them. They're a bunch of bullies and always will be. Tom doesn't know what he's saying. He's a grade A cunt. Please don't listen to them."

I push off her arm and ignore my trembling hands. "I said I'm fine."

Daisy remains walking beside me as I head towards my house, she keeps close but silent.

"I'm gonna go home," I mutter under my breath.

"Want me to come?"

"No." I shake my head as my heart clenches in my chest. "I want to be alone."

Daisy's eyes shift into a look of concern. "Ivy, I don't thi—"

"I said I want to be alone," I snap unintentionally.

"Okay." She frowns, looking uncertain. "I'll text you, yeah?"

I say nothing, but nod. Daisy stops walking, and I head towards my house as quickly as I can before the tears of agony start to fall.

CHAPTER 18
JJ WOODFORD

I'm home alone because Finn has work and I don't feel like going out today.

Callan and Joel said they're hitting the beach, but I'm enjoying my own company right now. As much as I like Finn's friends, I like having alone time too.

So settling for a new Viking series and the sofa is music to my ears right now.

A small thump against the door has me snapping my attention away from the TV. At first, I think it must have been a gust of wind because it wasn't heavy enough to be a knock.

I frown when I hear the noise again, as if someone's trying to pick the lock and break in.

I jump up from the sofa and inch closer. Then I hear keys drop altogether. My fingers press to the door handle, and I swing it open to find Ivy bent down, her fingers lingering over her keys as they rest on the floor.

"Ivy?"

A sound falls from her lips, somewhere between a sob and a shuddering breath.

I bend down to the floor instantly, but I can't see her face, it's clouded by her blonde hair. "Ivy," I lean over to grab her hand that is now touching her keys.

She's trembling like a leaf.

"What's happened?" I demand carefully.

I give her a once-over as best as I can in her crouching position, but I can't see any signs of injury. Her breathing becomes harsh, and I grab her keys with my empty hand and pull her up onto her feet and into the house.

Her legs barely work as she stumbles inside, flashing me her face for the first time. Tears are streaming down her cheeks endlessly and she sucks in a big breath, her chest going crazy as I shut the door behind her.

"Take a big breath," I say gently, gripping her shoulder. Ivy's eyes shut, and she chokes out a cry, then fails to take a breath, resulting in hyperventilation. "A big breath, in then out."

She's not listening. She's full-on sobbing.

My heart wrenches in my chest. What the fuck happened since this morning?

"Princess," I whisper, and clutch her cheek. "Listen to me."

But Ivy shakes her head, hands still vibrating. I tell myself to keep calm, to not let this situation escalate by panicking.

"Listen to my voice."

She raises those terrified, glossy eyes up to mine, full of tears and pain. My lips part at the strain on her face; whatever happened, she's losing control. She pants quickly, breathing still erratic and uneven.

"Ivy, please," I tilt her chin to force those green eyes to mine. "Focus on my breathing, copy what I'm doing."

Ivy's lips begin to tremble, and I inhale deeply through my nose for four counts, then I exhale through my mouth for four. Her eyes sweep over my face as I drop my hand from her cheek and grip her cold fingers instead.

"Copy me," I tell her again and focus on my breathing, keeping my gaze on hers.

She attempts at first, and I squeeze her fingers in encouragement. Tears continue to leak from her eyes, and seeing her this distressed makes me feel like a shattered man.

"That's it," I say supportively. "Now breathe out for a bit longer, until there is no air left in your lungs."

I watch as she swallows at my words. She attempts a nod, but she stops. Her eyes fixate on mine, and then my nose and my lips, trying to keep in control. I can still hear her quiet sobs, but her breathing is much calmer.

After a moment, she tugs her hand away from mine and shakes out her fingers, turning away from me slightly with that tortured expression again. I reach out for her, but I don't touch her, not when I don't know where her head is at.

She raises a hand to wipe her cheek and across her lips. "No one's ever going to let me forget." Her voice cracks as she continues to cry quietly.

My brows push together at her words. "Forget what?"

"I'm—" her chest rises quickly again, and I fear she'll bring herself back into a panic. "I'm always going to be reminded. People are always going to remind me."

I step closer and watch her with concern. "Of what, Ivy?"

At this point, I'm desperate. I'm desperate for her to open up to me and tell me everything that is on her mind, everything that has her up at night. Because I *want* to know.

Ivy turns and then turns again, eyes tired and body limp. She shakes her head, lowering it to the ground. "I can't do this. I thought I could, but I can't. I can't."

"Ivy—"

Her sobs become louder. They cut through my heart like a shard of glass.

A sound I *never* want to hear again in my life.

She steps towards me, collapsing into my chest completely. I wrap my arms around her in an instant, her cheek pressed against the centre of my sternum. My hand clasps the back of her head gently, cradling it like a baby.

Her fingers latch onto the back of my T-shirt, gripping on for dear life. The sound that rips from her chest vibrates through my entire body, and I close my eyes to shut it out, but I can't. Instead, I focus on the feel of her body, swaying us ever so gently as I lower my forehead to touch the crown of her own.

"It's okay," I whisper. "I've got you."

Ivy's cries begin to quieten after a few moments, keeping her as close as I can. I feel her fingers begin to ease their tightness on the back of my top, but she doesn't move away; she presses her head further into my chest instead.

I press a kiss to her hair again and listen as she exhales a little sigh, one of exhaustion.

The pain that she's been through, it's something I've never seen before.

And knowing something happened to her… something happened to her, and she's not the same person anymore. They've taken it from her, ripped it from her, and left her with nothing but a shell of a body, and I can't stand the thought.

I slide my hand from the back of her head and pull her back slowly. "Ivy," I say as I catch a glimpse of her face. Swollen eyes and red-stained cheeks.

She glances away, using her hair to hide her face. "I'm sorry."

"You have nothing to be sorry for."

Her eyes stay focused on the floor and I take her hand again, running my thumb across her knuckles soothingly. Slowly, she glances up at me, still shuddering through a breath. The tears have stopped, but I know she's still hurting.

"Come sit with me for a minute." I gesture my head towards the sofa.

Ivy's eyes glimmer for a second. "I don't want to disrupt your alone time."

I frown at her. "You're not interrupting anything," I assure her. "Please? I want you to sit with me."

She nods once, and I tug her hand gently to the sofa where the episode of my medieval program is still playing. I feel her perch beside me, but not close enough to touch.

"Have you seen this before?" I ask.

Ivy shakes her head. "It's not my kind of thing."

"We can change it," I say, reaching for the remote.

"No," she calls out. "It's fine. I don't mind."

I pause for a moment before leaning back, leaving the remote on the coffee table. "Don't ask me to explain what's going on because I have no idea myself."

Ivy laughs a little at this, and I celebrate the small success. "I think they make these series complicated on purpose."

"Agreed. I always wonder if it was actually like this, you know?"

"No way. This is completely glamorised," she says. "And they're always such horny people, yet I doubt they've washed out their mouths or bathed for weeks."

I cringe internally at the thought. "You're so right."

"To think they never had to use dating apps because there is always someone lined up for them," Ivy says with a subtle smile. "Like I'm sure most single people in the twenty-first century have used dating apps."

My shoulders raise once. "I've never used them."

Ivy's mouth falls open as she turns to me in shock. "You've never had to use them? Like… ever?"

The corner of my lip quirks. "Never needed to."

Ivy's eyes narrow in my direction again, but there is a ghost of a smile on her mouth. "So damn cocky," she comments, but her words are gentle.

"I think the key word here is confident."

"Yeah… trust me, I've seen the confidence."

I smirk at her. "And you liked it."

Ivy's cheeks turn beetroot red. This is the only time I've

managed to bring up our night together without her running away or shoving me back into my place. "I must have had concussion or something."

"Yeah, right." I laugh. "If that's what you want to call it."

She rolls her eyes and hides her face.

We watch the rest of the episode in comfortable silence.

"Thanks for earlier," she says when the credits start to roll. "I was a total mess."

"No, Ivy, you're human."

She presses her lips into a thin line. "I needed to hear that."

"If you want someone to talk to, I am here. Just putting the offer out there."

Ivy's chest quivers. "Thanks."

For a few moments we just stare at each other, and regardless of the fact she was crying her eyes out thirty minutes ago, she still looks so fucking beautiful it hurts.

Then she sucks in a breath and turns her attention back to the TV, moving away from me this time. "What's going on then? I'm secretly invested now."

I reach for the remote with a grin. "I'll start it from the beginning."

CHAPTER 19
IVY THOMPSON

I knew coming home would involve seeing the people who hated me the most. But I refuse to let them push me out. I ran the first chance I got, but now I'm not letting them take this from me, too.

As I stroll down the beach barefoot, allowing the sand to sink between my toes, I look out to the sea and watch as the clear water laps at the shore before retreating. I could watch the ocean for hours and never get bored.

The tranquility of all the sounds, the sights, the sensations, the smells.

Every part of being at the coast is like therapy.

I inhale the salty air and allow it to fill my lungs, the grains of sand pushing into the soles of my feet. The breeze flickers over the edges of my hair.

This is home.

A smile curves at my mouth as I walk back to the path, and dust off my sandy feet before attempting to slip on my sandals. I wobble, trying to hold myself up as a hand reaches for my wrist and the other for my waist.

I glance up to find JJ shirtless, sweat glistening off his

chest as if he's done a ten-mile run. I blink in surprise as I bring my foot back down to the ground before I fall.

"What is with you and unstable shoes?" he asks with a playful shake of the head. "These ones are flat."

My eyes narrow at his face—*anywhere above the collarbone, really.*

He's beaming down at me, a cheeky smirk that makes my heart miss a beat.

"If I don't get the sand out, they rub," I respond pathetically.

JJ's brows raise as he pulls his hands away from me. "Sure, sure. And it has nothing to do with your coordination?"

I raise a hand to shove at his shoulder, which was a big mistake considering all I can feel are the rock-hard muscles beneath his sweaty skin. I retreat my hand faster than lightning, but JJ laughs anyway.

"How far did you run?" I ask, folding my arms over my chest.

JJ swipes a hand over his buzz cut and pins me with his blue eyes. "Ten kilometers."

"I can't even run to the end of the street." I laugh to myself.

His lip twitches in amusement. "Want me to teach you? It's all about practice."

"No thanks, I'd rather not die this summer."

"I won't let you die, Ivy." He takes a tiny step towards me, and I swallow hard. "What have you been up to?"

I tilt my head an inch to look him in the eye. "Just went for a walk. I needed it after yesterday," I say before cringing at the state JJ found me in. "Thanks for what you did. It really helped."

"You don't need to keep thanking me. I just wanted to make sure you were alright."

My lips purse. "Yeah, I'm better now."

"Good. You wanna go grab a drink? I'm parched."

"It's eleven o'clock."

"No one said anything about alcohol."

I stare at him for a moment before glancing over my shoulder. It's harmless, right? And I don't want to go home just yet.

"Uh, okay. Sure."

We walk along the beachfront where the parade of shops is, before we head into a café to grab a strawberry cooler each. Then we perch on the edge of the wall and face the sea once more.

Silence washes over us, but it's far from uncomfortable.

JJ's bare arm occasionally grazes mine as he raises his drink to take a sip, and I'm well aware of the warmth it gives me. I glance down and stare at his tattoos on display. I've not really had a chance to see them up close and in the light, but they litter his arms in a patchwork style.

"What?" He chuckles when he catches me looking.

I shake my head and meet his eyes. "Oh, I just—" I pause to find a look of amusement on his face. "I'm being nosy."

"You can be nosy." He nudges me.

"Do your tattoos have meanings?"

JJ pauses for a moment, lowering his cup. "Not all of them. Some do. Some I got just because I liked them. I don't think every tattoo has to have meaning."

I spy the sparrow on his forearm with fine lines and light shading, then I glance up to find a cloud with a lightning bolt through it, and higher up is a leopard that sits on the outside of his bicep.

"What about these ones?" I gesture to his arm.

He places his cup down and twists his arm to have a look, as if he's forgotten which tattoos are there. "The sparrow was my first tattoo," he starts. "I read that sparrows represent resilience and freedom. I got it when I was freshly eighteen to keep reminding myself to do what I love, regardless of the life my father wants for me."

My forehead creases at his words. "Does he really dictate your life that much?"

JJ glances out to the sea. "We're working on it."

"And the cloud?"

"My tattoo artist had a flash sheet, and when I saw it, I liked it. Just a reminder everyone has bad days, but it doesn't mean it's a bad life, you know? Rain and storms usually clear up, just like bad days."

I nod, relating to his words.

"What about the leopard?"

His hand cups his bicep, stretching the ink over his muscles. "This one's my favourite." He beams.

"Why?" I smile as I study the tiny markings of the leopard, intricate and thoroughly detailed.

JJ shrugs. "Because leopards are my favourite animal. Simple."

"Which ones did you get because you just liked them?"

He flashes me his other arm, and on the inside of his forearm is a dark snake. "This has no meaning. I just liked the look of it and the placement when he put down the stencil."

When he straightens his arm, I get a peek of an abstract pair of faces on his tricep and some sort of card on the inside of his forearm.

"What's that?" I ask, pointing to it.

"It's a tarot card for strength. It's my newest one. I got it when my mum got sick."

I instinctively reach forward to take his elbow to get a better look. Inside is a woman hugging a lion with the moon and stars in the background. I'm amazed by the level of detail.

"I like this one," I confess as my thumb grazes the ink. "It's beautiful."

"Thanks." He smiles.

"Are you spiritual?" I ask, looking up at him.

JJ pulls a face. "Not really, but a friend at university did me a card reading and it was the first card I pulled. I guess it kind of gave me hope. I was afraid I'd pick the death card, but it didn't come up." He picks up his drink when I drop his elbow. "I know they're just a bunch of cards, but I felt something when she told me about the strength card, and it meant a lot to me."

I blink slowly as I take him in. My mouth becomes increasingly dry as he stares right back. He's a sentimental kind of guy, that's obvious in the way he expresses himself.

"What?"

My head shakes once. "Nothing."

"Tell me," he urges.

"I just like your tattoos."

He laughs softly. "That's not what you were going to say."

"I suppose people think tattoos are surface level, but they're not."

"No," he says in agreement. "They mean a lot to me."

"What do your parents think about your tattoos?"

JJ scoffs. "My dad hates them, but my mum likes them."

"I think both my parents would cheer me on if I got a tattoo."

His face lights up. "Yeah?"

"They're very into not letting anyone hold you back from being your true self."

"Would you get a tattoo?"

"I don't know if I could deal with the pain," I admit.

The thought of tiny little needles makes my head spin.

"They don't hurt too much," he brushes off. "You get used to it after a while."

My lips press together. "I suppose I don't know what I'd get."

"I wish I had that problem," he sighs with a smile. "I have too many ideas."

"Sometimes I want to push myself out of my comfort zone," I find myself admitting as I glance along the beach, the wind floating through my hair. "Do something unlike me."

"Why?"

To feel something again.

I raise my shoulders. "To try something different."

"Well." JJ shuffles impossibly closer until our legs are brushing. "If you want to go get a tattoo, I'll be there to hold your hand."

My teeth sink into my bottom lip. "Moral support?"

JJ flashes a grin. "Moral support, princess."

A flutter in my heart sparks at the silly nickname. "I'll let you know when I'm brave enough."

"You are brave, Ivy," he says sincerely. "I just don't think you see it."

I blink at him in surprise.

And I don't think either of us is talking about tattoos anymore.

CHAPTER 20
IVY THOMPSON

Tonight is another beach party. Daisy said I have to get myself out of the house. I know she's trying to help, but I'd rather curl up in a ball and watch movies alone. It's safe to say I've been feeling a little fragile since the run-in with Ben's friends.

I'm just glad Tom, Julian, and the rest of them are never invited because they've always been bullies since school, and no one wants them around. If they showed up, they'd soon be ushered out.

And despite my protests, we're here. On the beach. At the party.

The last thing I need is a drop of alcohol in my current emotional state. Those two don't mix well, and I'll end up a bawling mess if I'm not careful.

Isaac greets me with a hug and I sit with him, Daisy, and a few of our old school friends. I only speak when someone asks me a direct question, my eyes lingering on the roaring fire in front of us.

"Hey." Isaac nudges my knee with his when Daisy takes over the conversation. I turn towards him and look into his warm, friendly eyes. "Everything okay? You seem a little quiet."

I hum in response and flash another fake smile I've perfected. "Yeah. Just tired."

He doesn't take his eyes off me, analysing my expression. "Sure?"

"Sure."

"Okay."

I glance down at my almost empty cup of lemonade and stand from my seat. "I'm gonna grab a drink."

To get myself out of this conversation before it escalates, and I don't want to talk about my feelings at a party.

The sand rocks against my trainers, and I wrap my cardigan close to my chest. I lean forward for a can of Sprite and pour it into my plastic cup to pretend I'm drinking at least.

A familiar presence approaches at my side, and I don't have to look to know it's JJ. I can tell from the way the hairs on my arms begin to stand and my breathing changes. Whatever he possesses in his aura, it's incredibly dangerous.

He reaches for a bottle beside me and pours himself a drink. My eyes don't move from the table. I lower the empty Sprite can and turn away slowly. Maybe he didn't see me here, maybe he did—

"Hey." His deep voice makes my heart skip a beat.

I stop. I don't move. His voice practically hypnotises me and I wish—I fucking wish—it didn't.

"What's up?" I say as nonchalantly as possible.

JJ's brows crease and he studies my face. He can read straight through my fake expression.

"Are you okay?"

I hum and nod. "Yep. All good. Perfect."

"You don't have to lie to me, princess."

My heart quivers.

"It's easier than telling the truth."

He seems taken aback but recovers. "I haven't seen you for a few days."

"Yeah." I raise my cup to my lips. "Been busy."

"In your bedroom?"

"Yep. There are a lot of things you can do alone in your bedroom."

JJ's eyes narrow slightly, his lip curving. *Oh shit.* My eyes spring wide.

"I-I don't mean like that." I shake my head. Thank goodness the sun is already setting because I can feel my face heat up like a furnace. JJ's lips are now forming a smug smirk that makes me want to rip my hair out. "I don't mean I was being intimate… with myself." I pause and close my eyes painfully. "God, I don't even know what I'm saying. I'm gonna go now."

Without looking in JJ's direction, I speed walk to the seat I was occupying before, ignoring my heart thrashing against my ribcage. Why the hell did I say that? I should have stayed at home.

I try to pick up the conversation between Daisy and our old school friends when her words begin to slur. At least one of us is having fun.

Later on, I'm standing with Daisy by the fire, trying to keep warm now that the night is upon us. "You're my best friend, you know that?" She wraps an arm around my shoulder and slumps her weight on me.

I huff out a laugh. "I know, Dais."

"You're so good to me," she mumbles in my ear, almost tipping her drink down my arm. "I'm so grateful for you."

"I love when your drunk confessions come out."

She gawks at me. "What do you mean confessions? I tell you all the time how much I love you."

I smile. "I know."

Daisy whips her head over her shoulder and then jumps. "JJ!" she yells, and I find myself tensing. Oh god, *don't come over here*.

"You guys good?" JJ's voice floats through the air.

I close my eyes in defeat. "Yeah!" Daisy exhales as JJ stands in front of us. "I was just telling Ivy how amazing she is, she's amazing, right?"

For some unknown reason, I decide to look JJ directly in the eye. He smiles straight back at me and nods. "Sure is."

She points her finger between us as she sways on her feet slightly but doesn't let go of my shoulder. "I know about you two. I know about your date. I know your dirty little secret."

My blood runs cold, and I step out of Daisy's hold. I know she's drunk, but I didn't expect her to bring it up at a party, surrounded by people who know us. JJ doesn't seem startled by her confession, which has me raising my brows in confusion.

"Daisy," I warn her.

She scowls at JJ. "I can't believe you told me Ivy wasn't even your type," she slurs. "But you said I'm your type."

Everything begins to slow as I take in her words.

"That's like saying she's not attractive. Do you even find her attractive?"

I blink and look at JJ, he's staring back at Daisy in horror, and I feel like the size of a grain of sand on this beach. *Absolutely nothing.* Of course I'm not his type. I'm not surprised someone like Daisy is his type. A busty natural beauty who has enough confidence that she could give a top model a run for their money.

The ache in my heart isn't unexpected, but it still hurts. I glance away because suddenly my breath has slowed. I could have spared myself this embarrassment.

"Right," I whisper, my voice becoming hoarse as I step away. "I'm gonna go."

Before Daisy can protest, I walk towards the main road as quickly as I can, wrapping myself up in my cardigan and keeping my eyes on the ground. Pressure builds behind my eyes, but I refuse to cry.

My insecurities crash down on me once again.

I never want to compete with Daisy, but sometimes it feels like I am, and I despise it. I've lived in her shadow for almost ten years and now this... I almost laugh. This is the cherry on top of the cake.

Who was I even kidding?

JJ is JJ, and I'm... no one.

"Hey." I hear a voice behind me, but I don't turn. "Ivy."

Isaac touches my arm gently and stops me from walking any further. One tear rolls down my cheek because I know he's going to ask me what's wrong and it's going to set everything off. *Everything.*

"What's the matter?"

I duck my head, but he tilts my gaze towards him.

"Hey." He clutches my cheek and wipes away my tears with his thumbs. His face turns to panic. "What happened?"

My lip trembles. "Nothing."

"You're crying, Ivy. It's not nothing."

"It's stupid."

"Nothing you say to me could ever be stupid."

I chew on the inside of my cheek as I glance up at him. "I'm just tired of feeling like I'm never good enough."

His eyes soften at my words. "What do you mean?"

"Is it selfish to admit that sometimes I envy Daisy?" I confess quietly. "She's beautiful and bubbly, the complete opposite of me. And sometimes I just want to feel seen, that I actually exist. It's something I've always struggled with because I have never felt good enough in my own skin. I'm invisible to others."

Isaac shakes his head. "That's not true."

"It is."

His jaw locks before he exhales a short breath. "I thought you were beautiful from the second I met you. I remember we were lining up in the science corridors, it was our first day with Mr. Harrington, and you were standing there, your hair in two braids, and you had bright blue braces. He sat us together, and I remember so vividly that I could barely look at you because I was so terrified that I was going to make a fool out of myself."

I sniffle and pull away slowly. "You remember meeting me?"

Isaac grins. "Of course. And even now, you're still beautiful to me."

My heart feels like it's going to fall out of my chest. More tears leak from my eyes; I can't stop them. He continues to wipe them away with his thumbs and then I laugh, shaking my head. "I don't even know why I'm crying. I'm being pathetic."

"Ivy, we all have our own insecurities." He holds me gently. "Feeling like this isn't stupid, insecurities that stem from school stay with us for a really long time. Trust me, I should know. But I've always seen you, you've never been invisible to me."

I blink once and tears roll again. I'm not sure if they're sad or happy anymore. I'm a fucking mess of emotions right now.

"Come on." He beckons with his head away from the beach. "Let me take you home."

I don't protest, I walk towards the main road with him because there is nothing I want more than my bed right now.

"My car is over here." Isaac points down the street. "I haven't been drinking tonight."

My feet halt for a second, and I tighten my fists in my cardigan. Isaac notices my sudden discomfort and his expression warps to realisation.

"Or I could walk you home," he offers instead. "I'm happy with whatever you're comfortable with."

I swallow the lump in my throat and smile. "No, it's okay," I say, even though my mouth tastes like shards of glass. "It's just down the road, we can drive."

Isaac tilts his head, trying to read through my mask. "Alright. As long as you're sure?"

"Yeah, I am."

We walk to his car, and I gingerly place my fingers on the door handle. Isaac watches me carefully before I get in, and I look at him over the top of the car. "Can we listen to some music?"

Isaac smiles gently. "Of course. Whatever you want."

"Thanks." I slip into the passenger seat.

He hands me his phone that is already connected to Bluetooth, and I scroll for the perfect song for this two-minute journey. I watch Isaac's arms as he puts the car into gear and backs out of the space.

"I'll drive slow," he tells me, and I give him a small smile back, glad my tears have finally dried up.

"Thanks, Isaac."

He shrugs it off and turns the steering wheel gently. "No need to thank me. Party was lame anyway, I enjoy your company far more."

We stay silent for a few moments, and it really doesn't take long to reach my house, but Isaac drives at the speed of a snail, which puts me at ease. When he pulls up outside, I take off my seatbelt.

"Thanks again," I say softly.

He shakes his head and raises his eyebrows. "Please, stop thanking me."

I stare at him for a few moments before I lean over and wrap my arms around his neck. Hugging in a car is always awkward, but we somehow make it work. He laughs gently into my ear. "The seatbelt is strangling me," he comments.

After a second, I pull away, and he stretches the fabric away from his neck. "I'll see you soon?"

He hums in my direction. "Most definitely."

"Bye." I step out of the car and give him a little wave.

"Bye, Ivy."

And with that, I walk straight up to my front door and towards my bed, where I vow to sleep until lunchtime tomorrow.

CHAPTER 21
JJ WOODFORD

Watching Ivy walk away feels like the most painful form of torture; the look of hurt and vulnerability that crossed her face circulates in my brain on repeat. I should have said something, I shouldn't have let her walk away.

I turn back to Daisy, who is now latching onto me, stumbling about in her drunken state. Her cup sloshes everywhere, the liquid pouring onto the golden sand. I remove her hand, and her blue eyes flash with confusion.

"Why did you say that? I know you're drunk, but that was totally uncalled for." I try to keep my voice as quiet as possible because I know Finn is lurking somewhere, and I don't need this broadcast to the entire party.

Daisy scowls. "You're the one who said it. Not me."

My stare hardens. "I said it to you in confidence. I didn't even—"

"Didn't even what?" Daisy stops swaying as her eyes partially roll into the back of her head.

I bite my tongue. There is no point in this. She's wasted, and I don't need her causing a scene, not when I know that Ivy is upset because of what *I* said.

"Forget it," I grumble before turning away from her.

I search for Ivy amongst the crowd of people, and dart from the drinks table to the logs. Then I glance up at the road and find Ivy's blonde hair flapping in the wind, her back to me. My jaw tenses when I spot Isaac in front of her, his facial expression is soft.

He raises his hands to her face and rubs his thumbs against her cheeks.

Shit.

I stop walking, my feet sinking further into the sand. From this distance, I can't see what Isaac is saying, but he's smiling at her, continuing to wipe her face. After a few moments, he beckons with his head towards the road, and she walks with him to his car. It seems like she's apprehensive at first, but she joins him after a few moments.

My fists clench beside me. Fuck, fuck, fuck. What have I done?

The only reason I told Daisy that Ivy wasn't my type was because I didn't want her getting suspicious. I didn't want her to know I still think about our night together. I said it because I thought it might defuse the situation, not make it worse.

I watch a car leave the beach and head in the direction of Ivy's house.

I slip away from the party without anyone noticing, knowing it only takes me ten minutes to walk. When I reach the front door, there aren't any unknown cars outside, and I pray that Ivy didn't go home with him. I *need* to talk to her.

Drawing my keys from my pocket, I slip them into the lock. When I step inside, I don't see her in the kitchen or the living room.

There is a slight scuffle upstairs, feet pattering on the hallway floor. "Finn?" Ivy calls out, and I shut the door behind me.

My eyes snap to her blonde hair as she emerges from the stairs, and her eyes find mine instantly. She stops on the middle step, her throat bobbing at the sight of me. Her eyes are red, and even from this distance, it's obvious she's been crying.

You're such a fucking idiot, JJ.

I never want to see her like this again. I should have been the one comforting her, pushing those tears away. Not Isaac.

My chest rises rapidly at the strong energy surrounding us. Ivy blinks once and then frowns at my presence. "Why aren't you at the party?"

Her fingers pick at the chipping bannister; I register her anxiety.

"You're upset," I state pathetically.

"I'm not upset."

My jaw ticks at her defensive words. "Don't lie to me, Ivy."

Ivy's eyes ripple with tears again, and her chest heaves irregularly. Her body turns rigid, and she refuses to speak. I take one step closer, but there is still so much distance between us.

"What Daisy said—"

She scoffs loudly and plucks her fingers away from the bannister, crossing her arms instead. I watch as she trembles with the action, she's trying to be brave, but I know deep down something is eating at her.

"I really don't care anymore, JJ."

"What she said isn't true," I say with sincerity.

She blinks at my statement, clutching her fists together that rest over her chest. "Then why did she say it?"

I sigh and brush my hand over my head, eyes shutting briefly. "I didn't mean it. I said it becau—"

"It's fine, JJ." Her voice cracks, and I hate the way she says my name with a clipped tone. "I know you like her."

My expression falls because I'm astounded by her words.

"Like her?" I snap suddenly, my face twisting into a scowl. "You think that I like her?"

Ivy rubs her eyes viciously and sighs. "I'm too tired for

this conversation right now." She deflates and takes a step back up the stairs and towards her bedroom.

Before I know it, I'm right behind her. A couple of steps. That's all that closes the distance between us.

"Why do you keep doing that?" I demand. "Run when you get the chance."

Ivy keeps walking as she approaches the upstairs hall. She turns around and stares me down with her burning green eyes. Emotions of rage, hurt, and confusion shine in them. "Because I don't know what the fuck is going on with"—she flicks her hand between the two of us—"this."

"Oh, so there is a 'this' now? Because I was under the impression you were trying to shut me out despite what we both felt the first night we met."

Her eyes burn and she takes a shuddering breath. "What we felt was lust. Nothing more."

"Lust?" I laugh sourly and take two steps forwards, her eyes watching me with thick intensity. "You think what we felt that night was lust?"

Ivy takes a step until her back hits the wall, stabilising her. I stop directly in front of her, close enough that our chests brush when she breathes. Her eyes are now dilated like the night sky; there might be lust, but I know it's more. *So much more.*

My gaze travels down to those perfectly plump pink lips. The ones I've tasted before and craved ever since. She follows my eyeline, and a small whimper escapes her mouth as I pin her against the wall until there's no space left.

"I dare you to tell me this *only* feels like lust." I lower my face to her level, whispering against her jaw.

With one hand, I grip the side of her cheek. I tilt her face towards mine and lay my lips over hers. At first, she's stunned, utterly stunned, but when I coax her mouth open with my tongue, she answers by gripping onto my T-shirt.

I clasp my other hand around her jaw and twist my head,

brushing my lips against hers in yearning strokes. My tongue glides into her mouth, and she releases a moan of bliss. I push her further into the wall with gentle force, her fingers still latched onto the fabric of my top in a death grip.

Fuck. I can't get enough.

I've missed these lips, the way they feel, the way they taste.

Ivy relaxes into my body as I shove my chest into hers, angling her head so I can kiss her deeper, harder. She whimpers and I grunt at the same time, the air around us becoming hotter and thicker until I forget that we live on Earth and she isn't my entire existence.

Something sizzles and cracks against my lips, fire roaring in my heart. I've never felt more alive. This will have me dreaming of Ivy even when I'm not asleep.

After a few moments, Ivy presses a palm flat to my chest and pushes me off. When I open my eyes, I glance down at her, panting heavily to catch my breath. Ivy closes her eyes and purses her lips. "Wait, JJ," she heaves. "Stop. We can't do this."

I don't remove my hands from her face, instead, I slide my fingers into the back of her hair and tug gently. Her delicious lips part, and she stares up at me with heated eyes that would make me submit. My legs begin to wobble at the sight of her like this. At my mercy. And I'd happily get down on my knees for her if she asked.

"Why?" I ask deeply.

She closes her eyes, pursing her lips. "We can't."

"Tell me why." I dip my lips to her jaw.

Ivy shudders beneath me, her heart thrashing against mine. "Because it's not fair to Finn. He won't allow it."

"Allow it?" I raise my voice, and Ivy's eyes flutter open. "He's not your keeper."

"But he's my brother." She pushes me off, and my hands fall to my sides. "And this is a bad idea, we both know it."

I watch her, suddenly feeling cold without her presence. She slips away from the wall, putting distance between us again. But my lips are still tingling from the kiss we shared.

"Finn doesn't get to tell us what to do," I say, chest trembling.

"You don't understand."

"Then enlighten me, Ivy. Please."

Her lips wobble as she approaches her bedroom door, but she shakes her head and lowers her eyes. "I can't. It's too much."

She steps into her room and shuts the door behind her. I stare at the spot she was occupying seconds ago. The high of the kiss now dissolves into nothing. I should have just told her how I feel, that I lied to Daisy because I tried to push my feelings for her away.

I want her laughter. I want hours of nonstop talking. I want playful flirting.

I close my eyes in defeat and wish I was good with words to express how I truly feel.

CHAPTER 22
IVY THOMPSON

My body feels mummified when I pry my eyes open. Every inch of flesh and muscle aches like I've run a marathon. I slump into my pillow, not bothering to move. I reach over to my bedside table and grab my phone.

Shock. No notifications.

I raise a hand to rub my crusty eyes. I quickly replay last night, Daisy confidently spouting that JJ said I wasn't his type, Isaac dropping me home, JJ kissing me against the wall.

My heart lurches in my chest, making me feel like I'm about to go into cardiac arrest.

He cupped my cheek and held me with tenderness that I could only dream of. My skin flushes with a new desire for his tongue against mine. Fuck. It felt so good, *he* felt so good.

But I know this is the right thing to do. Not only would it destroy Finn, but I'm putting myself in a tricky position. We were lusting after one another, we had great sexual chemistry—probably down to the four cocktails I drank that night.

It's best if we leave it alone.

My phone buzzes in my hand and my brows furrow. My stomach twists. I don't want it to be Daisy. I need some time away from her. I'm pleasantly surprised to find Isaac's name pop up on the screen.

ISAAC:

Hey, how are you feeling this morning?

I smile at the simple message. *Checking in.* He has no idea how much it means to me. I nuzzle my head back into the pillow as I hold my phone above my face.

IVY:

Hey, I'm okay. I'm sorry about last night, total mess haha

ISAAC:

Don't apologise, everyone has emotions. It's okay to get upset.

IVY:

Well thanks for being a good friend anyway, I really needed you last night.

His response takes a little longer than normal, so I get out of bed and hurry to the shower. It's still early, which means I probably won't bump into JJ, and I'm counting on it.

When I get out of the shower and shut my bedroom door, I get changed into fresh clothes. My phone finally vibrates on my bed as I pull down the white cropped jumper over my chest.

ISAAC:

No problem... Are you doing anything today? Wanna go for a morning walk?

I glance out of the window, the sun gleaming through the room. Some fresh air and getting out of this house will help clear my mind a little. There is only so much *Gilmore Girls* I can watch without wanting to gouge my eyes out.

IVY:

> Sure! Shall we meet at the beachfront in twenty?

ISAAC:

Perfect, see you then

As I walk to the beachfront, my phone vibrates in my pocket, and I pull it out to see Erin's name on the screen. I press down on the green button and hold it to my ear.

"Hey, Erin," I exhale. "I'm so sorry I haven't called."

"It's okay," she chuckles. "I just wanted to make sure that you're alive."

I smile. "Alive, just about."

"Everything okay?"

No. Not really.

"Yeah, I've just been so busy. I feel terrible."

"Don't be," she says. "I know this is a big thing for you. I just wanted to check in, hear your voice."

My heart thumps. "You're too good to me, Erin."

"What are you up to?"

"Actually going to meet an old friend right now," I say. "But I'll call you later when I get home and we can have a proper chat?"

Erin hums in agreement. "Sounds good. Miss you."

"Miss you more," I say before hanging up the call.

Isaac is already waiting for me at the beachfront when I arrive. I smile at him as I approach, and he pushes off the metal railings to meet me halfway. "Hey," he brings me into a hug.

I rise up onto my tiptoes to match his height. My arms wrap around his body, and I press my face into his shoulder.

"Hey," I murmur into the fabric of his T-shirt. "How are you?"

"I'm good." He pulls away. His warm hands grip my shoulders gently, those dark eyes inspecting my face. "You sure you're okay?"

I nod even though I'm fighting that ongoing battle inside my brain. "Yeah." I force a smile. "Let's walk."

Isaac falls into step beside me and we walk down to the seafront, the waves gently lapping the soft sand beneath our feet. "I was worried about you yesterday," he admits after a few moments.

I tuck my arms into my chest, clutching onto the granola bar I haven't found the courage to eat yet. "No need," I say. "I was overreacting. It was nothing."

"You've struggled with living in Daisy's shadow?"

When he says it like that, I groan internally. It sounds so pathetic. "Yeah." I sigh as the ocean crashes into the shore, the sound like music to my ears—peace. "It's stupid. It doesn't matter; it's something I need to get over."

"No." He shakes his head. "It's not stupid. We all have insecurities; best believe I was a fucking wreck at school."

This time, I look at him and tilt my head so the sun isn't shining directly in my eyes. "A wreck?"

"I mean, Ivy, you know I wasn't popular at school." He laughs hesitantly.

"Neither was I."

No one is around when we perch on the sand and sit to face the sea.

"But we were on different continents," he says, lips curling. "You were the pretty girl with the blonde hair and braces for days. Literal days. How long did you have them for?"

I shove his shoulder playfully. "Shut up. It's not my fault my teeth were all wonky to the point where they considered giving me an operation. It was only for three years."

Isaac grins down at me, wrapping his arms loosely around his knees. "Three years," he chuckles. "But I still liked you."

"Well, that's kind of you." I smile and look down at the patch of sand beneath my crossed legs.

"No, I mean…" He pauses and then clears his throat. My eyes peek up at him slowly. "I liked you a lot, I was just too scared to say anything. Biology haunted me because I used to be so nervous and excited at the same time. I thought I would pluck up the courage, but I never did."

A pulse hits my throat. "Why didn't you?"

"Because someone like you was never going to like someone like me."

His words echo around my head, and suddenly I feel guilty. Every fibre inside my body begins to vibrate because how Isaac feels is exactly how I feel about JJ, and it's messing with my head.

"I might have," I admit. "I always enjoyed your company. I guess the thought of us being together in that way never crossed my mind because I believed we were such good platonic friends."

Isaac swallows harshly. "Don't say you might have." He lowers his head. "Because I don't want to kick myself any more than I already do."

My lips slip into a subtle frown. "I wouldn't have been ready for a boyfriend at that age anyway," I say slowly. "I was struggling so much with my body, my flaws, always being second best. I would have been a complete fucking mess, but I'm glad that we're still friends, Isaac. I really appreciate you."

He stares at me, and I fear I've said the wrong thing. But when he nods, I take a small breath of relief. "I'm glad you're back." He drops a hand to trace shapes in the sand. "I was worried I'd never see you again."

"I needed time away."

"Of course, I completely get that. I'm just glad I have this time with you."

A genuine smile creeps up on my face. "Me too," I say quietly, the sound of the waves building. "I really need a real friend right now. I'm sorry I left and said nothing, you deserved better than that."

"Well." He clears his throat. "We can make up for now. Can't we?"

"Most definitely."

He beams down at me, and I beam right back. Allowing the comfort of his company and my home to rid myself of any past emotions, to let go and allow myself one moment of peace.

I think I owe myself that at least.

After spending the entire day with Isaac, I come home feeling refreshed.

We no longer spoke about past feelings or insecurities, we changed the conversation to university, jobs, our futures, what will make us happy.

A conversation like that is worth more to me than anything else.

Although I know deep down in my heart I don't like Isaac like that. A part of me wishes I did because he would treat me like a queen. But that spark of fire and longing isn't there, and I don't think I could ever see him as anything more than a friend.

When I walk through the front door at five o'clock, I find Finn and JJ sitting at the kitchen counter with bowls of noodles. I catch my brother's gaze, and he smiles at my entrance.

"Hey," he calls out.

"Hey."

JJ rips his eyes away from the bowl in front of him, as if he was lost in thought and didn't even hear me walk through the door. His gaze flicks to mine within a second. I try to ignore the way he looks at me, like I'm the only person on this goddamn Earth to exist.

That look must be a fragment of my imagination. Surely.

"Where have you been?" Finn asks curiously before stuffing his face with noodles.

I drop my bag on the floor and shut the door behind me. My teeth sink into my bottom lip as I edge closer to the counter, JJ's eyes still burning a hole in my face.

"With Isaac," I say truthfully.

Finn hums in response. "Isaac's a nice guy," he says as I plate myself up and sit beside my brother. "I approve."

I stupidly meet JJ's stare, noticing his hand that's latched around his fork becoming deathly tight. His knuckles begin to turn white.

JJ's jaw tenses, and I swallow down nothing but shakiness

I can't, for whatever reason, take my eyes off him. Finn is too distracted in his own bubble to realise that we're having a silent standoff.

I finally drag my gaze away from his and take my fork with a wobbly hand. "How was your day?" I ask Finn calmly.

"Fine. Work is long, but I like the money, so I can't complain," he mumbles through a mouthful of food.

I grimace at the sound and the visual. "Close your mouth, you animal."

"Make me." He narrows his eyes towards me, and I shoot him a glare back.

"Gross."

He slinks an arm around my shoulder, weighing me down. Then he rubs his knuckles against the top of my head like we're ten years old again, and I squirm in his grip. "You're so annoying," I grumble.

Finn chuckles. "I know, but you love me."

CHAPTER 23
JJ WOODFORD

Ivy was with Isaac *all* day.

After our kiss.

After I pushed her against the wall as she moaned into my mouth and fisted my shirt.

After I heard how aggressively her heart thumped against mine.

After I told her that what we felt was not lust.

When in fact the desire to have her is so strong, I can barely function knowing she purposely avoided me while Finn was at work.

I've never really been good at voicing how I feel or what emotions I'm experiencing because I grew up thinking it was a sign of weakness. But when my mum got sick and I couldn't keep everything bottled up anymore, it all came out and I realised… expressing how you feel isn't too bad.

Last night I wanted to say a million different things, but none of them would have come out right. I probably would have pushed Ivy further away, knowing she was already in a fragile state. That's the last thing I wanted after already upsetting her once.

The next morning, I wake up fairly early and decide to

take a run down at the beach. It's better to run in the mornings when it's quieter and cooler; it helps me function, and it clears my mind.

My chest burns as I run down the seafront, earphones blasting music with my eyes set forward. I never realised how running in a beautiful setting like this would help calm the storm inside my head.

When I circle around and find myself slowing to a jog from where I started, I stop my watch and look down at the damage I've done. Yeah, I definitely needed this this morning.

My legs shake as I ease into a walk and catch my breath. I glance up at the beaming sun and shield my eyes for a moment. I turn back to the beach front, plucking out my earphones as the water crashes against the shore softly. A calm day. A day to refre—

"JJ?"

My head whips to the sound of my name, only to find Daisy at the other end of it. Beside her is a massive golden retriever who is heading straight towards me.

The dog licks my arm and I grimace because I'm so incredibly sweaty. I dip my hand down and ruffle its head and scratch its ears as Daisy walks towards me in a tiny sundress.

"Hey," I say politely.

Her blue eyes glitter at me, her teeth sinking into her bottom lip. She doesn't bother to hide how she's openly roaming her eyes over my sweaty body and arms. "Hey." Her voice drops into a tone of seduction. "Went for a run?"

"Yeah." I smile gently. "Who's this?"

"Rufus." She grins and strokes his back. "He's such a good boy."

His tongue hangs out as he looks up at me and I have to give it to him, he's fucking adorable. "He's sweet," I say, stroking his soft, velvet-like fur again.

Daisy sways from foot to foot in front of me, but I keep my

eyes on her dog. She clears her throat to get my attention, and I glance up at her slowly. My gaze flicks to her hand as she twirls a piece of hair around her finger and flutters her eyelashes not so subtly.

"You look so good right now," she says with a glint of playfulness in her tone.

My hand raises to scratch the back of my head. "Bit sweaty," I laugh.

"Hey." She leans forward and grabs onto my bicep suddenly, my eyes gravitating to the action. "So I was wondering, we should go do something soon. Like just the two of us, we could—"

"Daisy—"

"—go for a walk or go for dinner, then maybe we could go somewhere a bit quieter and—"

"Daisy—"

"—I don't know… have a bit of fun."

I suck down a breath because this can't keep going on, I have to end this now before it gets messy and out of control. She deserves to know the truth, she shouldn't be parading around after me like a cheerleader.

"What?" She blinks.

I lower my head to the ground as I attempt to bring together my thoughts without making them seem rude or blunt.

"You're a great girl, Daisy," I say, and her eyes light up at my words. "But I don't like you like that. I'm sorry if I led you on, but this isn't going to work out. We're different people."

Her tan complexion turns to the colour of a sheet of paper, like she's seen a ghost. "Is it something I've done?"

"No." I shake my head. "I just want to be honest with you and myself, and I realise that this isn't going anywhere. I don't want to upset you, but I can't keep stringing you along, and you know that wouldn't be fair."

She swallows thickly and glances away for a moment. "Right," she whispers. "Silly me."

"I'm sorry," I say sincerely. "But you will realise this when you find the one, it's just not me, Daisy."

Daisy turns her back and grabs Rufus. "No worries, J," she says, dark hair falling over her shoulders. "Thanks for being honest. I'll see you around."

She walks away so quickly that she almost stumbles down the steps towards the beachfront. I huff out a sigh and head back to the house, ready for a shower and a gallon of water.

When I get home, I know Finn is already at work; he's been called in to pick up a lot of shifts this week. I don't know if Ivy is home or out—probably with Isaac. That thought sends tsunamis of frustration through my body.

After I shower and get changed into fresh clothes, my phone buzzes with a message from Cal, asking if I want to grab a beer with him and Joel over lunch.

I head into town to meet them at a pub with a beer garden. It's fairly quiet for the week, but at least the weather is pulling through despite the clouds that are rolling in. I greet them both and find out they've already ordered me a beer for my arrival.

"How's it going, man?" Cal asks, swiping a hand through his mousey-brown hair.

I take a sip of my drink. "All good, just went for a run this morning. Nothing crazy."

"Can't believe Thompson got himself a job," Joel chuckles. "I cannot imagine that guy serving tables."

The corners of my lips twist. "Me neither, but money is money at the end of the day."

Cal raises his glass as a salute and nods. "True. What's he need all that money for anyway? His parents are well-off."

My eyes flick between the pair of them, and I realise they don't know what he's like at university. Spending almost every last penny on alcohol, going out, takeaways. I have no idea what's changed in that guy recently, but getting a job is the most responsible thing he could possibly do right now.

"He's an animal," Joel comments. "He told us some crazy stories about your time at uni."

I almost snort into my drink. "Most about him then?"

They both laugh. "Of course."

"Did something happen a few years ago to make Finn…" I pause for a moment. "I don't know, a bit off the rails?"

Joel and Cal share a glance, narrowing their eyebrows. "You mean when Ben became a total asshole and changed fucking everything? Then yeah."

I lean forward on the bench. "Who's Ben?"

"He was a friend of ours," Cal comments, resting his lips on his glass. "Dated Ivy for a bit."

My heart skips a beat. One of Finn's friends dated Ivy? I didn't know that.

My gaze switches between the two of them frantically, desperate to know more. "What happened?"

"I can't believe Finn didn't tell you." Joel scratches his head, clearly feeling awkward about the conversation. "Maybe he just wanted to forget."

"Forget what?"

My skin crawls with the desperation to know. With the way Finn's been acting, it's clearly bad.

Something has happened between them—Finn, Ben, and Ivy. Did he do something to her… is that what this is about?

"Finn should probably be the one to tell you. I know he hated how people gossiped and spoke about it behind his back; that's why he's so protective of Ivy. He's got to be. Ben was a really close friend," Cal explains, and now I'm left feeling even more confused.

What the fuck did this Ben guy do?

"Did Ben hurt Ivy?"

Cal sighs and glances at Joel quickly. "Put her in the hospital."

"He what?"

The poison that drips through my veins is sharp. My nostrils flare at Callan's words. He put Ivy in the hospital. *Ivy in the hospital.* Those are words that should never end up in the same sentence.

I hope this man is dead because if he's not, best believe I'm—

"He didn't put his hands on her like that," Joel clarifies. "But yeah, he put her in danger."

I lean back slightly and let all this information sink in. They're right, Finn or Ivy should be telling me this, but at the same time, how did I not know? He's kept this bottled up for three years.

Now things are starting to make sense. Ivy was so adamant that Finn couldn't know about us because it would be unfair to him. Because he's already been through that pain once, he couldn't possibly do it again with another friend.

Then I think back to Ivy. Who on earth could even think about hurting her? My chest turns to stone at the thought of her lying in the hospital. Confused and scared. I have to close my eyes to shut out the haunting thoughts.

My stomach churns. She didn't deserve that. Finn didn't deserve that.

When I open my eyes, I remember the scar running down her chest, when she said that she was in an accident a little while ago, and she almost died. It doesn't take a genius to put two and two together. *He did that.* He put that scar on her body, and I feel my fists begin to tighten.

That scar she hides with shame. All because he took away the confidence she once had. Her body is beautiful, perfect in every way, with each freckle and scar. I would kiss over any insecurity and flaw she believes she has to prove to her that it's all in her mind.

God. I want to wrap her up in my arms and promise her

happiness. Because I knew someone or something had sucked the soul out of her body, leaving nothing but a hollow shell.

She's not living, she's just surviving.

And I want to help bring that soul back, a soul that is in need of some tender care.

Even if Finn forbids it.

CHAPTER 24
IVY THOMPSON

After I hear the door close for the second time today, I know JJ has gone out. Finn has been at work since this morning, and I haven't left my room. I pick up a book and spend the morning with fictional characters instead of real ones.

An hour or so ticks by when my phone vibrates beside me. I put down the book and glance at the screen to find Daisy's name pop up, and I frown at it. She hasn't even bothered speaking to me since the party, since she got drunk and decided to run her mouth for no reason.

I roll my eyes and reluctantly press the green button. "Hello?" I say dully.

She sniffles from the other end of the line. "Ivy?"

My body twists, and I press my feet to the floor. "What's the matter?"

"I'm outside your house, could you let me in?"

"Coming," I say before sprinting down the stairs to my front door.

My fingers latch onto the handle and open it to find Daisy sobbing on the other side. I open my mouth, but she falls into my arms. Even though I'm still angry at her for the other night, I can't deny her friendship right now, so I embrace her in a hug.

"What happened?" I ask as I smooth down the back of her brunette hair.

Slowly, she pulls away from me, blue eyes filled with tears. "I feel like shit," she chokes.

I move my head away. "Why, what happened?"

She shuts the door behind me, and I beckon with my head for us to sit outside. Her footsteps follow me, and I perch on the edge of the sunbed. She sits down right beside me.

"Stupid boys," she grumbles.

"What happened, Daisy?"

Her attention turns to me, and she wipes her eyes. "JJ," she whimpers. "I saw him at the beach earlier and he told me that he's not interested and that I'm not the one for him."

My forehead scrunches together, confused as to why she's this upset. From what I know, they went on one date, and they haven't even kissed.

"I'm not trying to sound insensitive, but you barely know him."

Her eyes blaze with fury at my comment. "I'm sitting here crying, Ivy, and that's all you've got to say?"

I recoil from her tone. "All I've got to say?" I scoff. "You haven't even talked to me about what happened at the party."

"What?"

"The comment you made about JJ, Daisy. It was a shitty comment to make."

The tears in her eyes begin to ease up, and she presses her lips into a thin line. "I don't even know what you're talking about."

"Of course you don't, because you were drunk and you wanted to put me down so you could look superior to him."

Days' worth of frustration and anger begin to build.

"What are you talking about?"

I throw my hands up in the air. "Forget about it."

"No," she grumbles. "Tell me what you wanted to say."

My eyes flick between hers, and I huff out a small laugh. "You had to bring up that JJ said I wasn't his type. My whole life, you've made this into some competition, and it's exhausting. I never wanted to compete with you, but this time I can't stand it; it's as if my feelings don't matter."

"I didn't rub it in."

"You did," I state simply. "You always have to make sure you're above everyone else. Every day throughout school, I literally hid in your shadow, I was so insecure because I didn't understand why I got treated differently to you."

Daisy's jaw clicks, and her eyes narrow at me. "You have no idea what I went through in high school," she mumbles. "All the shit I had to go through."

"Like what?"

Her nose twitches. "Everyone thought I was a stuck-up bitch. Being gossiped about. Having girls hate me because boys were interested in me. Those days were some of the worst times of my life."

My eyes narrow. "Oh man, imagine people hating you because you're pretty."

Something burns in my chest, and I'm not proud of it. Daisy sniffles and stands from the sunbed. "You don't understand, Ivy."

"I went through years of bullying, Daisy," I say harshly. "Years of rude, backhanded comments that have sat with me until this day. People tripped me up in the hallway because I was your stupid sidekick who followed you anywhere, and they'd do things to get your attention. Sticking gum in my hair because boys found it funny."

She folds her arms over her chest and glances away. "You endured boys asking for your number and girls being bitchy because they were jealous! I spent years fearing going to school, not understanding why we got treated so differently. We all have feelings, yet I would go home and cry because I wanted to know why I wasn't good enough for anyone to look at and see a person who mattered."

"It's not my fault boys didn't like you, Ivy."

A laugh passes my lips. "No, that's not your fault. But you've played up to it the entirety of your life, and you don't even know it. Everyone knows you're beautiful, Daisy, but it seems like you always can't wait to kick me while I'm already down."

"That's not true." She shakes her head.

"Remember when we found out that Ben liked me?" I say in a whisper. "You made little comments when you could, acting shocked that he asked me out when he didn't even look in your direction. You couldn't believe that someone liked me and not you."

Daisy sticks her tongue into her cheek. "Those comments were nothing."

"They might have been nothing to you, but they stuck with me, Daisy."

She glares at me, and I look away. I could list a hundred other things she's made comments about because I'm sick of keeping them to myself. But this conversation isn't doing me any good, and I'm over it.

It might not be malicious, but when they begin to build up, I feel like a target that I can never escape, and I don't need friends who bring me down.

"You're actually unbelievable," she rasps harshly.

My eyebrows shoot up. "I'm unbelievable?"

"Yeah," she spits and steps towards me. "I came here upset, and you're the one who decides to lecture me, that's not what a friend does."

A sour chuckle escapes my lips. "A friend? I don't understand why you want me to be your competition."

"I've never seen you as competition, Ivy. That's just ridiculous."

"Alright," I throw my hands up in defence. "Whatever."

She scoffs in my direction. "See, you don't even care how upset I am about JJ!"

"I'm sorry you're hurt, Daisy. And I know it feels shit." I press my hands to my face. I can't be dealing with this right now. "But it's a rejection. It happens to everyone, all the time. I guess you don't know what that's like, because it rarely happens to you."

Daisy's eyes fill with tears again, and she shakes her head. "You're not being very nice, Ivy."

My heart quivers inside me, and I never intended for this conversation to take this turn. "Yeah, well, that makes two of us."

"Screw you," she grits and stalks away, slamming the front door behind her.

My fists tighten at my sides, and I resist the urge to scream at the top of my lungs.

The comment to JJ was the final straw. I shouldn't have told Daisy to get with JJ. I should have told her the truth. It might have made things easier. Maybe this is my fault.

I inhale a big breath, burying my hands into my hair. A part of me wishes I never came home at all.

I knew it would end in disaster.

Footsteps echo behind me, but I don't turn around. I really don't care for any conversation right now. My head has already started thumping, and I've barely done any thinking. The rest of the day is going to be hell.

"Ivy?"

JJ's voice rings in my ears.

"You good?" he asks softly.

I nod once, staring ahead at the blue sky. "Yeah," I rasp and drift my eyes to the side to find him standing against the patio door.

"You sure?"

My eyes shut for a second. I hum in response.

"Can we talk… about the other night?"

I stand from the sunbed and grab my things. "Not right now." I focus on the floor. "I have a headache and I'm not feeling up to it."

When I walk towards the door, he doesn't move out of the way. "Want me to grab you some paracetamol?"

I meet his blue eyes, and I curse him silently for being so sweet. After that argument with Daisy, I really don't want to sit around and talk about my feelings for a second longer. I'm done with this crap for today.

"No, thank you." I swallow and attempt to move around him.

His arms are folded over his chest, and I try not to stare at his muscles and broad shoulders, but they're in my direct eyeline, and I can't stomach looking back into his eyes again.

When he doesn't move, I have no choice but to glance up. He's watching me with a cautious expression, and it has blood thrashing through my system like there is no tomorrow.

"Princess, I just want to talk."

My heart pauses for a simple beat, and I close my lips again. I can barely form a sentence right now, let alone listen to what he has to say. "Can we talk tomorrow?" I squeeze my eyes shut. "I'm really not feeling too good."

"Alright," he says after a few moments and steps out of the way.

I walk straight upstairs and into the bathroom, where I take a few moments to breathe. Sometimes I wish I knew what exactly was going on inside my head, rather than having one hundred different emotions attacking me at once.

When I exit the bathroom and head towards my bedroom, there is a packet of paracetamol and a cold bottle of water lying in front of my door. I pause and glance down at it, then look over my shoulder.

Why is he doing this to me? I don't need to fall for him any more than I already am.

Things are too complicated. I'm actually losing the plot.

I bend down to collect the items and shut myself in my room, wishing this day never happened.

CHAPTER 25
JJ WOODFORD

I greet Finn for breakfast the next morning. Yesterday felt like a fucking whirlwind.

At least my shoulders feel ten times lighter now that I've told Daisy the truth.

"You got work today?" I ask as I grab the milk from the fridge.

Finn shakes his head. "Nah, man, party tonight. I got someone to cover my shift."

I snort quietly and peer over my shoulder at him. "Already?"

He shrugs effortlessly. "They offered, why would I decline? It's my turn to get absolutely smashed."

"Great," I murmur to myself and pour some cereal into a bowl, followed by the milk. I perch beside Finn as he reads through something on his phone. "Can't wait for that."

Finn's idea of a good night is getting so blackout drunk that he has no recollection of it, what he's said, what he's done, and how he got home. I started noticing his increase in drinking at university.

He's always loved to drink, but over the last year, it's

become increasingly worse. He's not drunk every day, but it still concerns me, and I fear bringing it up in case he takes a bad turn.

So I wait for a better time, especially if he repeats history tonight.

I hear the floorboards creak upstairs. I still haven't had my conversation with Ivy, even though she said we'd talk eventually. I've gone over what I want to say in my head a thousand times, but I already feel myself cracking under pressure and going off script. I didn't even want a script in the first place but if I don't think about it, it's going to be an absolute shit show.

I glance up to find Ivy walking towards us, her eyes down on the floor. I wait for her to look at me or even Finn, but she doesn't. Something has been bothering her since yesterday, and I want to know what it is.

"Hey," Finn calls out. "You good?"

Ivy hums as she reaches the fridge and pours herself a glass of apple juice. "You okay?"

"Yeah, party tonight. You up for it?"

"No, I'm gonna stay in."

"Why?"

I watch as Ivy drags her tongue across her bottom lip and turns towards her brother, barely acknowledging me. She seemed somewhat fine with me yesterday, what has changed all of a sudden?

"Not feeling it," she sighs.

"You might later," Finn says quickly. "Why don't you invite Daisy? Haven't seen her around for a few days."

I cringe at the sound of her name. Finn doesn't know I've turned her down. It's not been something I've wanted to talk about, not when all I can think of is Ivy, and I can't exactly tell him that.

"No thanks." She raises the glass to her lips. "I'll pass on inviting her."

Finn turns to her slowly. "Is that why she hasn't been around? Has something happened between you two?"

"Don't know, don't care," she mumbles into the glass before emptying it and placing it inside the dishwasher.

"Iv." He reaches out to grab her wrist, and she stops walking. "What's going on?"

Ivy tilts her head to the floor. "Nothing."

"*Nothing*? It's not nothing, what happened with Daisy?"

She raises her eyes to meet her brother. "We fell out. It's not a big deal."

My brows hike. They fell out? Shit. I wonder if it has anything to do with her drunken non-confessions of mine the other night.

Finn tugs her back gently and twists in the stool. "Come out with us tonight, I don't want you to be alone if you're all sad. I'm sure Isaac will be there."

I resist the urge to roll my eyes. Right, sure, Isaac will save the day, the ultimate cock-blocker.

But Ivy said we'd talk, and I will do everything in my power to get her alone, so I can drop all my feelings on the table.

Even if the thought alone terrifies me.

"I'm not feeling it," she whispers.

"For a little bit? It might make you feel better. I promise I won't make a fool out of myself."

Ivy's lips tilt at his comment. "You always make a fool out of yourself. What are you talking about?"

He gasps loudly, and her smile brightens, turning my stomach into a clump of cement. *I wish she'd smile at me like that.* And yet, I might as well be dead to her right now because she hasn't even acknowledged me.

"Well, I'll try extra hard today then." Finn puffs out his chest.

"Please don't. None of us needs that. And I'll think about

it," she pulls away from his grip. "I wanna go into town and do some things, I'll see how I feel later."

"Alright."

Ivy turns, catching my eye for the first time, and I offer her a smile. "How are you feeling today?" I ask.

I feel Finn's eyes boring into the side of my face, but I couldn't care less what he thinks right now. I have to talk to her, even if it's for a second, before I drive myself to the brink of insanity.

"I'm okay." She smiles weakly.

"What was wrong?" Finn frowns in our direction.

Ivy sucks in a breath and grabs a yogurt from the fridge. "I had a headache yesterday, and JJ left some painkillers at my bedroom door. Thank you for that."

Her eyes collide with mine when she speaks, and I stare back into those stunning green irises. God, my chest is crumbling. "You're welcome," I say softly.

Ivy's gaze lingers for a moment too long before she thinks better and finally looks away. I immediately miss the warmth of her eyes.

I'M pleased when I spot Ivy as she joins the party on the beach.

I'm not pleased when the first person she goes to is Isaac.

Daisy is nowhere to be seen, which is convenient. Now I'm curious about what happened between the two of them.

I keep track of Ivy as she sits with Isaac and a group of people I vaguely recognise. I'm at the beer pong table next to Cal, and on the other side, Finn stands next to Joel. He said he wouldn't make an idiot out of himself if Ivy came but he's already halfway to fucked.

As usual.

I sip on my drink, not wanting to be intoxicated when I

finally get to speak to Ivy tonight. It's been too damn long, and I can't stand another second of her thinking that I don't find her attractive, because I do. It's unhealthy how much the chemicals in my brain alter when I look at her.

After losing three games because Finn is too busted to even throw the ball, I spot Ivy walking towards the drinks table alone, and I excuse myself, saying that I need the toilet. But I make a beeline straight towards her. She's covered up despite the warm weather, and her wavy blonde hair rests against her shoulders with half of it shoved up and wispy pieces framing her face.

I clear my throat as I approach her. "Are you avoiding me? You said we'd talk."

Ivy glances up at me as she fixes herself a drink. "No. I've been collecting my thoughts."

"What happened between you and Daisy?" I straighten out my spine, suddenly conscious of the height difference between us.

Her eyes close tightly. "You mean where she came crying to me because you said you didn't want anything to do with her anymore?"

I feel my brows pinch together painfully. "How is that my fault?"

"Because you decided to have a conversation about me with her." She turns to me with deep frustration burning in her eyes, and I realise how hurt she really is. "I don't know why she brought it up, probably because it made her feel good knowing you guys went on a date. It's not the first time she's had to make it obvious that I'm never anyone's first choice."

Her words ripple something inside my chest. I've never heard her speak so freely about her struggles, about how I made her feel. Guilt clouds my mind, and I wish I could go back in time and change how everything played out, but I can't.

I can only try and fix the future.

"I'm sorry about what I said to her, I didn't mean it. I was—"

"Look, JJ, I don't care." She folds her arms over her chest, shaking her head as if this situation could just go away. *I wish it would.* "I don't care about this anymore. It's such a mess and it's exhausting."

She takes a step away, and alarm bells start ringing in my mind. I have to take control of this situation. I have to say it now, even if the words are barely forming on my tongue. I reach forward and take her wrist in mine, tugging her back gently.

Ivy glances up at me, and as I look at her pretty face, the words fall a lot easier than I thought they would. "Don't you realise that every time you catch me looking at you, it's because you are so damn beautiful that I can't tear my eyes away."

She blinks once, and her throat bobs, a small sound falling from those lips.

"The night we met, I told you you were gorgeous. And I said it because I *meant* it."

Never in my life has my chest felt so tight and so relieved at the same time. She stands there in surprise, but she doesn't move, so I take a slow breath and run my finger along the inside of her wrist in soft motions.

Ivy's lips are now parted, inhaling as much air as she can. Goosebumps run along her skin as I continue to move my finger over her wrist, warmth stretching through me.

I step closer to her, my body towering over hers. "From the second I saw you, Ivy. I—" I pause to admire her all over again. Those big eyes are staring at me with awe, they're crumbling, and I hope she realises that everything I'm saying is true. "I had to have you. Even if it was for one night. But I don't want just one night with you. I *never* wanted just one night."

My heart pounds against my ribcage. I've opened my heart and laid it out for her.

"JJ—"

Listening to her whisper my name makes me shiver. My spine tightens and then relaxes because it doesn't come from a place of mistrust. She's trying to wrap her head around this, too.

"I wanted you to stay," I confess. "I wanted to wake up to you."

Ivy's throat bobs. "I didn't want you to wake up and regret it."

"That wouldn't have happened." I shake my head. "All I regret is not asking for your number that night."

"I-I didn't feel good enough for you," she exhales.

My forehead aches from frowning so deeply. "What are you talking about? You are more than enough. You will always be enough."

Her eyes glitter at me before she pulls away, but I continue to hold onto her.

"Come back to the house with me. Away from the party. Let's just talk. No one to distract us."

"Finn will know we're gone." She glances over her shoulder, but I couldn't give a shit who is looking at us right now.

All I see is her.

"Then we make something up."

Ivy's lip trembles for a second, but she doesn't remove her wrist from my grip. She lets me hold her. "I can't do this to him. Not again." She sounds so defeated. I wish she'd do things for herself, not for anyone else.

"Not again?" I repeat. "Ivy, I don't understand."

Her eyes falter for a second, and I notice her jaw tenses at my question.

"Is this about Ben?"

Ivy rips her hand from my grip, eyes glittering with

sadness, within a matter of seconds. My fingers turn ice cold without the comfort of her skin, and I regret it.

Shit. Why did I say that?

"Did Finn tell you?"

"No."

"Then who?"

"Joel and Cal. They didn't say much, but they mentioned him."

Ivy lowers her head, and she's back to hiding away in her shell. I had her for thirty seconds and I fucking ruined it. She bunches her hands into her cardigan and attempts to shield herself from me.

"*Stop*. Stop shutting me out." I plead with her.

"I can't help it." Her voice tears through my soul. "I can't talk about the past when it still hurts."

I step closer, but I don't attempt to touch her. "I would never judge you."

"It's not about being judged, it's about—" She pauses. "It's about having my chest ripped open again, having to go through those memories, when the last thing I wanted was to come home to relive them. I want to move on."

"I'm sorry for pushing you," I rasp when I see the twisted agony in her eyes.

"What's going on over here?" Finn's voice echoes into our space. I groan internally as he pauses between us. "Why do you both look weirdly cosy? I told you not to flirt with my sister, Woodford. And I meant it."

Ivy is still looking at me, and I draw my eyes away from her to look at Finn. "I'm not flirting with her." I clear my throat, mentally murdering him for interrupting us. "We're talking about Daisy."

The lie is quick and easy.

Her shoulders relax when I don't tell him the truth, not when she's so caught up in what happened in the past.

"Oh." Finn frowns. "Ahhh, well, let's ignore her for tonight. Let's have fun."

He wraps his arm around Ivy's shoulders, and she slumps under the weight of him. "Yeah." She nods before pursing her lips. "Sure."

When he pulls her away from the table, I grind my molars. The conversation might not have been as in-depth as I wanted, but at least now she knows where I stand.

CHAPTER 26
IVY THOMPSON

It's been three days since the party. Three days since my head has been scrambled like a goddamn egg.

JJ knows about Ben. I'm not entirely sure how much, but he knows something.

Joel and Cal can never keep their mouths shut.

I should have known that Finn wouldn't have told him. I know that he's not over it. He blames himself for what happened to me, for allowing the relationship to happen. Which is why he'd pin JJ down and kill him before he ever got the chance to be intimate with me again.

I spent the afternoon having a walk on the beach. I grab an ice cream and sit on the seafront, kicking off my flip-flops so I can dig my toes into the sand.

I wrap my arms around my legs and inhale the salty air, taking my time to study each wave as it plummets onto the shore. It's therapeutic because every wave is different in the way it looks and sounds.

My phone vibrates in my pocket, and I tug it from my denim shorts before staring at Daisy's name on my screen. I press my thumb to the notification, and the message fully pops up.

DAISY:

Hey, I know I'm probably the last person you want to talk to right now. But could we meet up? I've had the week to think about everything, and I'd like to speak to you in person. No shouting, just talking.

I blink rapidly at the text. She wants to talk again in person?

Daisy isn't the usual type to start shouting and spurting her words, but when she's upset and hurt, that side does tend to come out.

I rest my thumbs over the keyboard and contemplate how I should respond. A part of me wants to ignore it altogether, but I know that having this argument between us has made my anxiety spike.

IVY:

Hey... uh sure. Do you want to talk today?

DAISY:

Yeah, I do. Everything is eating me alive.

IVY:

I'm on the beachfront if you want to join

DAISY:

Okay, I'll be about twenty minutes

I don't reply, I lock my phone and throw it onto the sand before lying back. I stare up at the baby blue sky, my eyes flickering across the candy floss-like clouds.

As I count down the seconds in my mind, I tell myself not to freak out. This might be good, might give some closure to our past. It was messy when we last saw each other, and considering we've been friends for almost ten years, I don't think it should have ended like that.

I glance to my left and sit up, watching as Daisy strolls

towards me. Her dark hair is up in a ponytail, and she's dressed down in a simple pink playsuit that makes her tan glow even more than usual.

"Hi." She pauses, and I place my hand over my eyebrows so I can see her.

"Hi," I respond. She stands awkwardly for a few moments until I clear my throat. "Do you want to sit down?"

"Thanks," she whispers before perching beside me.

The air is filled with silence, and I swallow.

"I'm sorry," her voice trembles. "For how I acted the other day. I was out of order and I said some really nasty stuff. This time apart has made me think about our relationship in school."

I stay quiet and let her do the talking.

"I wanted the attention, I always did. But I get where you're coming from with your insecurities, thinking you were competing with me. I found myself becoming insecure with the girls who would judge me and spread nasty rumours about me because I was catching boys' attention," she says gently, and I finally turn my gaze to meet hers. "I struggled with my own image because I wanted to look the best, be the best. Hell, when I was sixteen, I wanted lip filler, which is crazy because I was a child."

My lips purse, and I play with the sand between my fingers. "But what I'm saying, Ivy, is I understand how you felt. I'm sorry for not paying better attention to it at the time. I should have been a better friend, and I wish I didn't care about what other people thought of me, but I did, I still do."

Emotion clogs my throat as I glance at her to see the sincerity and honesty etched onto her expression.

"And you were right; rejection is hard for me because I take it out on myself. It does happen to everyone." She drags her tongue over her lip. "I'm sorry for what I said to JJ at the party. I was pissed out of my mind, but I meant it positively, that if you're not his type, then fuck him. I'm sorry if it didn't sound like that. You are beautiful, and you don't need to be defined by someone's type. You don't need to conform to societal norms about beauty, because everyone is beautiful in their own way. And it's taken me a while to realise that."

"Why didn't you tell me how you were feeling in school?"

Daisy shrugs and releases a long sigh. "I thought if I ignored my problems and my insecurities, they'd go away."

"I felt the same," I admit. "We could have helped each other."

"I know," she says, her shoulders drooping slightly. "I wasn't a great friend because I was too busy focusing on my social status, but I want to be better. I want to be that friend who doesn't give a fuck if a boy doesn't like them or when I don't look like a top model from Instagram. I'm over having to compare myself to everyone. I just want to be me. I just want to be happy."

I swallow quietly. "We're not perfect. None of us are. And I know, high school was a crazy time with all our fresh hormones. But I want you to be happy, too."

"I know, Ivy."

"And I'm sorry. I wasn't being a good friend when you came over the other day. I should have been more supportive than bitter," I sigh. "I wish we had just talked it out instead, and I feel awful."

She chews on the inside of her lip as I look at her out of the corner of my eye. "The reason you got so upset when I said that thing to JJ is because you like him, don't you?"

My mouth falls open and I attempt to shake my head, but somehow I can't move.

"I know I asked if I could talk to him, Iv, but if you had told me you liked him, I would have backed off. I would have never gone there; I got the impression that you didn't really like him," she says slowly.

"I lied," I blurt. "I lied about the night we met."

Daisy frowns. "What do you mean?"

"Well, I didn't lie. I withheld the truth."

"Go on."

"I slept with JJ the night I met him."

Daisy's eyes widen. "What the hell, Ivy? Why didn't you tell me? I would never have tried to go after him if I knew that."

I shrug. "I don't know. I guess it was so out of the blue and unlike me, it felt weird voicing it to you."

"Did you think I'd judge you for it?"

A sigh escapes my lips and I roll a hand down my face. "I thought everyone would judge me for it, not just you."

"I don't care who you sleep with, Ivy. As long as it's consensual and you're safe doing it," she says sincerely. "Fuck, I wish you told me."

I close my eyes for a brief second. "All my emotions have been a mess since coming home."

"Which is understandable, given you haven't been here in years. I wish you had said something to me so I wasn't going around making an absolute fool out of myself around him when it's obvious he likes you. I thought maybe he was just protective, considering you're Finn's sister, but he looks at you with stars in his eyes," she says, and a lump forms in the back of my throat.

"It won't work out."

"Why?"

"Because of Finn, because of everything in the past."

She shuffles closer to me on the sand. "I know you're not the same Ivy since before the accident." Her hand rests against mine. "But you deserve to be happy, you deserve to do what you want with your life. If Finn doesn't like it, he doesn't have to. But it's not his choice."

"It would break him." I press my hand to my chest and take a long breath. "Not after how guilty he felt after the accident. Ben was his friend. A friend he trusted. He'd never trust any of his friends with me again."

Daisy hums. "Yes, and I get his concerns. But you can't be bubble wrapped for the rest of your life; any guy could turn out to be an asshole. It might not be his friend, but it could be someone; he can't protect you from everything."

I stay silent for a few seconds.

"So it's true… you like him?"

My eyes fixate on the clouds resting above the sea. My stomach churns as I open my mouth. "Yeah," I whisper. "I do. I have since the day I met him. He teased me, he bantered me, he tried to understand me. And then he treated me with care, he was gentle, and it felt so real. Like we had known each other for years."

"Does he know?"

"I'm scared to admit it to him."

Her arm slides over my shoulder, I can't remember the last time we had a heart-to-heart like this. It's been years, but it makes me feel so comfortable and seen. It's rare I talk about my feelings, but right now, I want to pour them out to her.

"Sometimes, Ivy, we just need to take life by the horns. Things are going to be difficult and tricky, but that's how we get the best out of it. How will we ever know if we don't take risks?"

My head falls onto her shoulder gently. "I'm not the sort of girl who takes risks." I laugh quietly to myself.

"No…" She trails off. "But it might be the one risk that is worth it."

Her words stick with me for a few moments, and I keep my eyes on the ocean and the way it crashes into itself.

"Finn will come around eventually." She squeezes my arm. "You're an adult, Ivy. You make your own decisions, and I have a feeling that JJ is the type to be an absolute gentleman."

The corners of my lips twitch because I already know he is.

My head turns to Daisy, and she stares back at me with

her pretty eyes. "I feel awful for what I said," I tell her. "We weren't very nice to each other."

She breathes through her nose with a laugh. "Tensions were high, I'm glad we had this talk. I promise to be better; I never want you to feel like we're competing for anything. We're best friends, not on rival teams."

"I know. It was an explosion of feelings."

"Do you forgive me?"

"Yeah," I say gently. "Do you forgive me?"

Daisy grins. "Obviously."

"I think we need some more deep chats like this, without the boy drama. More about ourselves, and how we're feeling. I could do with a support system for life in general," I say.

She tugs me into her side again. "Me too," she murmurs against my head. "I feel like I just got my best friend back."

"Same."

CHAPTER 27
IVY THOMPSON

When I get home, the sun has already set and the orange sky is fading into darkness. I don't hear anyone when I get in and I decide not to call out, Finn might be at work or asleep—who knows.

I head to my room where I get changed into my silk pyjamas and I climb into bed, reaching for the book that sits on top of my bedside table. I sink into my sheets and fold back the page, exhaling a little breath.

This is the life.

My eyes scan the words, and I find myself smiling. The events of today have put me in a mood I didn't realise I needed. I allow myself to be sad far too often, but why would I want to be sad? Daisy was right, I deserve to be happy.

Taking a chance with JJ might upset Finn, but it might be worth the risk.

What if it works out?

A noise echoes from outside my window, and I turn my head towards my blinds. I frown at the noise, it sounds like a whimper or a quiet cry. When it doesn't happen again, I turn my attention back to my book and try to engross myself in the story.

I chew on my lip as I flick my eyes over the words, only for the sound to reach my ears again. It's now louder than before, and I feel my heart hammer in my chest because I know it's coming from the garden, which is directly below my bedroom.

Without hesitation, I push back the covers and walk to my window. I tilt the blinds slowly and glance outside, but I can't see anyone or anything. I hum to myself and turn towards my door.

I lean over my desk and grab my dressing gown before sliding it over my arms and around my body. I crack open my door and head downstairs to find the back door shut but unlocked, someone must be home.

My fingers wrap around the handle and I pull it back. As I step outside onto the patio, I instantly regret not putting on any shoes because the stones are freezing now that the sun has gone down.

I glance down the side of the house, my eyes squinting as I find a body hunched over, head in their hands. A sob wracks the back of their throat as they choke, the sound making me pause for a moment because it's haunting.

"JJ?" I call out.

He doesn't move as I take a few steps forward, not wanting to startle him. When my bare feet come into his view, he sniffles and wipes his nose with his wrist before more tears spring out of his eyes.

A surge of panic rushes through me.

I lower down to his level and flick my eyes over the shadows on his face from our dim garden light, and it shatters my heart to pieces when I find his eyes red and cheeks damp from his tears.

"JJ," I whisper his name this time, the two letters becoming lodged in my throat. "What's happened?"

I study him as he buries his palms into his eyes and shakes his head. My eyes wander to his wrist, and I dig my teeth into my bottom lip. I want to comfort him, but I don't want to push him away if it's not what he needs right now.

"Oh fuck," he curses and glances up, then he sniffles again.

This time, I don't hold back. I can't let him sit here and sob his heart out without a bit of comfort, even a light touch to let him know that I'm here and he's not alone. I lean forward and place my hand on his inked arm ever so gently.

He twists his head towards me, and I flick my eyes over his face. If he doesn't want to talk, he doesn't have to. I'm the queen of bottling things up, so I understand if he doesn't say a word.

I'm certainly not one to judge.

"Do you want to talk about it?" I offer softly.

JJ glances down at my hand as I smooth it over his forearm in slow circles. He watches the action as I do it, and I notice that his breathing finally begins to even out after a few seconds.

"My mum," he says hoarsely.

My heart twangs. Oh god. Oh god. Please, *no*. My palms begin to sweat when he speaks.

"The treatment she's having." He takes a shuddering breath. "It's taking too long to work, and now I'm starting to worry that there is nothing that can help her. This was our last hope, and I'm fearful of what it means."

My face crumbles at the sadness in his words. I sit up on my knees and lean forward to wrap my arms around him, his head resting on my shoulder as he sniffles.

"I am so sorry, JJ," I exhale as I hold him tightly. "But don't give up hope. There might be something, and the treatment might start working, or they might have something new for her to try. Don't give up. She needs you to stay positive for her."

His arms snake around my back and he grips onto my dressing robe, fisting the material as his body shakes against mine. I close my eyes and tell myself not to cry, even though my throat feels like I swallowed razor blades.

But I need to be strong for him.

He's far away from home; he's far away from his parents. My lip wobbles at the thought, he's here and can't do anything to help. I couldn't even imagine that pain and isolation.

I tilt his head up from my shoulder and hold his handsome face between my hands, using my thumbs to push away his tears that keep rolling. "I know it's easier said than done, and you have every right to feel the way that you do right now. But there is still time, there is still hope that something might work for her. She's in the best place she can be, where all the treatments are and the best doctors."

JJ squeezes his eyes shut. "But what if there isn't?"

"Try not to think about the what-ifs. You could spend hours, days, spiraling, thinking about what might be. Instead, channel that energy into positive thoughts. She needs your love and support right now," I whisper and tilt his head a little. "I know this is hard for you and your family, but don't give up. Keep going. I'm right here with you."

His eyes glisten, water in his lash line. He raises his arm and wraps it around my waist before tugging me into him. I practically tumble into his lap as I latch my arms around his shoulders and cup the back of his head.

JJ's face remains in the crook of my neck as I drop my head and swirl my fingers into shapes over the skin above the neckline of his T-shirt. "Don't give up," I say softly. "There is still time."

He squeezes me harder, and I listen to how fast his heart rattles inside his chest.

After a few moments, I pull away, feeling his arm slip from my back. I reach down and take his hand, attempting to tug us onto our feet, but he is literally twice my size. "Come," I beckon towards the grass and lower to the ground, patting the space beside me. "Stargazing always helps to calm me down."

JJ steps forward and lies beside me, both of our heads parallel to each other. I glance at him out of the corner of my eye. We lay there, our hands merely an inch apart. I reach out my finger and brush his, and I listen as he takes a deep breath.

Then I reach for his hand, giving it a light squeeze. I shouldn't enjoy the way his hand fits against mine, but I do. It practically swallows mine whole.

For a moment, we both look up at the night sky, stars shining across our beautiful galaxy. It humbles me in a way because I always think there is so much out there that we don't know about, why do I fret over the small things I can't change?

"Tell me about her." I smile, turning my head towards him. "If you want to."

His eyes flick over the stars, and I notice that his tears have dried up and his chest has slowed down. I give his hand a quick squeeze again, to which he returns it, sending a zap of comfort to my heart.

"My dad has always been hard on me and my brother," he says after a few moments. "In a good way, he wants the best out of us. But our mum, she just wants us to be happy. Whatever it may be that we do, she only wants us to be happy."

I smile at him, but he doesn't glance my way; his eyes continue to roam the night sky.

"She got me into ice skating, remember when I told you?"

"Of course," I hum.

"But when it didn't work out, she was never angry with me. She was just happy that I gave it a shot. She always came to my football games to cheer me on. When I wanted to start video production, she was always my first viewer." He smiles at the memories. "And she was always so biased. I remember my first video was so crap but she told me it was amazing and how she wanted to show all her friends."

My lips lift to a grin at his words. "Biggest fan."

JJ turns to me this time, the light in his eyes beginning to show again. "Original fan club member."

I chuckle gently. "I love her already."

His throat bobs as he flicks his gaze to my eyes. "She always puts other people first, no matter her situation," he carries on. "I like to think I took after that trait of hers, it's one of my favourite things about her because she cares so much. If she had five pounds on her and someone else needed it, she'd give it away in a heartbeat, even if she needed it herself."

"People like her are the best type of people," I say sincerely.

JJ rolls onto his side, our bare knees brush, and I forget that I'm in nothing but a tiny crop top, shorts, and my dressing gown has come undone. But right now isn't the time to care, not when this moment with him feels so raw and real.

I want to make sure that he's okay. That he doesn't have to go through this alone when he's miles away from his family, when he feels like no one can relate to him. I might not be able to, but I want to support him regardless.

"Are you close with your brother?"

JJ hesitates. "We're not super close because we're very different, but I still love him. We're just not best friends."

"I get that."

"Thank you," he tells me sincerely. "For being with me."

"I'd never leave you out here by yourself." I focus on his silver nose ring because those eyes are too much for me right now. "I'd never want you going through this alone."

JJ squeezes my hand again, and I glance up into his eyes. I notice how close we are as I roll over. Noses merely inches apart from one another as we lie against the cool grass and listen to the silence of this small town.

Peaceful.

"I wish I could be with them," he admits.

"Could you go out to visit?"

His head shakes once. "My dad said the fewer people, the better. We don't want to cause her stress or increase pressure. I mean, it broke my heart when he told me, but I understood. Sometimes I think he forgets that she's my mother, not just his wife. It hurts."

I bring up our entwined hands and press an instinctive kiss to his knuckles.

Feeling that way must be agony, and I wish I could take his pain away.

JJ's lips fall open when I pull my hand away, his eyes staring at my mouth and then our hands. His expression is a look of surprise, I suppose I've never really shown true affection towards him before. But it feels natural.

"Well, you might not be able to support her in person, but you can support her in spirit," I whisper. "I'll keep her in my prayers, too. And I'm sorry your dad thinks that way."

"We've always had a strange relationship." He sighs. "I know he just wants to see us succeed, but in the way he wants. And it's exhausting sometimes."

I hum. "Well, I'm glad to hear that you're still doing your video stuff, despite what he thinks. It's your passion, and you shouldn't give up on it."

"I just don't want to let him down," he rasps.

I push myself up a few inches as I stare down at him. "You couldn't let him down. You're smart and creative, and if making videos makes you happy, then never stop. I bet they're both really proud of you, regardless."

JJ makes a sound before closing his eyes. "I don't think my father has ever told me he's proud of me."

My heart sinks at the pain in his voice. "Does he struggle to voice his emotions?"

"Yeah, I get that from him, too, I think."

"I don't think you struggle with your emotions."

He exhales a tight laugh. "Trust me, I do."

I purse my lips before frowning. If anything, I'm the one who struggles to voice their emotions.

He releases a sharp breath and glances down at my arms as a gust of wind whips against my skin. "Are you cold?"

I shake my head, even if my skin rises in goosebumps.

The corner of his mouth twitches. "Liar."

"I'm not lying." I try to hide the shiver that runs down my spine.

JJ's hands move forward and snake around my body within two seconds, tugging me into his warm chest. My leg rises and lands between his, his muscly arms swarm me, and I rest my head over his beating heart.

I take a shallow breath as I melt into his arms. A place I've secretly wanted to be since I met him that night at the bar. And now I've given in because I can no longer deny myself the sensation of being close to him.

I flick my eyes across the stars in the sky. When I was younger, I always tried to find as many constellations as possible. I'd Google when they were most visible and what time to look out for them.

"Look!" I point my finger up. "You can see Scorpius. Well, half of it anyway."

JJ flashes me an unsure look. "Scorpius?"

"That's its name."

"Where?"

I take JJ's fingers and point to where I can spot the upper portion of the constellation, as the lower part isn't visible here. Our cheeks are merely inches from one another. "There."

My head turns slightly as I watch JJ squint into the sky. "Still can't see it."

"Try harder," I laugh. "It's right there. Can you see that really bright star? That's Antares. It's the easiest way to spot Scorpius."

"Where?"

"Oh my god, JJ. It's right there!"

JJ turns to me with a grin, our lips could easily brush if I leaned in, but I freeze. "I'm just teasing, princess. I can see it."

I roll my eyes and drop his fingers.

"Are you into astronomy?"

"Finn bought me a telescope when I was sixteen, and I literally was out here every night trying to see all the different constellations." I laugh to myself. "It was the best gift I've ever received. There's something calming about looking out at the stars and wondering what else is out there, you know?"

JJ hums in agreement. "Yeah, I get that. It's an interesting thought, and there is no way we're the only intelligent life in the universe."

"Exactly! And it's rare to see Scorpius so brightly, so think yourself lucky."

"I'm a Scorpio."

"That explains a lot," I mumble with a smile.

JJ turns to me and grips my hand again, dropping it to his chest, entwined with his. "What's that supposed to mean?"

"Nothing…" I trail off, my fingers vibrating against the beat of his heart. "They give good advice, but sometimes they're bigheaded."

His mouth falls open, and he tugs me impossibly closer. "That is a lie."

"Is it?"

JJ rolls to his side but keeps my leg over him. "Actually, they're loyal, patient, and protective."

I study the shape and curve of his lips as he whispers the last word, and I know I shouldn't be looking at his mouth right now—not in his vulnerable state. My heart beats out of my chest, the air between us becoming thinner and thinner.

"You're freezing," he says as he rubs his hands over my arm, and it sends waves of fire across my skin.

"Doesn't bother me, I like summer nights," I murmur into his T-shirt.

His other hand cups the back of my head, and he smooths down my hair, the motion making my eyes flutter shut.

Something is telling me that this is right, and I need to stop pushing him away.

"Your heart is beating incredibly fast," he comments.

My eyes ping open, and when I try to push myself off his chest, he doesn't let me. He cages me in with his large arms.

"Because you're crushing me," I gasp with a chuckle.

I feel his lips press to the crown of my head, and I melt back into him again, not wanting to fight this feeling. It's like peace has found me all at once.

Because in this moment, there is no one else. It's just us.

CHAPTER 28
JJ WOODFORD

I slept a lot better than I thought I would.

When my father rang me with the news about my mother's treatment, I went outside to let everything out because I didn't want to disturb anyone. I failed that mission as soon as I saw Ivy crouch down beside me and flash me a look of concern.

At first, I didn't want her there. I didn't want her to see me like that. But when she placed her hand so delicately on my arm, I couldn't help but fall into her chest. I needed her comfort and company.

Anything to make me feel human again.

I'm miles away from my parents, and I was struggling with the loneliness of it. Until Ivy lay down with me and we looked up into the sky with our fingers entwined and her head on my chest.

We went up to bed before Finn could catch us cuddling on the grass. Although I could have easily spent the night out there with her. I thought it would take me hours to fall asleep. Instead, I took Ivy's advice and tried to think positively. My mum needs me to be strong for her, and I will.

All my prayers are with her right now, and I hope

someone out there will give her another chance at life because she doesn't deserve this. I don't want to lose her. I can't imagine life without her.

But it's not the end.

I wake up earlier than usual, no doubt my mind is working overtime, but at least I got a solid seven hours of sleep. I stand from my bed and jump in the shower before heading downstairs.

I make myself breakfast and sit at the kitchen island in silence, dwelling on last night and trying to digest the phone call, forcing the pessimistic thoughts away.

Finn walks down the stairs twenty minutes later, he's shirtless and rubbing his eyes.

"Morning, bro," he calls out as he makes his way to the fridge and drinks orange juice from the carton. "You good?"

"Morning." I nod as I take my plate to the dishwasher. "Yeah, fine. You?"

Finn studies me as he leans on the fridge. "You don't sound good."

I shrug it off. "I got a call about my mum last night," I admit, and Finn's expression softens. "But I don't want to talk about it."

"Okay," he says gently. "But if you do want to talk, I'm always here. You know that, right?"

I chew on my lip and meet his green eyes. "Yeah, of course."

"Shall we head out today?" he suggests. "Grab some lunch at the pub, have a drink, go for a walk. What do you say? It'll keep you distracted."

His plans sound like exactly what I need. If I stay in this house all day, I'll find myself staring at my phone hopelessly, waiting for a call to tell me that everything will be okay. But realistically, I know that's not going to happen as these things take time, and I don't need to torture myself with that possibility.

"You're not working?"

"Nah." He shakes his head. "Got today and tomorrow off. So let's head out, I'll buy you a beer."

I perch back on the stool and smile as he downs another gulp of the juice. "Are you sure you're not broke?"

"That's why I got a job." He holds up his hands in defence. "And note how I only said *a* beer."

A small laugh passes my lips. "Alright, fine. Sounds good."

Soon, another pair of footsteps makes it down the stairs, and I glance up to find Ivy dressed in one of those summer dresses that make men go feral. What is it about them? Most likely the way you can flick up the back and pull down their panties easily, sexy and cute all at the same time.

I almost slap myself for having such thoughts when her brother is standing right beside me.

Her hair is slicked back into a tiny ponytail, and I get a good view of those cheekbones and plump, glossy lips. The blue dress that clings to her body has me quivering in my seat after last night.

I want her wrapped up in my arms. Even if Finn will never allow it.

I'd kill for a moment like that again. Just us and the stars.

Yeah, I've gone soft for the woman I should be staying away from.

Her eyes collide with mine as she inches closer. "Hey," she calls out to both of us, but doesn't look away from me. Her expression is warmer than I've seen in the past, and it makes me want to take a picture and hold onto it forever.

"Hey." I offer her a smile.

Ivy turns to Finn, and she grimaces. "Ew, why do you always do that? I don't want to drink your saliva."

Finn spills some of the orange liquid down his bare chest, and I cringe at how sticky he will be. "I'll buy some more."

She snatches it from his hand and scowls at him. "You are

a monster. Wait till Mum and Dad get home and you can't parade around like a caveman anymore."

He rolls his eyes. "Like they'll care."

"When are they coming home?" I ask.

Ivy flicks her eyes to mine and grabs a napkin to wipe the lid of the carton. "Next week, I think," she comments. "Who knows. They like to extend their holidays at the last minute."

"What are you doing today?" Finn asks Ivy.

She shrugs and pours herself a glass of water and starts making breakfast. "Not sure," she says. "The weather's nice and I didn't want to waste it in bed."

"Want to come down to the pub with us for lunch?" he suggests, and Ivy blinks back at her brother.

"The pub?" She quirks a brow.

Finn blows out a breath. "For food."

Ivy glances over her shoulder, our eyes meet again, and I notice the way the corner of her mouth tips up in deliberation. *Please say yes,* I beg pathetically in my head. Having her in my eyeline today will definitely be the distraction I need to stop looking at my phone.

"Sure." She nods. "I could do with some good food."

My chest eases off its tightness, and I grin.

"You spoken to Daisy lately?" Finn asks as he slumps on the stool beside me.

Ivy reaches for a knife to butter her toast. "Yeah, we spoke yesterday, actually."

I turn my head to her with intrigue.

"Oh, really?" Finn asks. "How did that go?"

"We spoke about our differences, we apologised to each other, and we made up. Not much more to it."

"Well, I'm glad," Finn says loudly as Ivy walks past with her breakfast. He leans over to tug on her ponytail gently. "So, out for lunch and a drink?"

Ivy sits opposite me, and I have no shame in keeping my eyes on her. She picks up her toast and takes a bite, crumbs sticking to her lips. I study her tongue as she extends it to lick them clean, and I hate myself for being mesmerised.

Lips that have been imprinted into my brain from when she wrapped them around my cock the first night we met. *Fuck.* Blood rushes to my crotch, and I glance towards Finn instead to somehow distract myself, but immediately start feeling guilty.

"What time?" Ivy asks as she dusts off her hands over the plate.

"Twelve?" Finn suggests, tapping the screen of his phone.

She hums and hops off the stool, placing her plate in the dishwasher. "Sounds good to me."

As she walks away and back up the stairs, I find myself staring at her ass and the way her hips sway without intention. After last night, I've fallen another thousand feet for this woman, and everything she does makes me feel like I've touched an electric fence.

I run a hand over my head, grazing my buzz cut. Yeah, I'm fucked.

"I'm going to go and shower," Finn calls out.

"Alright," I respond as he leaves me alone in the kitchen.

I TAKE back what I said; having Ivy with us is a terrible idea. Especially because I'm sitting with Finn, and when I find myself staring at her, I want her to myself. Not wanting to share her attention with him.

She's still got on that baby blue sundress; one I'd love to hike up to run my fingers across her round ass and silky thighs. I shake my head subtly. *Stop it. Stop it.* Her lashes are now darker and curled, they're so long they almost touch her eyebrows.

I glance down at her sternum. The dress is high enough to cover the scar on her chest, but gives off a beautiful view of her shoulders, collarbones and neck. I clutch onto my beer and grind my teeth down against one another.

She's fucking torturing me and has no idea.

Ivy laughs at something that Finn says, and someone might as well dig me an early grave because at this rate, I won't make it to the end of the day. Not when I can't act how I want around her with Finn in the picture.

God, I want to clasp the back of her neck and tilt her head until our lips meet. Listen as she pants out my name before I press a kiss to those lips that have been begging for attention since I last kissed her.

My fist clenches, and I glance away. I'm not doing myself any favours by fantasising.

"I can't believe the lobster attacked you." Ivy chuckles and lifts her glass of wine up to her lips. "You're such a crybaby."

Finn gawks at her. "It hurts, alright?" He holds up his fist that has a massive blue plaster across his skin. My eyes scan the plaster, and I smack his hand, only for him to jolt back. "You asshole."

I look at Ivy. "You're right, total crybaby."

Ivy's cheeks heat, but she continues to smile at me before her eyes slip to something behind me. That smile disappears from her face within seconds, and I tense.

"What?" Finn asks, noticing her change in expression.

He glances over his shoulder, and I do the same. My eyes collide with a group of guys, but I don't recognise any of them. Finn's shoulders tremble as he turns back to the table.

"Ugh," he murmurs and drags his hand down the back of his head. "Ignore them. They won't come over here."

Ivy gulps, and I despise the way her face pales. "They did before."

"What?" Finn hisses under his breath, and for a moment, I see fear flash behind his eyes. "When? W-what did they say to you? Did they say anything?"

She nods, and her hands immediately begin to judder, and

I despise every second of it. I resist the urge to cup them with my own, to calm her, to do something. But I can't. "When I was with Daisy." She takes a breath. "They came over then."

Finn curses. "Why didn't you tell me about it?"

Ivy's eyes flick to mine, and she gulps. My brows draw in together. "I-I don't know," she stammers.

"What did they say to you?" I ask, leaning into the table more.

"Just being assholes. As usual."

"Did they mention Ben?"

Ivy drags her eyes to Finn, and she pauses for a moment before nodding again.

"I hate them," he grumbles, his jaw tensing so hard that I can see a vein pulsing in his face. "I knew they'd do something like this, backing Ben for his disgusting behaviour. They will never change."

"Do you want to leave?" I ask Ivy, sensing her severe discomfort.

After a few moments, she shakes her head. "No," she rasps. "I don't want them to win."

Finn leans over and presses a hand to her shoulder. "It's fine, we're here. Nothing is going to happen, Iv. I promise."

Ivy blows out a shuddering breath. God knows I'll deck anyone who dares to belittle her. I don't care who they are.

"I know." She flashes him a wary smile and then covers her mouth with her glass again.

Finn changes the subject, but it's obvious Ivy isn't in the conversation; her eyes keep moving between our heads and glancing at the group behind us. They get louder and louder by the minute, intoxicated by alcohol and slurring their words.

"You need to get your grades up this year," I tell Finn. "You barely scraped a 2:2."

He waves him off and takes a big swig of his beer. "I'll make up for it this year, I was too busy partying and—"

"Fucking," I cut in.

Ivy pulls a face of disgust. "Please, let's not go there."

I chuckle, and Finn sighs. "Trust me, there won't be any of that. I don't want anyone else but h—" He cuts himself off before finishing the sentence, then he clears his throat. "I'm going to be different next year, promise."

"Anyone else but who?" Ivy asks curiously.

No surprise he hasn't told Ivy about Maya.

As I open my mouth to speak, a chip lands directly on our table and splashes into Ivy's wine. We all jump back startled and I glance over my shoulder at the same time Finn does, of course it's the jackasses Ivy was worried about.

"Hey, Finn." One of them flashes him a cocky grin.

"Do you mind, Tom?"

He pushes himself off the bench and walks towards us. I don't take my eyes off him, but I'm ready to go if he pulls any stunts. "Funny how you distanced yourself from us after Ben went to prison." Tom sighs heavily.

Finn pushes himself up from the chair, and I watch Ivy's eyes fill with dread as he squares up to Tom. "Funny how you guys backed a guy who tried to kill my sister."

Tom scoffs. "Because girls make guys fucking nuts, you trying to say that your precious sister over there was the perfect girlfriend? We all know she wasn't. *You* know what she did, Finn."

This time, I stand up and tower over him by a good four inches. He stares at me and then scowls.

"Shut the fuck up, Tom," Finn grits. "What Ben did was fucking disgusting and you know it."

"Do I?"

"Yes," Finn snaps.

Tom shrugs. "A good guy went to prison over one little mistake; a lot goes on behind closed doors. We all know Ivy was… getting around, shall we say."

Finn steps right into Tom's chest and pushes him backwards. "Say one more word, I dare you."

"What's the problem? It was you who—"

"Shut the fuck up, Tom," Finn growls.

I feel a grip on my wrist, and my head turns to find Ivy standing there. "Let's just go, please." She latches onto Finn's hand and tugs him too. Finn glares at Tom before he steps back. "*Please.*"

My blood boils because Tom deserves to have his teeth knocked out, but Ivy doesn't want us to cause a scene, and right now, she's the priority. Finn wraps his arm over Ivy's shoulder, and we step away. Tom smirks in our direction.

"That's right," he calls out. "Walk away like a bunch of cowards. It doesn't take away from the fact that Ivy was probably a little bitch to Ben, she deserved it. Whores always get what they deserve. You sleep around, you find ou—"

Before I think about what I'm doing, I turn around and swing my fist directly into Tom's face. He staggers backwards, blood dripping from his nose. I take him by his shirt and shove him into an empty table.

"What the fuck did you say?" I bellow at him.

A groan falls from the back of his throat as he stares at me through hazy eyes. I pull my fist back again and hit him in the jaw, blood splatters against his T-shirt and across my knuckles.

I grip his shirt between my throbbing fists again and drag his face to mine. "I said, what the fuck did you say?"

Finn is beside me, pushing off a group of boys who are storming towards me.

Then the next thing I know, chaos erupts in the beer garden.

I'm not proud to say the police were called, but they deserved it, and I don't regret what I did.

None of us were arrested, but never have I seen two police officers so angry in my entire life. Luckily the pub didn't want to press charges; they barred us instead, which doesn't bother me.

I glance down at my bruised knuckles and smirk. Worth it. Totally worth it.

As we get back to the house, we're all silent.

I can still hear Ivy's voice cry out for us to stop. Thank god the staff managed to separate us seconds before the police came, we definitely would have been arrested then.

Finn grumbles something about needing to take a shower to cool off. I don't blame him. Ivy sighs as I walk over to the kitchen, and she follows me. I pause by the sink, and she grabs the first aid kit.

She stops for a moment and glances over her shoulder, those fearful green eyes roam my face. I don't want to know the damage; adrenaline is still pumping through my body, so I'm not feeling the pain yet.

"Why did you do that?" she whispers under her breath.

I fold my arms over my chest and lean into the counter. "I wasn't going to sit there and let them talk shit about you, Ivy."

She chews on her lip before dampening a clean cloth and walking towards me. "Let me," she says gently. "Please."

I don't fight her as she raises the cloth and brushes it against my bleeding lip and cut cheek. She takes in a quick breath and shakes her head. "You didn't need to do that," she says again. "You got hurt because of me and I—"

Her eyes remain low, and I dip my finger under her chin and tilt her gaze to mine. "I don't care about that. All I care about is you. They don't get to talk about you like that. I don't care who it is, *no one* talks to you like that."

Ivy's gentle caress of the cloth against my face has my

heart rate slowing and my rage calming. After a moment, she pulls away, and I glance at the blue cloth that is now stained with red splodges.

"They've always hated me," she says after a few moments, her eyes falling again. "A rumour went around, and they all used it against me, anything to make me the punching bag."

My brows crease. "What rumour?"

Ivy cups her hands over her elbows, stepping away from me. "That I cheated on him." Her throat bobs. "That's why they hate me so much."

"They're assholes." I attempt to calm my tone. "And I swear to god, if they ever come near you again, I'll do more damage than I did today. I mean it. Do not listen to them when they say you deserved it; nothing you could have ever done would have made you deserve it."

Ivy swallows harshly and looks into my eyes.

"Thank you," I whisper as I dip my head towards her. "For cleaning up my face."

"It's the least I could do for what you did."

Our mouths are merely inches from touching. She stares back at me with those big green eyes, and I almost lose myself again. *Fuck.* I can't help myself.

This time, I press my lips to hers, only a simple peck. It's sweet and light, and I feel *everything*. My shoulders droop with relief and contentment, emotions I didn't know I needed at this moment in time.

Ivy whimpers ever so quietly, and the sound has me clutching her tighter. The kiss lasts no more than a couple of seconds, and I pull away. Her eyes dilate, and I will never get over the way they expand when she's around me.

Her lips taste like summery wine, and when I look at them, I tell myself not to kiss her again. Not after last time. I should take things slow, not scare her away. If I want to make her mine, then I have to be patient.

I know she wants me, even if she hasn't convinced herself of it yet.

CHAPTER 29
IVY THOMPSON

"*Stop dreaming about me. I know you're dreaming about me.*"

My thighs clench at the sound of his silk-like voice, but somehow rough around the edges. I gasp and bury my head further into the pillow.

I'm not dreaming, am I?

"*Yes, you are.*" He chuckles, and I lick my lips, squirming against the sheets. "*You always dream about me, but you don't want to admit it. Don't you, princess?*"

I shouldn't be affected by that silly nickname.

Why do I have to go weak at the knees every time he says it? It's like a trap I always fall for. He's got me in the palm of his hand, but I'm not even annoyed about it.

I want it. I want him. All of him.

"*Turn over. Let me taste that sweet pussy again.*"

I whimper into the bed, and my body shifts. I've been commanded and I have to obey. I press my shoulder into the soft sheets and twist my hips. A laugh tickles my neck, and I feel his presence behind me.

"*So fucking eager,*" he purrs, and I nod in agreement.

Too horny to care about anything. I want him to touch me.

"*You want me to what?*"

Touch me. *I beg.*

A kiss is pressed to my shoulder blade, and I shudder, then another to my neck and then my jaw. "If I slipped my hand between your thighs, would I find you wet, Ivy?"

My teeth clamp onto my lip so harshly that I expect it to burst. All I can do is moan in response. Yes. Yes. Yes. I want it all. Fuck. Touch me before I explode.

JJ's laugh haunts me again. "You desperate little thing."

He kisses my earlobe and bites down on it gently. Nibbling as his hand rolls down my chest, across my torso and dances along the skin on my stomach. "Mmmm," *he hums.* "So soft. So beautiful."

I gasp at his words.

Words that bring tears to my eyes.

"So beautiful," *he says again, his fingers tucking into the thin waistband of my lace panties. My throat exhales a groan, and I muffle it by pressing my face into the pillow again.* "And I can't wait until you ride out your orgasm on my fingers."

I raise my head gently and feel his entire body cage around me. Warm, safe, protected.

Please. Please. Please. *I chant in my head.*

"Glad someone taught you some manners," *he says teasingly.* "Because good girls get what they want. And you want my fingers buried so deep inside your cunt, you have to bite down on your pillow to stop yourself from screaming."

Everything inside me pulsates. Over and over. I'm pretty sure I'm about to short-circuit.

His fingers slip beneath the fabric of my panties and tease the skin above my aching clit. I open my mouth and release a cry of desperation.

"More?" *he asks playfully.*

I clutch onto his wrist, fearful he will pull away. But he doesn't, he sinks his hand lower until the tips of his fingers graze across my soaked core. I'm dripping like a fucking waterfall and I'm not even ashamed about it.

"Fuck," *he rasps in my ear.* "So wet. And it's all for me."

My lips press together and I groan when his finger circles over my clit. I almost scream out, but he clamps a hand over my mouth. "Shhhhh," he whispers darkly. "Don't want anyone hearing us, now do we?"

My eyes roll into the back of my head as he sinks his fingers into me, I pant into his hand and feel his grip tighten around me. I'm choking, choking out with pleasure and euphoria as he begins to pump those fingers.

"Mmm," he grumbles. "You perfect little thing."

A gasp falls from my lips as he speeds up, getting closer and closer and closer and closer, until…

I scramble in my bed, pushing myself up from my sweat-infused sheets and taking a quick breath. I slap my hand on my chest and feel how fast my heart is rattling.

My mouth aches from the dryness, and I stare blankly at the wall. I try my hardest to ignore the ache between my thighs, but when I push them together, I find my panties slick and my skin moist.

Holy shit. I actually had a sex dream about JJ… and I kind of liked it.

Kind of? I was living it like a movie.

I throw myself back onto my bed and cover my face with the pillow, shaking my head over and over. Oh god. I can't believe that happened. I can still hear his voice in my mind, whispering all those filthy things.

My thighs press together again, and I whimper at the sensation growing there. If I placed my hand inside my pants, I'm sure I could bring myself to a climax within seconds, but I don't want to give myself that satisfaction.

Not when I'm thinking about my brother's best friend and what I want him to do to me.

You want my fingers buried so deep inside your cunt, you have to bite down on your pillow to stop yourself from screaming.

No. No. I need to stop.

I stand from my bed. I need to get out of here, go grab

myself a cold glass of orange juice and slap myself back into reality. Then I can shower and get on with my day, without thinking about JJ and his dirty voice.

I grab my silk dressing gown and throw it on before making my way downstairs. I need something cooling, something distracting, otherwise I'll climb back into bed and masturbate into oblivion.

There is nothing wrong with giving yourself a well-needed release, but right now, I shouldn't be getting off to the thought of JJ's body against mine. Not when Finn could be down the hall. It feels wrong on all levels.

As I approach the kitchen, I turn my head to the garden. At first, I spot Finn, he's got two weights in his hands and is wearing a white T-shirt that is soaked through with sweat. Then JJ walks towards him, taking the hem of his T-shirt and removing it from his body.

Holy fucking shit. Someone slam my jaw back together.

I glance down at his abs to find them rippling with sweat, and muscles on his shoulders and arms. My core tightens and I feel my clit throb harder than before. He flashes Finn a smile, and I suddenly don't know how to use my legs because I'm just standing here ogling him with my brother in view.

JJ takes a different set of weights, and I scurry to the kitchen when he turns in my direction. I open the fridge door and take out the carton of orange juice and a cup. I place it down onto the counter and begin pouring.

Don't look. Don't look.

Of course I fucking look. My eyes can't help themselves. JJ is doing reps with the weights, and his chest looks as hard as stone, sweat trailing down his face and onto his neck. I suck in a breath.

This is not good.

My gaze floats to his biceps that flex and showcase impressive muscle. I saw his body the night we hooked up and at the beach, but seeing him all pumped up from his workout, this is a game-changer.

I don't think I'm ever going to see right again.

JJ stops for a moment to catch his breath, his eyes glide across the patio doors, and then rests them on me. I feel like a deer caught in headlights, especially when the orange juice begins to overflow the cup.

Suddenly, I jump back and shake my hand, the liquid rolling down my fingers. "Shit," I curse to myself and my cheeks heat.

I slam the carton down onto the counter in frustration and stupidly take another glance up at JJ. He's watching me with a smug smile.

I snatch the full glass from the side, not even bothering to clear up the spillage or put the carton away. I head straight upstairs and shut my door behind me. The glass of orange juice barely makes it to my bedside table before I collapse onto my bed.

One time. I tell myself. *One time.*

My fingers latch onto the drawer beside my bed and I fish out my pink vibrator. I throw the covers up and over my knees and sink the silicone toy down the inside of my thighs and towards my core.

I turn it on and dip it beneath my panties. My hips buckle within a second, eyes floating shut, and my body humming at the instant pleasure. "S-shit," I groan as I increase the speed.

One of my hands balls into the sheets beside me and tears build behind my closed eyes. Oh god. Oh god. Here it comes. I'm about to fall over the edge, any damn second…

Then the vibrator stops, and I gasp, snapping my eyes open and pressing the button over and over. But it doesn't start, it does nothing. I groan and drag the vibrator into sight, my eyes hazy and my heart thrashing in my chest.

"Fuck's sake. No, *no no no*." I shake my head, trying to get it started again.

Of course this would be the perfect time for the batteries to run out.

I want to scream, so I do, out of pure frustration.

My entire pussy is hot and pulsing. I can hardly catch my breath because I'm so fucking turned on that I don't know what to do with myself.

The sound of feet pounding against the floor echoes down the hall. "Ivy?"

Finn.

I throw the vibrator under the covers and yank the sheets to my chin. The handle is pressed down, and Finn pokes his head inside. I try to act normal, not flustered at all.

"I heard you scream," Finn says as he drags his eyes over the room quickly to inspect. "Are you okay?"

My lips are pressed together as I hum. "Yeah, I thought I saw a spider." I lie straight through my teeth.

"Thought?"

"It was a bit of black thread, sorry." I cringe at the sound of my own voice.

Finn presses a hand to his chest. "You scared me, Iv."

"Sorry," I say as my cheeks redden.

He waves me off and then shuts the door behind him. I sink into my pillows and press a hand to my boiling face. Oh fuck.

CHAPTER 30
IVY THOMPSON

A day at the beach is the distraction I need.

When my feet hit the golden sand, I inhale a quick breath. The sun shines down over the people littered across the beachfront. I spot Daisy standing with Harriet and Isaac. I head over and greet them all, feeling Isaac's eyes on me.

"Hey." He smiles, his brown eyes glittering.

"Hey." I beam back. "Haven't seen you in a little while."

Isaac nods. "I know, I'm kind of bummed about it. How have you been?"

"Mmm, fine. Just relaxing before the dreaded thought of going back to university. What about you?"

"Same," he sighs and shoves a hand through his thick hair. "My sister is getting married this weekend, so that's something to look forward to."

My eyes light up at his words. "Oh, that's amazing, tell her I said congratulations."

Isaac's lips curve into a smile. "I will."

A hand wraps around my wrist as I glance over my shoulder to find Daisy. "They're gonna play football." She winks at me.

"Who?"

"The boys."

My eyes flick past her long brown locks to find Finn, JJ, Joel, and Callan, amongst their other friends. She tugs my wrist again, and we sit on the empty logs, facing their makeshift football pitch.

I watch as Daisy leans forward to grab a bottle of beer before cracking the lid open. "You want one?"

"Didn't think you liked beer." I grimace.

She shrugs. "It's growing on me."

Harriet sits down beside me on the log, Isaac on the other end.

"I hope they take their tops off," Daisy leans over to whisper in my ear.

I snort. "That's my brother you're talking about."

She turns to me with those big blue eyes. "He's not the only one playing. And besides, it wouldn't be too disheartening if JJ took his off, I know you want a bit of that eye candy."

"Shut up." I shove her shoulder as she giggles.

I don't need to see JJ topless again today. Not after this morning. I need it erased from my memory for my sanity. I shift uncomfortably, the tightness inside my core growing.

I should have just finished the job myself, but after Finn came into my room, it ruined the mood. Despite that fact, I've been throbbing uncontrollably. If I can keep myself together for the next few hours, then I have all night to myself.

Finn walks towards us, JJ close behind him. "Take my phone," he says, thrusting it in my direction. "I don't want to break it."

My fingers latch onto my brother's phone. "Good luck."

"Good luck?" he repeats with a chuckle. "We're going to win."

JJ stands beside him, blocking the sun with his ridiculous height. I can't look at him. Not after the dreams that fill me with shame. "I'm gonna get a drink." I excuse myself and walk across the beach to where the coolers are resting in the sand.

I grab a bottle and crack the lid, taking a large gulp.

A presence beside me makes the hairs on my arms stand. I glance over to find JJ fishing for a drink of his own and shift my eyes away. Fearful of my wandering gaze and the damage it's going to cause my cheeks.

"What's up with you?" he asks as I lower my drink.

I shake my head. "Nothing."

JJ twists his body towards me, narrowing his eyes. "Nothing? You're acting weird. You can barely look at me."

Somehow I manage to swallow back the lump in my throat and stare up into those mesmerising blue eyes. Oh fuck. Mistakes have been made. My stomach clenches, and those butterflies erupt all over again.

"I'm looking at you now," I say with a slight tremble in my voice.

JJ tilts his head at me and then smirks. "Alright, you weirdo."

When he walks back towards Finn, I blow out a heavy breath. I raise the bottle to my lips again and take a generous mouthful, letting the sugary taste invade my tongue. I head back to Daisy, who is now chatting away to Harriet.

I sit down and cross my legs, regretting my choice instantly. My core throbs, and the pulsing between my thighs is almost unbearable.

The boys begin to play football, and some of the girls cheer them on. I try my hardest not to focus on JJ, but every time I look away, he runs right into my eyeline.

After twenty minutes, a few of them begin to shed their shirts. Including JJ.

I shouldn't notice how sweaty and delicious his abs look, but they're a little too inviting. To think I was once underneath that body—and in my dreams.

My teeth clamp down on my lip, and I groan silently. I

cannot tear my eyes away as he runs, tackles, and shoots. Then he grins at Finn and claps a hand on his back. My eyes are glued to his massive, inked biceps.

That's when my chest tightens and heat grows between my legs.

Now is *not* the time to get horny again. I've never regretted not finishing myself off more.

As I cross my legs, I rock to one side to adjust myself. My eyes sting at the wave of sensations that rocket through me. Everything is uncomfortable. My skin begins to heat, and I'm fanning my hair away from the nape of my neck.

When JJ scores again, the boys jump him, and he grins like a smug bastard. It's a good look on him. Shamefully.

He turns and glances my way, face still bright and full of joy. When our eyes lock and I hold his gaze, I suck in a breath when he subtly winks at me.

Oh god.

I stand up abruptly and place down my drink. "I'm going to the toilet." I excuse myself.

Daisy glances at me but says nothing. I walk in the opposite direction of the match and head towards the beach huts. I need two minutes to myself. Two minutes to get my shit together before I practically climax without even being touched.

I press my hand to one of the vacant beach huts, and I'm relieved when it's empty. I pace and I pace, wiping my hand across my forehead. "Calm down," I mutter to myself, taking one big breath. "Calm the hell down, Ivy."

But I can't calm down, there is a bloody fiesta in my pants.

My feet won't stop moving, and my ragged breaths are all I can hear, loud and aggressive.

"You can go home later and sort yourself out," I grumble under a harsh whisper. "So get your shit together and—"

The door to the beach hut opens behind me, and I whip my head to the sound.

JJ stands in the doorway. All six foot three of him. He's still shirtless, and his chest is sweaty and sprinkled with grains of sand.

He stares at me. He stares at me like he's about to fucking pounce.

My core throbs, and I can't deny it anymore. I want him. Hell, I want him so badly it hurts.

He takes two steps towards me.

"JJ—" I pant.

My voice doesn't stop him, he continues to walk until he reaches me. He clasps his warm hands around my cheeks and tilts my head towards him. His eyes flick down to my lips, and I shudder.

JJ's thumb sweeps over my cheekbone, and everything inside me melts like butter. I part my lips with anticipation when he inches closer until his mouth falls onto mine. I whimper the second we touch, and when he takes another step forward, my back hits the wooden wall with a thud.

He widens the kiss with his tongue and clutches me tighter, angling my mouth so he can kiss me deeper. My head vibrates, and I cannot think of anything else but him. I grip onto his wrist, and the other rests against his bare chest.

I kiss him back fiercely. I can't deny that I want this, even if it should make me feel guilty. All I feel is him.

JJ nips my bottom lip and I gasp, his tongue brushing against mine in a passionate stroke. My knees begin to quiver, and I fear I'll fall, but he holds me tighter, an arm wrapping around my lower waist as he arches my back and pushes me further into the wall.

His hands graze down over the curve of my ass and hoist me up around his waist as if I weigh nothing.

"We shouldn't be doing this," I whisper between kisses.

He groans into my mouth, another stroke of his tongue. "I know it seems wrong," he grumbles. "But I can't help it when it feels so fucking right."

My head spins at his words. He's right. It does. Even if I didn't want to admit it before. This isn't a kiss, this is so much more than that. It's breathing and existing and living.

When our lips meet again, he slows down and I lose sense of where we are.

He drops one of his hands from my ass and runs it down the middle of my stomach, my core tensing at the touch of his fingertips. With a flick of the button, my shorts become undone.

JJ smiles into the kiss. His hand rests just above the line of my underwear and he pulls his lips away from mine. "What do you want, Ivy?" He asks hoarsely.

I rest my head back against the wall, watching him with heated eyes. I pause for a moment, incapable of words right now.

"Tell me," he whispers over my lips.

I glance down at his mouth and tremble. "*This*. I want this."

The corner of his mouth twists upwards and he moves forward, pressing his lips to mine again. He slips a finger inside the fabric of my thong, and I suppress a moan. He's not even touched me, and I'm ready to commit a thousand sins. I wrap my arms around his shoulders, pressing my hand to the back of his head and feeling the bristles of his hair against my palm.

JJ chuckles when I whine pathetically, teasing my skin with his fingers before he dives them deeper into my panties. I gasp when his hand brushes over my slit and he bites down on my earlobe when he slides a finger inside me.

"Fuck," he rasps. "Princess, you're so wet."

My eyes begin to water as he pumps his finger. I clench around him desperately as he adds another, and I claw at his neck. A pathetic cry falls from my lips as he latches his mouth onto my neck, pressing slick kisses across my hot skin.

"Oh god," I moan aloud.

He smirks into my shoulder, and I want to curse him for being so smug, but I can't find it in me to care right now. Instead, I channel the feeling of his fingers inside me as he fucks me slowly, my wetness pooling all over his hand.

"That feels so good," I murmur as he begins to pick up the pace, touching me right where I'm sensitive and most pleasurable. "Don't stop. Please don't stop."

He grunts again and kisses me fiercely. "I'm not stopping until you're coming all over my fingers."

My lips quiver at his words. He pumps his fingers in and out of me quicker, my breathing becoming harsh and uneven. "JJ—" I moan, eyes falling shut for a second.

Everything inside me throbs, and I know if I'm not careful, I'm going to be falling over that finish line pretty soon. I don't want it to be over. Hell, I want this to go on all afternoon.

JJ nudges his head into mine, our eyes colliding with force. My lips part as I stare back at him, his fingers moving perfectly and hitting my G-spot with each stroke. I'm shaking against his hold and whimpering even when I try not to.

He draws his face even closer, tracing the tip of his nose against my cheek and down my jaw. I bite onto my bottom lip as I feel myself get closer, everything pulsating with desire and need.

"JJ…" I warn him, digging my nails into his shoulder.

"Come on, Ivy," he taunts. "Come for me. Let me hear those sweet moans again. God knows I've been dying to hear them."

Tears swell in my eyes as he fucks me with his fingers, he doesn't speed up, he doesn't slow down. It's the perfect tempo, pace, and rhythm. All of it together is a lethal combination.

One last pump and I buckle in his arms. My mouth widens and I release a loud groan full of curse words and JJ's name in staggered exhales. He buries his face in my neck and smirks. "Ohh, that's it," he says gruffly as I ride out my high on his hand. "That's my good girl. You like coming on my fingers, princess?"

Yes. Yes. Yes.

A low scream escapes my throat as my entire world bursts around me.

After a few moments, I calm down from my earth-shattering orgasm, and JJ slows his hand. He plucks his fingers from my panties, and I shudder as he gently places me back down on the floor, my legs shaking.

We glance at each other. No doubt I look like a hot mess.

He raises his fingers, slick with my wetness and presses his index finger to my lips. I freeze when he smears it over my mouth, and I shake at the sensuality of it.

"Have a taste," he says with a wicked glint in his eye.

My tongue shoots out and I lick my lips, tasting myself for the first time.

"Mmm." His eyes flare before he pulls his hand back and slips his middle finger into his mouth and sucks. "God, you taste so fucking good."

I stare back at him in shock, cheeks burning red.

His gaze twitches with delight and hunger, sending my stomach catapulting.

We stand staring at each other for a while, the heat in the room doesn't evaporate—it increases. I should have known receiving an orgasm from him wouldn't relieve the tension.

It's only intensified it.

CHAPTER 31
JJ WOODFORD

The taste of Ivy resting on my tongue makes me unbelievably hard.

Thinking about the way she whimpered into my mouth and clutched onto my shoulders for support—it's doing nothing for the current situation in my pants.

As we stand facing each other, catching our breaths, we both know we need to leave before we're caught and people start asking questions.

"See you out there." I give her one last smile before I exit the beach hut.

My cock begins to soften as I watch the boys group up again. Yep, there is no way I'm going to be hard in public, especially not around Finn.

When I approach the drinks table, I crack the lid off a beer bottle and take three large sips before beginning the second half. I'm trying to keep focused, but I can't stop thinking about the way Ivy's mouth moulded to mine, how our tongues brushed over one another, how I pinned her to the wall.

Good girl. I cooed. And fuck. She came all over my hand so fucking hard.

The ball slips past me and I curse to myself. A hand swats my shoulder, and I find Finn in my direct eyeline. "What's the matter with you?" He scowls.

I don't know why he's taking this so seriously, it's just a bit of fun.

"It's hot," I grumble, which isn't an entire lie.

Finn rolls his eyes, and I ignore him. I continue to play the game—or at least attempt to, because I can't focus for more than two seconds.

When the game is over, reality hits that we lost *badly*.

Music starts blasting and people begin to build a bonfire for when the sun starts to set. I purposely didn't look out into the crowd whilst playing in case my eyes met Ivy's.

Then it would have been a dead giveaway.

I hate to admit the idea of sneaking around with Ivy gives me a sick thrill.

Finn is going to be furious if he ever finds out what went down between us, but right now it's probably best that he doesn't know. He'll have to find out eventually, but that's a future problem.

I float between groups until the fire is roaring and the sun has set, the sky lit up with stars that remind me of Ivy and our constellation hunting. My head turns towards the flock of people who are standing near the drinks table.

My gaze snags on Ivy instantly, she's standing with Daisy, Isaac, and a girl I don't recognise. Ivy is talking to Isaac and then laughs at something he says.

I raise my cup to my mouth and take a large gulp. Ivy chews on her plump bottom lip, the one I was sucking on a few hours ago. Her eyes wander from Daisy to the party around her and then in my exact direction.

Her mouth parts when she notices me staring, and I can't help but smirk.

Ivy's cheeks heat, and she looks back to Isaac as he speaks, but I can tell she's trying not to look back at me. I press my hand into my pocket and dig out my phone, scanning through my contacts. We swapped numbers in case of emergency, but really I just wanted her number.

JJ:

> Glad to know you're still a bit flustered. Can't stop thinking about me?

I hit send and flick my eyes back over to her. She plucks her phone from her pocket and glances at the screen, eyebrows pinched together. She shudders visibly, and I'm almost sure I can see her chest expand when she reads over the message.

She glances up at me from her phone and I drop my eye into a discreet wink. Her nostrils flare as she runs her thumbs across her screen quickly.

IVY:

> I'm not thinking about you. And I'm not flustered, I'm hot from the bonfire.

I smile, amused as I read over her text.

JJ:

> The bonfire? It's over on the other side of the beach. Just admit it, you liked riding my fingers. You most definitely liked coming.

Ivy's throat bobs and she takes a tiny step backwards. Her head shakes, and she locks her phone, clutching it to her chest with trembling hands.

I breathe through my nose quickly and type another message.

JJ:

> Are you embarrassed, Ivy? Because you shouldn't be.

> If only you knew what I've been dreaming of doing to you.

Ivy glances at her phone again and stares at the screen for what feels like an eternity. She doesn't look up at me, but her lip finds its way between her teeth again, and she slowly begins to type.

IVY:

Like what?

The smirk on my face is permanent. I knew it. She wants this more than she lets on.

JJ:

> You didn't think I'd tell you that easily, did you?

Something flashes across Ivy's expression. Blood rising beneath her skin as she swallows harshly.

IVY:

I see it's your turn to play games

JJ:

> No games, princess. Just admit you want me and I'll tell you every little dirty thing I'd do to you, right down to the last detail.

Those green eyes find mine within seconds. Her chest heaves quicker than before, something sizzling beneath her heated gaze. Yeah, that look alone will put me into an early grave.

IVY:

I might want you, JJ, but we know it's wrong.

I stare at those words for far too long. *I might want you.* That's good enough for me. It's more than anything else she's said.

She might not be able to admit it out loud, but it's obvious she carries around guilt like a dark rain cloud over her head. We're consenting adults, and if we do this carefully, Finn might be able to understand without murdering us both.

JJ:

> What we're doing isn't wrong, and even if it was, it's still not going to stop me from dragging my tongue down your sweet cunt and making you come with just my mouth.

> Then when I fuck you, I'm going to take my time with you. Until you're begging me to fuck you harder. But I won't. I'll tease you and torture you until you're crying and pleading for me to do more. And when I give you what you want, I'll make you thank me for letting you come all over my cock.

> Because this time, Ivy, this time... I am going to savour every damn second. And your pleasure will be my priority.

When I hit send, blood rushes through my veins. Yeah, I'm getting myself worked up thinking about listening to her sweet pleas.

Ivy reads over the message, her eyes widening. She raises a trembling hand to push back her beautiful blonde hair. Daisy catches her shoulder, and she quickly shoves her phone away.

I guess it'll give her something to think about tonight.

I've got another date with my fist after what happened in the beach hut.

"There is the worst football player of the year." An arm slings over my shoulder, and I turn to find Finn in my face. His eyes are bloodshot, and his words slurred. Of course he's drunk. "I forgive you for being shit."

I snort quietly. "Gee, thanks."

Finn removes his arm from my shoulder and sways in

front of me, bringing his bottle of beer to his mouth. "Who were you texting?"

"Hmm?"

He points to my phone in my hand, and I push it into my pocket, not wanting Ivy's name to pop up on the screen.

"Just someone from back home," I lie. "Nothing major."

"Fair enough. Oop, Daisy is strolling past."

"So?"

"So?" he repeats. "She's gagging for you."

I fold my arms over my chest, shaking my head. "I ended that ages ago, keep up."

Finn's mouth falls open. "Why?"

My shoulders rise. "I wasn't feeling it, and I didn't want to lead her on. No point forcing something that is never going to work."

"I can't believe you." He punches my side lightly. "Daisy, of all people. She's fucking incredible."

"Just not what I'm looking for."

Finn takes another sip of his drink. "Then what are you looking for?"

I run my tongue over my bottom lip. "Someone who I can have a real conversation with, someone who listens to me, who tries to understand me. Someone who is a little shy but comes out of their shell when they're with you because they feel comfortable and safe. Blonde, shorter than me, super smart."

I slam my mouth shut when I realise I went off on a tangent. I glance at Finn, who is staring me dead in the eye, one of his twitches and the other creeps me out entirely.

"Explain to me why you just described my sister," Finn demands.

"What?" I say instantly. "No I didn't."

Finn scowls at me. "Yeah... you did."

"Ivy isn't the only smart, quiet blonde I've ever met, you do realise that?"

He keeps looking at me with suspicion, and heat spikes the back of my neck. "So you're saying you don't fancy my sister?"

I groan silently. "She's pretty." *Beautiful.* "And she's nice."

"Uh huh." Finn pokes his tongue into his cheek as if he can't believe I just complimented his sister. "Don't ever say that shit again."

My hands throw up in defeat. "I don't really know what you want me to say, you want me to insult her to your face instead?"

"No!" he shouts and I suck in a breath. "But I don't want to hear you say how you find her pretty either, that shit is weird and I don't like it. You fuck with my sister, and I'll fuck you up."

Too late for that, Finn. Sorry to disappoint.

I huff out a breath. "Alright, then let's change the subject."

Finn crosses his arms, and I drop mine. He continues to stare at me.

"Actually, I'm going to get another drink and pretend this conversation never happened," I mumble before walking away.

Finn snorts. "Gladly."

As I approach the drinks table, Daisy turns to me as I pour a rather large drink, those blue eyes studying my choice in spirit. "Seems like you really needed that drink." She chuckles lightly.

My eyebrows raise, and I down it, the liquid burning my throat. "Yeah."

"Hey, look," she says after a few moments, and I turn towards her. "I'm slightly mortified about what went down between us. With how forward and annoying I was, I realise now that I was being extremely overbearing and I'm sorry."

I blink once, shocked by her confession. "It's alright, no hard feelings, Daisy."

She nods slowly and lowers her eyes. "You should have

just told me that you liked Ivy. At the time I didn't notice it, but after you said things between us won't work out, I saw the way you looked at her. It was so obvious."

"Don't say anything to Finn," I blurt.

She waves me off. "Of course not, it's not my business. I want to see Ivy happy."

"Nothing is really going on between us," I admit, because it's not. We fooled around for the first time today since our one-night stand. "I don't think Ivy is ready to commit to anything right now, and I understand."

Daisy flashes me a small smile before she grips my shoulder gently. "She'll come around soon, give her some time. She knows what she wants, and she'll take her time admitting it. She's not the type of girl to rush into things."

"I know," I admit.

Daisy leaves me by myself and walks to a group of people I haven't met before. I take another sip and grimace at the taste of my drink. Too damn strong.

I spot Ivy sitting alone by the fire, staring endlessly into the flames.

I don't think about my next move, I head straight towards her.

When I stand beside her, she doesn't notice me. "Deep in thought, are we?" I ask playfully. She snaps her gaze to mine, and I drink in that breathtaking face. "Dwelling over my text?"

"No," she grumbles, but her heated skin is a dead giveaway.

"Sure, sure."

Ivy rolls her lips together and then closes her eyes.

"I meant what I said," I say slowly. "Every word of it."

She stands up from the log so quickly that I take a step backwards. "JJ, we can't—"

"Can't what?" I cut over her. "I already know where her

sentence is heading. "Can't continue? Because every time I come onto you, you can't resist. Then you push me away."

Those wary green eyes drag to mine, and she wraps herself up in her arms, a way of protecting herself from her own vulnerability.

"Wanting something and being able to have it are two completely different things." She sighs, her expression dropping to a look of desolation. "And in this case, I can't do it again."

"Because of Finn?"

Ivy's watery eyes find mine. "Yes."

"Maybe you need to take control of your own choices, Ivy, rather than letting others dictate what you can and can't do. Otherwise, you'll live a very unhappy life, and I know that's not what you want."

Her lip wobbles slightly.

"Think about it," I say. "I'm not rushing you into anything."

When she says nothing more, I simply walk away.

I know she knows what she wants. I want her to admit it out loud because I know she's capable of doing so. I want her to prove it to herself first, rather than carrying around the guilt she doesn't deserve.

CHAPTER 32
IVY THOMPSON

JJ's voice has been on repeat in my head for the last two days.

Maybe you need to take control of your own choices, Ivy, rather than letting others dictate what you can and can't do.

Deep down, I know he's right. I can't keep living my life by Finn's rulebook, but we both know he's not going to be happy. Hell, after Ben, if he caught me with one of his friends again, he'd start throwing fists. Even if he trusts JJ.

Once upon a time, he trusted Ben, too.

I know Finn didn't handle the accident well, especially after the rumours went around about me cheating on him. He thought it was his fault because I met Ben through Finn. But when I think about being with JJ, technically, I met him before I even knew they were friends.

JJ is different. There is something about him that feels like home—and I haven't felt at home in a long fucking time. It's nostalgic and comforting, but I don't see Finn trying to understand that.

I fear it'll send him spiralling. He already took up drinking when I almost died, when he couldn't shift the blame from himself. He's still drinking now and refuses to accept that it's an issue. How would he cope if he knew I was with his best friend?

It wouldn't go down well at all. If anything, it'll tear us all apart.

That's what I'm afraid of the most.

I sit outside on the patio, sun cream smeared all over my face and arms as I scroll through my phone. A shadow is cast over my back, and I turn to find the culprit. "Hey," Finn says as he sits beside me. "What are you doing?"

"Nothing," I sigh as I lock my phone and throw it onto the grass in front of us. "Why?"

Finn wraps his arms loosely around his knees, drawing them towards his chest. "Look, Ivy, I need to tell you something."

My brows furrow, and I twist my body towards him, his green eyes flicking across the patio and onto the dark strands of grass.

"What is it?"

I know this look of my brother's all too well. Whatever he's about to say, it's not good news. It's never good news when he looks pained and lost for words. The man who never knows how to shut up, that's when you know it's bad.

"Spit it out," I urge him.

My heart pounds angrily in my chest when his mouth parts, and I lean forward eagerly. He shuts his mouth again and then clears his throat. I brace myself for what he's about to say.

"I found out that Ben is getting out of prison in two weeks."

All the air in my lungs is stripped away, and Finn dips his head slightly to check that I'm okay.

"W-what?" I blubber.

"Yeah," he sighs and runs a hand down the back of his head. "I heard about it this morning, checked around to see if it's true. He's being let out on good behaviour."

My entire body begins to shudder, and Finn scoots closer. "He's getting out."

Finn slings an arm over my shoulder and tugs me to his side. "I'm sorry, Iv. But you still have that restraining order, he can't come anywhere near you. I doubt he'll come back here after what happened. So many people turned against him and his stupid family, who continued to support him. I just thought that you should know."

"Right," I rasp even though I'm deteriorating inside. "Thanks."

He sighs, dropping his head to my shoulder. "I know this isn't the news you want to hear, but I'm going to be here for you, alright? I'm going to be the brother I should have been."

I pause at his words for a moment, and he raises his head. "What do you mean the brother you should have been?"

Finn shrugs but keeps his arm around me supportively. He tenses a little but relaxes a moment later. "I was a shit brother back then. I-I did things I'm not proud of."

"Like what?"

He shakes his head. "I—" he pauses. "I should never have let you get with Ben."

"He was good to me for the first part, and you know it, even you were shocked at how charming he could be."

"Shit," Finn curses and presses his hand to his face. "That's not the point. I still wasn't there for you. I wasn't there for you when he hurt you. I wasn't there for you when you almost died, Ivy. I should never have—"

"Have what?"

Finn looks at me this time, and the guilt that rests behind his eyes is evident. "I shouldn't have let you guys get together. I shouldn't have done what I did."

My heart cracks like a porcelain doll. I know Finn was upset about what happened, but I've never seen him… break down. I clutch onto his shoulder this time as he squeezes his eyes shut, a tear escaping one of them.

"Finn." My voice is quiet, afraid it'll crack if I say any more.

"I was a shit brother," he sniffles. "When you were in the hospital, I went back to uni and drank myself half to death most nights. I wasn't there for you when you needed me because I couldn't live with the guilt and the sickness I felt almost every night. I couldn't shake what happened, I still can't."

My throat burns from how hard I'm trying not to cry. "It wasn't your fault."

"It was," he murmurs. "It was."

When my mouth parts, I begin to tremble. "It wasn't. I've never blamed you."

Finn turns towards me with red eyes and watery lids. His lips part as if he's about to say something, but shut a second later. I study him carefully, his shoulders are shaking, and his face is scrunched up.

"I failed you, as a brother, I failed you."

"You had no idea what he was capable of, Finn."

He wipes his face with the back of his hand, and I rest my head against his shoulder. "If he comes anywhere near you or us, I'll kill him."

"I know," I whisper. "But you shouldn't. He's not worth going to prison for."

"He is if he tries to hurt you again."

We glance at each other, and Finn bundles me into his arms this time. I can't remember the last time I hugged my brother like this, but it makes my heart settle, both needing this moment to calm down. "If I could erase him from our memories, I would."

"Me too," I agree. "But I want to be happy. That is the only thing I want."

"I want that for you, too, Ivy," he says, clutching me tighter. "So much."

"Everything okay out here?" JJ's voice from the back door

startles us.

I glance up at him, and he flicks his concerned eyes between the pair of us with blotchy cheeks.

"Yeah," I croak and rid myself of any rogue tears. "All good."

JJ flashes us an apprehensive look but doesn't press. It's probably for the best, I know Finn struggles to open up about what happened. But I want to move on because otherwise, I don't think I'll ever heal.

THE SOUND of the front door being ripped off its hinges echoes through the house. I whip my head over my shoulder to find Finn barely standing in the doorway. As soon as I'm on my feet, I walk towards him, and the strong odour of alcohol wafts through the room.

It makes my stomach churn. It's a Monday afternoon. Jesus.

"Are you okay?" I call out to him as he hangs off the door and slams it loudly behind him.

His eyes are so bloodshot that I can barely see the white. I grab him, but he waves me off, stumbling into the wall and latching onto the curtains. "I-I have to get ready for work," he slurs.

"Work? Finn, you can barely stand up."

I watch him cautiously as he attempts to walk towards the kitchen, and I follow him slowly. My arms wrap around myself as he latches onto the counter. "I'm going," he spits, his eyes unable to focus on a single thing. "I have to or they'll fire me."

"How much did you have to drink?"

He turns to me with a sneering scoff. "That's none of your business, *Mum*."

The tone of his voice cuts through my chest.

I walk towards him and grab his wrist gently, trying to get him to look at me, but he refuses. "You can't go to work like this, Finn. You need to go to bed and sleep it off."

"Don't tell me what to do!" he yells, which makes me flinch.

"What's going on?"

I didn't even hear JJ's footsteps as he joins us in the kitchen, but I'm relieved he's here to help me with Finn. I don't know if I can handle him on my own.

"I'm g-going to work," Finn mumbles as he jerks his wrist away from me and then points at JJ.

My head twists, and I see JJ stare him down with a cold expression. "Don't be stupid," he says loudly. "Turning up at work intoxicated sounds like such a good idea, doesn't it? You'll be fired, and then you'll have no money to fund anything."

Finn's eyes light up with fire. "You sound just like her."

"We're trying to look out for you," JJ states, his shoulders turning rigid.

"What's going on? Why are you drunk right now?" I ask.

Finn twists to the counter, gripping it with two hands, turning his knuckles deathly white as he groans. JJ looks at me immediately, but I don't take my eyes off my brother. "I want to forget," he continues. "I want to forget everything because if I see him—"

Ben.

My entire body trembles at the pain behind his eyes.

JJ walks past me as he stands in front of Finn. "You're going to bed, and you're going to say that you're sick. You are in no fit state to go to work. I don't care what you say, sleep it off because this isn't the Finn I know."

Finn stares at JJ, and something flashes past his eyes. Almost as if he knows not to argue with him right now. His shoulders slump, submitting to his orders, and JJ takes hold of his arm and begins to climb the stairs.

My hand covers my face as I take a shallow breath.

This can't continue. His drinking is out of control.

JJ returns five minutes later.

"You okay?"

I sigh with heavy eyes. "We need to do something."

"Agreed, are you going to tell your parents?"

"Yes, when they get home. They deserve to know," I say simply.

"Are you okay?" he asks again.

My chest clenches as I struggle to inhale. "I-I don't know."

JJ's lips slip into a frown, and without another word, he steps forward and wraps his arms around me. I didn't realise how badly I needed a hug until this moment. My eyes close as I press myself into his chest and inhale his comforting scent.

I release a jagged breath and clutch onto his T-shirt.

He cradles the back of my neck with one hand and kisses my forehead tenderly. I open my eyes to find them wet, but I don't let any tears fall. "I'm here with you," he whispers into my hairline. "You don't have to go through this alone."

And I believe him.

CHAPTER 33
JJ WOODFORD

The next morning, I head downstairs to find Finn outside sitting on the edge of a sunlounger. His head is buried in his hands as he grunts—no doubt hungover as shit and feeling sorry for himself.

I lean on the patio door and clear my throat.

Finn glances at me over his shoulder, bags heavier than I've ever seen.

"Morning," I say as I walk towards him.

"Hey, I'm sorry about yesterday," he says hoarsely as he flops back onto the sunlounger and groans. "I got a little carried away."

My brows hit my hairline. "Carried away? Finn, that was a borderline hospital trip."

"Don't be so dramatic." He waves a hand.

My nostrils flare in frustration. "Dramatic? You really don't see what you're doing to yourself. Do you?"

"It's fine. Just a bit of drink."

"Fine?" I repeat. "Finn, you and I both know that you're not fine."

"What do you want me to say?" His voice is harsh, but I don't take it to heart.

I look up at the sky and exhale a long breath. "I want you to tell me the truth, to be honest with me. I've seen the way you've been deteriorating this summer, drinking any chance you can get. It's not healthy and it's not a way to cope with things."

Finn tuts as if he's heard this a thousand times before. He pushes himself up from the seat. "I don't need to hear about this shit right now," he grumbles and attempts to walk away.

I shoot up and lock my hand around his wrist, tugging him backwards. When he faces me, his eyes are full of sorrow. I'm sick of him feeling sorry for himself and pushing everyone around him away. Soon, he'll have no one if he doesn't attempt to open up.

"You *do* need to hear about this shit." I lower my voice but keep it stern. "You're covering your problems with drinking. Don't you think I saw how bad it was at university? Well, it's a hundred times worse now. You were trying to go to work drunk, you were being rude to Ivy. This isn't the Finn I know. Talk to me."

He lowers his head as I move my hand to his shoulder, caging him in. "I—" He pauses. "Can't." His chest sounds like it's about to give out any second.

Instead of pressuring him into speaking, I bundle him into a hug. He presses his forehead down onto my shoulder as I rub his back in soothing strokes. "Breathe," I instruct him when he starts choking on air. "Inhale really deeply, hold it if you can. Then back out again."

Finn takes a few moments to take in what I'm saying. I pull away and hold him at arm's length as he hangs his head. His breathing slows, but I can still hear his pain. It's destroying him from the inside out, and I wish I could somehow take this away from him, from Ivy, from this entire town.

"I feel like I'm losing sense of everything," he says between breaths. "I-I don't even know who I am anymore. All this guilt has eaten me alive, and I'm living a lie. A fucking lie."

I dip down to see his face, but he closes his eyes. "Guilt about what?"

"About Ivy!" he shouts, taking a step back. "I hurt her. It's all my fault. It's always been my fucking fault."

I don't know much about their past, but all I know is it haunts them daily.

"I should never have let her get with him. My friend. *Ever.*"

His words slash through my heart, bleeding out of my chest. "But Ivy is still here. She's getting on with her life. You should be doing the same. This guilt is eating you alive because you don't talk about it with someone who could help. Have you ever thought about going to a therapist?"

Finn rolls his eyes and glances out at the grass. "No. Therapy doesn't work."

"You ever been?"

"No."

"Then how do you know it won't work?"

Finn bites down on his bottom lip and shakes his head. "Because sitting there an hour a week with someone who is getting paid to listen to my shitty struggles doesn't sound like fun to me."

"Therapy isn't supposed to be fun, Finn. It's meant to be painful, but it's meant to get you out of your own head. It's meant to make you get things off your chest, dig deeper into root causes. It's not to punish you even more, it's to take the load off, it's to make you realise that what you've been thinking all along isn't true."

He sighs. "My head is too fucked up for a therapist to sort through."

"There is no such thing."

Finn closes his eyes and turns around before sitting back down again, drawing his knees up and resting his elbows over them. I join him. If he doesn't want to talk right now, fine. At least he's not down the pub drinking whatever he can get his hands on, even with this terrible hangover.

"I-I—" he starts and closes his mouth. I remain silent. "I hate how I feel when I'm hungover, it makes me feel fucking depressed. But that's why I drink again, so I stop feeling like that."

My head twists towards him. "It's not healthy, Finn. One bad choice and you could end up in a ditch or out in the sea. You could get too cocky and think you can swim to the nearest island. This is really fucking with your head and you know it."

"Yeah," he says quietly. "I know."

"I think you have an addiction," I say bluntly.

He says nothing; all we can hear are the seagulls flying through the air.

"Do you think you have an addiction?"

"Maybe."

I hum silently. At least he's not denying it.

"You need to seek professional help, Finn," I state after a few moments. My entire body moves to face him, but he refuses to look at me. "I don't want to lose you. You're my best friend. Problems like these don't just go away."

His eyes gravitate to the grass. He doesn't run off, which makes me think I've said something right, even if I'm being harsh. I listen to his calm breathing, almost in rhythm with the breeze.

"I didn't think anyone cared." His voice is so deflated, it crushes me to pieces.

My arm slides over his shoulders and I tug him into me. "What are you talking about?" I exhale. "I love you like a brother, man. I care about you too much, you'll think it's soppy."

A small laugh falls from his lips, but I know it's not the

time to make jokes. Instead, I keep going because he clearly needs to hear this.

"And I should have been there for you more, and I'm sorry that I wasn't. But I'm here now, telling you that I'll support you through your journey of getting better. You are never alone, you have amazing parents, an amazing sister. I get that reaching out is hard, but we will support you regardless." I give his shoulder a quick squeeze.

Finn swipes a hand through his hair and then nods. "Thank you," he says, though his voice is strangled. "It's just hard to accept it for what it is. I know I'm the only person who can make a difference with my life, but sometimes it's so easy to slip down that hole of self-pity."

"And we all get like it," I admit. "But that doesn't mean we have to continue to follow that path."

He exhales a breath and falls back to the grass. I follow his lead and look up at the sky with him.

"This conversation makes me want a drink," he grunts. "Is that bad to admit?"

I pause for a moment. "Not bad to admit, only bad if you give in."

"I think you'd side tackle me if I went to the pub right now."

A snort falls from me without thinking. "Too right, but I'm here for you," I say sincerely. "You're never getting rid of me now."

He turns to look at me as he sniffles, his eyes looking less pained than they did ten minutes ago. "Yeah, you're a pretty great friend."

CHAPTER 34
IVY THOMPSON

When my parents stumble through the door the next day with their thirty suitcases and glowing tans—I have no idea how I pulled the short end of the stick with my pale complexion—I'm relieved to finally see them after what feels like years.

"Sweetheart!" my mother, Andrea, chimes. "You're home."

She wraps me in her arms, and I get a whiff of her natural, earthy perfume. When I inhale, it wraps tightly around my heart because she has always smelt the same and it's a comfort.

"Hi, Mum," I mumble into her chest. "How was your trip?"

"Oh, it was amazing!" She pulls back. "Wasn't it, James?"

I turn my head to find my dad gleaming at me. "It's good to see you, kid," he says as he walks towards me and ruffles my hair. Then I'm tugged into his hard yet soft chest. "How have you been doing?"

"I'm good," I say softly. "Enjoying summer before going back to university."

"I guess we've got a lot to catch up on," he says as he pulls back and winks at me.

A laugh rumbles from my chest. "I guess we do."

Finn says hello and helps them bring their luggage into the house. Knowing my mum, she probably bought the entire tourist shop full of knick-knacks and memorabilia.

The stairs creak from behind us as JJ descends. "Uh, Mum, Dad, this is my friend JJ. JJ, these are my parents, Andrea and James," Finn introduces them.

He walks straight up to our mother and offers her a polite hug before smiling at her. "Hey, it's lovely to meet you. Thank you for letting me stay over this summer, it's been a lifesaver."

My mother's hand rests on JJ's shoulder as she inspects him. "Oh, don't be silly, JJ. We are a family who loves to share, who loves to get everyone involved. Once you step into this house, you're a part of the family already."

Then he greets my father. JJ places his hand out politely, but my father grabs it and draws him into a bro-like hug. We're not very formal here, and my parents are certainly the type to put on a circus act.

I love my parents, but they're definitely a lot different than normal parents.

Sometimes my dad likes to share stories of when he went travelling in the eighties and took crazy hallucinogenic drugs that changed his life. *We're that sort of family.*

"So, what's for dinner?" My father rubs his hands together and glances between Finn and me.

I hear my brother breathe out air with a chuckle. "Dinner? You'll be lucky."

My father launches at him playfully. "Cheeky sod," he says with a chuckle.

"Shall we order in?" I suggest as I walk towards the kitchen to flick on the kettle.

"Yes," Finn says. "Most definitely."

My mum sighs exasperatedly and turns to my dad. "First night back with our children and we're already guilt-tripped into getting a takeaway."

"We raised them well," he says under his breath.

I can't help but smile. I didn't realise how much I missed them until now.

My heart fills with love and the familiarity of being back home.

When my mum heads upstairs to get freshened up, I follow after her.

"Everything okay, honey?" she asks as I linger by her door.

I glance over my shoulder before shutting us inside her room. "Yeah, I'm doing okay," I say. "Actually, Mum, there's something I need to tell you. And I know you just got back, but I can't keep it to myself."

Panic covers her face. "What's the matter?"

"It's Finn."

"What about Finn?"

I sigh and drag a hand through my hair. "He's been drinking a lot. Almost too much. He tried to go to work drunk the other day, and at every party we attend, he gets almost blackout drunk. If he's not careful, he'll end up in the hospital."

My mother blinks. "Okay." She nods. "Are you sure he's not just having too much of a good time?"

I shake my head. "He's suppressing what happened with my accident," I sigh. "And JJ has spoken to him about getting help, but I don't know if he will, and I'm really worried about him, Mum. We need to do something before it gets worse. I fear it will."

She's silent for a long moment. "Oh god." Her eyes close. "Thank you for telling me. I'll talk to him and keep an eye on him."

"He'll probably be defensive and downplay the severity of

it," I admit. "But I know he needs help. He's self-destructing and I'm scared."

My mother steps forward and wraps her arms around me in a hug. "It's okay. We'll get him the help he needs if things get worse, but I'll try to talk to him, see if he can open up to me."

"He's literally terrible at opening up."

"I know, but it's worth a shot."

"Yeah." I twist my lips to the side.

She rubs my back before pulling away. "Come on, let's get pizza."

CHAPTER 35
JJ WOODFORD

I've never met anyone like Andrea and James. Take away the fact they're Ivy and Finn's parents; they might as well be the fun older auntie and uncle.

We order pizza and sit around the kitchen counter as we discuss their latest travels. It seems they go away often.

"You guys are too old to be going to clubs." Finn covers his eyes with embarrassment. "Let alone being kicked out of them."

Ivy is sharing the same amount of shame as she flicks her eyes between her parents. "What did you guys do to get kicked out?" she asks.

"You are never too old to go clubbing." James points at Finn.

Andrea covers her mouth to suppress a laugh. "Nothing bad." She shrugs with a cheeky smile. "Nothing bad at all."

Finn rolls his eyes. "Yeah, like I totally believe that."

"We might be older than you, but we're still allowed to have a good time," Andrea exclaims and grabs her glass of water.

Ivy snorts. "Having a good time or being menaces and getting kicked out?"

"When did we adopt two teenagers?" Finn directs to his sister.

James swats his son's shoulder gently, but his expression is comical. "When did we have two children who might as well belong in the old people's home?"

Finn wrestles back with his father gently until they're laughing. As I watch them, it makes me miss my family dearly. I wish I could hold my mother through her treatment and be there for my father.

But being here with Finn and Ivy's family heals a tiny hole in my heart. It makes me feel like I belong.

"So, what's been going on around here then?" Andrea asks as she looks between us all. "Enjoying your summer, I presume? The weather is delightful today."

Ivy hums softly. "It's been nice being home. Weather is definitely a bonus."

She gestures between Finn and me. "These two have been looking after you, I hope?"

Her throat bobs and I tear my eyes away, focusing on Finn as he smiles. "Of course," he says.

Andrea slides her hand over the counter and squeezes her daughter's fingers. "How have you been holding up?"

"Fine," Ivy murmurs. "Just looking forward to going back to university now. It's been long enough."

James chuckles gently. "Trust you to be excited to go back to school." He flashes her a grin. "Always been so proud of you, sweetheart. Reach your dreams, don't let anyone stop you."

"Thanks, Dad." She shares a genuine smile.

That comment meant a lot to her. Anyone could see it.

If only my father felt the same.

When the bell rings, Finn jumps off his stool to answer the door and retrieve our pizza. I listen to James as he starts talking about a moment from their trip, a scholar they met who wrote one of the world's most incredible theses on the galaxy.

My eyes flash to Ivy's, and she stares right back. A moment between us, both of us remembering the night together in the garden under the stars.

Finn lays the pizza in front of us, and we all dig in. "So, JJ," Andrea says as she chews on her food. "How are you?"

"All good." I smile at her. "I love it here."

James snorts. "That's interesting, most people under the age of thirty would find this seaside town boring. There isn't much to do."

"Might not be a lot to do," I admit. "But it's been nice meeting Finn's friends and having a quiet summer for once. Summers at my house are usually quite hectic. I've enjoyed the sun and parties. It's a nice balance."

Andrea leans forward for another slice. "You usually spend summers at home with your parents?"

"Yes." I nod. "But they're not here this summer."

"What are they up to?"

Her question throws me off, and a familiar pair of eyes rest on my face. My throat tenses, and my palms begin to sweat. Talking about it with strangers isn't something I enjoy. I don't mind sympathy and condolence when it comes from the right place, but I don't want to discuss it with all of them in the room.

Doing it with Ivy is enough. She knows more than Finn. And that's because I wanted her to know. Now, my tongue is tied, and I want the conversation to move on.

"They're in Germany," I say after a few moments.

Andrea's eyes light up. "Oh, how wonderful. Germany is beautiful. We spent a few weeks in Bavaria. I would love to go back. Whereabouts are they staying?"

My lips part, and I raise a slice of pizza to my mouth. "Uh, Berlin."

"Berlin is one of my favourite cities." She clasps her hands together. "You must tell them to check out this restaurant we went to." Her voice drones out as she reaches for her phone and scrolls. "Oh my, it was wonderful. We even went for this walk, I think we discovered a new path, and it was breathtaking. Once in a lifetime opportunity, certainly for the bucket list."

Suddenly my chest constricts like my lungs have shrivelled.

"Mum," Ivy says sharply. "Please stop."

"What? I wa—"

"Mum." Her voice is harsher now. "Just, *stop*."

I glance up slowly and hate the silence that washes over us. Shit. She was trying to be nice. I'm the one who is overthinking this.

I turn to Finn, who is staring at Ivy, flashing her a rather strange look. But I ignore it and turn to Andrea again. "Sorry," I tell her. "I'd just rather not talk about it."

Andrea slaps her lips together and shakes her head. "No, I'm sorry, JJ. I'm always overstepping, always talking. Goodness, I apologise. If you ever need me to shut up, just tell me to, and I will."

I flash a quick smile and excuse myself. "I'm going to grab another drink," I say before heading out of the back door towards the ice bucket.

As soon as the fresh air hits me, I drink it down, filling my lungs to maximum capacity.

A hand touches my shoulder. "You okay, brother?"

"I'm okay," I say as I stare at the skyline.

"I'm sorry about my mum," Finn says after a few moments.

"It's not her fault. It's just raw, and I don't like talking about it."

Finn hums softly. We remain silent, but he doesn't move from my side.

"Did you tell Ivy?"

My eyes tighten. I knew this was coming.

"Yeah," I blurt.

"I see," Finn responds. "You guys have been getting close, huh?"

"We live in the same house." I shrug. "She's been a good… friend."

The word friend doesn't settle well with me, but it's better to lie than open this can of worms the night his parents get home. I'd rather not sport a black eye today.

I grab some more drinks and clear my throat. "Let's go in," I say, avoiding his eyes.

"You sure?"

"Positive."

"Alright." He sighs as he takes a can from my hand.

When I settle back at the counter, Andrea and James don't make a scene when I stroll back in. Ivy, on the other hand, her eyes might as well be lasers tracking me.

I finish a few more slices of pizza and listen to James tell more crazy stories.

A part of me can't believe these two are alive with their risky adventures. They really love to live life on the edge, doing whatever the hell they please. I'm glad they can do something that gives them a thrill. What is life if you're not living?

At one point, Finn helps his parents take their luggage upstairs. I pack the pizza boxes away and empty beer bottles. Ivy keeps her eyes on me as we clean the rest of the kitchen.

"Hey," she says as she steps beside me.

"Hey."

"I kind of feel like you've been avoiding me."

"I'm giving you space to decide what you want. Especially after what I said the other night, I meant it. I'm not going to rush you."

"And I heard you loud and clear," she says under a

hushed breath in case they can hear us from upstairs. "I'm still processing things, JJ. This isn't as simple as you expect it to be."

When my eyebrows rise, she leans back and places a hand on her hip. Half of her blonde hair is thrown up with a blue clip, with loose strands framing her face. She looks so effortlessly pretty like this. Prominent cheekbones. Darkened freckles from the sun. Softened eyes.

But that is not what I should be focusing on right now.

"What do you want me to say?" she asks desperately, her voice cracking.

She looks so tiny right now as she hugs her arms to her chest. Emotion runs through her eyes. I've never seen her look so vulnerable and raw.

"I want you to claim back your life, Ivy."

She flashes me a confused look. "What does that even mean?"

"You need to stop worrying about everyone else and think about yourself."

Ivy's lips tremble, and she blinks slowly. Her breaths become shallower as she takes in my words. "I am thinking about myself."

"No, you're not. You're worried about Finn and everything else. What do you really want?"

Her mouth parts, and she blows out a little breath

"I want to move on," she whispers. "And I want… to spend more time with you."

The words give me a fraction of relief, but I can still hear the reservation in her tone. She's not ready to let go yet, and it's written all over her expression.

"But it's not just about that…" She pauses. "It's about me and my body."

My forehead creases in confusion.

"What about your body?"

"I just haven't felt like myself since—"

"The accident?"

She nods and lowers her head an inch.

"Ivy, your body is perfect," I say honestly.

And I can't believe she doesn't see it, how breathtaking she truly is.

Her eyes waver for a moment as she looks up at me.

"Do you still believe wanting something and actually having it are two different things?" I ask.

She hesitates for a moment and averts her gaze.

I hum and lean into the counter, folding my arms over my chest. Ivy's eyes glance up and flick across my biceps beneath my T-shirt before returning to my eyes sharply.

"It's clear that you're still not ready," I admit. "And I'm giving you time to think this through. Like I said, I'll wait. But I need you to come to this decision on your own, when you're ready to. And if there are bigger issues at hand, you can talk to me about them, Ivy. I'd never judge you, you know that."

She stares up at me with her big green eyes, fingers fumbling together.

I lean down slowly, my lips beside her ear. "You say the word and I'm yours, princess."

She quivers, and I hear her breath hitch. A smile covers my lips.

"I-I," she attempts, but her head tilts backwards, and I resist the urge to clasp the back of her neck and give her a punishing kiss. My lips graze the curve of her neck instead, her pulse against my skin.

The stairs of the floor begin to creak, and I pull away from her, dampening the cloth in the sink. Ivy is still rooted to the spot, staring at me with dilated eyes. God knows if I had a minute more with her, she might have opened up to me a little bit.

"You don't even want to see what those two brought home," Finn comments as he joins us in the kitchen. He's shaking his head in disbelief, and I can only imagine the worst.

I glance up at him and smile. "No sex toys, I hope."

Finn grimaces. "If that's what I saw, I'd be bleaching my eyeballs right now."

A chuckle passes my lips.

CHAPTER 36
IVY THOMPSON

I've been sitting on the edge of my bed for the last twenty minutes.

My eyes are glued to the window, watching the white clouds sweep across the sky. No chance of sunshine today. I sigh and grab my phone and ring Daisy.

She answers on the third ring. "Hey, you okay?"

A hum mumbles off my lips. "Hey," I say as I flop back onto my bed. "I'm alright. I need to talk to you."

"I'm all ears." The sound of shuffling echoes in the receiver. "What's up?"

"I want JJ."

Daisy laughs quietly. "Yeah, I think we all know that."

"But—"

"Oh god, there is a but."

"Shhh," I say over her, and she chuckles again. "This is serious."

Daisy pauses for a moment. "Okay, go on. I'm listening."

I inhale a deep breath and stare up at my ceiling, twirling a piece of hair around my finger. "I know things will get complicated with Finn if I start something with JJ," I start. "He thinks it's because of Finn, but it's also because he doesn't know what happened with Ben. I want to tell him, but I haven't found the courage to yet."

"Are you worried JJ could be like Ben?"

I pause for a moment before shaking my head. "No."

"Then what?"

"I've felt different since the crash, like this body and mind aren't mine. I don't know. It's stupid."

"Ivy, it is not stupid. You are beautiful inside and out."

Her words don't even comfort me because I can't seem to believe them.

"I—" I trail off, my throat clenching. "I don't feel like it."

"Are you worried about being naked around him or something?"

My lips roll together. "I'm worried about being vulnerable in front of him."

"Ivy." She says my name with purpose. "I hate to break it to you, but JJ has already seen you naked. You've already allowed yourself to be completely vulnerable with him by sleeping with him."

The thought has my stomach rolling. "That doesn't count." I shake my head. "We were drunk. The alcohol gave me stupid amounts of confidence I'd never have had if I was sober. There was a moment I hesitated, but then I forced myself not to care what he thought about my body, because I didn't think we were going to see each other again. We both wanted pleasure, and we got it."

"Well, he saw you, Ivy," her voice crackles through the line. "He saw your body and scars, and he still wants you. I wish you could see yourself how we see you. You need to pick up that confidence and show him who's boss."

An awkward laugh escapes my mouth. "Show him who's boss… have you ever met me, Daisy? I don't know how to be confident."

"No…" she trails off. "But you can learn. You can learn to love that body of yours by making yourself feel sexy."

"How?"

Daisy doesn't talk for a few seconds until she eventually says, "Meet me in town in thirty minutes."

"Wait—"

"No, *nope*. No excuses. Thirty minutes."

Then the line goes dead.

I pull the phone away from my ear and stare blankly at the screen. My eyes shut, and I try to ignore my racing pulse. Knowing Daisy, she's going to pull out all the stops for whatever she's got planned.

A LINGERIE SHOP is Daisy's idea of confidence boosting.

It's safe to say that I've never purchased a sexy set for myself or anyone else. Not even when I was with Ben. I didn't want to see myself naked or in lacy undergarments, let alone flashing it off to someone else. Sure, I've owned a thong, but I've never gone into a lingerie shop to pick anything up.

"Ooooh, this is cute!" Daisy exclaims as she tugs off a matching black bralette and thong. My brows furrow as I step closer and examine it. "It's super hot."

My fingers run down the fabric of the bottoms, and then I gawk at what I find. "Daisy, there is a hole in the middle of the pants."

She chuckles gently. "Yeah, they're crotchless. So you don't have to take them off." She winks.

Boy, I've been living under a rock my entire life.

"Maybe not black," I say, dropping the fabric from my fingers.

Her blue eyes flick to me, and she smiles. "Well, at least you're considering it."

I shrug with a sigh, turning and glancing at the mannequins. "It might work," I admit. "Or I might put it on and decide this is the stupidest idea."

Daisy slings her arm over my shoulder. "You never know until you try. Personally, it's liberating. Remember, this is for you. No one else. It's okay to love ourselves, it's okay to be perfectly imperfect because everyone is beautiful in different ways."

I hum gently. I wish I had that mentality.

"So not the black set?" Daisy asks, trailing after me.

I gnaw on my lip. "I think black is too sexy, maybe something else."

"Oh my god!" Daisy gasps as she beelines across the shop. She walks towards a teal lace set. It's not as sexy as the black, but it's still gorgeous. The detail is breathtaking with the mesh material and small thong. "This colour would look amazing on you."

As I approach her side, I take the set off the hanger. "Yeah," I agree. "I love this colour."

Daisy beams beside me. "It's perfect, it's literally you all over. Not too sexy but still sexy enough to give you all the confidence and self-love you need."

"Should I buy it?"

"Is water wet?"

My head turns to her slowly with raised eyebrows. "I'm being serious."

"So am I." She nods encouragingly. "You need to own this."

I stare at the garments for another few moments and blow out a breath. "Alright. I'll buy it."

Daisy claps her hands together. "Yes," she hisses through her teeth. "I'm so proud and pleased for you. You're going to look incredible. I can't wait for you to try it on."

And for once I'm a weirdly excited too.

When I return home with my new purchase, no one is in.

Finn is at work, and my parents have gone out to dinner with their friends. JJ is nowhere to be seen, and I ignore the thought of him because I have other things on my mind right now.

I drop the fluorescent pink paper bag on my bed and remove the lingerie set. I take a few steps back and stare at it. The back of my neck begins to sweat.

I lean forward and pick up the set. The lace feels soft and delicate between my fingers. *Don't overthink it. Just put it on.*

I strip away my clothes and slip into the sexy two-piece. My eyes hesitate to glance in the mirror, so I grab my pink silk robe and slip it over my arms to build myself up gently. I close my eyes and tell myself to breathe.

Three, two, one.

My body twists, and I face myself in the mirror, arms slack at my sides.

Blood rushes to my face as I take in my body. I startle. The tips of my fingers tingle as I rake my eyes over my appearance, taking in every little detail of my half-naked body.

The bralette cups my chest perfectly, enough to show off cleavage in a way I wasn't sure was possible. My eyes float down to the way the straps of the thong cling to my hips, giving the illusion that I actually have some.

And considering I've always believed I'm short, my legs look… *long.*

When I drag my gaze back up, I'm quivering because, for the first time in forever, I didn't focus on the scar across my chest. I barely even acknowledged it because it's not important. *It doesn't define me.* It never has.

My phone buzzes and I reach for it, opening the message from Daisy.

DAISY:

How's it going?

> IVY:
>
> Better than I thought.

> DAISY:
>
> Let me see!

I don't even think twice as I open up the camera and pull back the silk robe gently, letting it fall from my shoulders as I pose in the mirror. I take a quick snap and send it to Daisy. The thought of sharing it with her would normally make me feel anxious, but right now, I don't feel that way at all.

I'm proud of myself for even taking this step.

> DAISY:
>
> HOLY FUCKING SHIT
>
> You look incredible
>
> Oh my god, you are a goddess

A laugh falls from my lips gently, and I bite down on my lip to suppress a smile.

> DAISY:
>
> Send it to him

My smile falls and my eyes bulge out of my skull.

> IVY:
>
> What?

> DAISY:
>
> You said you want him, prove to him that you do. He will go feral, I promise you.
>
> I know we said this was for yourself, but it can be for him too ;)

I snort to myself. There is no way.

> IVY:
>
> I can't

DAISY:

Excuses, excuses

I stare at her text for a moment and slump on my hip. What is this going to prove? He might hate it. *Or he might not.*

A breath escapes my nose as I draw up my last texts with JJ from the beach party a week or so ago. I click the attachment and press on the picture, watching it float into the message section. My thumb hovers over the send button.

No. I can't do this. My body trembles. This was for me. Not anyone else.

Building confidence for myself. For my own self-love.

I shake my head and rest my finger over the exit button. My thumb presses down only for a blue line to stretch across the bottom of the screen and for the image to pop up in our messages.

My eyes widen so far that my face nearly splits in two.

No, no, no. NO, NO, NO.

"Shit," I chant once pathetically. "Shit, shit, shit!"

My fingers fly over the screen, attempting to recall the message, but I have no idea how to—if it's even possible. Nausea creeps up my throat, and I resist the urge to vomit everywhere.

I begin to pace, skin heating up as the word 'delivered' pops up underneath the picture.

Holy shit.

What the *fuck* have I done?

I press my hands to my forehead as I burn a hole in my carpet. Every last drop of saliva in my mouth evaporates within seconds. I rush to Google, trying to figure out how to recall a message. I scan my eyes across the screen and rush back to the message, only for my heart to fall out of my chest.

Read 18:05

A sob falls from the back of my throat, and I choke. "Oh god," I whimper, still pacing because I don't know what to do with myself.

Fuck. *Fuck!*

I brace myself on my desk, hunching over it because I'm struggling to catch my breath.

This cannot be happening.

My eyes burn when I hear the front door open and slam. I'm shaking as I glance over my shoulder, footsteps becoming louder as they race up the stairs. The handle to my door twists, and I clutch my robe around my body as it opens.

JJ stands in the doorway like he just ran six miles without hesitation. His chest puffs out aggressively, his eyes set on me like he's a hungry lion and I'm nothing more than his silly little prey.

I don't know how long we stand here staring at one another, but it's not long enough to process the situation.

CHAPTER 37
JJ WOODFORD

I'm grateful I can spend time with Joel and Cal whilst Finn is at work. They're nice guys and welcomed me with open arms. We didn't plan much, a quiet evening on the beach to watch the sunset.

"I'm impressed with Finn," Joel comments, bringing his beer bottle up to his lips. "I didn't think he'd be able to keep this job for this long."

"He clearly needs it," I comment.

They both hum in response. "Agreed." Joel nods. "Although there's no doubt he'll be getting drunk at the beach fair in a few weeks. Plus, we all heard the news."

My brows crease. "About what?"

Joel and Cal share a glance. "About Ben."

"What about him?"

The sound of his name makes my blood boil. I might not know what he did, but I know he hurt Ivy, and I know he's an asshole that deserves a lot more than just prison time. My phone vibrates in my hand as Cal waffles on.

But I'm not listening because Ivy's name pops up on the screen. She never texts me.

Something must be wrong.

I press the notification and wait for our messages to pop up. Except, when it does, all the air from my lungs evaporates and I feel like I've been winded by a seven-foot rugby player.

Holy fucking shit.

She's wearing nothing but a matching greeny-blue lace underwear set, her pink silky robe slipping down her shoulder. I let my eyes roam over the image again, and my heartbeat begins to increase in speed rapidly.

Ivy sent me this. Ivy. Sent. Me. This.

"JJ?" Cal says, forcing my eyes away from my phone.

I jump up from the sand and slide my phone in my pocket. "I gotta go."

"What?"

"I'll tell you later," I rush out a quick lie before darting off. "Sorry, I'll see you guys later."

Joel laughs and waves. "Alright… bye."

I take off towards the house as quickly as possible. It doesn't take long to get from the beach back to their home, which I'm thankful for.

The image has been burned into my mind. But goodness, I want to see it in real life.

I draw my keys from my pocket and hurry to shove them in the door, failing the first time but successfully getting it the second. As soon as I'm inside, I slam the door behind me, scoping the living room and kitchen to find no one here.

My legs race up the stairs as I approach Ivy's door. I don't knock, I don't wait. I can't physically breathe.

I press my hand to the door and let it creak open. Ivy glances over her shoulder at me, those green eyes bright with surprise. Her hand clutches her robe together in a death grip.

She literally just took the photo. Merely ten minutes ago.

Oh fuck.

My chest heaves as I study her face, those perfect pink lips and precious little freckles. I step into her room, shutting the door behind me with a click. For a moment, I lean on the door, hands behind my back.

Her breathing becomes louder, backing away into the desk as if she's trying to put as much distance between us as possible. But something crackles in the air, it's been here since the first night we met.

After a few seconds, I push off the door and stroll towards her with agonisingly slow strides. Ivy studies me, and I flick my gaze down her attire. "Are you purposely trying to kill me?" I ask, my voice a lot deeper than I expected.

"No, I—" She stops talking to lick her bottom lip. "It wasn't meant for you."

I quirk a brow, her hands slide against her desk for extra space, but there is nowhere else for her to go. "It wasn't meant for me?"

Ivy's chest heaves. "No, it was for—" She cuts herself off. "It was for—"

I'm inches from her now. She looks so small as I move even closer. "Tell me who it was for, Ivy." My voice is calm. *Still.*

She looks up at me from under her lashes and shakes her head, glancing away. I close myself around her, taking her chin between my fingers to tilt her gaze back to mine. When she finally looks at me again, I whisper, "Tell me, *who* was it for?"

Ivy shivers. My words resting on her parted lips. I glance down at them once and scold myself because now I want to taste them, bite them, suck on them until she's crying out for me to do more.

My head races with positions I'd love to put her in. Listen to her whimper and beg to be touched. I grind my jaw and tell myself to calm down. I know underneath her tiny gown is that mouthwatering underwear set she was wearing in her picture.

It's taking every ounce of patience not to rip it off her.

I stroke my thumb across her lip, and she whines at the touch. "Tell me," I demand.

When she swallows this time, her eyes remain on mine. "*You.*"

A deep sense of pride and relief washes over me. "That's what I thought," I grunt before pressing my lips to hers in a gentle kiss. It's not possessive or urgent. I said what I meant in those texts, I'm going to take my time because I want to live every damn second of being with her.

I slide my hand against her cheek as I kiss around her mouth, jaw, and chin. Ivy exhales a low sigh of satisfaction, and the smile that etches its way onto my face is smug. I know exactly who and what she wants.

"JJ—" she whimpers, and I pull back slowly.

Her eyes are dilated. I can barely see the green, all black. *All desire.*

I groan and slam my lips down onto hers and tilt her head back, pushing her into the desk and slipping my fingers through the back of her hair. My teeth graze her bottom lip, and she quivers against my chest, her fingers latching onto my forearms as I devour her mouth. Her tongue is eager against mine, and I grant her what she wants. As soon as they brush, we moan at the same time.

Holy fuck. I'm not going to last three seconds.

My hands abandon her hair, and I slip them down the softness of her silk robe, over her back, and across her ass. I grip her thighs gently and haul her upwards, her legs clinging to my waist effortlessly.

Ivy's arms wind around my neck, our chests flush to one another. Her head twists, and I get another delicious taste of her tongue. The passion is enough to tear my head right off, and if I don't claim her right now, I might die. No exaggeration.

I draw her away from the desk and walk towards her bed, both of our hearts thrashing loudly. I drop her onto the bed softly, pulling my lips away from hers. Her lashes flutter open, and I stand up straight, her champagne locks splayed across her light bedsheets.

I reach down to the knot of her robe in the middle of her stomach and gently tug at the material before Ivy covers my hand with hers. I meet her eyes and the reservation behind them. We both pause until she inhales and removes her hand, giving me silent permission to carry on.

For a few moments, I don't do anything. I focus on her expression and make sure that she doesn't make a last-minute decision to change her mind. But something flashes in her eyes—encouragement. So this time, I tug on the material that's keeping the robe together, and it falls to her sides.

A hiss escapes my lips as I take in her heavenly body. "Ohhh fuck." I swipe a hand over my mouth to make sure I'm not immediately drooling. My eyes widen at that delicious underwear set against her pale skin.

Ivy stares back at me with uncertainty, and I shake my head, exploring her with my eyes again. Her bra cups her breasts, her thong resting against the tips of her hips. This colour is an absolute dream on her. *Perfect.*

I lower myself down to the bed and press a kiss to the centre of her stomach. "You are beautiful, Ivy," I whisper against her skin. "So beautiful. It should be a fucking crime to look this pretty."

She arches her back away from the bed as I clutch her waist and kiss a little higher. Up and over her chest, neck, shoulders. My eyes latch onto her scar that rests beside her heart, and I press one simple kiss to the centre of it before venturing downwards.

Ivy wriggles against my hold, tiny little whimpers escaping her lips as I reach the hem of her underwear. I smile up at her, back arched and fingers kneading into the duvet. I've barely touched her, and I have her in the palm of my hand.

I hook my fingers into the strap of her thong and tug it down her legs smoothly. Her eyes find mine as she pushes herself up slowly. I wait, giving her time to tell me to stop, but all she does is nod, and I press a kiss to the centre of her stomach again. I wrap my arms around her legs and tug her to the bottom of the bed, her ass hanging over the edge, and a yelp falls from her mouth.

A chuckle escapes my own, and I kiss the insides of her thighs. Her skin is soft against my face, and I close my eyes, enjoying the warmth and closeness after all the space I've given her.

And now I get her all to myself.

My eyes settle on her glistening pussy. I groan at the sight, desperate for another real taste. It's been months. *Months* too long. Satisfied that she's wet and ready for me, I lower my mouth to her core and latch my lips around her throbbing clit. Ivy moans loudly and claws at the bed. The taste of her explodes on my tongue, and my eyes almost roll into the back of my head.

I push her thighs apart, spreading them wide so I can lick and devour her. My thumbs press into her flesh as her hands find their way over my head, her fingertips grazing the bristles of my buzz cut. Sometimes I wish I didn't shave my hair off so she could tug on it as much as she wanted, that would make me rock fucking hard.

My tongue rolls over her clit generously, feeling it grow bigger beneath me. I pull back and give it a little peck. Ivy's entire body jolts, and I smirk at her sensitivity. I'm living for her. Fuck, I'm living for the taste of her.

I suck on her clit again.

"JJ," she moans aloud.

Her breathing becomes irregular, and I keep up the pace, tasting her arousal as it pools between her legs. She hums softly, her breath hitching every time I rock over her bundle of nerves.

My tongue continues to lap at her, enjoying every damn second of being between her legs. Her clit pulsates against my tongue and I pull away, knowing she's close. She pushes herself up from the bed and gasps at me, eyes heavy.

I grip onto the neckline of my T-shirt and strip it from my body in one swift movement. Ivy's eyes float over my bare chest, and she shivers, shutting her legs slowly. I shake my head; I'm nowhere near done with her.

Instead of returning to my previous position—the taste of her on my tongue making me crave more—I slip my arm underneath her waist and tug her towards me. She flashes me a look of surprise, but she doesn't fight me. This time, I spin her around and face us towards her floor-length mirror that rests against the wall. I climb onto the bed behind her, both of us sitting on our knees.

One of my hands wraps around the front of her waist as she settles between my legs. My head is above hers as she rests her back against my bare chest. I stare at her in the reflection and study her gorgeous, flushed face. I sink my fingers down her stomach, and it goes taut beneath my touch.

Then I rest them above her core, and Ivy whimpers as I tease her. Unable to help the smirk on my face at the way her eyes fall shut when I slip my finger down her soaked core. She latches onto my hand and exhales an innocent whimper.

I grip her jaw and force her eyes to the mirror, but she doesn't open them. I chew on the inside of my lip and slide my middle finger directly into her wet pussy, and she gasps, muffling a moan as best as she can.

My thumb runs circles around her clit, stopping when she comes too close to the edge. I can't take my eyes off her face in the reflection, her frustration showing fast because she wants to come.

When I plunge my fingers back inside and press on her clit, I release instantly. Ivy moans and then snaps her eyes open to me, lips parting. "Please," she pants, her hips trying to grind down on my fingers, but I take them away. "*Please*."

I slide my hand up her sternum and over her neck as I feel her throbbing pulse. Her skin rises in goosebumps at my touch, and I grab her chin and twist her head to let her eyes focus on herself in the mirror, but she looks at me instead.

Oh fuck. She is breathtaking. A fucking goddess on her knees in front of me.

"Look at yourself in the mirror and tell yourself that you're beautiful."

Her lips tremble. "JJ," she whimpers, and her eyes look anywhere but at herself.

I circle her clit once again and she moans, sinking down into my hold and moulding herself into me with ease. Her wetness coats my fingers, and I thrust them inside her slowly as her eyes begin to shut.

When she's close, I remove them, and she looks at me with fire behind her eyes. "Tell yourself that you're beautiful," I state again.

Her lips purse for a moment. "I'm beautiful," she mumbles timidly.

I tut at her weak attempt. I grip her chin harder and turn her head, forcing her to look at herself in the mirror. *Finally.* "Say it like you mean it."

This time, I swirl my fingers across her core for long moments. Ivy throws her head back to my shoulder, but her eyes are open, just about. I drop my hand from her chin and brush my fingers across the smoothness of her chest and the base of her neck.

I press my lips behind her ear, and she shudders. "Say it," I whisper.

She chews down on her lip as my fingers pump in and out of her. A gasp escapes her pretty mouth, and she shudders against me. "I'm beautiful," she calls out.

"Look at yourself and say it again," I demand.

Ivy's dilated eyes flick to the mirror as she lowers her head, panting as I slowly continue to fuck her with my fingers. She meets her reflection and stares directly at herself as she whimpers, "I'm beautiful."

"Damn right you are," I grunt against her earlobe.

Her clit throbs beneath the tips of my fingers and I graze over it softly with my thumb. Her neck stretches, and a breathy moan falls from her pouty lips, echoing around the room.

Ivy doesn't take her eyes off of us in the mirror, she watches my fingers as they slip in and out of her. "Look at you." I grin as she grinds down on my hand.

Her pretty pink nipple pokes out of the top of her lacey bra, I slip my fingers down her chest to roll it between the tips, pinching and tugging gently. "So fucking wet for me and so fucking beautiful."

Her eyes remain glued on mine as she shakes in my hold, coming all over my fingers with an almighty cry. Those moans. Oh god. *Those moans*. She falls into me, and I cage her between my arms as she crashes back down to planet Earth.

I give her a few moments to calm her breathing, her eyes now shut, and her head rolling back onto my shoulder again. I can't stop the smile that covers my lips, and I press them to her neck, peppering kisses across her hot skin as I slip my fingers out of her.

When she finally opens her eyes, I loosen my grip on her. She twists in my hold and takes my face between her hands, pressing our lips together, a groan erupts from my chest as she pushes me backwards, completely mounting my body.

Yes. I chant in my head. This is the confident Ivy I want to see. Confident enough to do whatever she wants around me because I know she feels comfortable.

Her mouth slides over mine as my back hits the duvet. I shove off her silk robe so I have access to her luscious skin. I'm greedy. I want it all, I want to touch every inch of her.

Ivy dips her tongue into my mouth, and I slide one hand down her spine and the other into the back of her thick hair. She hums as she tastes herself and it makes my cock throb uncontrollably at the vibration.

When her little hand presses to my bare chest, I bite her lip at the sensation. She pulls back and stares me directly in the eye as her hand brushes my crotch. I groan and silently beg for her to touch it.

She smiles at the expression on my face, and I tug her mouth back to mine. I can't stop. I don't want to stop. The gasp she makes when she slips her fingers inside my undone trousers makes me feel like a smug bastard.

"Bigger than you remember?" I rasp as she grips the base of my cock and my stomach rolls with pleasure.

Ivy pulls back gently and strokes her hand over me. I fist her hair tighter and her eyes light up with fire and want. "Yeah," she admits deeply. "It is."

I can't take it any longer. I wrap my arm around her waist and roll on top of her, holding her weight into my body before dropping her back onto her bed. I fucking thrive off her being in control, but now it's my turn.

We both attempt to kick off my trousers and boxers as fast as possible. My cock springs free and Ivy's eyes are like magnets towards it. "Shit," she curses under her breath, and I attempt to push away my smirk.

"Are you blushing?"

"No."

"Touch me, princess."

And she does. Those dainty fingers wrap around my length, and she begins to pump. I can't tear my eyes away from the erotic sight. My cock looks ridiculously big against her palm; it makes me throb harder.

She smears her thumb across the tip, and I shudder, gripping her chin for another punishing kiss as I groan into her mouth. She takes down my sounds and strokes harder, eager for me to make more.

"Do you have a condom?" I ask against her lips.

Ivy's green eyes flick between mine slowly. "I'm on the pill," she murmurs. "I haven't slept with anyone since you, or for a long time before that. And I've been tested."

"Me too," I admit, and her eyes flare with relief. "Are you sure you want to?"

Her hand grips the back of my neck, and she swirls patterns against the skin, eyes watching me closely. "Yes," she whispers. "I really do."

I pull back slowly. My eyes stare down at her body beneath me; I nudge open her thighs and pin one of them to the bed as I fist my cock and position it against her glistening pussy. She watches with eagerness as I tease her core for a moment.

A whimper falls from her lips, and I smirk at her, our eyes meeting in a blaze of heavy desire. "You want this, Ivy?"

"Yes." Her voice sounds strangled. "Please. Oh god. *Please*."

I suppress a groan and clench my jaw before I press the tip into her and thrust. Ivy gasps loudly, wrapping her arms around my shoulders as I sink halfway into her. Her nails dig into my skin, and she pushes her head back to the bed, taking a moment to adjust. She's tight, so fucking tight that I'm grateful for the pause.

My hand cups her cheek, and I press the tip of my nose to hers. "You okay?"

She hums out a breathy moan. "Yes, don't stop."

I rock my hips into her another inch.

"JJ," she cries aloud. "Fuck. *Fuck*."

My lips press to her throat, right above her pulse. "Relax," I exhale into her skin. "You're with me, princess."

She swallows slowly. "It's been a while."

"Then we'll take our time," I mumble before meeting her eyes again. "I don't want to miss a second of you."

Ivy's eyes flick between mine, and her lip trembles at my words. She pulls my head back down to her mouth and claims my lips, but slower than before. I push myself deeper until I'm filling her completely. We both groan when I thrust again, our tongues tangling with heated desire and feral need.

"Please, move." Her voice is quiet but desperate. "Faster. Anything."

I smile into the kiss. My hips retreat, and I slide back into her, her chest grazing mine as she arches her back. Our mouths part for a second, and she moans so sensually that I nip at her throat in response.

"Like this?" I say huskily as my thrusts become harder.

Ivy's eyes fill with tears as she nods and holds onto my shoulders for leverage. "Yes. Fuck, yes."

I fuck her deep and hard until I'm gasping for breath at how incredible she feels. The sound of her whimpers, her moans, her cries. *Fuck*. I bury my head in her neck and peck her skin, the way our bodies move as one and melt together.

My hand moves down her stomach and I play with her clit, matching my thrusts. "So fucking wet," I groan. Our eyes meet and she holds my stare as I fuck her, the legs of her bed rocking into the floor and I'm grateful no one else is in. "All for me."

"JJ—" She grips my wrist.

"Close?" I tease.

Ivy's eyes fall desperate. She doesn't have to answer, I already know she's building again.

I move my hand away slowly. "Want me to stop?"

"No!" she gasps in displeasure, eyes pleading for me to let her finish. "Please, don't."

Oh, I'll let her finish, alright.

My thumb returns to her clit as I generously apply pressure, rubbing her until she throws her head back once more.

"I like it when you beg. I like knowing how badly you want me."

I thrust harder, pounding her core until the wetness is seeping down her thighs and onto her bed. Her breasts jiggle beneath the fabric of her bra with each stroke, and I am mesmerised by her stunning body, by every inch of her.

"F-fuck," she stammers. "Right there. Yes. Fuck. Yes."

Not once do I slow down. I massage her clit with more determination, and I kiss her the second her orgasm explodes. She jolts in every direction, but I wrap her up in my arms and I hold her through it. "That's it," I groan as she continues to scream with pleasure. "Oh, that's my girl. Let it out for me."

I give her a moment to calm down from her high before I flip her onto her knees with ease. Her back arches, ass high and juicy. I grip it with one hand and grunt out a curse word before slapping it gently.

"Oh god," she groans as I look down at my glistening cock.

My tip rubs against her pussy and I push back into her. Ivy curves her spine even more and moans loudly, fingers curling into her duvet as I take her from behind. "Fuck," I rasp and study the art that is her. "You're so perfect. You take me so fucking well."

Her ass ripples against my lower stomach as she bounces back, meeting me stroke for stroke. I bite down on my lip, slip my hand up her spine, and take her hair in my fist, yanking her backwards slightly.

"Oh fuck," she moans as my cock fills her deeply at this new angle.

I groan at the sight and sensation. "Ohh, fucking hell," I hiss behind her.

The thought makes me feel fucking wild and slightly unhinged. I wrap my arm around her chest and haul her to my body, thrusting upwards as Ivy whimpers.

She's still not done. She's still moving against me.

Desperate for more. I want to give it to her again and again and again until we're physically spent.

"One more, princess," I whisper in her ear, my hand pinching her hardened nipple. "Give me one more."

Ivy's forehead creases as she presses her head back into my chest. For a moment she concentrates as I fuck her, but then she shakes her head. "I can't," she gasps.

I know she's sensitive. Super sensitive, but that won't stop her. *It didn't before.*

"You can," I demand, thrusting deeper, making both of us pant for breath. "Do you not remember when you came on my cock the first night we met? Because I remember the way you screamed when you came for the third time, and you still begged for more. Such a fucking dirty, dirty girl."

This time, I slam into her and play with her nipple between my fingers. Ivy's eyes roll into the back of her head, and she vibrates aggressively against my hold. "Uhh, JJ!" she cries as she crumbles around me. "Fuck."

"Yeah, that's what I thought," I grit through my teeth as she comes all over me. "Good girl."

She's whimpering, barely anything falling from her lips. I've well and truly exhausted her. Her entire body quivers in my hold. I take her throat in my hand and grip gently, tilting her head back.

"Now thank me for making you come," I say darkly, feeling her pulse thrash against my fingers.

"Thank you," she says without hesitation. Her voice is breathy, still coming down from her climax. *"Thank you."*

"For what?"

"For making me come."

The sound of her voice sends me straight over the edge. Two more thrusts and I'm a goner. I lose myself in her as she clutches onto my arm with one hand and buries the other in her duvet. She continues to moan as I fuck into her and she calls out my name, making my orgasm last an eternity.

I bury my head into the back of her neck as I finish inside her. Her pussy clenches around me, making me spasm with how fucking sensitive and euphoric I feel.

I hold her body close to me, her heavy breaths are still heightening my climax until I can barely see, I can barely think. All I know is her.

We slump forward, my cock slipping from her. Ivy falls onto the bed, eyes closed. I smile down at her and gather her in my arms before lying against her pillows. She doesn't push me away or rush to cover her body, she lets me cuddle her as the room is filled with the sound of us trying to recover.

My fingers stroke down her back, and I watch her. Warmth covers my body, and I smile. Never in my life have I experienced sex like that. Intimate, passionate, *real*.

Every second of it was real.

Something I won't forget for a long fucking time. *I know she won't either.*

CHAPTER 38
IVY THOMPSON

I'm well aware that my head is resting on JJ's shoulder.

I'm well aware we've been sleeping in this position all night.

He held me tight. He brushed his fingertips over my skin in slow circles. He pressed a kiss to my forehead as my eyes fluttered shut and I drifted off into a perfect night's sleep.

It wasn't late when JJ barged into my room, shortly after I sent him the picture. But it's safe to say once wasn't enough. We laid there for a while, enjoying the naked feel of one another, then one kiss led to more touching and more touching led to more fucking.

JJ bent me over my desk, and I watched all my belongings fall to the floor. Then I turned around, sank to my knees, and opened my mouth.

Never have I felt so alive.

Never have I felt so in control.

It felt relieving to let go. I practically handed my trust over to him. Whatever he did, I knew it would be pleasurable. He possessed me and took charge, and I submitted. Without hesitation.

I've been awake for the last thirty minutes, but I refuse to open my eyes. I might not have been able to admit it to myself before, but I've wished for this moment more times than I can count.

And besides, I don't want to wake him up after the performance he gave last night. I bet he's tired.

My core certainly is.

I flick my eyes open for a brief second, and JJ's head turns as if on cue, his body twisting around me as he stretches. His lashes flutter open, exposing those beautiful blue eyes in my direction. His sleepy face makes my heart quiver. I didn't get this experience last time. Now I wish I stayed.

JJ offers me a lazy smile, those eyes shutting for a second before opening again. He flicks his gaze across my face and leans down to peck my cheek, my chin, my neck.

Heat spreads everywhere. If he struck a match, I'd be up in flames.

"I'm pleased to know you're not a serial up-and-leaver," he says through his deep, sleepy voice. "I was worried I'd wake up in an empty bed."

"Not this time," I whisper, finally finding my voice.

He twists his arm underneath my head and shuffles me half on top of his chest. My bare breasts press against his torso, and I try to ignore the negative thoughts, especially after he witnessed my naked body last night and looked at me as if I were the most expensive painting in the world.

"How are you feeling?" he asks, brushing my hair away from my eyes.

I purse my lips, attempting to pull the covers up to hide my naked back. JJ clocks it, and his arm becomes tighter around my waist.

"After last night, I thought you'd know better than to try and shield yourself from me," he murmurs into my temple. "Unless you need reminding?"

My lips tremble at his words. I glance up at him, my heart

pounding against my ribcage. "Not yet," I say timidly, and he smiles, his eyes flicking down to my lips.

"Good," he says heavily. "Because I would have been doing something terribly wrong."

I press my hand to his chest, slide it up over his collarbone, and clasp the side of his jaw. "You did absolutely nothing wrong," I find myself admitting. "Everything was… perfect. Like the first time."

The corner of his mouth twitches in amusement. "Perfect?"

My lips press together in a soft hum. "I came lots of times, it doesn't get better than that."

JJ exhales a low and throaty laugh, which spreads warmth through my entire soul. "True." He nods, a glint of arousal playing in his eyes before kissing my chin again. "You sure you're okay?"

"I feel safe with you," I blurt.

JJ's hand stills on my bare back, and the room turns silent for a moment. "And I'd be an entire failure if you didn't."

I release a quiet sigh. The scar over my chest begins to throb, and I know my body is trying to tell me something. I trust JJ, of course I do. I want to open up and tell him everything that happened with Ben. Why I am the way I am, and my stupid insecurities that come along with my trauma. But I don't want anything to ruin this moment.

My head shifts on his chest, and I rest my chin on his muscly shoulder. JJ looks down at me and brushes back my hair with his fingers, over and over. "I know you're waiting for me to talk about my past," I whisper.

JJ's brows crease. "I'm not entitled to anything, Ivy," he states simply. "If you want to tell me, then I'm ready to listen, but if you don't, then that's your decision. Not mine."

"I want to tell you." I flick my eyes down to the curve of his neck and along his collarbone. "I want to share that part of my life with you because I trust you. I think it will help you understand why I've been putting this off, and why I think the way I do."

He places his hand under my chin and tilts slowly, our eyes meet, and I melt at the security and comfort that lies there. "Even so." He shrugs lightly. "If you're not ready, then you're not ready. I'm still going to be here."

"I'm almost ready," I admit. "But after last night, my head is a little clouded with other thoughts."

JJ's other arm snakes around my back, and he hugs me close, our hearts pounding in unison. "Then I'll be here to listen when you are."

When I take a breath this time, it's like a thousand tonnes have fallen off my shoulders, giving me a chance to stand tall. I might not have told him what happened, but openly declaring I want to, that is a step I never thought I'd take.

I haven't spoken about it in years. Only to my therapist.

JJ takes my hand and twists my palm towards him before kissing the centre of it. Butterflies flicker across my sternum and down to my stomach at the soft gesture. I can't take my eyes off him. He's so effortlessly handsome, I can't believe he's here in *my* bed.

"Is this good enough proof that I want you?" I plead before he places my hand down in the middle of his chest. "And that I'm ready to try."

JJ's eyes light up and simmer as he nods. "Kiss me."

I swallow back the tight lump in my throat. How am I nervous to kiss him when he was deep inside me last night? My eyes flick down to his lips, and I'm not surprised to find a proud smirk lying there. He knows exactly how he affects me and he's living up to every moment.

I slowly shuffle upwards, our lips hovering over one another's. He glances down at my mouth, still smirking, and my head spins. His hands glide up my bare legs and ass before he grabs my waist and forces me to straddle him.

I gasp when my core touches his cock. He's not wearing

any clothes either. He's hard and warm and I bite my lip as it rolls down the centre of my pussy. I shudder, and he clasps the back of my head with his hand. "You're hard."

He's staring at me with dark, hooded eyes, breathing heavier than before. "That's a given when I'm around you."

My lips tremble at his words. Our mouths brush, and I clasp the side of his jaw. The kiss is instantly deepened as he dips his tongue inside my mouth and bites down on my bottom lip. I hiss and he smiles, twisting his head to plunge his tongue deeper.

Somehow, I find my hips rocking against him, planting his cock against his stomach as I slide up and down his length. What the fuck am I doing? I don't even know, but I love it.

God, I love it so much.

"JJ—" I moan into his mouth when my clit grows bigger.

"Holy fuck," he groans into the kiss and fists my hair.

I glance down as JJ's fingers knead into the flesh on my thigh with one hand. His eyes are dark like onyx, not a speck of blue in sight. "Fuck, princess," he rasps. "That's it. Use me. Make yourself come all over me."

Tears swell in my eyes as I rock harder, faster. My clit grazes the ridge of his tip and I clench my core, my stomach, *everything*. "Oh fuck," we exhale at the same time as he stares at me with hungry eyes.

"Come on, Ivy. Don't you want to come for me? I know you want to," he grumbles darkly as I grind harder.

My hand latches onto the base of his throat, and I pin his neck down to the bed as his cock twitches against my pussy. "I want you to come," I whisper breathlessly. "I want you to come for me, too."

JJ's eyes flare up at me as he tightens his fingers in my hair, both of us whimpering and groaning. "Princess," he says through gritted teeth. "You're playing a dangerous game."

My entire body jitters as I rock forward again. "Then come

for me," I gasp as I roll over his tip and back again, and we both release a moan. "Oh god, I'm close."

Close is an understatement. Everything lights up, and my world is somehow brighter, livelier. Even my mind goes silent and allows me to have this moment of pure bliss and harmony.

He tugs my head down to him, and our lips collide. The second we touch, I burst around him. I see stars, I see moons, I see the entire galaxy as I grind my orgasm out on his throbbing cock.

"Fuck, Ivy," JJ says through gritted teeth. "Take it. It's yours."

When I moan a little too loud, JJ slams his lips to mine again. The sound is muffled as I whimper into his mouth, and when he bites my bottom lip, he groans out the pleasure of his own orgasm, coating his stomach.

"Oh my god," I cry out, pressing my forehead to his chest.

"Fucking hell, Ivy," he groans as I lift my head. "You are—"

A knock at my bedroom door startles me. JJ's mouth hangs open, and we stare at each other with wide eyes. "Ivy?" Finn's voice floats through the door. "You awake?"

"Shit, shit, shit," I chant quietly before jumping off his body. My legs tremble as I step back, now feeling uncomfortable with the wetness between my legs. "Get up."

JJ leisurely lies back against my pillows, one hand behind his head like he's at a five-star hotel. I reach for my robe and wrap it around my naked body, his eyes following my movements.

I grip his clothes and throw them at him. He's smiling smugly again. "*Get up*," I hiss under my breath.

He sighs and starts to put on his clothes, until Finn knocks on the door again. "I can hear you shuffling around in there," he says as the door handle twists.

My eyes almost lurch out of my skull. I shove JJ into my

closet with his clothes and shut the door firmly. I hate that he's enjoying this. Granted, sneaking around should be fun, but not when I know Finn might actually murder JJ if he finds out.

I run to the door and grab the handle, keeping it slightly ajar as Finn's face appears. "Do you mind?" I say as I catch my breath. "I was getting dressed."

He blinks once, taking a step back. "Yeah, sorry."

"What do you want?"

"Have you seen JJ?"

My mouth turns bone dry, and I somehow manage to shake my head. "No," I exhale slowly. "Why?"

He shrugs. "He's just not in his room. Not answering my texts. Just wondering if he's okay because it seems like he didn't come home last night."

My eyebrows rise. "Oh." I clutch my robe tighter to my chest. "Now that I think about it, I'm pretty sure I heard the door shut early this morning. Maybe he went for a run or something."

Finn's brows crease, but eventually he nods. "Alright." He steps away. "Thanks."

I shut the door and take a calming breath. My head flicks over my shoulder as I see JJ emerge from my closet, a tissue in hand as he cleans up the mess he left on his abdomen. His trousers are on, but he's still shirtless, and those muscles and tattoos never miss a beat. They're fucking beautiful.

He strolls straight up to me and takes my face between his hands, then he kisses me. Deeply, passionately, *fiercely*. For a second, I forget my brother almost caught us because being wrapped up in JJ is like forgetting the world exists entirely.

We part gently and he stares down at me. My chest shudders. "JJ," I whisper. "You need to go. Finn will get suspicious, and I really don't need that right now."

JJ hums and pecks my lips one last time. He drops my face and walks towards the door until I press a hand to his chest. I shake my head, pointing to the other end of my room. His eyebrows rise as he follows my direction.

"The window?" he says in disbelief.

I fold my arms over my chest and raise a brow at him.

"Wow," he chuckles to himself. "Talk about the walk of shame."

"Do you want your head on a stick?"

JJ's lips swish to the side in an amused smile. He leans forward again and kisses my lips, this time longer and softer. "I'll take my chances, princess." He winks before opening my bedroom door and scoping the hall before shutting it behind him.

I stare at the wooden door for a moment. When I don't hear shouting or a physical altercation, I take a breath of relief.

Let's pray JJ has a good backup story of where he was last night.

CHAPTER 39
IVY THOMPSON

Later that evening, I head downstairs to find my mother cooking dinner. I stand beside her while I peel a pot of potatoes.

"So, how have you been since being home?" she asks curiously.

I hum as I run my thumb across the skin with the peeler. "It was a challenge at first, but I'm alright now."

"I heard about Ben, and his release is soon." Her voice dips.

"Me too," I whisper.

I haven't thought about it for a few days, but when I do, realisation slams into me once again.

What if I see him?

What if he tries to contact me?

We live in the same town. Something is bound to happen.

"I'm sorry we weren't here when you came back." She steps closer to me, and I stare up at her dark blue eyes. "My baby." She frowns before kissing my head. "I didn't realise you'd be coming back for summer so soon. I wish we were here to welcome you home with warm hugs."

The corners of my mouth tug. "Finn was here," I say

before turning back to my peeling. "And JJ. I've had Daisy, too, and even Isaac. It hasn't been as lonely as I thought it would be."

"I'm proud of you, Ivy," she says, and my eyes build with pressure. "So proud. We both are."

I drop the peeler into the pot. "Don't make me cry."

"Oh, baby." She wraps her arms around me completely, then kisses me again. "We're always here for you; you know that, right? If you ever need anything."

"I know," I sniffle into her shoulder. "I know, Mum."

The front door opens, and my mother lets go of me. I peer over my shoulder to find Finn and JJ strolling inside. "Oh, right on time," my mother calls out. "You guys can help with dinner."

Finn groans, turns around, and walks back to the door, but JJ grabs him and pushes him in the direction of the kitchen. "Don't be an ass," JJ grumbles.

I blink at him and feel my face flush when he smiles in my direction. "Chop these for me, love?" she directs Finn as she points to a bunch of vegetables on the chopping board.

"Yes, Mum," he sighs, although it sounds like he'd rather bash his head into a wall.

I'm still focusing on JJ as he walks behind me. His fingers delicately brush the backs of my bare thighs, and I tingle all over, goosebumps rising on my skin. My lips part, and he shoots me a wink.

My core clenches at the subtle action, but it affects my body in ways I can't explain.

"JJ," my mum says, and he snaps his eyes away from me instantly. "You can be in charge of the cooking."

He nods once. "Yes, ma'am."

"Please," she laughs loudly. "Call me Andrea, don't make me feel any older than I already am."

JJ plants himself behind me and starts up the pan with a

slab of butter. I feel his eyes flick down to my face as I continue peeling the potatoes.

As we prepare dinner and plate up, we sit around the table and eat. "So there is a fair at the beach on Saturday," Finn comments as he stuffs his face full of food.

My mother rolls her eyes. "Close your mouth when you eat, Finn," she huffs. "You're not five, and we don't want to see it."

"I heard. You going?"

"Yeah, we're going." He uses his fork to gesture between himself and JJ. "Are you coming?"

I glance at my brother and then at JJ, who is staring at me hopefully. "Sure. Should be fun."

"How lovely for you all," my mum says gleefully. "So glad you're all getting along."

My face heats. Yeah, getting along really well with Finn's best friend.

"Where's Dad?" Finn asks.

"Out playing pickleball, he'll be back later."

Once we're done with dinner, we clean up, and soon after, I head to bed. I'm exhausted after last night.

As soon as I'm in my bed and in my pyjamas, I scroll through my phone. It buzzes in my hand, and JJ's name pops up at the top of the screen. My heart misses a beat when I click on the text instantly.

JJ:

Thinking of me?

IVY:

Why, are you thinking of me?

JJ:

Always.

I shamelessly squeeze my legs together at that one word.

Desperate for a bit of pressure because now all I can think of is the way I came around JJ over and over again.

IVY:
> Will I see you at the fair on Saturday?

JJ:
Yeah, I hope so.

I chew on my lip for a moment, my thumbs hovering over the screen. The fair will be a good time to tell him. It's the closest opportunity I have to being alone with him this weekend. I can't keep this to myself anymore. I want him to know.

A part of me believes he deserves to know. Especially if he decides he doesn't want my extra baggage. I can't trap him into this. He should know how fucked up I've been since.

IVY:
> Yeah. I want to tell you something. When we're there.

JJ:
Okay... good or bad?

IVY:
> Neither? Meet me at the Ferris wheel, that way we won't be distracted.

JJ:
Can we at least kiss at the top?

IVY:
> Depends.

JJ:
On what?

IVY:
> If what I say doesn't scare you off.

JJ:

Don't give me that bullshit, princess. Anything you tell me will not change how I feel about you.

IVY:

You don't even know what I'm going to say.

JJ:

No, but I know you and I'm not going anywhere. You're worrying about nothing.

IVY:

Maybe.

JJ:

So that kiss?

My heart pounds in my chest. If he sees past the messed-up parts of me, this might work out. Emphasis on the *might*. So I suck down some confidence and type out a response.

IVY:

It's yours.

CHAPTER 40
JJ WOODFORD

The fair at the beach is in full swing. Rides, food stalls, games. Music blasts across speakers, and children run about the sand with candy floss in their hands. Even the sun is peeking out behind the pearly white clouds for a perfect day.

I walk together with Finn, Joel and Callan, and the four of us grab a drink and perch on a railing, facing the sea. I cautiously eye Finn, and he demands it's just one, but I don't believe it.

Joel starts talking about a house party tonight, when all I can think about is Ivy.

She wasn't at the house all morning, I can only presume she went over to Daisy's to get ready before the fair.

We agreed to meet at the Ferris wheel at seven o'clock. I swear, time couldn't be going any slower right now.

I'm a deprived man. It's barely been four days, and that's far too long for me.

There is nothing I want more than to wrap my arms around her and feel her delicate touch. I've been dreaming of it.

Finn clinks his beer against mine, snapping me out of my trance. "Cheers to a good summer, may it last forever."

I raise my eyebrows as Joel and Cal's glasses meet ours. "Forever indeed."

I continuously watch the clock as we walk around and grab some food before Finn becomes intoxicated. I keep my eye on him because I don't want him to go overboard tonight.

When it reaches five to seven, I chew on the inside of my lip and shove my phone into my pocket. "Guys, I gotta go take a call," I lie.

Finn turns to me and grabs my shoulder. "Who is it?"

"I'll tell you later," I say, moving away from his grip. Joel and Cal nod as I take a step backwards. "I'll be back in a bit."

"Alright." Finn holds up his hand as I turn around and head straight towards the Ferris wheel.

I almost stop walking when I spot Ivy in the distance, her fingers laced together in front of her as she glances from side to side. "Oh my," I whisper to myself as my eyes rake over her attire.

She's wearing light denim wide-leg jeans with a white crop top that showcases a sliver of midriff and the top half of her scar. She normally covers that scar. But not tonight.

My fingers twitch at the sight of her.

Her hair sweeps over the tips of her narrow shoulders in gentle waves. Big green eyes flick over every person until they land on mine. Then she smiles. *She smiles.* And my entire world slows down.

I take long strides to reach her, and when I do, I tower over her short frame. I grip her cheeks between my fingers and draw our noses tip to tip. Ivy releases a quiet gasp as I bring our faces together.

"I want to kiss the hell out of you right now," I murmur heavily.

Her eyes light up at my words, and then she glances around. "Same," she confesses. "But—"

"I know." I drop my hands from her face. "Later."

"Later," she agrees.

"You look so beautiful," I admit, my eyes taking a journey over her again.

Ivy's cheeks heat as she presses a hand to her chest. "Oh, this is just—"

I clutch her chin between my thumb and finger, tilting her eyes to mine until she stops talking. "Take the compliment, princess, or I'll make you."

She gulps. "Okay. Thank you."

"That's more like it," I say as my mouth curls to the side.

We queue up for the Ferris wheel and I pay for both of us. She thanks me, and I motion for her to go first, taking her hand as the cart rocks gently. We pull the barrier close to us, and it begins to move.

I glance down at Ivy, and her hands are tight against her thighs. "You okay?"

She hums and then brushes her hair behind her ear. "Yeah. You?"

"I am now," I say, smiling as I take in every little detail of her perfect face.

Pink creeps up across her freckled cheeks as I extend my arm across the back of the seats, my fingers tickling her bare arm. "I like what you're wearing," I say as I take it in again.

"I thought I'd step out of my comfort zone again," she says timidly.

"Again?"

A hesitant laugh falls from her lips. "Buying that lingerie set and taking a picture of myself. That was very out of character for me."

I flash her a grin as I scoot closer. "Well, I like you stepping out of your comfort zone. It's like seeing another side of you. I like it."

Her lashes brush her cheek. "I'm getting there." She lowers her head.

"What did you want to talk about?"

Ivy glances up at me. "Everything." She releases a jagged sigh. "Excuse me if it takes me a while to get through it all."

"Then I'll keep paying the ticket guy until you're done."

"Thanks." She laughs softly, and it's so peaceful compared to the loudness of the fair. "I'm sorry it's taken me so long to tell you, but I doubt it's something I'll ever get over."

"Don't apologise," I whisper.

She sucks in a breath. "I know you've heard about Ben."

I run my tongue along my lip. "I only heard about him, I know nothing about what happened."

"It was probably for the best." She attempts a smile, but it doesn't meet her eyes. I continue to caress the back of her shoulder because I need to touch her, I need to be close to her. "I wanted to be the person to tell you, not anyone else. People tent to twist the truth."

"Whatever you want to tell me, I'd never demand answers."

Her eyes glance over the fair as we reach near the top. "Ben used to be one of Finn's friends. We met at a party and clicked instantly. Obviously Finn hated the idea of it because they were friends. But we dated for a year and everything was going well, then I started getting these strange vibes from him."

My brows crease. "Like what?"

She pauses and pivots to look at me. "At first, I never got any feelings that he was possessive or super jealous, but the closer we got to leaving for university, he started acting out. He became too attached, clingy. He said that I probably wouldn't say no to other men when I went to university."

I keep my eyes on her carefully as she continues. "I couldn't handle it, being accused of something that I would never do. Then these rumours came out, they spread like wildfire. Someone said that I cheated on Ben with some guy I met at a club, but it wasn't true. I'd never cheat on anyone and hurt them like that."

I nod in agreement, not wanting to interrupt her.

"So, one evening he was dropping me home from a day at the beach and we got into an argument about the rumours. I was trying to convince him they were lies, but it kept getting more and more heated. I couldn't control the direction of the conversation, he barely let me talk."

Her voice falters, and I take her fingers in mine, giving them a little squeeze. When she glances up at me, her eyes glisten. Her chest is now moving quicker than before, so I hold her hand tighter and brush back her hair with my other.

"We were in his car but he started freaking out, crying, shouting at me. I-I was terrified. He kept speeding up, going faster and faster until my heart literally felt like it was going to burst. He was demanding I admit that I cheated on him, and said he would slow down if I admitted it."

Her eyes flutter shut, the memory too painful to think about. I watch her and wish I could push away all her agony.

"I've never seen him so angry." She shivers. "He literally switched. One moment his eyes were on the road, the next he undid my seatbelt, opened my passenger door and threatened to throw me out of it."

Jesus Christ.

"He grabbed me here," she says as she brushes her hand over the base of her throat. "So tightly. I couldn't breathe. I couldn't get him off me. He hung me half out of the car, and if he didn't throw me out, I thought he was going to suffocate me. We were easily going one hundred miles an hour, and then he started to loosen his grip. I thought he was going to let me go. And I'll never forget the look in his eyes. Filled with hatred over something I didn't do."

My hands start to shake from the fury rolling through me.

"I cried at him to stop and slow down, but he refused, and I could see a bridge ahead of us." Her fingers now tremble in my hold, and I raise them to my lips and give her knuckles a little kiss. "I thought I was going to die. It's a feeling I don't even know how to describe."

A single tear rolls down her cheek, and I brush it away with my vacant hand. I never want to see her upset, it brings out emotions I didn't even know I had. "But he kept going," she gasps, and now I wrap my arms around her and tug her head into my chest. "He told me I was his and that I did this to myself. Then he purposely slid into the the side of the bridge, and the car fell into the water. The windscreen smashed and I was pierced by a piece of metal that missed my heart by like two centimetres. I was knocked out when it happened, and I was barely alive when they found us. I should have died; I should have died right there."

I shake my head over and over. "No, princess," I whisper into her hair before pressing a kiss to her crown. "Don't say that."

A fire lights in my stomach knowing Ben put her in danger like that. He tried to hurt her. *He did it on purpose.*

"I was so scared," she chokes out. "I thought that was the end."

My eyes burn at the thought, the panic, the fear.

"After the accident, I was never the same." She peeks her eyes up at me, filled with sadness. "It took me a while to recover. Weeks in the hospital. Then I fell into this shell that I hated. I haven't been myself in years, my insecurities got stronger, and my anxiety has been so bad that I don't even recognise myself, let alone my body."

"Ivy," I rasp and press my forehead to hers.

Her lips tremble. "I felt like the scars that cover my body —especially the one on my chest—define me. It wasn't just what happened that had an effect on me; it was the aftermath, too. It affects the way I see myself, and I started overthinking it because I believed others would see me that way, too. All of Ben's friends, outside of his friendship with Finn, were blaming me for what happened, that I deserved it for what I did. When he went to prison, it made everything a thousand times worse. That's why I left this town."

"None of your scars define you, Ivy." I dip my finger underneath her chin and force those green eyes to mine. "They never have and they *never* will."

"I know that now." Her lips stretch into a wobbly smile. "It took a while to realise it. The first night we met was the first time I allowed myself to be vulnerable with someone else."

I clutch her chin a little tighter, not wanting to let go. "I'm so fucking sorry, Ivy. I'm so sorry you had to go through that. I understand why you didn't tell me. Jesus. He tried to kill you. He put you in danger on purpose. That is not okay whatsoever."

"It gets worse." Her eyes fall. "He's getting out of prison next week."

My eyes blink rapidly. "What?"

A sigh leaves her mouth. "Finn told me. I still have a restraining order against him, but I wouldn't put it past him to come back here and act like nothing happened."

"Are you scared of him?" I ask which sounds stupid considering he literally tried to kill them both.

She meets my eyes this time, and she nods.

If I ever meet this fucker, I am going to make him wish he died that day.

"Princess." I let my eyes shut for a second. "I promise I won't let him hurt you again. *I promise.*"

"I haven't seen him in years, and I'm terrified to see his face again." Her body trembles against mine. "I don't want all of my progress to disappear."

I cup her face between my hands, flicking my eyes between hers slowly. "Your progress will not disappear when you see him, Ivy. If you do see him, you will remind yourself how strong you are, how far you've come. That he is nothing, that what he did doesn't make you who you are. The only person who makes you *you* is yourself. The smart, amazing girl that I have completely and utterly fallen for."

Ivy exhales sharply, two fresh tears rolling down her cheeks. "I thought I'd tell you this and you'd do a runner."

"Why? This changes nothing. Absolutely nothing."

She shrugs. "Because being with me isn't easy. I know that."

"I don't want easy." I kiss her cheek again, her salty tears dampening my lips. "I want you just how you are."

Her head presses into my shoulder, and she releases a breath of relief. "I wanted to tell you because I trust you."

"I'm honoured that you trust me, but just know, I'm always going to be here."

She holds my stare. "Finn blames himself for what happened. That's why he's been drinking so excessively." Her voice cracks a little. "I worry about telling him about us. You're his best friend, and I know he doesn't want history repeating itself."

I chew on the inside of my cheek for a moment. "History won't repeat itself. I would never hurt you, Ivy. I'd rather jump into incoming traffic than even think about hurting you."

"I know," she admits quietly. "I didn't mean it like that, I mean that Finn carries this guilt, and he'll spiral if he finds out about us."

"Thank you for telling me," I say as I slip my finger underneath her chin again. "For allowing me in."

Her lips curve slowly, but tears are still evident in her eyes. I hate seeing her like this, it makes me feel like a failure of a human being. I wish I could do something to change how she feels, show her how incredible and brave she is. But it's something she'll need to work on herself. There is no doubt in my mind that she'll get there.

"Are you okay?"

"When I'm with you, yes."

"So, about that kiss?" I smile softly, glancing at her mouth.

She shuffles closer to me, our lips grazing. "I told you it was yours as long as you didn't want to bolt a thousand miles away from me."

I place my hand on the nape of her neck, tilting her head. "Trust me, you're not getting away from me that easily. Nothing could push me away. *Ever.*"

"Good," she whispers, relief washing over her again.

I lean forward and press my lips to hers in a gentle caress. She whimpers into the kiss, and I graze my tongue against hers softly. Her little fingers bunch against my T-shirt, trying to get as close to me as possible.

I smile when I feel her smile. It's contagious.

This moment might not be one of full happiness, but I hope she realises that this changes nothing and I'm not going to bail at the first hurdle.

Life isn't easy, but being with Ivy is.

Falling for her is the easiest thing I've ever done.

CHAPTER 41
IVY THOMPSON

When it's our turn to get off the Ferris wheel, I exhale a silent sigh of relief. It was difficult telling JJ the truth, but I immediately felt better for it—he deserved to know.

He listened, he asked questions, *he reassured me.*

He makes me feel seen.

But as we reach the bottom, reality slowly begins to slap me in the face. The bubble around us now bursts, and my heart weeps.

JJ helps me out, and I thank him. He glances over his shoulder briefly before landing a quick kiss on my lips. I'm smiling as soon as I feel the warmth of his skin. "I wish we could stay here all night," he murmurs against me, lips slipping downwards with disappointment.

"Me too," I admit, enjoying the rawness of his blue eyes.

As we exit the ride, JJ pulls his hand away from mine, and my fingers turn to ice cubes. I wrap my arms over my chest as the night comes creeping in, the sun slowly setting and lighting up the sky with the most perfect shade of orange.

"There you are!" I hear from behind me.

I whip my head to find Daisy, Isaac, and Harriet approaching us. My mouth morphs into a forced smile as I see them, my heart hammering in my chest because I know I'm standing right beside JJ.

"Where have you been?" she asks as she slinks an arm over my shoulder.

I quietly clear my throat. "I went to the toilet; the queue was long. Then I bumped into JJ for a bit."

Daisy glances up at JJ, who has his hands shoved into his pockets, smiling down at us. She muffles a laugh. "Yeah, 'bumped'... *sure*." I glance up at her to find her winking at me.

I twist my head and look over at Isaac and Harriet, who are talking to each other, but Isaac catches my eye and offers me a timid smile. "Let's go get a drink," I say.

"Hell yeah," Daisy cheers as we walk towards the bar.

JJ tags along with us, and Finn is already there with two beers in hand, Joel and Cal beside him. My chest tightens at the drinks he's holding, and I pray he doesn't go crazy tonight.

Finn beckons us over and asks JJ where he's been. I try not to listen in on the conversation, but JJ mutters something about a call, and he didn't realise how long he was gone.

I grab a drink with Daisy when my brother appears at my side. The stench of beer wafts into my nose, and that's when I know he's drunk. I curse to myself when he beams at me with a wonky smile.

"Why are you intoxicated already?" I ask.

Finn scoffs. "I'm having fun, Iv. Lighten up."

I bite down on the inside of my cheek before I make him worse.

"So are you coming to the house party tonight?" he asks.

Daisy's eyes light up. "Party?"

"Fuck yeah," he slurs. "We're gonna have a wild night."

I roll my eyes before pinning him with a stare. "You're already having a wild night."

"Shhhhh." He presses his finger to my lips, and I swat him away.

"We're at a civilised fair; you couldn't wait until later?" My eyebrow raises.

Finn laughs loudly. "Alright, boring."

"We'll be there," Daisy replies, and I glance at her, sighing.

Finn glances at something behind me, and his expression twists into a look of pure anger. "Motherfuckers," he spits, and I furrow my brows.

I make the mistake of looking over my shoulder to find Tom, Julian, and a group of their friends. My body shakes at the sight of them, but they've already clocked us and are making their way over.

Joel and Cal step towards Finn, knowing what's about to go down.

"Shit," I hiss under my breath.

Why can't they leave us the hell alone?

I sense someone beside me, and I glance up to find JJ moving closer. His eyes aren't on me; they're zeroed on Tom as he strolls over to us cockily.

"Look who it is," he sings patronisingly. "Cute little family meet up."

"Back the fuck off, Tom," Finn's slurred voice booms across the fair and draws attention to us.

"What?" Tom drawls as he shoves his hands into his hoodie pockets. "Can we not come and say hi?"

Finn's shoulders tense as Joel places his hand on his arm to pull him back before he causes a scene. I wish they'd just ignore us, let us go on with our lives, but they've got a vendetta against me.

My stomach acid crashes into my sternum, bile rising in my throat.

"You can fuck off," Finn grumbles, taking a step closer. "I don't know what your obsession is with us. Unless you want a repeat of the pub."

Tom tilts back his head and barks out a laugh. "Obsession?

More like trying to get justice for our friend. Who was once upon a time, your friend, too, Finn."

I see the hatred in Finn's eyes. I haven't taken a single breath, I don't know if I can. "He tried to kill my fucking sister, you asshole. What justice do we need to serve other than for him to rot in jail forever?"

"Because that bitch cheated on him, made him go crazy," Tom shouts.

Finn's fists clench, and I flinch from the aggression in his voice.

"But you'd know all about that… wouldn't you, Finn?"

"Shut up," he growls.

My brows furrow as I glance between them, not fully understanding.

"What?" Julian laughs. "Doesn't she know?"

Every bone in my body begins to tremble as I dart my eyes between them pathetically.

"Oh god. She doesn't know." Tom swats Julian's shoulder.

"Know what?" I bite.

Tom chuckles before poking his tongue into his cheek. Then his eyes flick to mine, and I freeze. "That your brother gave your secrets away. He came straight to us as soon as he found out you cheated on Ben."

Suddenly, I'm being knocked off the Earth's axis.

No. No. That can't be true. Finn wouldn't do that to me.

My eyes find Finn's, and I see the sheer panic behind them.

Everything crashes into me at once, so intense I can't breathe.

I blink, and a tear rolls down my cheek.

"Please tell me that's not true," I rasp to him, barely recognising my own voice.

"He's lying," Finn dismisses, but the guilt is written all over his face. "I didn't say anything, Ivy."

Tom snorts. "Really, Finn? I still have the text messages. If you want to see them, Ivy. To know that your own brother stabbed you in the back, but rightfully so, brought you to justice."

I shake my head over and over, staring at my brother in disbelief.

"Tell me that's not true."

"Ivy—"

"How could you do that to me?" I whisper beneath my rolling tears.

"Wait—" He steps forward.

"How could you lie to them about that?"

"Ivy, listen—"

I take a large step back. "No. Don't you dare. Don't you fucking dare."

My hands begin to shiver uncontrollably. I spare him one more glance before I walk away as quickly as possible.

"Ivy, wait. Let me explain."

My head remains low as I fold my arms over my chest.

"Ivy, I fucked up, okay? Ben, he was—"

"I don't care what Ben was doing." I whip my body towards him and grit my teeth. "I care about the fact you made up a lie that put me in the fucking hospital. Ben only freaked out because someone told him I cheated, he reared us off a bridge because of that reason. I almost fucking died, Finn. How could you do that to me?"

Finn's face crumbles, red eyes glistening. "I-I panicked, okay? I never thought it would lead to that. I knew he wasn't good enough for you, I know you needed to break up with him."

"Then why didn't you just talk to me like a normal human being?" I laugh, but my voice is hoarse. Tears continue to stream down my face at the humiliation of what he's done. "I don't understand why you'd do something so cruel."

I shake my head dismissively and turn back around again, needing to get out of here before I break down.

"Ivy—"

"Leave me alone, Finn. I don't want to talk to you right now."

Or ever.

Finn doesn't follow me after I speed off through the fair. An arm clings onto mine, and I feel Daisy step into me. "That's so messed up." She brings me into a hug. "I'm so sorry, Ivy. I can't believe Finn would do something like that."

I sniffle, incapable of words right now.

We stay like this for a long while, and I'm grateful she doesn't say too much, she holds me tight as I cry into her shoulder whilst she strokes my arms.

We might have had our differences in the past, but I know she has my back.

CHAPTER 42
JJ WOODFORD

I don't want to believe what I just heard, but Finn's guilt is imprinted into his body language.

Ivy walks away with Daisy, and when I move to go after her, Tom steps towards Finn. "Oops, did I say something I shouldn't?"

"You fucking asshole." Finn raises his fist and attempts to swing, and I tug him back at the last moment. He's too drunk and fired up to fight right now, and even though I'm annoyed at him for his choices, I'm not going to let him get into a brawl.

"Let me go." He wriggles in my grip.

"Not a fucking chance."

I glance at Tom, who raises an amused eyebrow at us. The rest of the boys behind him look equally entertained. Joel and Cal tug Finn back before he gets himself arrested.

We drag him to the beach, away from the fair.

Finn releases a long groan and eventually rips himself from us, and when I stare back at him, his eyes are red-rimmed.

"What the fuck are you doing, Finn?" I ask angrily. "This is a family event."

"I need a drink," he slurs.

I shake my head and shove him lightly to snap some sense into him. "Are you hearing yourself right now? You're wasted and you're not going to do yourself any favours."

Finn's chest heaves as he swipes a hand over his jaw.

"Why would you do that to her?" I lower my voice.

He scoffs. "What do you care?"

"Because that is not something you do to your sister."

"Don't you think I've lived with that guilt for years, JJ?" He steps towards me but stumbles in the sand. "Don't you think the reason I drink is because I know I almost killed her?"

I blink at the harshness of his voice.

"I hate myself for it. Every single day."

My head turns to Joel and Cal as they look back at their friend with deep concern.

"Yet you kept lying to her," I state. "You should have told her."

Finn squares up to me, his beer-tinged breath fanning my face. "Stop telling me things I already fucking know."

I clench my jaw. "This could have been resolved and worked through on your own time, now she's found out through that fucking idiot. Do you even care about your relationship with her?"

"You know nothing about us," he hisses.

"Oh, I know plenty."

His eyes narrow at me, and he shoves my shoulder. "Oh fuck off." He waves a hand. "If you're going to stand there and try to tell me what I should and shouldn't have done, I don't want to hear it. I don't care."

I raise my brows. "You don't care that you hurt her?"

"Fuck off, JJ," he spits. "Just get out of my face."

My tongue pokes into my cheek at his words. "Keep pushing away your friends, Finn. Soon you'll have no one left if you keep acting like this."

"I don't need you." His nostrils flare. "I've never needed you."

His aggressive words strike my chest.

"You don't need me?" I rasp. "Like I haven't had to pick you up after every time you passed out from drinking too much, all the times I've tried to encourage you to get help, all the times I've sat with you when you've cried."

Finn's eyes water, but he turns his nose up at me. "Leave me alone," he grits through his teeth. "I don't fucking need you, JJ."

"So you can drink yourself stupid? No."

"Come on, Finn." Joel steps in. "Stop this. Let's get you home."

Finn's expression twists. "I ain't going home."

"Yeah, you are," I say, folding my arms over my chest.

"No."

I reach for him and he swerves my grip, his fist raising in response. I pause and stare at him without moving.

"Go on then," I heave. "Hit me. If that's going to make you feel better. Hit. Me."

Finn's teeth clench together as he watches me. He eventually lowers his fist and steps towards me. "Leave. Me. Alone," he says, each word a punch without the action. "Go, JJ. I don't want you here."

I shake my head in disbelief. "You really want me to go?"

"Fucking leave me alone!"

My gaze flicks to Joel and Cal, who share uneasy glances with me.

"We've got him," Cal says quietly.

"The fuck you do." Finn waves a hand and begins to walk off in the opposite direction with a sway in his step.

I watch as he moves away, and Joel and Cal follow after him.

A curse word falls from my lips as I turn back to the fair

and draw my phone out from my pocket. I call Ivy and raise it to my ear.

"Hi." Her voice breaks.

"Ivy, I'm so fucking sorry."

"It's not your fault." She sniffles.

"Are you okay?"

It's a stupid question. Of course she's not okay.

"No."

"Where are you?"

Ivy's silent for a few moments. "Aren't you with Finn?"

"No, he made it evident he doesn't want me to be around him. Joel and Cal are with him. I'm not going to be his babysitter. I want to be with you. Where are you?"

"By the candy floss stand."

"Don't move. I'm on my way."

I cut off the call and head back into the fair, keeping my eyes out for a candy floss stand. It doesn't take long for me to spot Ivy with her hands wrapped around herself, with Daisy beside her.

After pushing through the crowds of people with a determined stride, she turns her head, and her eyes find mine. I roam her blotchy face, my lips twitching downwards into a frown.

When I reach her, I don't say anything, I pull her into a hug, and she exhales a sigh of relief. "I'm sorry," I whisper into her hair. "I'm so fucking sorry, Ivy. I can't believe he would do something like that to you."

She squeezes her eyes shut as I cradle the back of her head with my hand, embracing her firmly but gently.

I pull back and take her face between my hands. "I know you're not okay, but I'm not gonna leave you. Okay?"

Daisy hikes her thumb over her shoulder. "Uh, I'm gonna go. I'll text you, Ivy. And whenever you need me. I'll be there."

"Thanks, Dais." She glances at her quickly, flashing a grateful smile.

When she leaves, we make our way home.

"Finn's going to be a mess. No doubt drinking himself into oblivion."

I kiss her head again. "It's okay to be angry at him right now, regardless of his issues."

"I tell myself I don't care, but I do."

"Of course you're going to care," I admit. "But you need to think of yourself right now, and if you want space. That's perfectly valid."

I stop us, wrapping my arm over her shoulder and tugging her into my side.

"Yeah."

"Do you want to talk about it?"

"No," she whispers. "I'd rather ignore it for tonight because I'm breaking inside."

I rest my forehead on the crown of her head. "Whatever you need, princess. I'm gonna be right here."

CHAPTER 43
IVY THOMPSON

The entire journey home, I felt numb.

JJ held my hand and brushed his thumb over my knuckles every few seconds as we walked back to the house in silence. Every step made my shoulders sink lower and lower until I was completely weighed down.

How could he do that to me?

Why would he do that to me?

I'll never understand.

The house is quiet when we return, and my parents are most likely asleep. We creep upstairs, and JJ follows me into my bedroom. I strip myself of my clothes and climb into bed with JJ behind me.

I lay my head on my pillow and stare up at the ceiling. JJ shuffles next to me, wrapping an arm around the back of my neck and tugging me into his bare chest. I exhale a long sigh.

My eyes burn, and no matter how much I want to cry, I refuse to.

He made his decision. He chose to humiliate and betray me.

"Stop thinking so loudly," JJ whispers into my temple. "Sleep."

I screw my eyes shut and shake my head. "I don't think I'm going to be able to sleep."

"Then talk to me," he murmurs before rolling me onto my side so we face each other.

"I don't know why he would do that. I can't wrap my head around it. It's spiteful and completely uncalled for, and yet, he still didn't tell me. He lied to me this whole time, he watched me fall apart. It makes me so angry."

JJ purses his lips. "I don't know either. He clearly wanted to break you guys up, and went the wrong way about it. I'm trying to understand, but I can't because I would never even dream of doing that to someone, let alone my sibling."

"He could have spoken to me," I mumble harshly. "That's all he had to do."

"I know, princess, I know. I'm not agreeing with him." He strokes a hand down my back. "Finn has always dealt with things the wrong way, and he needs to understand that his choices have consequences."

I nod in agreement. "I've tried to talk to him about his issues, but he refuses to get help. I don't know what else I could have done."

"It's hard to help someone who doesn't want to help themselves," he says simply. "As tough as that is to hear, you can't save him if he's not ready to save himself."

My eyes close in defeat. A wave rolls through my stomach, churning like cement.

"Sleep," JJ says delicately in my ear, and I take a breath.

I nuzzle my head into JJ's chest and attempt to sleep, knowing I'm here with him and no one else.

A LOUD CRASH coming from downstairs stirs us both from our sleep. JJ's arms tighten around me in defence. I push my hand into the bed and sit up, blinking through my hazy eyes.

"What the hell was that?" I rasp.

"I don't know." JJ shakes his head before leaping from the bed. "Stay here."

"Hell no," I say under a harsh breath.

JJ turns back to me with a pinned stare before he opens the door and checks downstairs. I grab my dressing gown and slip it over my arms before walking onto the landing and peeking my head over the bannister.

"What on earth is going on?" My father's voice has me jumping out of my skin as he emerges from their bedroom.

"I-I don't know."

"Finn?" JJ's voice echoes through the house. "Finn. Fuck. Someone call an ambulance."

We both scurry down the stairs, mortified at the sight of Finn lying on the floor with broken bottles around him. JJ is on his knees before him as he chokes up froth. JJ attempts to roll him onto his side as he vomits across the wooden floor.

"Oh my god." I raise a shaky hand to my lips before rushing back upstairs to grab my phone.

With trembling fingers, I call an ambulance as my parents surround my brother, panic laced through their voices as I try to answer the questions they're asking me as best as I can.

"He's having a seizure," JJ cries out, and my father snatches the phone from my hands, demanding an ambulance come now.

I stand back, tears leaking from my eyes.

My stomach rolls. I knew this was going to happen. I knew he'd get himself into this state. I pray he didn't overdo it this time because I'll never live with the guilt.

We've been sitting in the hospital waiting room for two hours.

Finn needed to have his stomach pumped, and I hate to

imagine how much alcohol he drank after we left the fair. Now they're making sure he's stable before we can go in to see him.

My parents haven't said much after we explained what happened.

They might blame me, but I was protecting my own sanity at that moment.

I take a walk down to the cafeteria, but because it's late, it's closed. JJ follows close behind me.

"Ivy," he calls out.

"It's my fault."

"Stop." He shakes his head, reaching for me. "It is not your fault."

"They're going to blame me."

JJ's jaw ticks. "No. They're not. It's not your fault. Do not think that."

My eyes sting as I glance up at him. "We should have stayed with him. What was I thinking?"

"You were processing the information, Ivy." He cradles my face with his hand. "You had every right to take some space."

My bottom lip trembles. "He could have died. He could have been somewhere unsafe."

"He's okay, princess," he says to reassure me. "He's in the best place he can be."

I squeeze my eyes shut, and fresh tears stream down my face. JJ pushes them away with the pad of his thumb. We stand there for a while before he takes my hand and guides us back to the waiting room.

My mother glances up at me as we reappear, she doesn't even try to smile, and it shatters me to pieces.

"I'm sorry," I whisper when I reach them.

"Why are you sorry, honey?"

"I should have been there."

My father clears his throat, eyes set forward. "We should

have helped him sooner, after you told your mother about his habits. We should have done more. I didn't think it would ever lead to this."

"I think he needs to go to a rehabilitation centre," JJ says simply. "I don't know if he's going to be able to heal if he doesn't."

My parents share a glance, and the thought alone puts into perspective how out of control this has become.

"We all failed him," I croak.

JJ smooths over my knuckles with his finger. "Maybe so, but we've all been going through shit."

I watch as my mother stands and wraps her arms around me. I cry silently into her shoulder as she smooths back my hair with her hand. "It's not your fault." She shakes her head adamantly. "We should have taken action when you told me. I didn't realise it was this serious. I tried to talk to him about it, but he downplayed it, and now I have to live with knowing I ignored the signs. God, I'm an awful mother."

My father steps to our side and attempts to draw her into a hug. "You're not an awful mother, Andrea. We just need to be there for our son now."

The doctors let us in to see Finn when he's stable. My eyes roam over him as he lies in the hospital bed with tubes taped to his arms and hooked up to the machine beside him. He looks broken beyond belief.

My parents rush to his side. Finn says nothing, he looks disoriented and confused. I stand back as JJ patiently stands beside me, his fingers gently brushing my hip, but we know we can't show affection at a time like this.

Not when he's recovering.

Finn listens to what my parents say, managing a nod here and there until his eyes flick around the room and land on me. I freeze and swallow at the sadness that washes over his face.

"I'm sorry," he chokes out as my parents turn to look at me. "Ivy, I'm so sorry."

My throat feels like razor blades as I attempt to speak. I wrap my arms around myself and hold on tightly.

"You should rest," I say instead.

Finn's mouth opens, but when my father rests a hand on his shoulder, he closes it again. "She's right. You should rest."

"Do you think you could give us a moment?" my mum asks and subtly flashes us the leaflet the doctor gave her about rehabilitation treatment.

We both leave in understanding. This isn't going to be an easy conversation, but it's important, and Finn's health needs attention.

Once we're outside in the waiting area again, JJ holds my hand in my lap. We stay quiet because I don't know what there is to say, and I'm grateful not to be bombarded by a million different questions.

An hour later, they emerge from Finn's room. My mum wipes her eyes, and my dad wraps an arm around her shoulder. I hold my breath as I watch them, unsure if I want to know how the talk went.

"He wants to see you," my mother says softly.

"Okay." I lick my lips.

I glance at JJ, who offers me sincere eyes. "Do you want me to come with you?"

"I think I need to do it by myself." I suck in a breath.

"Of course." He gives my fingers a squeeze. "I'll be here if you need me."

CHAPTER 44
IVY THOMPSON

It takes me a moment to pluck up the courage to enter Finn's hospital room. My shaking fingers raise to the door, and I push myself in before his green eyes settle on me. I enter quietly, allowing the door to shut as I walk to the end of his bed.

Finn's chest shudders as he studies me with dark bags under his eyes and cracked lips. It hurts to see him like this, a spear to the chest, but something inside me is pulling me back.

"Ivy," he croaks with watery eyes. "I'm sorry. I never meant to hurt you."

My lips purse and I look down. His gaze is far too intense for my liking.

"I wish I knew why I did it, but—"

"You must have known why you did it," I say, snapping my head back towards him. "Because you continued to lie about it."

Finn swallows as he watches me. "Ben wasn't good enough for you."

"So you decided to make up a lie that made me look like a cheater?"

He curses and covers his hand with the cannula hanging out the back. "No, I didn't do it to hurt you. You deserved better. I wanted better for you, but my plan backfired. I just wanted someone who actually cared for you."

I sniffle and fold my arms over my chest. "Why didn't you talk to me about it?"

"I tried," he admits. "But you thought I was just trying to cause a rift between you."

My eyes narrow at him. "You brought it up once, and you never said anything about him not being good enough for me. All you said was that you didn't like it, and I decided to ignore you because that's not a good enough reason to break up with someone."

I stare back at my brother as he sinks into the pillows.

"What's the real reason you wanted us to break up?"

Finn's mouth remains closed for a moment, and I tilt my head at him.

"Tell me, Finn."

He heaves a heavy breath. "We went to a party on the other side of town, and he thought he was being clever and sneaky, but I saw him flirting and getting close with other girls," he admits, his gaze lowering. "I don't know what else happened, but I didn't like it. I confronted him about it, and we almost got into a fight, but he said what he was doing was friendly and that he loved you. I hated his guts after that."

I flinch from his words. "Why didn't you just tell me that instead?"

"Because I knew you wouldn't have believed me. You would have assumed I was only saying it to get between the two of you."

My forehead creases at his words. "I would have believed you because you're my brother."

His lips part, inhaling a breath. "I went about it in the wrong way."

I don't respond, sweeping my gaze over his face.

"And I'm sorry." His voice cracks. "I wasn't thinking. I should never have lied and made you the bad guy. If I knew what he was going to do, I wouldn't have ever said anything."

I shudder at the devastation in his voice.

Finn blinks, and a tear rolls down his cheek. "I've lived with this guilt for years, and every time I see your face, I'm reminded of what I've done. I almost lost you because I stupidly made up a rumour to get you away from him, when I should have just told you the truth. I don't know what I was thinking. I was fucking desperate, and I'll live with that regret for the rest of my life."

"Finn—"

"No," he breathes out sharply. "Let me finish."

I manage a nod.

"You might hate me," he whispers beneath his flooding tears. "I *want* you to hate me for what I've done and what I've caused you, but I want you to know that I have hated myself every single day since I lied to them. I knew what I did, and as time went on, I struggled to tell the truth because of the shame that swarmed me. That's why I bury myself in alcohol to make the pain go away, to make me forget that I'm a bad person, to make me forget that I almost lost you."

My throat aches as I attempt to swallow. "You're not a bad person. You just made a really bad choice."

"I am," he shoots back at me, eyes burning. "I'm a fucking monster, Ivy. I won't blame you if you never want to speak to me again for what I've done. I deserve it."

Two more tears roll over his cheeks, and it cracks my heart into pieces.

"I want you to get better," I confess.

Finn's gaze strains.

My lips roll together as I take a step closer to his bed. "You need help, Finn. We've been trying to tell you for months, but you don't want to listen. And just now you've admitted you use alcohol to push away your pain and make you forget. That isn't healthy. You need professional help."

He glances away and raises his hand to brush his tear-stained cheeks.

"You had to have your stomach pumped," I continue. "You could have seriously hurt yourself last night, Finn. We could have lost you."

"Probably would have been for the better," he mumbles.

I stare at him incredulously until he finds my eyes again. "Why would you say something like that?"

Finn shakes his head.

"You might have done what you did, but you're still my brother, and I still love you."

He squeezes his eyes shut, as if the words are too painful for him.

"I want to see you get better," I grind out between my teeth. "I don't want to see you give up or end up drunk in a ditch somewhere no one can find you. I want my brother back. I need him. Don't you want to get better? I know you don't want to keep relying on alcohol the way you do."

Finn curses and rolls his head to look up at the ceiling, eyes glossy. "They want me to go to a rehabilitation centre," he grumbles with a clenched jaw.

"It's probably the best place for you. Then you can talk to professionals and get a therapist, and try to work through everything in your head. I want to see you get better, and I want you to want to get better. Because this isn't you, and I want *you* back."

"It's not going to help." He blows out an exasperated breath.

"It won't with an attitude like that."

Finn wipes his eyes once more.

"If you don't do this," I say after a moment of silence. "Then I don't know what will be left of our relationship."

He whips his head towards me. "What?"

"I'm not threatening you," I shake my head. "But you need to work this through with someone and figure out your own head. I want to see you get better, but I can't guarantee that if you continue on like this, that I'm going to be there time and time again when I'm literally begging you to get help."

He buries his head into his hands. "Fuck."

"Please, Finn. Please. You can't keep going on like this. Mum and Dad are in pieces. You need to see that you need help."

He glances away as another tear rolls down his cheek.

"This could have ended up far worse, and I don't want to see you in this position again," I whisper. "Please think about it. For yourself. I know you're not pleased about it, but there is no shame in getting help. We will all support you through it."

"I don't want to lose you," he breathes.

My lips tremble. "Then do this for yourself. Please."

Finn turns back to look at me, fear evident in his eyes. When I think he's not going to say anything more, he eventually says, "Okay."

CHAPTER 45
JJ WOODFORD

The last few days haven't been fun, to say the least.

Seeing Finn in that hospital bed, disheveled and broken. It hurts.

But it hurts more knowing he made up lies about Ivy to get her to stop seeing Ben, which could have resulted in her death.

We all noticed his drinking habits; I should have tried to do something about it sooner before it ended up like this. Now he's been taken off to a private rehabilitation centre. He needs it. He needs to find his peace again.

He carries so much guilt and hatred for himself; it's something he needs to work through on his own and with professional help. I might be mad at him, but he's still like a brother to me.

I fear that if I push him away, it won't help his recovery.

When I head downstairs in the morning, Ivy is sitting at the edge of the back door with her feet on the patio and her knees drawn towards her chest.

I pause behind her and glance down at the way her head is tipped back and admiring the clouds, not sensing I'm here.

I perch beside her, and she flinches a little at my unexpected arrival.

"Uh." I clear my throat. "I've been thinking, I should probably go home."

Ivy's face falls. "What? Why?"

"Because I don't want to be in the way, your parents probably need the space—"

"No," she cuts over me. "Don't go."

I blink at the sudden fear in her voice.

"Please." She exhales and reaches for my hand. "I want you to stay."

My eyes flick down to our entwined fingers. "Are you sure?"

"Yes. I need you here."

"Okay," I say softly.

"My parents don't mind that you're here at all." She shakes her head. "They would have said something by now if they did. You're not in the way; you could never be in the way."

"Okay," I whisper as Ivy's face relaxes. "How are you feeling?"

She shrugs once. "I don't know. A little numb, but I know it's what's best for him. It's going to take some time to get over what he did."

"Yeah, I think so too."

"I kinda just wanna get out of the house. Distract myself, you know?"

"Then let's get out of the house."

"And do what?"

"I have an idea or two," I admit, something that would be good for both of us.

I glance over her perfect face, and the need I've felt to film her returns. I've had so many visions of her, creative visions, dream visions. Real visions.

"What are we gonna do?" she asks.

I study her mouth. "Remember when I told you that I like making films?"

"Yeah…" She trails off, sounding confused.

"Well, I wanted to create something this summer, although I didn't really know what I wanted to make it on," I start, and she holds me with those big eyes. So curious. So beautiful. "But when I got here, I realised that I only wanted one test subject."

She blinks once. "The beach?"

I smile at how innocent she can be sometimes. Instead, I shake my head. "*You.*"

"What?"

"Yeah," I whisper. "It's all I can think about."

"Why?"

"Because you'd look incredible on film."

Pink bleeds into her cheeks, and she laughs hesitantly. "Incredible is a bit of a stretch."

I tilt her chin softly, exploring those eyes again. "To me, you are."

"What would you want me to do?"

"Stand on the beach. I want to capture you with the sand and the waves."

Ivy blinks in surprise. "As charming as that is, I don't think I'm cut out for it."

"Why?"

"Because I'm not photogenic."

"Liar."

She tilts her head to the side and shoots me a knowing look. All I do is grin back. "It's a no."

"Ohhh come on," I say optimistically. "Don't ruin the fun. You wanted a distraction, and this is the perfect distraction."

"I'm sure hundreds of other girls in this town would eat up the opportunity. They'd look better doing it, too," she says before wrapping her arms around her knees.

"I don't want hundreds of other girls. I want you. I've made that very clear."

She watches me for a long moment, eyes a little weary. "What if they come out rubbish?"

I slip my arm around her waist and tug her to me. She exhales a small breath. "No such thing, princess. Come on, do something out of your comfort zone with me. I promise it'll be worth it."

She swallows apprehensively. "Fine," she huffs. "But only for thirty minutes."

A smile stretches over my face. "That's all I'll need."

An hour later, we head down to the beach.

It's still early, and we've seen only a couple of people out walking their dogs. Ivy's hands bunch together in front of her, tugging at her fingers. She's wearing a lilac sundress with white flowers that makes me feel out of control. Her blonde hair is resting on the tips of her shoulders, and a splash of make-up—although her freckles are still on full display.

"You're going to have to tell me what to do," she says as she paces the beach barefoot.

I grip my camera in my hand and smile. "Don't worry. I've got you."

When I click record, I already have her perfectly in the frame. The lighting of the sun rising behind her is spot on—an equal mixture of the blue and yellow skies from the beautiful sunrise, down to the clear water and golden sand—and then there's Ivy.

In that purple dress that makes my brain short-circuit.

It's a stunning shot, and all she has to do is stand there.

Everything else seems to fade away.

She is the vision.

"Walk towards me," I direct, and she does. Very, *very* slowly.

"Like this?"

"Exactly like that," I rasp.

The wind makes an appearance every few moments, allowing strands of her gorgeous hair to flap around her face. I move closer until Ivy places her hand over the camera. "That is too close."

I keep filming her and smile. "Trust me, it looks good."

She huffs out a breath and drops her hand. Her eyes look anywhere but at the camera.

"Look at me," I demand softly, and she does reluctantly.

I bring the camera in closer, getting a flawless shot of her bottle-green eyes. Her lashes brush her cheekbone with a caress, and when those eyes open once more and she stares directly at the camera, I know nothing will ever look as sensational as her.

The wind whips her hair again, and she tucks a piece behind her ear that becomes stuck against her eyelashes. Her movements are delicate, which looks so smooth and fluid on film. There is no possible way I can take my eyes off her.

"You're so beautiful, Ivy," I comment, not being able to keep it to myself.

Her cheeks flush, and she laughs. "Stop."

The way her eyes light up, even though she's embarrassed. And her laughter. Oh, that pretty laugh. She is a movie in herself. To be studied every minute of every day, without fail. A case study, because how can someone be this breathtaking?

"Complimenting you? Never."

Ivy follows my lead after I ask for shots against the sand, dipping her toes into the sea. She might not think she belongs on camera, but she does. I can't wait to edit together what I shot today because I want her to see how I see her, how breathtaking she is. This will be in my heart and memory forever.

"Are we done now?" she asks. "It's been longer than thirty minutes."

It has. A lot longer.

Instead, I place the camera onto the ground, still recording. I walk over to her, and she stares at me with confusion in her eyes. But I reach down and hoist her up around my waist, clutching onto her soft thighs. Her arms automatically latch onto my neck as I tug her towards me.

I waste no time in pressing my lips to hers, spinning us around as she squeals against my mouth and laughs. The feeling is euphoric. She clasps a hand on the back of my neck and deepens the kiss, our tongues brushing together.

Our hearts flush against one another, beating in sync as I clutch her tighter, enjoying every second with her. I place her down and hold her waist in my hands before picking her up, and she screams. "No," she heaves. "Don't throw me into the water."

"I wasn't going to," I chuckle.

"I don't believe you for a second."

I fake gasp. "How dare you think so low of me."

And then we laugh, my hands remaining at her sides as I bury my hand into the back of her hair and tug her lips to mine again, desperate for another taste.

The kiss is filled with passion and longing, and it lights up my heart with pure fire.

A droplet of water hits my cheek, but I don't pull my lips away from hers. It starts to rain as if we've been in a drought for the past two months. We gasp for air, the sky rumbling and grey clouds looming over us quickly.

"Well, shit."

I grab her hand and run over to my camera and our belongings. We chuckle like teenagers, a thrill of excitement zapping through me. Even if my T-shirt is beginning to completely soak through.

Instead of rushing back to the house, Ivy runs towards the beach huts and throws herself into the closest one. We both stare at each other, wet, and chests heaving as we attempt to catch our breath. I drop my stuff down onto the floor, and Ivy's eyes flare with heat as she strolls past me and grabs my camera.

"What are you doing?"

"Distracting ourselves." She bites her lip before hitting record and placing it on a table. "And besides, I think the cameraman should get some screen time. He's far too handsome."

Holy hell. My cock throbs at her words as she stops directly in front of me.

There's my confident girl.

"Whose beach hut is this?" I ask breathlessly, not wanting to be interrupted.

"Don't know, don't care," she says before raising onto her toes and catching my mouth in another hot kiss.

I don't bring up the question again.

When I taste raindrops on her tongue, I groan. My fingers knead into the sides of her body, and I shove her into the wall, trying to avoid the furniture and objects that occupy it. I pull her up around my waist again and press my crotch into hers, she groans at my growing cock.

I pull my mouth away from hers and dip my lips to her neck, teasing the skin. "I've dreamt about fucking you in a dress like this," I rasp, and she whimpers, gripping onto me tighter. "I've wanted to bend you over your kitchen counter and fuck you until you can't take it anymore. While this dress is hoisted up around your hips and your panties are at your ankles."

"Yes," she whines.

I press her further into the wall with my weight and drop

a hand to slide between her legs and over her thong. I groan when I find her wet, soaked through the material. "Mmm," I hum into her skin. "My filthy, filthy girl."

When I sink my finger inside her, she cries out, and I love that we don't have to be quiet. I want to listen to every moan, whimper, and scream that I draw from her.

Slowly, I pump, and her wetness drips down my fingers. "JJ—" Her head falls back slowly. "Yes."

I tease her clit with my thumb as I continue to push my fingers inside, feeling her walls clench around me. "You feel so good, princess," I whisper against her lips. "But I bet you'd feel so much better bouncing up and down on my cock."

A cry escapes her throat. "Fuck me," she begs. "Please. I want you to fuck me."

My eyes flare at her pretty little voice. I take my fingers out of her pussy, removing her underwear and pulling down my shorts, fisting my stupidly hard cock. I line it up against her soaked core and press her into the wall again. She slides down onto me as I guide her slowly.

"Ohhh fuck," she cries out as I push halfway in and we both groan. "Fuck. Oh fuck."

I kiss her jaw tenderly. "Relax, princess. Relax for me."

Her muscles loosen as I begin to thrust, but I don't push myself all the way in, not yet.

"That's it," I whisper as she slides down on my cock without resistance. "Hold on."

She does and I fuck her. She cries out and whimpers at the same time. The sounds floating around my head are like pure ecstasy. "Oh god." She bites her lip. "That feels so good."

I move my hands under her thighs, pinning them to the wall so I can fuck her deeper. Ivy cries out at the new sensations, and her entire body shakes around me as I pound her, but not too hard that the wall hurts her back.

"Come on," I grunt in her ear. "Come all over my cock. I

want you to come for me. Show me how much you fucking want it."

She screws her eyes shut before her walls tighten again. I know she's close because I recognise her breathing rhythm that always changes when she's about to climax, and I want to watch every second of it.

I drop my thumb back to her clit and generously swirl circles over her as she shudders in my hold. Her fingernails dig into my skin for leverage, and a minute later, she shatters around me. I fuck her harder and claim those lips as she whimpers into my mouth, calling my name, which only turns me into a savage beast because I can't get enough. I'll never get enough.

"Ohhh, fuck. That's it. 'Atta girl."

Ivy spurs nonsense from her mouth as she rides out her climax as I pound into her, until she's spent and panting.

I rip her from the wall and take a seat on the big lounge chair in the corner, bringing Ivy with me. She straddles my hips as I sit back. I slap my thigh and smirk at her, flushed cheeks and dazed eyes. That orgasm must have sent her head spinning.

"Come take a ride," I say deeply. "Show me what you've got."

A part of me expects her to shake her head in protest, but to my surprise, she raises herself over my cock, lifting her dress before lowering herself down. We both moan at the same time. And then she rides me. She fucking rides me.

"Like this?" she asks, holding my gaze.

I fist the back of her hair. "Yes," I grunt. "Just like that."

My eyes don't move from hers. I can't physically look anywhere else. I tug down the neckline of her dress, straps falling over her shoulders. Glancing at her scar, it's clear she doesn't seem to care that her chest is exposed to me.

She shouldn't care, because this woman is a form of art.

Beautiful in every sense.

Beyond words.

Beyond measure.

She's fucking mine.

I move closer, kissing her delicate skin but resisting the urge to flip her over and fucking devour her. She throws her head back as I kiss her scar and gently move down to her hardened nipples.

The way she's grinding down on my cock is like the most addictive drug. Her hip movements make me forget where I am, and what my name is. She's hypnotising and I'm not even ashamed to admit it.

"Never let anyone treat you less than what you're worth," I whisper into her skin, keeping my hand in the back of her short hair. "Because you are worth everything in this world. And you're fucking mine."

Ivy gnaws on her lip as she moves quicker, squeezing the life out of my cock. I'm so deep inside her that I'm close to shooting my load, but I hold off for the time being. "Because you're beautiful," I tell her, tightening my fingers against her scalp. Those eyes ping open to mine, full of light and safety. "Tell me. Tell me you're beautiful."

"I'm beautiful." She doesn't hesitate, and I smile, kissing her with pride.

"Yeah, you are," I say over her lips. "And you should be told every single day."

Her body jolts and she screams, riding out her orgasm on me. I watch her fall apart, and I come straight after because there's no way I'm able to listen to her cry for me and not fall headfirst over the finish line.

I'm too wrapped up in her.

I'm too obsessed.

I'm too… attached.

My girl.

The climax we experience together goes on for a while, both of us having some kind of out-of-body experience.

One of a kind.

Because it's us.

She slumps into me, my cock throbbing from its sensitivity, but I don't want to remove myself from her yet.

I clutch the back of her head and smooth down her hair, kissing her temple. "God," I grumble. "You're so fucking hot when you let go."

Her eyes peek up at me, and she laughs, slightly embarrassed, but I know it'll go away with time. "I like being on top," she admits with a shy smile.

"Me too." I grin. "Let's do it again."

CHAPTER 46
JJ WOODFORD

After a long run on the beach, I'm sweating from every crevice of my body to the point I had to go shirtless for the last twenty minutes. Even though the beaming sun was dipping in and out of the clouds, the sweltering heat was blistering.

I purposely left my phone at home because I needed some alone time. Especially after knowing everything going on with Finn.

I don't know how long Finn is going to be in rehab, but I want to be here when he gets back to tell him that I'm here to support him, even if I don't agree with what he did to Ivy. He needs stability, otherwise I fear he'll end up in a worse state.

Soon, summer will be over, and I won't have the luxury of visiting this beach. It's the perfect spot for refreshing your mind and body—lungs included.

My chest heaves as I reach the house. Andrea is in the kitchen making food. I catch my breath, and she glances up at me, red rings around her eyes.

"Hi, Andrea," I greet as I throw my sweaty T-shirt back on. "How are you?"

"So-so." She forces a smile. "How are you doing, JJ?"

I shrug. "I'm okay. Have you heard from Finn or the doctors?"

"Yeah, a little."

"How is he?"

Andrea's face tightens before she exhales a long breath. "Struggling," she confesses. "I feel so awful, I had no idea his drinking was this bad. I should have listened to Ivy when she told me. God, I hate myself for it."

My heart strains. "I saw the signs, and I should have done or said something sooner. I didn't know he was struggling with what happened to Ivy."

"Me neither," she sighs. "We've been away a lot and I blame us—"

"You can't blame yourself. Finn shut us all out, I just wish I did more."

Andrea nods. "Me, too. At least I know he's getting the care and attention he needs."

"If there is anything I can do," I say gently. "Or if I'm in the way, please tell me to go."

"No." She gives me a sincere smile. "You're not in the way, JJ. Not at all."

"I want to see him before I leave. I don't know when he's coming home, but I would like that."

Andrea places her hands on the counter. "Yeah, I definitely think he needs his loved ones around him."

"Of course. I'm gonna go shower."

"I'm making lunch." Andrea turns back to the kitchen. "So come down when you're ready to eat."

"Thank you."

After I head upstairs and jump straight in the shower, my phone lights up on my bed as I get changed. My heart stops in my chest when I find three missed calls from my father.

"Shit," I curse before reaching for it and tapping on the notification.

I return the call and place my phone against my ear,

anxiously chewing on my lip. I haven't heard from my father in a few days, but multiple missed calls? Something is wrong.

My stomach flips like a rollercoaster. Oh fuck.

I perch on the edge of my bed, my knees giving out because I physically can't stand anymore. My teeth clamp down on my lip so hard I taste blood in my mouth.

Fuck. Fuck. Fuck.

"Pick up the phone, Dad," I heave, dropping my head into my hands. "Pick up."

The line cuts, and I hear his voice. "Hi, son."

"Dad?" I gasp, lifting my head and staring straight at the wall. "Is Mum okay? What happened? Did something happen?"

Every question I want to ask falls from my lips. All I can think about is Mum. My eyeballs burn, and I shake my head. My father breathes, and I grit my fist together. "JJ—" he starts. "Everything is okay."

I exhale a breath of relief. "Okay?" My voice wobbles.

"More than okay, in fact," he says, and I can hear the smile in his voice.

My chest blooms with warmth.

"Tell me," I beg.

"The new treatment the hospital has been trying with mum," he says slowly. "She's been showing results. Good results."

Tears gather in my eyes. "Really?" I whisper under a shuddering breath. "Oh my god."

"Amazing, isn't it? We've still got a long way to go, but it's a start, and she's been fighting." My dad's voice cracks, but there is so much happiness and relief behind the words. "She's always been a fighter, and us being here, supporting her every step of the way, is exactly what she needs right now. She needs as much optimism as possible."

I drop my head into my hands and release a small sob.

"Fuck," I curse because I don't know what else to say. My chest feels a thousand times lighter than it did before. The most amazing news I could possibly hear. "She's getting better?"

My dad hums softly. "They say it's very promising. They'll have more to report next week. That way they can see what exactly the treatment is doing, but they're certain it's going in the right direction."

"Can I talk to her? Is she there?" I mumble out my words, wiping my face free of tears.

"Of course," he says before I hear a muffled sound on the other line.

I clutch my phone tight to my ear, desperate to hear my mother's voice. "JJ?"

I'm crying again, cheeks damp and vision blurry. "Mum," I rasp as I shatter into pieces. "How are you?"

"I'm doing okay, my boy. And you?"

My head shakes. I don't want to talk about myself. This is about her. "Fine," I say as I straighten my spine. "I heard about the treatment. That's amazing, Mum. So amazing. I can't wait to see you. I miss you."

I hear her sniffle, and my lungs painfully squeeze. "I miss you too, so much," she says, as if she's trying not to cry herself. "I'm so proud of you, you know that? I've always been so proud of you. I hope you're having a lovely summer away. Be sure to send pictures. You haven't sent any!"

A laugh rumbles from deep inside my chest. "Okay, okay." I grin. "I will. Sorry."

"What's been going on with you? Tell me, I want to hear what you've been up to."

"I met someone." I smile.

My mother gasps. "You have?"

"Yeah, and she's great."

"Oh, JJ," she swoons. "That's amazing. What is she like?"

I bite my bottom lip as Ivy flashes through my mind. "She's beautiful, and she's lovely, and she makes me so happy."

"Oh my goodness." Her joy radiates through the phone. "I'm so pleased for you."

"Hopefully soon she can meet you," I say optimistically.

"I'd love that. I can't wait to meet her. What's her name?"

"Ivy."

"Beautiful name."

"Beautiful indeed."

"Lots of things to look forward to when we get home," she says cheerily.

My cheeks ache from smiling too hard. "I can't wait."

"Me too, my boy. The doctor is coming over to check on me in a bit, so I'll let you go," she says, her voice full of warmth and hope. "I love you."

"I love you too, mum." I release a shuddering breath. "I'll call you soon, okay?"

"Of course, speak soon. I love you more."

"Not true."

When she laughs, my heart expands, and I wish I could be there with them, holding her hand and supporting my father. A family. But I know I'll see her soon, when she's better. "Take care of yourself, JJ."

Her words have my chest tightening. "You too."

The call ends and I pull the phone away from my ear. I stare at the screen for a long moment. A smile etches its way onto my lips, and I soar with an emotion beyond relief—it's all-consuming.

Sadness I'm not there, but reassurance that she's getting better.

And the first person I want to tell is Ivy.

After getting dressed and heading downstairs, Andrea is setting the table with Ivy, James plating up the food. She catches my eye and offers me a smile as sweet as sugar. I return the gesture, even though my eyes are still slightly blurry from crying a few moments ago.

Her head tilts, as if she knows something's up. I stare at her for a moment, signalling that I'll tell her later. She nods, and I smile further, our silent conversations mean the world to me.

She fucking gets me. We get each other. Without even trying.

That's what I adore about her. She's always observant, always watching, always understanding.

We sit and eat lunch together, talking about light topics because I know Finn has been the main conversation, and it's clear they need something else to talk about.

As soon as we clean up after our meal and dismiss ourselves from the table, I grab hold of Ivy in the upstairs hall. She blinks those massive green eyes at me, fanned by her long lashes.

"Hey." She smiles, making my soul melt.

She has no idea how powerful that smile is. One little flick of her lips and she could send me into an early grave.

"Grab ice cream with me," I say, tucking a strand of blonde hair behind her shoulder.

Her head tilts. "Ice cream?"

My eyes gleam with joy. "Yeah, please? I need to tell you something."

"Sure," she says before rising up onto her toes and kissing my cheek. "I'll meet you downstairs in a second."

I bathe in the warmth of her kiss, pleasantly surprised by the action, not taking it for granted. Her affection is my fucking weakness. I could live off her acts of tenderness for the rest of my life.

When I go downstairs and wait for her in the kitchen, I notice her parents watching a movie in the living room.

They're cuddled together, holding hands, and despite their position, they look restless. I can't imagine how difficult Finn's situation must be for them.

Ivy comes downstairs a few moments later. "Ready to go?" I ask when she joins me.

"Yeah." She smiles brightly.

She tells her parents we're going out, and they tell us to have a nice time. I lead her down the street until we reach the beachfront, the sun still high in the sky.

"What did you want to tell me?"

I suck down a breath and shove my hands into my pockets. "I got a call from my dad today."

Ivy's face falls slack. "Is everything okay?"

"Everything is good." I turn to her, not being able to fight the smile on my face. "Great, actually. Mum's new treatment has had good results, and they think it's the one that will make her better."

She claps a hand over her face, both of us stopping outside the ice cream shop. "Oh my god," she gasps through her fingers. "JJ, that's amazing!"

Then she's up on her toes and wrapping her arms around my neck, tugging me as close to her as possible. I smile gently and bury my head into her shoulder, telling myself that it's okay to be emotional.

"You're the first person I wanted to tell," I say into her ear, holding her tighter than before. "I was getting worried, I hadn't heard from my dad in a while."

"Thank you," she murmurs into my T-shirt. "For sharing it with me. I'm so pleased for you, JJ. I'm pleased for all of you."

I press a kiss to her neck and pull away slowly. My hands stay on her arms as I'm looking down at her. "I remember when you wished my mum a healthy recovery with your shot of sambuca on our first date."

Her eyes light up like fireworks. "You remember that?"

"I remember every moment with you, princess." I lean down to nuzzle my nose with hers. "Even if I wanted to forget, I couldn't."

Ivy's eyes flutter shut for a moment, and she presses a soft kiss to my lips. "You are so special," she whispers, and her words make me shiver. "To me, to Finn, to your parents. You are a breath of fresh air in this world. We're all lucky to have you."

I fist the back of her hair, tilting her neck to get better access to her lips. "Don't make me cry. I've already cried today, and that's one too many times for the year."

She laughs against my mouth, and it comforts me to the bone. "Let it out, JJ. I don't care, but you have to know how much you mean to me. In the short time I've known you, you've changed my life in ways you can't understand."

"I do understand," I groan, kissing her deeper. She hums in surprise when my tongue invades her mouth. "Because you've done the same to me."

Ivy gasps into the kiss, gripping my shoulders. For a moment, I forget we're standing outside the ice cream parlour until the man behind the counter clears his throat. I pull away from her but keep my arms firmly around her shoulders.

She buries her head into my chest, embarrassment swarming her, but I'm grinning ear to ear. "Sorry, man," I say to the owner who stares at us like disgusting horny teenagers. "We'll get whatever she wants."

Her head raises, and she walks to the counter, looking through the glass at the different selections of ice cream. I watch her cheeks remain tinted pink as she folds her arms over her chest. I smile at her innocence.

"Can we get hazelnut and strawberry, please?" she asks.

The man nods, and I sweep my arms around her from behind. "I wish I could tell Finn." I lower my head. "He always asks how she's doing."

She glances up at me over her shoulder. "You can soon. When he's home and better. I pray it helps him."

"I know." I sigh in agreement. "But I'm sure it will. I know he doesn't want to live with those demons anymore."

"He will get better," she says confidently.

"I think so too."

CHAPTER 47
IVY THOMPSON

The hazelnut and strawberry ice cream combo is unbeatable.

JJ doesn't agree as we sit on the wall, facing the sea as we munch on our sweet treat. "This is wrong on so many levels," he grunts.

I roll my eyes. "It's good."

"I promise you, princess, it's not."

I gently nudge my shoulder into him, and a dark splatter of ice cream hits his white T-shirt. I open my mouth in horror as I clap a hand over it to muffle my words.

"Oh my god, I'm so sorry," I say with a chuckle.

JJ glances down and shakes his head with a growing smile. "You are a menace." He laughs playfully.

His ice cream begins to melt in his hands, dripping down the curve of his fingers. He releases a grunt. "I'm going to get cleaned up. Never order those two flavours together again."

"Spoil sport." I grin as he walks towards the bathrooms.

I finish my ice cream before wiping my hands down with a napkin. I stretch my arms above my head and turn around to the beach shop behind me. The sunglasses display snags my attention as I try a pair on and look at myself in the mirror.

"Ivy?"

My entire body freezes at the sound of my name.

I don't tear my eyes away from the mirror as a presence behind me sends alarm bells ringing in my head. I snatch the glasses from my face, and I turn around to face the person I've been dreading seeing.

Slowly, I begin to back away from him. I doubt he'd try something in public, but at the same time, he drove us off a bridge with the intent of killing us. How can I trust him at all?

"You shouldn't be here, Ben," I rasp. "You're not allowed to talk to me."

Ben's dark eyes soften towards me as he takes another step forward. "You think I'm going to hurt you?"

I say nothing as I watch him cautiously, and every movement he makes until my back hits the wall of the shop.

"Ah, come on," he grunts. "I've been away for two years. Don't you think that's enough punishment?"

Hell no. He deserves life for trying to take mine away.

"Leave me alone, Ben," I say through gritted teeth. "You're breaking your restraining order."

Ben scoffs. "I live here, Ivy. It's not my fault you're here too."

My hands grip onto the wall as he takes another step, and my stomach flips with dread. He towers over me, and I prepare my knee, knowing if he takes another step, I'll drive it straight into his balls for thinking he can try and intimidate me.

"Come on, just talk to me," he exhales. "Please. I thought about you almost every day, and I'm sorry—"

"Everything okay here?"

The relief that washes over me as I hear JJ's voice is instant. I glance up at him, standing behind Ben. JJ steps forward with his arms folded over his chest and a face like thunder.

"Yeah, everything's—"

"I wasn't talking to you." JJ scowls at Ben, pushing him back by the shoulder to step between us. "You okay?"

My mouth opens, but my tongue feels heavy and numb. "Can we go?"

JJ doesn't hesitate to lean down and take my hand, wrapping an arm around my front protectively before he leads us out of the shop, making sure I'm not left at the back. He stares at Ben with narrowed eyes but thankfully says nothing more.

"Ivy, wait—"

My eyes clamp shut, and JJ tenses at the same time I do.

"Leave me alone, Ben," I spit. "I'm not having this conversation with you."

JJ's eyes almost bulge out of his head as he looks down at me. "This is Ben?"

I nod wordlessly.

JJ's hand swipes across his jaw as he tucks me behind him and steps towards Ben. "I suggest you get the hell out of here and never come near Ivy again. Do you fucking understand me?"

Ben flinches but then laughs. "Who the fuck are you?"

"Her boyfriend," he grumbles. "And you're about to be in a casket if you don't leave her alone. You've broken your restraining order, you can go back to prison for this, and you know what? I'm fucking glad about it."

"I ain't going back to prison." He rolls his eyes as if it's the most ludicrous thing he's ever heard. God, he's more delusional than I remember. "I didn't even touch you."

My jaw clenches. "You don't need to touch me to break it."

JJ steps towards him, fists clenched. I tug on his arm, desperately needing him not to fuck this up for me. "Please, let's just go."

"You come near her again," JJ threatens. "And you'll fucking regret it."

Ben laughs, and the sound irks me. I won't let him win. I won't let him bring me down for a second more.

"Are you okay?" JJ asks as he checks over his shoulder to make sure we're not being followed.

Our eyes meet, and I flash him a wobbly smile. "I didn't think he was going to do anything, but there is always this little thought in the back of my mind that he might. He did it once before, he can do it again."

"I won't let him hurt you," JJ says adamantly.

"I know."

JJ practically vibrates as we walk home, neither of us says anything more, and I'm not sure what there is to say. He doesn't remove his hand from mine; he holds me tight. I know he'd protect me in a heartbeat.

When we reach my front door, I slump against it. "We should call the police, or your old case handler, or someone, so we can get the CCTV from the shop and send it off." JJ drops my hand to brush a few strands of hair from my face. "He can't be breaking his restraining order and getting away with it. It's not fair, Ivy. I'll end up killing the man if he tries to talk to you again."

My throat tenses at the thought. From the venom in his eyes, it looks like he's being deadly serious.

"Okay," I whisper.

The second we step into the house, I'm greeted by my parents. We tell them what happened with Ben on the beachfront, and soon the police are over to take my statement, along with JJ's.

My dad has been pacing with fury, telling the officers that this is unacceptable and that my safety comes first. JJ is right beside him, agreeing that it's not fair that I'm the one to suffer from it.

I wish I could lose this chapter of my life and move on, but little things always have to draw me back.

My mother pulls me into a hug. "I knew this was going to happen," I murmur. "It's a small town. His parents still live here."

"Doesn't mean you have to live with it, honey," my mum mumbles into my hair before pulling away. "Are you okay?"

I tremble at the thought of how it could have ended, but JJ was there. He never fails to make me feel safe.

"Just a bit shaken up from it," I admit, my hand trembling.

"Do you want some dinner?" my father offers, now somewhat calmer.

"Not hungry," I admit. "Gonna take a bath instead."

"Okay, we're here if you need anything. Alright?"

My lips curl into a forced smile. "Yeah, I know."

I glance at JJ as I pass, and he stands back as I mount the stairs and walk to the bathroom before filling the tub. The second I slip beneath the scalding water, I release a low groan along with the tension in my muscles.

I lay here for what feels like hours, until the water goes cold and I'm numb again.

CHAPTER 48
JJ WOODFORD

The door to my room opens, and my gaze shoots to the sound as it creaks. A small figure appears in the doorway, and I shuffle up in my sheets as I spot Ivy as she steps inside.

"Hey," I whisper as she shuts the door behind her. "Are you okay?"

She says nothing but walks straight to my bed as I scoot to the edge. I can barely see her through the dimness of my bedroom, but I can tell that her body language is off from earlier, which I expected it to be.

She wanted space, and I gave her space.

I wrap my arms around her waist, and she drops her head to mine, pressing her lips to my mouth swiftly. The kiss is quick, and it makes my head spin, but I don't want her doing anything when I know she's not one hundred percent in herself. But this isn't a good night kiss, this is much, *much* more.

"Wait." I pause against her skin, my hands sliding down her back slowly. "I'm not going to take advantage of you when you're like this."

Ivy whimpers against me and kisses me again, this time

harder. She opens my mouth with her tongue, and I groan silently at the touch and taste. *Everything*. She has my skin rising in goosebumps.

"Ivy," I say, deeper. "Are you okay?"

She nods once. "Yeah, I just want to be close to you."

"Are you sure?"

I don't want to deny her what she wants, but at the same time, I don't want to encourage her in this emotional state.

She pulls away and stares at me through the darkness. "Let me do this," she pleads. "I need you. I need this. I need to know that this is real, right now."

I tug her down onto my lap, her thighs straddling my own. My lips press to her bare shoulder. "Everything between us is real, princess," I whisper against her warm skin. "It always has been. From the moment I saw you. I knew you were going to be mine."

A sound falls from her lips as she moves my face to take my mouth again. This time, she pushes me back, and I allow her. I promise myself one thing: I'm not going to be rough. I'm going to give her everything she needs right now.

Real fucking love.

I brush my fingers along the hem of her crop top, tugging gently. "Can I take this off?"

"Please," she begs.

I hook my fingers underneath and tug it off her body in one swift movement. I drop it to the floor and run my hands over the backs of her thighs and the curve of her ass. The shorts she's wearing do nothing to cover her but I fucking love it. Her skin feels euphoric beneath my fingers.

She grinds her core down onto my crotch and I groan into her mouth, clutching the back of her head with one hand and the other firmly on her ass. Blood rushes through my body until I feel myself getting harder. She barely has to do anything for me to get it up.

"More, please," she says breathlessly. "I need you to touch me."

I clasp my arm around her waist and roll her onto her side, pressing her back into my bed. I cover her body with mine and lower my head down to her chest, pressing soft kisses over her scar and erect nipples.

Her dainty fingers slide down the back of my head, gripping my neck. I latch onto the waistband of her shorts. "Can I take these off, too?"

"JJ," she moans aloud, but she sounds frustrated. "Stop being so gentlemanly and just touch me. I can't stand another second withou—"

Before she finishes her sentence, I tug off her shorts. Now she's in nothing but a tiny thong as I trace the outside of the material.

"Thank you." She throws her head back to the sheets.

I trail my fingers down her sternum and over her stomach. Then I dip my hands inside her panties, her wetness coating my fingers instantly. "Yes," she whimpers, pulling my head back down to her lips so she can kiss me as if her life depends on it.

Ivy whimpers when I touch her clit softly, rolling it around and feeling it grow bigger beneath my fingertips.

"F-fuck," she stutters.

I peck her lips over and over as she becomes more aroused. I push one finger inside her pussy and she clenches around me, her hands clutching onto my shoulders. Those nails, fuck. Those nails make my teeth clench because I want to give her so much more, but I take my time.

"How does that feel, princess?" I ask along the curve of her neck.

She nods desperately. "Good. So good. Keep going."

I slip another finger inside and listen to her breathing change. My lips press to her neck as I lick and suck at the skin, being careful of making marks. I raise my thumb and massage her clit at the same time.

Her legs spread wider naturally, and I speed up, curling my fingers inside her to hit that spot I know will set her off.

"Yes, yes, yes," she chants, arching her back into me.

"Let go, Ivy." I drag my mouth over her neck and across her jaw. "Let me have it. I've got you."

Ivy presses her lips together, but seconds later, she releases a loud moan. "I want you to have it," she pants.

"Yeah?" I grunt.

I press down on her clit as I fuck her pussy with my fingers, using just enough pressure and speed to bring her to the edge. "Oh god," she cries quietly. "Yes. Right there."

My mouth claims hers once more, and she falls apart beneath me. The way she moans into the kiss has my head spiralling into never-ending lust and desire, making my cock throb in my pants.

"JJ," she moans my name as she comes all over my hand.

"That's it, princess." I bite down on her lip, and her hips jolt into my hand, attempting to ride it for more friction.

My eyes turn hazy, her moans grow louder. I resist the urge to slap my hand over her mouth because I don't want anyone to hear, but right now, my pride grows stronger. I want to hear exactly how I make her feel.

"Fuck, fuck." She shivers beneath me as she slowly recovers from her climax.

I stop moving my fingers, but keep them deep inside her. She clenches around me until she's spent and lying back against my sheets, breathing heavily.

"More?" I ask quietly.

She hums with her eyes closed. "More."

My arms wrap around her body again, and I twist us so I'm sitting and she's straddling my hips. We fight to take off her thong together, until her beautiful body is completely naked. I tug my boxers down and let my cock spring free as I worm it between her drenched core.

"Come down," I whisper as she perches at the tip.

She bites her lip and slowly eases her way down. At first, she takes a couple of inches as she stretches and accommodates to my length.

"Holy shit." She throws her head back.

I clench everything inside me. My arms snake around her back, and I tug her bare chest against mine. She hovers, and I don't rush her; I want her to do what feels good.

Tonight is about her and no one else. She needs this, and I understand that.

Ivy shifts and sinks lower, another inch. "Fuck!"

I press a kiss to the edge of her shoulder, trying to keep it together, but she feels so damn blissful. I stay still, my hands exploring the silky skin on her back. She moves on top of me, sliding up and down.

"Oh fuck," she cries again. "I never want to stop. Ugh. You're so big."

My nostrils flare at her comment, stroking my ego. Shit. I could bust any second. "Yeah," I agree. "But it fits you so well."

With that, she sits all the way down on my length and groans, throwing her head back again, exposing her throat to me. I draw my hand up her back and hook it over her shoulder, keeping her against me.

My eyes close at the sensations that wash over me. Then she starts rocking and riding. I fucking lose my head and every part of my sanity to this woman who glides over me like an ice rink.

"Oh yes." She latches onto my shoulders, sliding her arms around my neck.

"You're so beautiful."

She nods, and I smile at her response.

Then her head buries into my neck, and she moans,

making me shudder. "I love the way you make me feel," she whispers breathlessly. Pleasure erupts everywhere as she continues to ride me. "I love that you make me feel seen."

I cradle the back of her head in my hand, threading my fingers through her hair before hooking them onto her shoulder and tugging her down onto me as we move as one. "I've always seen you, Ivy," I state and groan when she drops back down again, taking me completely. "*Always.*"

Her lips tremble as she angles her head up to the ceiling. She rolls her hips harder, clenching around my length. "JJ, I'm gonna—"

"Come again?" I finish for her.

"Yeah. Fuck."

"Come on, Ivy. Take what you need," I grunt into her shoulder, biting down on her flesh lightly. "Make a fucking mess for me."

Moments later she explodes, and I can't help but follow after her. I jolt my hips upwards, meeting her strokes as she crumbles and moans and rides me until we're both gasping for breath. Crying out each other's names as we fall back onto the bed, sweaty and entwined.

"Oh my god." She shakes as she presses herself into me.

My cock slips from her pussy and I keep my arms firmly wrapped around her. "Fuck, you are so hot when you're on top."

She smirks at me through the darkness. "You've said that before."

"And I need to say it every time."

When she chuckles, it lights up my soul. "Can I stay here tonight?"

"Always."

"Naked?"

"Naked indeed."

We lay and listen to our rapid breaths.

"As much as I want to lay here knowing my cum is

leaking out of you," I rasp. "You should pee first before you give yourself an infection. Let me clean you up."

She pushes herself up from the bed and stares down at me, not bothering to cover her body as the sheets fall around her waist. "Wow, I'm surprised you know that rule."

I gasp in mock shock. "I know a lot of things, thank you very much, and your health is one of them."

A smile flashes across her face. "You're so cute."

"Yeah, when it comes to you." I cup her cheek. "Come on."

I pick her up with ease and carry her towards the bathroom.

"Then we can cuddle?"

"Yeah, princess, then we can cuddle."

CHAPTER 49
IVY THOMPSON

A pair of soft lips presses to the back of my shoulder as I stir from a dreamless sleep. I knew I would pass out after spending the night with JJ. I wanted to stay awake to savour the sensation of being in his arms, but he made me feel too relaxed, and I couldn't fight my heavy eyes.

My heart has been empty for a long time. A great big gaping hole directly in the middle that I didn't think would ever close again. But here I am being proved wrong, so damn wrong.

JJ kisses me again, but this time on the middle of my spine. I can't stop the smile that forms on my face as he pulls me closer, our naked bodies tangling together. He brushes my hair away and places another kiss that makes me tingle.

I shut my eyes at how good his lips feel, how delicate a few pecks can make me feel absolutely everything.

"Mmm," he whispers against my skin. "I want to wake up to you in my bed every day."

"Me too." I nod in agreement. "Good morning."

"Morning, princess." He nuzzles his head into my shoulder. "How are you feeling?"

I hum softly. "I think I'm okay," I say quietly. My fingers

run along his bare arm, the one that is wrapped around my waist. "I'm just glad that I'm with you. I don't want to be anywhere else."

He squeezes me somewhat tighter without suffocating me. "I don't want you anywhere else either," he grumbles in that sleepy voice that still hasn't gone away. "I love being with you."

Heat spreads across my cheeks as I close my eyes, exhaling a breath of relief and contentment. "I love being with you, too."

Our eyes meet when JJ turns me around. He cradles the side of my face as he flicks his gaze over every inch, taking in every freckle. "This summer has been one of the best."

I raise my eyebrows. "Really?"

"Yeah," he rasps. "I met you. My mother's treatment is going well. I get to spend it in one of the most beautiful places. I hate that Finn isn't doing well, it's tough not having him here, but I'm glad he's getting the help he needs."

For some reason, a lump forms in my throat when I realise that summer will be over soon. We'll have to go back to university for another year, and I don't know how it's going to work out.

JJ instantly realises something is wrong because his brows press down into a frown. "What?"

"We'll be starting university soon," I say under my breath.

"I know."

I chew on my lip because I'm not sure if I can find the words right now.

"Talk to me, Ivy. What is it?" He swipes his thumb across my cheekbone gently.

"Is this like—" I pause, pressure building behind my eyes at the thought of the question. "Going to—"

JJ lifts his head off the pillow. "End?"

My breathing catches in my throat. "Yeah."

"Do you want it to end?"

"No," I admit. "I love what we have going on, but I'm scared that when we go back, things will get complicated."

He pulls me closer and our lips brush. "If you think you're going to waltz into my life so you can waltz right back out, then you are deeply mistaken, princess. You're not getting rid of me that easily."

The tone he uses sends warmth through my body. "But what about—"

"Shhhh." He presses his thumb to my lips. "I don't want the ifs and buts. I want you, Ivy, and we're going to make this work. If you're willing to make this work with me. I want you to be on board."

"I am," I whimper. "I am. But—"

Before I can speak another word, he presses his lips to mine, shutting me up. "No," he states, cupping the back of my head with his large hand. "No more talking. I said what I said."

His lips close around mine, and I sigh into his mouth, pressing myself up against his chest. My head moves like waves in the sea. Kissing JJ is electrifying, and I can't get enough, especially the way his tongue explores my mouth.

God, I'll never get bored of this. It feels incredible. *He* feels incredible.

I pull back this time to look at him, pressing my hand to his shoulder. "What about Finn?"

JJ blinks rapidly. "What do you mean?"

"We need to think about when we're going to tell him."

"Do you think that's the right idea, especially right now?"

I sigh. "Maybe not yet, but when he's home and more stable."

He keeps his eyes trained on me for a long moment. "Do you want me there?"

"Yes. I think it'll be better if we're both there. I should also tell my parents. Although I feel like they might already know from the night Finn went into hospital."

He nods slowly. "Yeah, it needs to be done. I don't want to have to sneak around anymore. Not touching you when we're not alone has been fucking torture."

The corners of my mouth tug upward. "That bad, huh?"

"Don't act like you're not the same." He flashes me a knowing smirk.

I roll my eyes playfully. "I'll catch you downstairs," I say, leaning over to peck his pillowy lips.

"Sure, princess." He cups my ass as I shuffle past him, giving it a light squeeze.

A squeal falls from the back of my throat. "Stop. Do you want my parents to hear us?"

"I like teasing you."

I huff out a laugh. "Don't I know it."

Seeing Finn's rehabilitation centre put my mind at ease.

It's small but not overcrowded. I guess my parents paying for private care has its benefits, and I know they'd do anything to see their son get back on his feet again. No matter the cost.

After we sign in, the doctor takes us through the building before we walk out onto a patio with garden furniture. I glance around to find Finn sitting down with a mug in hand.

His eyes lock on us, and he stands up.

Mum and Dad surround him instantly, bringing him into a hug as I watch them shower him with love and affection.

Finn pulls away from them and glances at me, blinking in surprise.

"Ivy." His breath hitches. "I didn't think I'd see you."

My mouth curls to the side. "I wanted to see how you were doing."

He sniffles. "I'm doing okay."

"Yeah?" My mother beams.

Finn clears his throat as we sit down in the chairs. He picks up his mug and takes a slow sip. "I guess hearing other people's stories and their determination to change their lives puts mine into perspective. It made me realise I was in a dark hole."

My dad places his hand on his shoulder. "Are they good to you here?"

"Yeah," he says. "They are. I've been seeing a therapist two to three times a week and doing group therapy as well. It's been… weird. But I don't want to keep ruining my life, I don't want to ruin your lives either."

"You could never, honey." My mother leans over to kiss his temple. "We just want you to get better. That's all. We want you to be happy."

Finn's eyes lower as he places the mug back down, and his elbows rest on his knees. "I think I've been really unhappy for a while. I was just… in denial about my addiction."

"We're so proud of you," our mother says.

Finn laughs awkwardly. "It's only been three weeks."

"Three weeks are better than nothing, son," my father pitches in. "Three weeks of progress."

"It's only a short-term program." Finn shrugs.

"But you'll be able to have all the resources when you come home," I say, and he glances at me. "You now have three weeks of knowledge. That's a lot."

Finn nods once. "Yeah, I guess."

We change the subject after the doctor told us not to focus too much on his treatment plan and to catch up on other things instead. We don't stay for long as they have group activities planned for the afternoon, and none of us wants to disrupt his schedule.

My parents hug Finn goodbye, and when they walk around me, Finn stares back with glassy green eyes. "It was good to see you, Ivy." He sighs despondently, his fingers twitching as if he wants to hug me.

"You too," I whisper.

He tucks his fingers into his back pocket before I have the chance to turn around. "I've written you something."

My brows crease as I glance at the folded piece of paper outstretched to me. "Why?"

"My therapist said that if I'm not good with my words, then I should write them down. And we're working together to fix the things I've broken. You don't have to read it, if you rip it up, then that's fair enough." He swipes a hand through his hair. "I don't think I can physically put together the words of how sorry I am for hurting you, because what I did is inexcusable. But this is all I can do, and I hope you can take two minutes of your time to read it. Even if I don't deserve it."

A ball forms in my throat as I look at the letter again. I raise a hand to take it, and Finn releases a low breath of relief.

"Okay," I say, despite my voice cracking.

Finn's eyes wobble a little as we stare back at each other. "Can I hug you?" he chokes out as a tear rolls down his face. "Please, I just really need to hug my sister right now."

My chest concaves at the vulnerability in his expression. I step forward and open my arms as he crashes his body into mine, burying his head into the crook of my neck as he sobs.

I squeeze my eyes shut, tears rolling down my cheeks. I hold onto him, my fingers fisting into the back of his shirt, his letter tightly between my fingers. He takes a shuddering breath, relaxing into me as we embrace each other.

After a few moments, we pull away, and I wipe my cheeks. "Uh." I clear my throat. "JJ wanted me to tell you something."

"Yeah?"

"JJ's mum's treatment is working, and it's looking positive."

Finn's face lights up with excitement and relief all rolled into one. "Are you serious?"

"Yeah," I sniffle through a smile.

"Oh my god." He grins. "That's fucking great."

My arms fold over myself as I tuck the letter into the crook of my elbow. "He wanted to tell you when he came home, but he couldn't wait."

"I'm so happy for them." His shoulders relax an inch. "Can you tell him that I can't wait to see him? I owe him a lot."

"Of course."

My eyes settle on my brother's as we stare at one another

"Can't wait to see you home and better," I confess.

Finn shoves his hands into his pockets. "Me, too."

When we leave the complex, I follow my parents to their car, but freeze as they open the door. "Wait," I call out to them, and they look back.

"What's wrong?"

"I need to tell you something."

My dad frowns. "What's the matter?"

I suck in a breath, my eyes bouncing between the two. "Me and JJ are together."

Neither of them says anything for a long moment until my father steps forward and presses his hands to my shoulders delicately. "Sweetheart," he whispers. "We know."

"Oh." I pull my head back an inch. "You do?"

"You haven't been so subtle over the last three weeks." My mother smiles.

I remain quiet as I try to gather thoughts. "And you're okay with it?"

"You're both consenting adults," she says simply. "Why wouldn't we be?"

My shoulders raise. "Because of Finn, and everything before."

"You're capable of making your own decisions, honey." She steps towards me. "Regardless of what happened in the past. We want you to be happy, too. But maybe just wait a little to tell Finn until he is home and settled."

"I wasn't going to ambush him with it," I admit. "I know he needs time to adjust first. But I wanted you guys to know."

"Well, thank you for telling us," my father says. "And I hope he makes you happy."

My cheeks heat, but I smile through it. "He does, Dad. So much."

"Good." He shoots me a wink. "Only the best for my girl. Come on. Let's go grab some pizzas and head home."

My mother nods, but there is clear reservation in her eyes. Not all of the family is here, and with Finn missing, it's taking a toll on them.

"Yeah, sure." She attempts a smile.

"We can have more pizza nights together when he's home," I comment. "Make up for the time he's been away."

"You're right, honey."

On the drive home, we grab pizza and sit around the table, with JJ by my side. Finn's letter burns a hole in my pocket, but I'm not sure if I'm ready to read it yet.

CHAPTER 50
JJ WOODFORD

After twenty-eight days, Finn is finally coming home.

If the doctors believe a short-term program is best for him, I'm not going to argue. We all know we have to come together to do better and support him in any way we can.

Andrea and James went to pick him up, and Ivy went to see Daisy because of the anticipation.

The second the front door opens, I push myself up from the kitchen stool and walk towards my best friend as he enters with a duffel bag slung over his shoulder.

"Hey, man." I smile, drawing him into a hug. "How are you doing?"

"Glad to be home," he sighs.

I pull back and hold him at arm's length. My eyes roam his face. "You look fresh."

"That's what a month of no drinking does for you."

"They give you things to work on at home?"

Finn nods. "Yeah, I still need to go and complete my therapy sessions and have them signed off by a doctor. Even though I'm not in the facility anymore, they're still keeping an eye on me. And want to continue to support me so I don't relapse."

"That's good. Proud of you, brother."

"Thanks." He smiles. "Ivy told me about your mum. I'm so pleased for you and your family."

My eyes burn. "Yeah, we think she's getting better."

Finn hugs me again and I close my eyes. "Best news ever."

I give Finn some time to unpack and find his bearings again. I head up to my room to tidy away the mess of clothes and a pair of Ivy's underwear, swiping them from the floor faster than lightning.

A knock at my door stirs me away from my chest of drawers. "Yeah?"

Finn pokes his head into my room. "Mind if I come in?"

"You don't need to ask." I chuckle.

"What you doing?"

"Just tidying. Not a lot."

"Oh."

I shove some clean clothes into the drawers and hang up a few hoodies before turning back around to face Finn. My stomach falls out of my ass when I find him holding my video camera.

Without hesitation, I lunge forward and snatch it from his hold a little too aggressively. My heart thrashes in my chest when I remember what exactly is on there and should never be seen by Finn's eyes.

Finn flinches and glances up at me as I twist the camera around. I release a silent sigh of relief to find clips of Ivy on the beach playing as she grins and the sea crashes behind her.

I place the camera down. "Sorry." I clear my throat. "That's expensive and I don't wanna break it."

He stares at me for a long moment, and I squirm under his scrutinising gaze. His eyes flick between mine as if he's working something out in his head, and the silence around us is near deafening.

"You're in love with my sister."

Well, talk about being blunt.

My brows pinch together. "What?"

Finn gestures to the camera, his eyes vacant. "You love her. Don't you?"

I suck in a breath and shift side to side, unable to hide this from him.

"Tell me," he urges, tone heavy.

"Yeah, I do."

And it feels like instant relief to admit.

Finn stares at me for a long time. I stand there rooted to the spot, unsure what to say or how to handle this. He runs a hand through his blond hair, then drags it down his face.

"Shit," he curses.

"Let's talk about this," I say before the situation blows up. "Let's go for a walk or something."

Finn doesn't move, and I wait for him to put up a fight or punch me square in the face. Neither happens when I walk out of my bedroom door, and he follows. We silently walk to the beachfront and sit on the stone wall.

I glance at him as he stares out at the ocean, shaking his head over and over. "Have you been sneaking around behind my back, hoping I don't find out?"

"No. We were giving it time. We knew your recovery was more important and neither of us wanted to disrupt your progress."

Finn scoffs. "So you lied to me?"

"Oh god, Finn." I close my eyes. "We just knew how you'd react."

"Like what?"

"Like this."

His eyes simmer, and even though he's calmer than I expected, I can see the betrayal in his gaze. We shouldn't have kept it from him for this long, but we both agreed that we didn't want to set him off before he had the chance to settle.

I want Ivy to be my girlfriend. I want her to visit us at university. I want all of it, and I don't want to lose Finn because of it. I want them both. But I know he won't accept it —not right away.

"A brother who is worried for his sister?" he grumbles.

My face recoils from his harsh words, and my chest turns to stone. "If you think I'd ever hurt Ivy, then you don't know me at all. We met before I came here for the summer. Our paths crossed before you got the chance to introduce us. We didn't meet because of you."

Finn's hands tremble in front of him, his forehead creasing.

"Wait—" His head shakes adamantly. "You knew each other before I introduced you?"

"Yes."

"And you both just pretended in front of me?"

"I didn't know how to react," I confess. "Neither of us did, okay? I didn't know she was your sister at the time."

Finn scoffs. "Would that have stopped you?"

I pause for a moment. "No," I say eventually.

I bite the inside of my cheek as I watch him. When he says nothing more, I decide to open up my heart and be honest. "She makes me happy. Isn't that what you want to hear? She is a fucking amazing girl and the way she has made me feel over the last few months is genuinely indescribable. This hasn't been easy for her, she didn't let me in until recently."

He scowls at me. "What are you talking about?"

"For months, she pushed me away and denied our connection, afraid of what you'd think. She didn't want to upset you. She ignored her own happiness because she was worried about how it would affect you. She had your best interests at heart. But I told her that she needs to do things for herself, not for anyone else's validation," I say, dropping my tone.

He looks at the ground, jaw clenching.

"Do you think I wanted this to happen? Do you think I wanted to keep this from you? I've felt guilty these last few months. But when I finally saw Ivy step out of the shell I know she's been in for the last few years, I couldn't bring myself to care anymore. Because you know what? She's happy. She's finally letting that light inside her shine like it always should have." My chest rumbles with all the emotions that I'm pouring out. "And I know I can make her happy. Isn't that what you want for her?"

Finn meets my eyes. His mouth opens once and then twice.

A wave of uncertainty washes over me when he looks like he's about to give me an ultimatum. My stomach churns at the thought, and I tighten my hands into fists.

"If you make me choose between you, then I automatically pick her," I state with all seriousness.

He blinks rapidly and then furrows his brows at me. "I would never make you choose. I just can't—" He abruptly stops. "This isn't something that I can accept and be fine with straight away."

"Because of what happened with Ben?"

Finn flinches.

"Yeah, Ivy told me. *Everything*. You know me, Finn. You fucking know me better than any of my other friends, and you know all I want is peace and calmness. And I want to make Ivy happy because we both know she deserves it."

His eyes gravitate to the ground.

"You blame yourself for what happened with Ben," I say gently. "I know you've got a lot to work through. But that girl has lit up my world in a few months and has given me hope for lots of things. And I don't want to lose her; I don't want to lose you, either."

Finn remains silent, and I don't know if that's a good or a bad thing. He's not screaming his head off, demanding to get drunk—so I guess that's a start.

"I'm sorry," I sigh. "For keeping this from you, for not saying anything. But I am *not* sorry for loving her."

He runs his hands down his face, releasing a strangled breath. "Knowing you guys have slept together and been intimate together is making me feel nauseous."

I grimace at his words. "It's more than the physical stuff, Finn. She was there for me when I found out the news about my mother's treatment. I was there for her when she came home in pieces when Tom and his shitty friends were harassing her. The moments you haven't seen."

Finn meets my eyes when I finish my sentence. "God, my head is spinning."

I sigh. "I know this isn't easy for you. After everything with Ben, the rumour, the car crash. But she's capable of making her own decisions."

"You're in love with her," he repeats absently.

I nod and say nothing more. I don't think he needs to hear me say it again.

"All summer?"

"Mostly. I couldn't stay away from her, and she put up a good fight."

Finn breathes out through his nose sharply. "You said she was being a good friend to you and now I realise… that's not what you meant."

"Please, can we not lose our friendship over this. I'm sorry for keeping it a secret, but Ivy wanted to wait, and I wanted to respect her wishes. She's been living with so much guilt herself, and she doesn't deserve that. We both know it."

"Yeah, I know. She should hate me," he rasps. "She should never want to talk to me ever again, but she has. I'll never understand that girl."

"She has a big heart," I comment. "And some people take it for granted."

"I promise I'll never hurt her."

"I know, bud," I say, grabbing his shoulder. "I know this is hard for you to accept, but if you want her full forgiveness, I think you need to accept us for what we are. Don't come in the way of her happiness again. I need to see her smile, Finn, more than anything."

He swallows audibly. "Okay," he murmurs, the word a struggle.

I chew on the inside of my mouth. "It's your turn to be happy, Finn."

"Doubt anyone is going to want my sorry ass. I've got an alcohol problem and I ruin people's lives," he grumbles. "And besides, the girl I want wants nothing to do with me. I fucked it up. It's all I keep on doing. Fucking up."

"You didn't ruin my life." I shrug.

Finn snorts. "Yet."

"No." I shake my head. "You won't, because you're getting the help you need."

"I suppose."

"And as for Maya, you know you can talk to me about her, right?"

Finn shrugs and looks away.

"I don't know what went down, but it's not healthy to let it fester. Talk to me about it. I know you love her."

He sighs deeply. "Maybe soon. I'm not ready to face it yet."

"Okay. I'm sorry you found out like this," I confess. "Ivy wanted to tell you first."

Finn's shoulders rise. "It's obvious now that I think about it. After the fair, and when you punched Tom, and the way you look at her, and those shots of her at the beach. When you described her to me when I asked what you're looking for in a girlfriend. I'm not stupid, JJ. I know when my best friend is in love."

I drag a hand down the back of my head. "Not so subtle, am I?"

"Nope," he exhales, a ghost of a smile gracing his face. "I guess I just didn't want to believe it. It's going to take some time getting used to this."

"And I totally respect that. We're both here for you."

His eyes shine against the light. "I'm starting to realise I don't deserve either of you."

I tug him into an embrace and slap a hand on his back. "Don't let that negative shit get into your head, brother," I say quietly. "We're here because we both love you and want to see you get better. You need your loved ones around. I'll be damned if we don't see you through your journey. Okay?"

Finn swallows and pulls away, wiping his eyes as if he didn't want me to see. "Okay."

My chest heaves as I take a breath. It's one step forward, but I pray it's not a million back.

CHAPTER 51
IVY THOMPSON

JJ:

He knows.

I'm sorry.

He asked if we're together and I couldn't lie to him any longer.

I've practically chewed the entirety of my finger off after getting home and expecting Finn and JJ to be here. But they're not, and the wait feels like agony.

I have no idea how Finn found out, although I bet I'm about to receive a lashing for it.

But he doesn't get to dictate my relationship this time.

My stomach crashes with nausea the longer I wait. I'm sure I've permanently marked the flooring in our kitchen from where I've been pacing back and forth like a woman who has lost her head.

I lean over the counter and press my elbows into it. My hands cover my face as I try to regulate my breathing. I wish I was there to listen to the conversation, to know exactly what is going to happen when they come home.

Whatever happens, I pray it doesn't make Finn want to pick up a bottle and drink himself stupid.

As the front door swings open, I blink and push myself up from the counter. JJ and Finn emerge, neither of them covered in blood or bruises, so I presume no fists were involved.

"Hey," I whisper.

Finn raises his eyes to me, and he looks like he's been to hell and back.

JJ shuts the door behind him and follows us over to the kitchen. My heart flutters when he looks at me and offers me a supportive smile, especially now that Finn knows everything. I draw my gaze to my brother and watch as he presses his palms to the counter.

For a long moment, he's silent, and I don't know if that's worse than him screaming at me. His gaze is low as he says, "I would like more answers."

I gulp and look at JJ, who steps to my side, his fingers brushing my bare leg out of Finn's eyesight.

"You okay?" he asks quietly.

My lips open, but I shut them and nod instead. Now is not the time to showcase our relationship in front of him. I twist my head and find Finn staring back at us, looking lost and startled.

"Why did it take you so long to tell me?" His tone dips, and I swallow.

"Because I couldn't find the right time to tell you."

Finn scoffs. "The right time?" he exclaims, and I flinch when his voice echoes around the kitchen. "There was never going to be a right time."

I blink once when his eyes focus on only me. "I'm not asking you for permission, Finn. I'm an adult. I can make my own decisions. And after everything that happened with Ben,

I really don't think you have the right to try and destroy this too."

His eyes waver for a moment, and guilt slashes through me.

"I said I was sorry, Ivy."

"I know."

Finn presses a hand to his temple. "You've been laughing at me this entire summer, haven't you?"

"What?" I recoil from his accusation. "No. We've been trying to figure out how to tell you without damaging your health."

His nostrils flare. "Oh, because you thought my alcohol problem would ruin everything, like I always fucking do." I tilt my head back when he walks towards me. "But ask yourself this, Ivy. Why do you keep dating my friends?"

Another step, and JJ is there like a flash of lightning. He presses a hand to Finn's shoulder and shoves him back lightly. "Step back, Finn. I fucking mean it."

The tone of JJ's voice sends a shudder down my spine.

Finn's comment rips a gaping hole in my chest, and I try not to take it to heart because I know this isn't the best news to hear when you've just got out of rehab.

Finn shakes his head, his face falling in shock, as if he can't believe what he said. "I-I didn't mean that, Ivy," he exhales jaggedly. "I'm just—"

"You're upset," I finish for him. "I get it."

He nods solemnly and drags a hand down his face. "It's hard to hear… *again*."

"That's not her problem," JJ snaps.

Finn shoots him a glare. "Oh, and it's my problem?"

"Yes." JJ folds his arms over his chest. "You're an adult, Finn. We're all adults, and you're acting like an immature child."

"Sorry that I need time to digest this information." Finn's

jaw ticks in frustration. "Unlike you guys. You've only just decided to tell me about it."

"You don't need to be rude to Ivy." JJ's voice is low and makes me shudder. "Who she dates isn't any of your business, and blaming her—"

Finn's mouth falls open. "I wasn't blaming her."

"No? Because that's what it sounded like, and I'm not going to stand for it."

"You're putting words in my mouth, JJ. That is not fair."

"Do you know what else isn't fair? Be—"

JJ's voice begins to fizzle out into a muffled sound. Finn starts shouting back. The kitchen explodes into endless bickering, but I can't hear a single thing they're saying.

My ears start to ring, and pressure builds in my eyes.

"Stop!" I say as loudly as I can. "Stop shouting at each other."

My knees begin to quiver as their voices become quieter until the kitchen is silent and all I can hear is my heavy, uneven breathing.

"Ivy." JJ's voice echoes through my ears.

His arm wraps around my waist. I attempt to catch my breath before I set myself off. I'm not falling down this rabbit hole again.

"Stop it," I say through gritted teeth.

JJ cups my face and I study his blue eyes, forcing them to bring me back to reality. "Breathe," he instructs me, and I do as he says. "Breathe. Slowly."

I shift my watery eyes up to find Finn staring at us with a look on his face that I've never seen before. He's not angry or disgusted—he looks dishevelled. His eyes are low and lids are hooded. There is something in the way that he blinks that makes me see a different side to his emotions.

"I trod on eggshells around you, Finn," I croak. "And I'm done putting your feelings before my own. This is what I want. JJ makes me happy, and if you can't see that, then I'm done with this. I'm done with you."

JJ buries his hand in the back of my hair and makes me look at him. He searches my face and wipes my tear-stained cheeks with his thumbs. "Are you okay?"

I shake my head. "No. I hate this. I hate—"

My body trembles again, and JJ clutches me to him. "Easy," he whispers. "Take a breath, Ivy. Take a breath."

My lips part, and I take in air and exhale once my lungs are full.

With JJ's arms firmly around me, I remind myself that I'm okay.

"Ivy—" Finn's voice is calmer now.

JJ stiffens behind me. "Finn, if you say another fucking word."

"I'm sorry." He trembles, shaking his head towards me. "I didn't mean to set you off."

"I think we need to leave this alone for today," JJ states, his fingers massaging the back of my neck delicately. "Emotions are too high right now, and we all need a night to sleep on everything."

Finn drifts his eyes between us and focuses on our entwined hands that are wrapped around my stomach, then to the hand that's in the back of my hair, soothing me.

"Fine," he agrees.

Then he tears his gaze away from us and slowly walks upstairs. I sigh and droop back into JJ's warm embrace. He drops his hand from the back of my head and caresses my arm gently.

"I'm sorry," he says. "I'll sit here with you for however long you need. I promise I'm not going anywhere."

My eyes sting, hating how emotional I am right now. I wish I could snap my fingers and everything would magically figure itself out. The last thing I want is this pain and guilt that looms over my head like a dark cloud of shame.

But we shouldn't feel guilty for wanting to be with each other.

Especially when I know it's right.

"I want to go to bed," I admit.

"Okay."

Without hesitation, he bends down and lifts me up. My legs sweep off the floor and wrap around his waist, my hands winding around his neck. I practically collapse into him, exhausted.

As soon as he starts moving, I cling onto him, but I already know that he's got me. *He's always got me.* We reach the stairs, and he climbs us to the top before opening my bedroom door and carrying us inside.

He kicks off his shoes before dropping us onto my bed softly. I bury my head into his neck, wanting to forget the entire day.

I pull my head back slowly and glance up at him through my swollen eyes. "I feel awful for doing this when he just left rehab, but what I said is true. You told me to claim back my life, and I am. This is what I want, and I'm taking it for myself. I'm done with putting others' happiness before my own."

"Ivy." He strokes my cheek, staring at me in awe. "I am so proud of you."

"I'm over worrying about what he thinks, because I know this is right. Being with you feels right," I whisper. "And I don't want anything else."

He kisses my temple.

"But sometimes…"

"What?"

I chew on my lip. "Sometimes I kind of wish we met under different circumstances, to save ourselves from all of this mess."

He exhales through his nose sharply, and I meet his eyes

again. He looks devastated, and that's not how I want him to feel. He drops his hand from my face.

"Do you regret sleeping with me the first time we met?" His voice is hoarse.

"No." I furrow my brows. "I liked you. I liked what we had—"

"But now?"

"But now I love you."

JJ's expression twists to a mixture of relief and reassurance, and my stomach lurches. The words I've been dying to say for weeks. The words I've felt for so long but been too terrified to voice.

"Do you regret sleeping with me?" I whisper.

He leans forward and presses his hand to my cheek, pulling our faces together again.

"I'm in love with you, Ivy. How can I regret anything when it comes to you?"

My lips part shakily, and I resist the urge to cry.

"You do realise that even if we didn't sleep together that night or if I didn't even meet you then, when I saw you here, I would have still wanted you the same. The fact that we slept together means nothing because I would have still been drawn to you." JJ swipes his thumb across my cheek. "And I know you would have wanted me, too. You cannot deny the connection we have."

I chew on my lip as he leans forward and kisses the corner of my mouth.

"When I woke up the morning after we met to find that you were gone, I was fucking distraught. I had no idea how to find you, how to get in contact with you. And then when I saw you here, I knew it was fate." He brushes his thumb over my cheekbone. "We had unfinished business."

My heart pounds in my throat because he's right, it was fate.

"Finn will come around, I promise."

"Knowing him, he might not."

"Then that's his issue. Not ours. If he wants to lose us both, then he's the one who needs to see the bigger picture. He's in shock right now. Hopefully over the next few days or weeks, he'll have a better attitude towards it." JJ tugs my bottom lip with his thumb.

I swallow. "Thank you for earlier."

"You don't need to thank me. It's not your fault, princess." He cups the back of my neck with his vacant hand. "And I'm always going to be there for you. *Always.*"

CHAPTER 52
JJ WOODFORD

Ivy's body lies on top of mine as I crack open my eyes. I smooth my hand down her back and then up again before cradling the nape of her neck. I peck her temple softly, careful not to wake her since she's still fast asleep.

Even though I slept fairly well, I couldn't stop thinking about everything that's happened. Ivy breaking down into a panic attack is something I never want to see, and trying to keep her calm and safe is my priority.

Ivy twists in my hold, and she releases a soft groan, nuzzling her face further into my neck. I kiss her again and keep my arms around her comfortably. "Good morning, beautiful."

Another groan. "It's so early."

"It's past ten," I chuckle.

She cracks those green eyes open to me and then smiles. "I clearly needed the sleep."

I hum in agreement. "Sure did, princess. How are you feeling?"

"Mmm," she huffs and rolls onto her back beside me. My hand slides over her midriff. "Okay, I guess. Worried to see Finn, but I'm glad it's all out in the open now."

I shuffle forward and press my lips to her forehead. "I think it's time you focus on what you want and how you feel, rather than everyone else."

She pulls back slowly and flicks her gaze over my face. "Yeah." Her lips twitch. "I think you're right. I do. And it's taken me a lot of courage to admit."

I press my hand to her cheek and swipe my thumb across her silk-like skin. "Can I ask you something?"

Ivy nods. "Of course."

"When was the last time you went to therapy?"

She blinks at my question and then stares at the wall. "I dunno, like a few months before I came back home."

"Do you think you still need to go?"

"Why are you asking this?"

"Because I can see that you still carry so much guilt, shame, and insecurity. Your panic attack last night was scary, Ivy. I want to make sure you're also getting the care and recovery you need," I whisper, focusing on her eyes, but she's not looking at me.

Ivy clears her throat and shoves her face further into the pillow. My heart pounds, thinking I've stepped over the line of her boundaries, but I have to admit when I'm worried about her. I want to know that she's getting the help that she needs.

"Princess." I move closer and let my fingers slide into the back of her hair. "I'm sorry. I just—"

"No." She swallows. "You're right. This summer has been a blur of different emotions. I've been up and down constantly. But yeah, I think I still need guidance with how to help myself, slow my triggers. My anxieties are still there, and it would be wise to get help when I know I need it."

Relief washes over my chest, and I can't stop myself when I wrap my arms around Ivy's body and tug her into my embrace. "I'll support you every step of the way. You know that, right?"

She nods into my shoulder. "I know, JJ. I wouldn't even need to ask for you to be there, I already know you will. It's inevitable."

"Completely inevitable."

Ivy pulls her head away and peeks her eyes up at me. "I want you to shower with me."

My eyes widen in surprise. "You do?"

"Please?"

I leap off the bed with her in my arms faster than I can blink.

After our shower, we head downstairs to make some pancakes for breakfast.

"What are you doing?" Ivy demands.

I stare at her, bewildered. "This is how you make pancakes."

She snorts, but I find it stupidly adorable. "That is not how you make pancakes, are you serious?"

"Yeah, it is," I dismiss her playfully as she walks towards my side. "If you don't like how I do it, get out of the kitchen."

Ivy pokes her head around my shoulder to get a better look. "Oh my god." She presses a hand to her head. "This is going to be a disaster. You've added way too many eggs, it's not an omelette."

"Just trust me." I scowl at her with a smile playing on my lips. "I know best."

She rolls her eyes and bumps my hip. "I'll believe it when I see it."

"Excuse me?"

Her arms fold over her chest, and fuck, she looks so damn cute when she's pulling a face of determination. "Here, taste," she says as she dips her fingers in the batter so quickly I barely see her move. The next thing I know, she's smeared it across my mouth and chin. "Taste right to you?"

"Oh, you're taking the piss," I say with a chuckle.

I lean forward to grab her, and she moves fast, but I reach her in time. She releases a squeal of laughter when I begin tickling her ribs. "How dare you ruin my perfect breakfast." I brush my lips all over her neck.

"Ugh!" she bellows with a laugh. "That's disgusting."

"Yeah, but you love me," I say, and she snorts again.

"Debatable."

My hands dig into her waist further. "What was that?"

"Nothing!" she yells with a breathless laugh, my own filling the air too. "I didn't say anything."

I grin at her. "Liar," I say as we continue to playfight.

I glance up at the stairs to find Finn at the bottom of them, watching us. I didn't even hear him or register his appearance until now. When I stop laughing, Ivy notices him too. Slowly and reluctantly, my arms move from around her waist.

"Hey," I say to break the silence.

Finn merely nods before walking over to the counter. "Hey."

Ivy stands there with her eyes down, her fingers entwined. "You good?" I ask Finn when no one says anything more.

"No," he states, shaking his head, and finally, Ivy glances up. "I'm sorry for how I behaved yesterday. It was unacceptable. I replayed everything I said and I fucking hate myself for being such an asshole, Ivy."

"It's fine."

Finn presses his hand to the counter as if he's taking a stand. "No." His voice is harsh. "It's not fine, Ivy. I'm sorry for what I said. It was uncalled for. But you guys have to realise that this is so new and alien to me. I can learn to deal with your relationship, but it's not going to be easy for me."

"We know, Finn," I state. "You need time to process everything. We understand that."

"Did you read the letter I wrote to you?"

Ivy darts her gaze to him and shakes her head. "Not yet. I've been struggling to open it. I'm still trying to figure out what's left of our relationship," she admits, and I couldn't feel prouder of her for doing things at her own pace. "You broke my trust, Finn, and that's something I'll need to take time to learn to deal with."

Finn remains silent for a long moment, and I resist the urge to sigh. "I get it. It hurts, but I get it. I want you to be happy, and if it's JJ who's meant to be that person, then I can't say anything after what I did to you. I might not want it, but there isn't anything I can do. I'm not losing my best friend and my sister because you both love each other, that would be stupid."

The corners of my lips lift. I've never been prouder of Finn. I walk around the counter and pull him into a hug. "This won't change anything, I promise."

I pull away and watch as he walks towards Ivy with his arms out. She glances up at him and gives in, his arms wrapping around her protectively. "Seeing you happy makes me happy," he whispers onto the top of her head. "I just wish you had better taste in guys."

"Rude," I call out, but they both laugh.

"I have great taste, actually," she murmurs into his chest.

Finn relaxes and flashes a small smile. "Mm, that's up for debate."

CHAPTER 53
IVY THOMPSON

"I can't believe how fast this summer has gone." Daisy pouts as she flings her arm over my shoulder.

I sigh and glance out at the sea as it laps the shore. "Same," I say sadly. "I hate it. I don't want to go back to university yet. I'm not ready for this to be over. Which is insane considering I was nervous about coming back."

She squeezes my shoulder with her hand. "Because you fell in love," she sings, and I roll my eyes, pushing her away. "Ivy fell in love."

"Okay, we don't need to declare it."

Her blue eyes glisten. "What? Are you saying it's not true?"

"No." I fold my arms over my chest. "I'm just sad thinking about it, and I don't want to overthink it."

Daisy frowns. "You worried about what it means for your relationship?"

"Yeah, we've spoken about it and said that we'll work out the long distance for the year, but it's still scary. To go from seeing him every day for two and a half months to barely seeing him at all. It's going to be tough, but I know we can get through it."

"You guys are gonna work it out." She squeezes my shoulder again.

I flash a quick smile. "I don't wanna talk about it anymore."

"Then let's not." She shakes her head and begins to pour me a drink. "Let's spend the last party having the best time of our lives."

I take the cup from her hands and clink it with her own before taking a few sips.

"That's my girl." She gently slaps my arm, and I smile back at her.

"Hey guys," a familiar voice echoes from behind me.

We both twist to find Isaac and Harriet approaching us. "Hey guys," I say as I lean forward to give them a welcoming hug. "Been a long time since I've seen you both."

"The fair was probably the last time," Isaac comments. "But it's good to see you, Ivy."

"You too."

Harriet falls into a conversation with Daisy, and I take another sip of my drink. "So, is it true…" he starts. "That you're dating JJ?"

I nod once. "Yeah, it's true."

Isaac's throat tightens, but then he smiles. "That's great, Ivy. I'm pleased for you, you seem really happy."

"I am happy." I raise my shoulders. "The happiest I've been in years."

"I'm pleased for you. We can still be friends, right?"

My forehead creases. "Of course, Isaac. We're always going to be friends."

"Good." He blows out a breath.

"Hey." Harriet grabs onto Isaac's shoulder. "Did you hear?"

I blink at her. "Hear what?"

"They're planning on a group skinny-dip at midnight." Her eyes light up, and Daisy snorts.

"Yeah, right. Half of these people won't have the guts to get naked." She waves off the idea. "I mean, to each their own, I'm not judging, but unless they're completely wasted, it's not happening, and that's a danger in itself."

Harriet grins. "I guess we'll see."

I glance over Daisy's shoulder to find JJ talking to Finn, Cal, and Joel. My eyes flick down to Finn's hand and the relief that sweeps over me to find he's not drinking. In fact, none of the boys are.

As if JJ can sense my stare, he finds my eyes like magnets. He stops talking and flashes me a panty-dropping smile. We said we'd stick by one another, but we knew it wouldn't happen that way.

I push off the spot I'm standing in, excusing myself as I walk across the sand. JJ meets me halfway and doesn't hesitate to wrap his arm around my waist. "Hey." I beam up at him.

"Hey." He leans down to press a peck to my lips. "How's your night?"

"It's been fun. Yours?"

"Better now that I'm with you."

"Cheesy."

JJ laughs and takes my hand. "Come over."

He brings me towards the boys. Finn glances down at our fingers entwined, and he smiles, which catches me by surprise.

"Hey, guys," I say, greeting them all.

"'Sup, Ivy." Cal grins.

JJ tugs me to his side and kisses my forehead in front of them. My eyes flick to Finn, who is staring back at us with a conflicted expression.

"I'm gonna go grab a soft drink," Joel says.

"I'll come with you," Cal dismisses himself, too.

Finn stands in front of us, and I swallow slowly. "You good, Finn?" I ask.

"Yeah." He shoves his hands into his pockets. "Just getting used to being here and not drinking. It's definitely harder than I thought it would be."

"I'm proud of you," I smile.

"We all vowed we wouldn't drink tonight," JJ says as I turn to look at him. "And we'd keep an eye on each other. We want Finn here, so we decided we'd do it together."

My lips widen into a grin. "You guys are cute."

"We did say we'd stay in together tonight," JJ continues. "But Finn said he wanted to prove to himself that he can be out and enjoy his time."

"Yeah." Finn claps his hands together. "I guess it's baby steps."

"Well, you have the best support system around," I say sincerely.

"Agreed," JJ adds.

I beam up at JJ as he squeezes my sides.

"I'm happy you guys are happy. Cherish her, man. She deserves it."

Then, before I know it, JJ is bundling us into a three-way hug. "I love you, man," JJ exhales, and Finn chuckles.

"I love you both."

"I love you, too, Finn."

My eyes close, and I take a quick breath. Maybe this will be okay in the end. It seemed impossible at first, but I know it'll work out.

I glance at JJ. "Could you give me a moment with Finn?"

"Sure," he says without hesitation and leans down to kiss my temple.

Finn flicks his gaze to me. "Everything okay?"

"Yeah," I purse my lips. "I wanted to tell you that I read your letter."

His green eyes glass over with sudden emotion. "You did?"

"Yeah."

Neither of us says anything for a few moments.

"I didn't expect it to be so long," I laugh in an attempt to lighten the mood.

Finn smiles softly. "Once I started, I couldn't stop. I wanted to get everything down."

"I appreciate everything you said and your honesty. I might not ever be able to understand why you did what you did, but I know how much you regret it. Especially the way you reacted after everything that happened." I watch his crumbling face. "And I know you want to do better, be better. And I forgive you, but please give me some time to learn to trust you again."

Finn nods, eyes glistening. "Yeah, that's more than okay. I'm just glad I still have you in my life."

My eyes ache with the need to cry. Instead, I step forward and hug him.

We stay like this for a while until Finn pulls back. "Thank you for not giving up on me," he whispers. "You, Mum, Dad, JJ, you all keep me going and I'd be lost without you."

"I'm always gonna be here, Finn," I say sincerely. "*Always.*"

When Finn steps away to go and mingle with Joel and Callan, JJ steps to my side once more. I wrap my arms around his waist and bury my face into his chest. "I'm gonna miss you so much," I whisper.

He caresses the back of my head soothingly. "Gonna miss you too, princess. But I'm not worried. I know what we have is special, and I'm not going to find it anywhere else."

"Me too," I admit as I peek my head up at him. "This has been the best summer ever—despite all the bad shit."

JJ's hand caresses my cheek, and he swipes his thumb across my skin. "And that just proves how strong you are. I know this summer hasn't been easy for you, but I think you truly found yourself."

"Thanks to you."

"Nah, don't give me credit for anything. You did it all on your own. Don't dampen everything you've overcome. *You* did it. No one else."

My lips curve at the thought, warmth swarming my chest. "I really, really love you."

"I know, beautiful."

I press up on my toes to capture his lips with mine, widening my mouth because I need him right now. In my veins, in my blood, in my soul, I need him *everywhere.*

"GUYS!" someone shouts. "It's time to skinny-dip!"

JJ glances over at the sound and laughs. "Skinny-dip?"

Suddenly, people start shedding their clothes and bolt for the sea. I've never seen so many happy faces and the vibrations of laughter. "Yeah, sometimes people do it at the last party of the summer."

"Should we?"

I narrow my eyes curiously. "You want to?"

"Hell yeah, let's go out with a bang. Not literally. Or we could, but later."

"Later," I say with excitement.

JJ grins devilishly, and it sparks fire in my soul.

My teeth clamp down on my lip. "Alright, let's do this, but underwear only."

"That still counts."

I raise my shaky hands and begin to undo my dress, and I let it fall to the sand beneath us. JJ throws off his T-shirt and slides down his shorts. He holds out his hand and I take it.

"Ivy." His chest heaves. "Will you be my girlfriend?"

My lips tremble, and I nod. "Yeah. Yeah, of course. I already thought I was."

"I know, I wanted to ask in the way you deserve to be asked."

JJ gives my hand a squeeze and kisses me one last time,

then we're running towards the sea like crazed teenagers, and I can't stop smiling.

Every second of being with JJ was worth it.

Because I've finally found myself again after being lost for so long.

EPILOGUE ONE - JJ WOODFORD

THREE AND A HALF YEARS LATER

When there is a knock at the door, I quickly walk across the flat to open it. Finn stands on the other side with a wide grin on his face, his blonde hair now longer and flopping over his forehead in beach-like waves.

"Hey, man," he says before pulling me into a hug. "You good?"

I slap his back. "Yeah, I'm good. How are you?"

As he steps inside, I close the door behind him and make my way back over to the kitchen where I'm preparing dinner.

"Yeah." He shrugs off his coat. "I'm good. Work is killing me, but I'm pushing through."

"But you like coaching?"

Finn blows out a breath. "I have to admit, some of those kids test me."

"You chose the job, bud." I snort.

"Skye is hard work enough," he murmurs. "God, I love her, but I can't wait until she's out of her toddler tantrum phase."

I grin. "Does Maya agree?"

Finn's eyes widen. "Oh, she agrees."

A chuckle falls from my lips. "How are you all?"

"Yeah, we're good. We're really good."

"I like to hear it."

"You know, I didn't realise this month will be three years of being completely sober," he states as if he's reading a boring article in the newspaper. "It's weird to think about."

"Finn," I exhale. "That's fucking incredible. I'm so proud of you." I pull him into a hug and smile into his shoulder.

"Thanks, brother. I appreciate it. Feels like a lifetime ago I was that low, honestly, sometimes can't believe that was the way I was living life."

"You're living better now," I say sincerely.

"Those girls saved my life," Finn's eyes glitter. "I can't say it enough."

"Because you became the man they deserved."

Finn smiles because he knows it too. "Where's Ivy?"

I pick up a spoon and stir the pasta. "Still at work."

"Swear that girl doesn't know when to call it a day."

"She has an important job." I pin him with a stare, and he raises his hands in surrender. "Neither of us could do what she's doing."

Finn snorts as he takes a seat at the kitchen island. "I pulled the short straw when she got all the brains and I got… nothing."

"You didn't get nothing." I shake my head.

Being a research scientist in the medical field must be incredibly tough, but the woman loves every second of it, and every time she comes home to me to say that she's had a breakthrough with something, it fills my heart with warmth.

I don't have a clue what she's talking about half the time, but I try my hardest to grasp the terms she uses and ask her about the projects she spends hours upon hours on.

When I plate up dinner, I keep my eyes on Finn as he devours the carbonara. There are words clinging to the tip of my tongue, words I want to say but can't bring myself to voice. I don't know why I'm suddenly nervous, he will be happy for us.

Of course I want to see my best friend, but I invited him over for a reason.

"Finn." I lower my fork, and he flicks his eyes to me.

"Yeah?"

"I'm gonna propose to Ivy."

A piece of spaghetti falls out of his mouth as he stares back at me in shock. "Y-you're—"

I freeze and study his expression.

Then he's barrelling off the stool before he wraps me up in a tight hug. "Holy shit," he gushes. "This is the best fucking news ever. When?"

A hesitant laugh falls from my lips as he removes himself from me. "When we finally get the keys to our dream home."

Two weeks, and I'm definitely not counting.

We've been looking forward to this moment for what feels like years.

Our very own beach house with sand for grass, waves for fences, and sunsets for days.

"Oh my god," Finn grins as he swipes a hand through his hair. "I can't believe this. Well, I can believe this, but holy fuck. This is happening. Wait—"

I blink up at him. "What?"

"Have you said anything to our dad?"

"Yeah." I smile. "And your mum. They already know and gave me their blessing."

Finn shoves at my shoulder. "I had no idea you were so traditional."

"I want to do this right. It has to be perfect for her."

"It will be," he says with another beaming grin. "That girl loves you so much."

My heart jumps with pride. *I know.*

"What did your parents say?"

"They're ecstatic." I grin. "Mum honestly couldn't stop crying."

Finn's smile increases. "I knew she'd cry."

"She loves love more than anyone," I chuckle.

"And your dad?"

"He's happy I'm happy. And he loves Ivy."

"She's hard not to love."

"Trust me."

"Have you got the ring?" he asks.

I nod.

"Can I see it?"

"Whatever you do," I say with narrowed eyes. "You don't say a single word to her."

Finn swipes his index finger and thumb over his lips before pretending to throw away the key. "They're sealed."

I leave the kitchen to go to the bedroom and find the little velvet box I tucked away into the back of my wardrobe. Too high for Ivy to reach when she decides to go on a cleaning spree.

When I return, I gently place the ring down on the table beside Finn's empty plate. He stares at it for a long moment before opening it, as if it's the most delicate thing in the world.

"Woah," he says as he blinks down at the jewellery I spent months designing myself to make sure it's perfect. "It's beautiful."

"You think?"

Finn nods eagerly. "Yeah, she's going to love it."

"I hope so."

He glances up at me with a cheeky grin. "Are you nervous?"

I exhale a ragged breath. "A little."

"Aw, JJ," he teases. "Don't think I've ever seen you nervous."

As I open my mouth to speak, there is noise at the front

door. The sound of keys jingling and the lock turning. I snatch the box on the table so quickly, it's gone in a flash and securely tucked into my trouser pocket.

Ivy steps into the flat a few moments later. Her blonde hair is thrown up into a messy bun with pieces falling around her pretty face. She blinks at us suspiciously.

Heat spreads over the back of my neck. That was a close call.

I've been planning this for months, and I don't want anything to ruin it now.

"Hello to you guys, too." She laughs softly before shutting the door behind her.

I quickly look at Finn and widen my eyes, and he shoots me a wink in response.

He better stay quiet, otherwise I'll tape his mouth shut.

She hangs up her coat, and I walk towards her. "How was your day?"

"Busy," she sighs. "But good. I think I'm almost finished with this project."

"Yeah?" I grin. "Sounds great, princess. Are you hungry?"

Ivy hums softly. "Famished."

I wrap my arm around her and kiss her forehead, enjoying the way she slides right into my side, her face pressed into my collarbone.

As Ivy greets Finn with a hug, I plate up her dinner as we all sit around the table. "So, the house," Finn says as Ivy eats. "It's real soon, huh?"

"Yeah." She smiles at him. "I can't wait. Not that I don't love this place, but we've grown out of it. I can't wait to live in a house and have the beach as a garden. You know? It'll be a brand-new start for us. We've worked so hard for this."

Ivy meets my eyes and I smile, the feeling of the box burning a hole deep in my pocket. Oh, how I physically cannot wait a single second more.

"Yeah, it's going to be the best day of our lives." I grin at her.

Her cheeks flush as she leans back in her chair. "Oh, don't I know it."

Little does she know, there will be two things to celebrate.

The house of my dreams. The woman of my dreams.

Nothing will beat this. *Nothing.*

EPILOGUE TWO - IVY THOMPSON

I clap a hand over my mouth, eyes watering at the sight of our beautiful new beach house. My hands shake, but JJ tugs me to his side and presses his lips to the top of my head.

"I can't believe we own this," I mumble in disbelief.

"Well believe it, princess. It's *ours.*"

The thought makes my eyes close in relief. Throughout the last four years, after finishing university and trying to find ourselves in the real world, we moved into some shitty apartment in the city.

It wasn't our forever home, but at least we were together.

We've always spoken about moving back down to the coast, where we know our story blossomed. But houses by the sea cost buckets full, and neither of us were in financially stable jobs to be able to afford our dream home.

So we waited, and fuck, it paid off.

Our beach house is stunning with a white and baby blue exterior, wooden features and beautiful golden sand all around the property. It looks out across the glimmering sea, and the sun sets along the horizon.

A single tear rolls down my cheek at everything we've done to get here.

"Don't cry," he whispers and takes my face between his hands.

"They're happy tears," I whimper.

He wipes them away with his thumbs and then brings our lips together. "We've worked so hard for this, Ivy. We deserve this. It's everything we've ever wanted."

"I know," I sniffle.

"I'm so proud of you." His blue eyes soften. "You've honestly worked your ass off."

JJ drops my face and takes my hand. "Let's go inside."

The moving vans aren't coming until tomorrow, but we said we wanted to have our first night in the house as soon as possible. We have a mattress we can put on the floor and not much else, but it's perfect. I wouldn't want it any other way.

We walk up the steps to our perfect home. JJ digs out his key from his pocket and twists in my direction, his eyes lighting up. "Do you want to do the honours?"

"We'll do it together," I say before placing my hand over his.

He guides it to the lock, the key slips inside, and we twist it together. I glance up at him, but he's already beaming down at me. "Forever, princess."

My cheeks hurt from smiling so much.

Once the door is open, we step inside. It's exactly how it was from the viewing we had, except all the furniture is gone. We're more than excited to decorate and add our own little beachy touches. The house is fairly old with lots of features that give the house character and spark.

JJ's arm wraps around my shoulder as we walk from the hall into the kitchen, then to the living room. It's everything we wanted and more. "I know it's not much right now." He kisses my head. "But it'll get there."

I shake my head. "I don't need convincing of anything. I know it's going to be perfect. I'm so happy."

He kisses my temple and I take a slow breath, feeling like the luckiest girl in the world.

"How about we have a little evening on the beach? We can make a fire, cook some food, and have a few drinks. Celebrate," JJ suggests, and I twist in his hold, nodding with enthusiasm.

"Yes," I say excitedly.

Thirty minutes later, we head down to the beach, which is completely empty. It's like our own private space. The sun is about to set soon, and JJ gathers some wood together to start a fire as I sit on a log and crack two bottles of cider.

Once the fire is roaring, JJ walks to his bag and removes his camera. I smile. "Are you documenting this?"

He looks at me with a soft smile. "Duh. This is an important memory."

"True." I smile before taking a swig of my drink. He sets up the camera on a tripod and aims it behind me and the fire. It'll be an amazing shot of the sunset.

Since leaving university, JJ didn't want to continue with engineering like his father wanted; he loved the idea of making his own art in the form of video production. Now he is a freelance filmmaker with a wide portfolio.

I adore his work. He has an eye for things some people just don't have.

He's talented, and sometimes I don't think he even sees it. He blows me away every time.

And even though it wasn't what his dad wanted for him, once he saw what JJ could do, he realised his son was super talented and to do what he loves most.

JJ slides onto the log beside me and takes the cider from my hands. I frown.

"I've got something better," he says before removing a bottle of sambuca from his bag.

I release a laugh as he takes two shot glasses and pours us

both a generous amount. "You don't like sambuca," I say, remembering the first night we met.

"I do, because it reminds me of you."

My cheeks burn from how bright my smile is. "I don't think I've drunk sambuca since the night we met," I confess.

JJ shakes his head. "Me neither. Cheers, princess. From the beginning to the end, this is us."

"Cheers," I say before knocking back the shot at the same time.

The liquid burns my throat, and I definitely can't drink like I used to at university, but this is a core memory that will stay with me forever.

"We did it." He wraps an arm around my shoulder.

I grin wider. "We sure did."

He nuzzles his head into mine and then grabs a speaker from his bag to play music. I watch as he stands from the seat and holds his hand out to me. "Dance with me."

I chuckle awkwardly. "Really?"

"Yeah." He nods. "Come dance with me."

I physically cannot say no to this man. I roll my eyes playfully. "Fine."

He tugs me up onto my feet as we stand in front of the fire. His fingers lace through mine, and we move to the soft music. Behind me, I can hear the sound of the waves crashing against the shore, and it's one of my favourite sounds—that and JJ's voice.

Our arms wrap around one another, and he stares at me like I'm the only person in the world—even after four years, and I still have his complete devotion.

JJ raises our hands above our heads, and I spin before stumbling into him as my bare feet sink into the sand. I press a hand to his chest and grin up at him, the fire illuminating our faces as the sun starts to set.

The sky's the perfect shade of blue and yellow. My favourite kind of sunset.

His hands find my hips, and he twists me towards the sea, our backs to the fire. "I want to get the perfect shot," he whispers in my ear.

I laugh as he steps away. "Okay…" I trail off. "What should I do?"

JJ is silent for a second. "Whatever you want. I want the silhouette of you. It'll look perfect against the sky."

"Okay." I bite back a smile.

My hair flaps in the wind, and I raise my hands in the air, letting it flow through my fingers. After a few moments, I hear nothing from JJ. "Now what?"

Silence.

I twist my head to find JJ on his knees before me, a box open between his hands. My eyes snag on the ring to find an aquamarine stone on a silver band with five circular diamonds on each side in different sizes. I stumble back, a trembling breath leaving my throat. My hand slaps over my mouth and releases a sob.

JJ's eyes sweep over me patiently, but I can't breathe.

"Ivy." His voice is rough, as if he's trying his hardest to keep it together. "You are everything to me."

I don't blink, but tears still manage to flow down my cheeks, my shaky hands lay on my face as I shift my gaze between JJ's eyes and the ring.

"The second I laid my eyes on you outside that bar when your heel broke, I knew you were it for me." He smiles, his eyes glistening with the reflection of the fire. "I didn't know how I was going to do it, I just knew I was. I couldn't let you slip through my fingers. I wanted you, and I wanted nothing more than to love you. And I'm so honoured you let me do just that."

My nose tingles at his words, eyes flowing endlessly.

"I've wanted to ask you this question for ages, but I wanted to find the perfect time. I also didn't want to scare you." He releases a chuckle, which I copy, but it sounds like

I'm drowning in my own tears. "You make me so damn happy. I couldn't imagine my life without you. So, please would you do me the honour of marrying me? I want to make you happy and make you feel loved for the rest of our lives."

I nod because words fail me, and I break down. My body turns numb from the surprise and the adrenaline that is pumping around my veins.

All I've wanted is to be happy.

JJ is my happiness, my sunshine, my soulmate.

"Yes," I whimper after a few moments when I manage to take a breath. "Yes. I'll marry you."

I lunge forward and wrap my arms around his neck. His arm closes around my back, and he stands up, lifting me off the floor completely. I'm still crying into his shoulder, sensing his nerves because he's shaking.

After he puts me down, he takes my face between his hands and plants a delicious sambuca-flavoured kiss on my lips.

JJ takes my left hand and slides the ring onto my ring finger. I watch in awe as it fits perfectly, sparkling back at me like all the stars in the sky. "I love it." I grin, admiring it for a moment longer. "It's so beautiful."

He tilts my chin and claims my lips again. "Yeah, you like it?"

"I adore it."

"I adore you."

I sniffle as I glance up and take his face between my hands. "I love you so much, JJ. I can't wait to marry you. I've only imagined it a thousand times."

He releases a raspy laugh and looks to the sand for a second. "Me too," he admits. "This ring looks so good on you."

I drop my gaze as he runs his finger over it delicately.

My arms clasp around his neck again, and he picks me up, my legs wrap around his waist, and I cling to him. I kiss him like it's our last kiss on earth. I pour every inch of my love into him.

"Thank you for loving me," I whisper against his mouth. "When I wasn't able to. Thank you for helping me to learn to love myself."

"Mmm." He kisses me again. "My favourite part was seeing you fall in love with yourself. To see yourself how I see you."

I grin, and he grins right back. "The number of times you made me tell myself that I'm beautiful."

"Only stating facts." He smirks at me. "I'm glad you agree."

My eyes roll playfully. "You're persuasive when you want to be."

"Nah. I'm just right."

I roll my hand down the back of his head. "This couldn't be more perfect," I say in awe.

"I'm glad you think so. I've been so nervous all day." He releases a breath of relief. "But it was worth feeling like that to feel like this right now."

My heart expands at the thought. I did think he was quiet earlier today, but I thought it was house nerves.

"Like I'd ever say no to you."

"I wanted you to be ready."

"I've been ready since we left university."

JJ stares back at me, eyes softening. "Well, it doesn't matter. We've got our dream house, and now we can have our dream life. It all worked out."

"It did. And I will love you forever."

"Forever doesn't seem long enough," he muses.

"Beyond the grave, then." I sink my teeth into my bottom lip.

JJ nods, agreeing. "Beyond the grave."

THANK YOU FOR READING!

If you enjoyed Risky Business, I'd be grateful if you left a review on Goodreads and Amazon!

You can find future updates on book 2 in the series over on my Instagram - savannaroseauthor

ACKNOWLEDGMENTS

Wow, I can't believe this is my third published book. I'm in shock myself.

Firstly, I want to thank you guys for reading and supporting. It honestly means the absolute world to me. More than you'll ever know. Being able to do this as a job is mind-blowing and I'm so grateful I get to create these stories and share them with you all. So thank you.

To G, my absolute rock. I don't know how many times you've had to pick me up when I've been having meltdowns, but I know I wouldn't be where I am without you. Love you to the moon and back.

I want to thank my beta readers, E, Josie, Jessi and Tylar. Your feedback and support has helped me in so many ways and I'm grateful for each of you. You're all superstars and I'm so proud to call you my friends.

E, I don't know what I'd do without you and our ridiculously long voice notes. Thank you so much for helping with this book and all your suggestions. Our friendship is everything to me and like I've said before, you're stuck with me.

Mum and dad, thanks for your endless support and always cheering me on!

Katie, thank you so much for your amazing editing skills and boosting me up when my confidence was low. I can't wait to work with you again!

Sam, thank you for this beautiful cover and bringing JJ and Ivy to life. It's one special cover!

And thank YOU for reading JJ and Ivy's story!

ABOUT THE AUTHOR

Savanna Rose is a romance author from London, England, who loves to write about strong women and swoony men.

When she's not creating one hundred new book ideas, she is either enjoying life with her boyfriend, reading anything with spice, hitting the dance floor with her friends, or sipping on a well deserved Aperol Spritz.

> Instagram/Tik Tok: savannaroseauthor
> Goodreads: Savanna Rose

Printed in Dunstable, United Kingdom